PRAISE

A Cosmic Kind of Love

"Wow. I've been reading Samantha Young for years, and she has actually managed to top herself with *A Cosmic Kind of Love*."

—Tessa Bailey, *New York Times* bestselling author of
It Happened One Summer

"With a premise that shines like the brightest constellation, Samantha Young delivers a refreshing and delicious rom-com about star-crossed lovers event planner Hallie Goodman and NASA astronaut Christopher Ortiz. [With] sizzling chemistry, a tangible connection, and complex characters I rooted for from the get-go, *A Cosmic Kind of Love* did in fact launch my heart into space and left me on Earth, starry-eyed and hoping for my own Captain Chris Ortiz."

—Elena Armas, *New York Times* bestselling author of
The Spanish Love Deception

"A stellar blend of upbeat and endearing, *A Cosmic Kind of Love* is classic feel-good rom-com entertainment!"

—Chloe Liese, author of the Bergman Brothers series

"*A Cosmic Kind of Love* will fly you to the moon and leave you star-gazing. This clever romantic comedy about two souls brought together by the stars is everything you need in your life, complete with swoons, smiles, and steam enough to power a rocket. *A Cosmic Kind of Love* doesn't just get five stars—it gets the whole galaxy."

—Staci Hart, author of *Wasted Words*

"Young makes the temperature rise in this sexy new novel, which blurs the line between friends and friends with benefits.... Readers will finish the novel craving more." —*Booklist*

"Young pens a wonderful romance with lovable, multifaceted characters who want what everyone wants—someone to love them, no matter what." —RT Book Reviews

"Full of tenderness, fire, sexiness, and intrigue, *Every Little Thing* is everything I hope to find in a romance." —Vilma's Book Blog

"Ms. Young delivers a character-driven storyline that is gripping from the get-go, injecting a beloved enemies-to-lovers trope with intense angst and eroticism." —Natasha Is a Book Junkie

"A really sexy book.... Highly recommend this one." —*USA Today*

"Humor, heartbreak, drama, and passion." —The Reading Cafe

"Young writes stories that stay with you long after you flip that last page." —Under the Covers

"Charismatic characters, witty dialogue, blazing-hot sex scenes, and real-life issues make this book an easy one to devour." —Fresh Fiction

Also by Samantha Young

The
Love Plot

Samantha Young

Berkley Romance
New York

BERKLEY ROMANCE
Published by Berkley
An imprint of Penguin Random House LLC
penguinrandomhouse.com

Copyright © 2023 by Samantha Young
Readers Guide copyright © 2023 by Samantha Young
Excerpt from *A Cosmic Kind of Love* copyright © 2022 by Samantha Young
Penguin Random House supports copyright. Copyright fuels creativity,
encourages diverse voices, promotes free speech, and creates a vibrant culture.
Thank you for buying an authorized edition of this book and for complying with
copyright laws by not reproducing, scanning, or distributing any part of it in
any form without permission. You are supporting writers and allowing
Penguin Random House to continue to publish books for every reader.

BERKLEY and the BERKLEY and B colophon are registered trademarks of
Penguin Random House LLC.

Library of Congress Cataloging-in-Publication Data

Names: Young, Samantha, author.
Title: The love plot / Samantha Young.
Description: First Edition. | New York : Berkley Romance, 2023.
Identifiers: LCCN 2022057983 (print) | LCCN 2022057984 (ebook) |
ISBN 9780593438633 (trade paperback) | ISBN 9780593438640 (ebook)
Subjects: LCGFT: Novels. | Romance fiction.
Classification: LCC PR6125.O943 L68 2023 (print) |
LCC PR6125.O943 (ebook) | DDC 823/.92—dc23/eng/20221208
LC record available at https://lccn.loc.gov/2022057983
LC ebook record available at https://lccn.loc.gov/2022057984

First Edition: August 2023

Printed in the United States of America
1st Printing

Interior art: NYC Icons © vectorwin / Shutterstock.com
Book design by Kristin del Rosario

For Billy

The
Love Plot

Chapter One

I'VE NEVER BEEN ONE TO SWOON OVER A MAN.

I'd felt attraction to gorgeous guys and had pretty good sex in my twenty-eight years on this planet. But swooning?

Nope.

In many ways, I was like the character I'd donned for the eight-year-old's birthday party that day. My strawberry-blond hair wasn't the right hue, so I wore a wig of tumbling, riotous bright red curls that were vivid against the teal velvet fabric of my medieval-style gown. I had a bow (fake weapon) looped over my shoulder and a brown belt slung across my hips, with a quiver holding plastic arrows attached to it.

It wasn't too hard to guess that I was Merida from Disney Pixar's *Brave*. This was a new character for me. I'd dressed up as many a Disney princess for parties, but it was the first time someone had paid me to play Merida. This character meant practicing a Scottish accent, and I didn't think mine was too shabby. Och, ah was quite proud o' it, so ah was.

The birthday party was hosted in the fanciest Upper West Side apartment I'd ever set foot inside, and I was feeling pretty connected to wee Merida because we were both independent women who had no intention of settling down with a man as a way of finding fulfillment in our lives. Merida would never *swoon*.

I was pretty damn annoyed that while I was in that moment, really feeling the character, making the kids laugh with my boisterous boasting and brogue, my gaze lifted for a second from the birthday girl and I saw *him*.

The sight of the stranger struck me in a way I didn't understand. But it was like all the air fled my lungs. It felt like that time I got mugged when I was nineteen and I tried to fight the guy instead of letting him take what little money I had. He'd punched me so hard in the gut, I couldn't breathe. It wasn't a pleasant sensation. It was discombobulating.

"Merida!" The birthday girl, Charmaine, tugged on my dress. "You were telling us about the Loch Ness monster!"

I blinked, dazed. Thankfully, I was a great multitasker, because I launched back into my story of being sent to kill the Loch Ness monster to protect my people only to discover that he was a hilarious big softy that I needed to protect *from* my people, and all the while I kept throwing glances at *him*.

Who was he?

What was he doing at a children's birthday party?

Whoever he was, he was a wondrous mix of male beauty and primal masculinity who just the sight of—once I got over the horrible breathless moment—made me tingle delightfully between my thighs.

Tall, very broad-shouldered, and from the thick forearms revealed by the pushed-up sleeves of his sweater, it was more than obvious he worked out. You could see the man's biceps shaping the fabric. I'd never been into working-out types. However, he was a very fine specimen, with his tapered swimmer's waist and long,

long, *long* legs. What was also puzzling about my physical response to the stranger was the fact he hadn't smiled once the entire time I surreptitiously eyed him up. I was into happy, funny guys. Not brooding, surly types. Usually, they were a hard pass. A frown marred his strong brow, and his full lips flattened into a grim line. That face. Boy, was that a face that could launch a thousand ships. All chiseled angles. I couldn't discern his eye color from across the room, but it didn't matter. He was just . . . sexier than a night in with hot chocolate and Netflix's *The Witcher*.

Yeah, I said it.

While, like Merida, I might not want to play arm candy to some man intent on being "my king," I wouldn't mind banging a headboard with a burly warrior in a kilt.

I imagined the stranger in a kilt and what I would do to him if we were alone.

Oh my.

That imagery was a keeper.

By the look of things, I wasn't the only person in the room affected by the gorgeous stranger. Three women currently surrounded him and he appeared rudely bored by them, while others eyed him from across the room.

"Are you hot, Merida?" Charmaine asked innocently. "Your cheeks are all red."

Wow, I was having sexual fantasies about a stranger at a children's birthday party dressed as a Disney character. There was nothing right about that sentence.

Forcing myself to ignore this shockingly strong physical reaction to a man I didn't know, I focused on the kids.

A little while later, when Philippa Whitman, the mom who'd hired me, appeared to lead the kids away for snacks, she told me I could take a break. I beamed gratefully and ignored the amused stares of the attending adults before I slipped out onto the balcony.

It wasn't every day I got to visit swanky New York apartments with balconies overlooking Central Park. While I held little stock in material things, I could appreciate a superb view.

"This balcony is occupied," a gruff and pissed-off masculine voice sounded from my left.

Glancing that way, I was delighted to discover Mr. Sexual Fantasy leaning on the railing of the narrow balcony. He glowered at me so ferociously, I wondered for a second if he'd mistaken me for someone else. Though it was pretty difficult to mistake me for anything other than a children's entertainer.

Intrigued by my outrageous and unusual attraction to him, I drifted toward him despite his less-than-welcoming comment. My bow got caught on the balcony door as it shut and I snort-laughed as I freed myself. The stranger didn't even so much as break a smile. I badly wanted to see him turn up the corners of his mouth, so I closed the distance between us. "I just needed some air. This is some view, huh?" I gestured with a grin over the city and the park.

Before his eyes narrowed on me, I noted they were a lovely denim-blue color. "So that's what you sound like when you're not butchering a Scottish accent."

My smile wavered, not sure if he was being mean or just bantering. I gave him the benefit of the doubt and responded in my awesome brogue, "Ah'll have ye ken that ah am the daughter of a Scottish king, dinnae ye ken."

"That sentence made little sense in English or fake Scottish." The stranger searched my face and then dragged his gaze down my body. He was studying me like I was a bug he'd never seen before. Inwardly, I bristled, but outwardly, my smile stayed in place. I'd adopted a "kill 'em with kindness" approach to mean people since I was a teenager. Some people couldn't help but melt under my niceness, and others got even more pissed at me. I found both reactions satisfying. "So, this is a job?" He didn't attempt to hide his disdain. "You actually do this for a living?"

Yes, you arrogant snob. I grinned. "Yeah. Isn't it great?"

He stared at me like I was babbling nonsense. "You think dressing up as Disney characters to entertain children is great? As a career?"

I shrugged. "I'm a costume character actor, so I dress up like lots of characters in pop culture to make other people smile on their special days. And, yeah, I think making people happy is a worthy endeavor. Don't you?"

He glowered harder at my bubbliness. "Are you acting right now? No one is this happy."

"Then you must surround yourself with a lot of miserable people."

He turned more fully toward me and the breeze caught his scent. Something citrusy with a hint of spicy earthiness. He smelled delicious. And very expensive. Who was he to Philippa Whitman? He wasn't her husband. She'd already told me her husband couldn't make their daughter's birthday party because he was on a business trip. "How old are you?"

His question took me aback. "Why?"

"Because you look old enough to know better than to goad a man who is clearly in a foul mood and certainly old enough to have moved on to more appropriate career paths by now. Disney princessing is for college students and failing college graduates."

Oh wow. I felt my attraction to him wilt rapidly. Refusing to let him see that his words bothered me, I tutted. "Oh, come on, surely you're old enough to know that we're responsible for our own dark moods and that expecting people, least of all a stranger, to rearrange their mood to accommodate yours is the height of arrogance and self-indulgence. It's the expectation of a toddler."

His lips might have pressed tightly together, but his eyes flared with surprise.

Before he could speak, I continued, "And many college students find it difficult to secure a job once they graduate, so I really don't think it's nice to speak of them in that tone." I grinned at him. "But since you're in a bad mood, I won't hold it against you. As for me, I'm genuinely happy in life. I don't know if many people can say the same, so I feel pretty awesome about the fact that I'm standing here rocking a Merida costume and a Scottish accent. I mean, of the two of us, which of us is in a *good* mood?"

"A good mood?" He pushed off the balcony railing and crossed his arms over his wide chest. "This isn't a good mood. This is passive aggressiveness. No one is in this good a mood after someone disparages their 'career.'"

He air-quoted the word "career" and I couldn't help it. My smile died.

Something flickered in his countenance as he studied me, but, thankfully, before I lost my grip on my usually easily accessed "kill 'em with kindness" attitude, a door opened behind us.

Philippa Whitman appeared. She took in the sight of me with the stranger and her expression grew puzzled. "Star, there you are. The children will be ready for you in five minutes. Why don't you go back inside and grab a quick bite to eat before then?"

It wasn't a suggestion.

Giving her a congenial nod, I turned from the stranger as Philippa stepped away from the door to let me pass.

The balcony door, however, didn't shut all the way over and I heard the stranger say, "Pippa, leave me alone and let me hide out here, please." He might have used the word "please," but his tone was demanding. It was not a request.

And he called her Pippa.

Was he her brother?

"Rafe, this is your niece's birthday party. You can't stand out here and brood."

So yeah, he was her brother. They looked nothing alike.

"Exactly. This is my niece's birthday party. Not an opportunity for you and my mother to foist every eligible woman in Manhattan on me, but, frankly, it feels like more effort is being put into that than Charmaine's party. A Disney princess, Pip? Really?"

"Your niece is eight years old and loves that movie, and Star came highly recommended."

"Star? That can't be her real name."

I scowled at the almost-closed balcony door. It was so!

"You seem awfully interested in my child's entertainer . . . and it's bad enough your brother can't even attend his own daughter's birthday party. I really don't need her uncle acting like he'd rather be anywhere but here."

Ah. He was her brother-in-law. Rafe Whitman.

Damn. That name suited him to a T.

There was a moment of silence, and then, "I'm sorry."

My eyes widened at his quiet apology.

"I had a terrible night in surgery last night and I'm just not in the mood for you to play matchmaker. Or to listen to that awful Scottish accent."

Moi? I pointed to myself. He needed to back off my awesome brogue.

"I think she's rather good," Philippa replied.

Thank you!

"But I'm sorry you had an awful night in surgery."

Was he a doctor, then?

That made sense.

Arrogance in abundance.

Though my easily forgiving side suddenly felt bad for him. He'd had a worse night than most people ever could at their job and then he'd come here only for his family to play matchmaker all afternoon. No wonder he was in a terrible mood. No one enjoyed being cornered. Not that that entirely excused his behavior, but I reminded myself that every single one of us had off days and acted out.

How was it a surgeon could make it to his niece's birthday party but her father couldn't?

"I'll try not to *foist* any more women on you today."

"Will you speak to my mother too?"

"Yes, I will. But, Rafe, you're going to have to settle down at some point. Your mother and I are just worried you'll end up alone."

"What does it matter if I'm happy? Happy and alone works for me."

I could totally understand that. Society needed to back off with all the trying to make people fit into their neat little boxes. *That* was the cause of so much unhappiness if you asked me.

"That would be fine if I thought for a minute you were actually happy. But the permanent scowl you wear suggests otherwise. Now, please try to be a little nicer to everyone in there."

"Including the woman who is too old to be dressed as a Disney princess?"

"Hush, Rafe. Don't be unkind."

I hurried away from the balcony door so they wouldn't realize I'd been eavesdropping. I hadn't meant to. Normally, I could not care less about anyone's private business. It was private for a reason, right? Truthfully, I did not understand my fascination with Rafe Whitman and, considering his disdain for me (whether it was real or driven by his awful mood), I was determined to erase that fascination from my brain and all my lady parts.

It was easy enough to do because after five minutes of being in the room, women surrounded Rafe again. This time, he really did appear like a cornered animal, his eyes wide, nostrils flaring. I felt a little bad for him despite his shitty attitude earlier. But when I looked over a few minutes later, he was gone, having, I assumed, made his escape.

It was only after most of the guests had left and Philippa had paid me in cash and was walking me to the door that I saw Rafe had reappeared. I glanced casually toward the living room and was shocked to see him sitting on the floor with Charmaine, grinning as she showed him what presents she'd received. He said something that made her laugh so hard she fell into him. Her uncle wrapped his arm around her to pull her into his side as he, shocker of all shockers, laughed with her.

And he went from unfairly attractive to "I might pass out from his sexiness" attractive.

Seriously, there went all the air out of my lungs.

Holy hot damn.

He looked up at that moment and our gazes met.

Rafe's smile died as his arm tightened around his niece, and I hurried out of the apartment before he could see my obvious reaction to him.

I'd learned long ago there was no point trying to make someone like you when they'd already decided that they didn't. It was much better to focus that energy on the people who already cared about you. And while I might find Rafe Whitman several levels of hot, I was only *physically* attracted to him. Bad day or not, judgmental snobs didn't really do it for me on an emotional level and, while I was anti-relationship, I still needed to *like* a guy before I'd let him into my bed.

As I took the elevator to the ground floor of that fancy Manhattan apartment, I shoved all thoughts of the man from my head and instead focused on the fact that I'd just added a character to my repertoire that had been a huge hit. Pulling my cell out of the pocket of my dress, I shot off a text to Dotty, my boss at We Bring Them to Life, the company that provided an actor to play almost any character you needed for your event.

> Put Merida at the top of my specialty list. I rocked her.

And no pompous, grumpy Manhattanite would convince me otherwise.

Chapter Two

"HOW CAN YOU DO THAT?"

I looked up from my e-reader to face three people in front of me. We were all waiting in line for the new iPhone. Even though I'd turned up pretty early, there were a lot of people already waiting. Considering my client was paying me to wait in line and every extra half hour was another ten dollars in my pocket, I didn't care how long I stood there. "Do what?" I smiled at the threesome.

The dark-haired girl who'd asked replied, "Read in the middle of a crowded street. You've been totally zoned out for the last hour."

Glancing around the busy street where the Apple store on Fifth Avenue was located, I realized it was now midday. Just as I realized that, my belly grumbled. Thankfully, I had packed a lot of snacks in my purse because the last time I waited on a new Apple product, the wait was six hours.

I had been here for four hours so far and was growing ever closer to the enormous glass-cubed entrance to the store.

Shrugging at the group, I switched off my e-reader and popped it into my purse. "I'm just good at drowning out noise, I guess. Are you waiting for the phone for yourselves or someone else?"

It turned out two of them were waiting for themselves, but the dark-haired girl, Yvonne, was, like me, being paid to wait for someone else. As we chatted about everything and nothing to kill time, I checked my phone and noticed I had a few texts from my client asking about my progress. Though I would never understand the urgency of owning certain material goods, I definitely appreciated it because it allowed me to do a job that didn't stress me out.

Yvonne was new to line sitting, and I was in the middle of recommending the best solo tent to buy for long waits during the winter when my attention moved over her shoulder and I spotted a familiar man.

He was so tall and broad-shouldered he was hard to miss.

And still spectacularly hot.

Rafferty "Rafe" Whitman.

Okay, so I might have googled him out of curiosity.

Rafe was the younger son of Greg Whitman, a shipping magnate. The Whitman kids could live off their trust funds and never work a day in their lives. But all of them did. The eldest, Hugo, Charmaine's father, was the new CEO of the family company. The youngest, Georgina, was some kind of computer genius. And Rafe . . . well, guess what?

He wasn't a regular surgeon. Oh no. It was much worse. Much more dangerous to my erogenous zones.

Rafe Whitman was a *veterinarian*.

He owned a vet clinic on the Upper West Side.

When I first read that, I had to admit I had to read it again. He did not seem like the cuddly animal-loving type at all, even with that brief glimpse of affection I'd seen between him and his niece.

What wasn't dangerous to my libido was the fact that he and I were so completely opposite to one another we were pretty much living on different planets. Which didn't explain my sudden urge to ruffle his snooty, wealthy feathers.

"Hey, Whitman, is that you?" I abruptly yelled, surprising my companions, who visibly startled.

The man in question was currently engaged in conversation with a shorter, older man, and he glanced predatorily toward the noise. When Rafe's scowling gaze moved over the line, I gave him a little wave and a grin so he could see who'd called out to him.

Recognition did not flicker across his irritated expression.

He turned back to his companion, ignoring me.

"Ouch." Yvonne chuckled. "The hottie doesn't seem interested."

I shrugged with a cheeky grin. "Last time he saw me, I looked a little different."

The line moved then and the girls turned toward it. I should have pulled some snacks out of my purse and forgotten Rafe.

For some reason, I couldn't.

I so wanted to mortify or annoy this man and I didn't understand the impulse at all. However, I went with my impulse. Smirking in his direction, I yelled louder, "Whitman!"

His shoulders stiffened, but he didn't turn.

I put my fingers between my lips and blew a piercing whistle at him. "We spend a beautiful afternoon together and now you're just ignoring me?"

People in line made oohing sounds, and I snort-laughed.

I had Rafe's attention again.

He glowered in my direction but didn't make a move toward me.

I shrugged. "The least you can do is say hi considering you got peanut butter and jelly all over my bedsheets!"

Laughter rumbled through the line and my shoulders shook with amusement as Rafe said something to his companion and then marched toward me. Wearing that thunderous scowl.

Butterflies swooped in my belly and I tried to bite my lip to contain my nervous laughter and failed. He wore a blue shirt, a fitted leather jacket, and a pair of dark suit pants, but he might as well have been naked for what it was doing to me.

"Look, I have no idea—" Rafe came to a sharp stop before me, recognition flooding his expression as his eyes darted over me. "*You*," he announced accusingly.

I grinned. "Me. What are the chances? Eight million people in this city and we run into each other twice in three days."

Rafe's eyes were even more attractively blue than I remembered as they wandered over my long strawberry-blond hair. "Your hair is different."

"Yeah, this is real. No wig."

His attention strayed down my body. I might have been feeling familiar tingles everywhere his eyes touched, but then he retorted, "Yet you're still in costume."

Frowning, I looked down at my maxi dress. While I dressed to suit how many hours I'd have to wait in line for something, when I knew it was just a half-day kind of deal, I dressed like me. And I liked dresses and skirts and a lot of florals. I also liked braid crowns and circlets. None of which was costumey. It was cute boho. "Uh . . . no."

He raised an eyebrow. "You look like you're auditioning to be a fairy princess."

I beamed at the compliment. "You're so sweet."

Rafe's lips pinched together for a second before he sighed heavily and glanced along the line toward the Apple building. "Is there a reason you catcalled ridiculous nonsense at me, or was it just boredom while you wait for a nonsensical gadget that's ruined the state of humanity?"

"Ooh, wow, there is a lot to unpack in that sentence, but to answer your question, no. I just felt like yelling at you." I shrugged. "And I'm not waiting for me. I'm a professional line sitter."

"You're a what?"

"A line sitter. I work for All on the Line. We're a group of line sitters. People pay us to wait in line for the things they want but don't have time to wait for. Phones, sneakers, theater tickets, gourmet coffee. I'm booked all this week to wait for all of those things."

He considered this. "People pay you to wait for stuff?"

"That's right. The company I work for created this app and people can post the jobs to it and if we want to do the job, we book it. The app takes care of the financials."

"And that's your job? Along with the Disney princess stuff? This"—he gestured along the line—"is what you do for a living?"

Okay, so maybe he wasn't just in a bad mood at his niece's party. Maybe he was just an asshole. "I'm not a Disney princess actor. I'm a costume character actor and a line sitter. Those are my jobs."

Silence fell between us as Rafe stared at me.

The longer he gazed into my eyes, the more I noticed his. His lashes weren't long, but they were unfairly dark and thick, making his eyes seem bluer. There were little silver striations in his irises that fascinated me. Refusing to break his stare because I knew I'd only linger over his gorgeous face (thus alerting him to the fact that I was attracted to his condescending ass), I remained still and quiet.

Then, true to form, Rafe pivoted and rudely departed without another word.

The mischievous teasing I'd felt earlier vanished, and I no longer experienced the urge to needle him with more catcalling. I stared after him but rather than feel insulted by his lack of interest in my life and seeming contempt for it, I felt sorry for him. He was clearly contained by the box that he'd grown up in and wouldn't know what an open mind was if it bit him on the behind.

I felt pity for anyone who was narrow-minded. It closed off so much of the beauty of the world to them.

Disappointed he'd turned out to be a cliché, I was looking away when movement caught my eye. I was shocked to find Rafe striding determinedly in my direction again. His broody face was more brooding than usual, so I braced myself.

Rafe Whitman drew to a stop before me and blurted out, "You'll literally do anything for money?"

Anger flared in an instant from the tips of my toes to the ends of my hair, so I didn't hear the *tone* in which the question was asked. I threw back my shoulders. Taller than average height at five-seven, I was still a good seven or eight inches shorter than this arrogant Manhattanite, but I was prepared to take him. Anyone who knew me knew I was a patient, laid-back kind of person . . . but Rafferty Whitman had crossed the line!

"What the hell does that mean?" I seethed. "Are you suggesting I charge money for sex?"

Rafe's blue eyes flashed with indignation. "No, I am not," he hissed at me, eyes darting around. "And lower your voice."

"I will not lower my voice." I crossed my arms over my chest. "I like most people, but you sure do make it difficult, Whitman. It's like you get off on being as insulting as possible."

He mirrored me, crossing his arms over his chest. "I'm not insulting you. If you'd paid attention, you'd realize the question was not meant to be untoward."

"Untoward?" I grimaced. "What, are you from the nineteenth century? Is that why you hate phones? Because if the technology is difficult for you to grasp, I can teach you how to use a phone." I was being a little shit now, but he brought it out in a person.

Rafe sneered. "How much will that cost me?"

Argghhh! I narrowed my eyes but smiled. "Oh, for you . . . twice as much as I'd charge anyone else."

"I see. Well." Rafe uncrossed his arms to reach into his back pocket. He removed his wallet and then a business card from that.

Holding it out to me, he continued, "I guess you stand to make a lot of money for doing very little. If you're interested, call me."

Flummoxed, I took the card. "Um . . . doing what?"

But he was already walking away.

"Doing what, Whitman?" I yelled after him.

He didn't answer, just casually strolled off. His suit pants molded perfectly to his sculpted ass. So unfairly physically perfect.

"Are you going to call him?"

I looked up from the business card that read WHITMAN VETERI-NARY CLINIC, DR. RAFFERTY WHITMAN.

His vet clinic was on the busy, tree-lined Columbus Avenue. *Nice location, Dr. Rafe.*

There was his phone number right beneath the address.

Yvonne grinned at me, and I answered her question. "Nah."

Her eyes bugged out of her head as her friends gaped at me in shock. "Uh, Clark Kent just asked you to call him, Star. You don't turn down Clark Kent."

"You do if he's an asshole. Life lesson, girls: an attractive face should not sway you if a pompous, arrogant, insulting, offensive turd lurks behind it."

Yvonne chuckled. "You did yell at him and try to embarrass him with the peanut butter and jelly stuff. That's not true, is it?"

I rolled my eyes. "No, it's not true." But she was right. I had antagonized him.

"You should make it true. I'd roll in a bathtub of jelly with that man."

Slipping the card into my purse, I shrugged. "Impossible. His ego would take up the whole tub. No room for jelly. Or me—I mean you."

"You're not the least bit curious to find out what he wants to pay you to do?"

"Considering how that sounds, nope. Not at all. Ooh, look, the line is moving. Yay."

But as the girls turned to move with the line, I knew I was lying.

I was so curious, my heart still raced from my encounter with Rafe.

Chapter Three

RIVER'S BAR, IN MY NEIGHBORHOOD ON STATEN ISLAND, HAD an energy my friends and I enjoyed. Vibrant but laid-back. Industrial meets boho. There was Edison bulb lighting, wrought-iron barstools and bistro sets, comfortable sofa seating in mismatched fabrics with wooden coffee tables. Every Friday night there was live music and on Saturdays they played an eclectic mix of music that didn't grate on the ears and was good to dance to.

I'd lived in the St. George area for the last few years, choosing to rent a tiny studio apartment because it was what I could afford. It wasn't in the best locale, but my neighborhood was what they called "up-and-coming." It was heading in what I hoped was a cool, artsy direction. There was already a great food scene. The major theater for Staten Island was in St. George, and there was a heavy metal scene in the neighborhood too.

My friends Roger, Kendall, and Jude had convinced me to move to Staten Island. I met my three closest friends when I worked as a bartender at a drag show and Roger's friend Adam had his bachelor party there.

Roger, a music producer who worked with Adam at the same studio, had attended and been completely enamored with me on a purely platonic level. And I with him. We shared the same sunny, optimistic outlook on life but with that contradictory dry, sarcastic wit, a combination that confused most people. He was kind of like my big brother.

With Roger came Kendall, an independent graphic designer and artist, and Jude, a full-time book editor and part-time writer for an online lifestyle magazine.

The three of them were in a long-term polyamorous relationship that made them happier than any three people I'd ever met in my life. Although sometimes it was hard to tell Jude was happy, but I knew him well enough to know that the big softy adored Roger and Kendall.

"Ooh, I'm likin' River's new signature cocktail." Kendall did a little shimmy in her seat, her short, dark curls bouncing with the movement.

I sipped at my beer as Jude slid his arm around the back of Kendall's chair, a fond smile on his face. "Let me try."

"You hate vodka," she reminded him.

"But you make it look so good."

I turned to Roger to see his reaction and found him studying me. I tensed. "What? Do I have something on my face?"

My best friend nodded slowly. "A secret."

"A secret?"

"Yeah. Why else would you be so quiet this evening? You've barely said a word."

"We've been here all of ten minutes."

"And by now, you've usually regaled us with something funny that happened at work." His dark eyes searched mine. "Did something *not* funny happen at work?"

Roger was one of those extremely observant people who noticed everything and genuinely cared too. I often pondered the fact that this facet of his personality helped keep the harmony between him, Jude, and Kendall. If one of them was unhappy about something, Roger could usually tell and sought to fix it.

I didn't think Roger could fix my problem.

Rafe Whitman.

Unfortunately, I hadn't been able to get the vet off my mind since we'd run into each other yesterday. His card was burning a hole in my purse.

I launched into my tale about the birthday party and yesterday outside the Apple store.

While there was some laughter, Jude scowled when I told them about Rafe's attitude toward my jobs.

"Forget about him," Jude advised, once I'd finished. "Don't call him."

Roger's ginger brows furrowed. "Why?"

"Because Star doesn't need some rich asshole filling her head with his toxic attitude."

I looked at Kendall. She wore an uncertain smile on her pretty face as she shrugged. "I'm on the fence."

Jude sighed. "What is it about bad boys that turns intelligent people into hormone-driven fools?"

She shoved him playfully. "Hey, you were a bad boy."

"Exactly. I'm speaking from experience. I was once that asshole that walked all over people and they let me. Don't call him, Star."

"I'm not sure he's a bad boy." I really wasn't. While Rafe was unpleasant, I didn't think that translated to bad boy.

Roger smirked at his boyfriend. "I took a chance on you even though I knew you were an asshole back then, and look how that turned out."

Jude frowned, but there was humor in his beautiful dark brown eyes. "I'm an anomaly. Reformed bad boys don't happen often."

"Again, I'm not sure Rafe Whitman is a bad boy. He's just a snob."

"A snob who turns you on?" Roger teased.

"Only when he doesn't open his mouth."

Kendall snorted into her drink.

"I say call him," Roger announced, reaching for my purse.

"Surprise, surprise," Jude murmured.

"What? Everyone deserves a second chance."

"Technically, this would be his third." I took another swig of my beer.

"Oh, just call him. Aren't you curious to know what he wants to hire you to do?"

"I swear, if it's for sex, I'll kill him," Jude practically snarled.

"It's not for sex," I assured him. "I'm not exactly his type."

Jude looked affronted. "You're everyone's type. If I weren't taken, I'd have tried to seduce you a million times already."

Kendall nodded in agreement, and I glowed at the compliment. My friends sure knew how to boost a lady's confidence.

"Call him," Roger insisted.

I wanted to. That was the problem.

"He could offer you a lot of money to do very little work. Maybe it would help with the road trip fund."

Ooh, he had me there. I'd fantasized about road tripping across the country since I read Kerouac's *On the Road* as a teenager. Not a likely choice, I know, but it inspired a love for road trip movies and books. Then, over the last few months, I'd grown restless and become attached to the idea that traveling would solve the problem. There was something about living life on the move, truly free of ties and commitments, that spoke to my bohemian soul.

"Don't call him," Jude cautioned.

Roger shook his head as he slid a hand over Jude's thigh and squeezed it, as if in apology, before turning to me. "Call him."

Staring into my friend's eyes, hearing Jude's wearied sigh, I contemplated it.

"You're just going to obsess over it until you do," Kendall threw in.

And she was absolutely right.

"Okay." I grabbed my purse. "Order me another beer, will you? I'll be right back."

"We want to hear all the juicy details!" Roger yelled over the music.

I threw a hand over my shoulder to let him know I'd heard him and then slipped out through the crowded bar and onto the street. The bar was on the corner of a busy cross section, so I wandered away from it to hear better. It was around nine o'clock, so I hoped it wasn't too late in the evening for Mr. Posh Vet. Pulling his card out of my purse, along with my cell, I quickly dialed his number.

He picked up on the third ring. "No, I do not want to buy what you're selling."

"Is that how you answer all of your calls?"

There was hesitation. Then he said, "Star?"

"You remembered," I teased gaily.

I could practically hear him rolling his eyes. "Your number came up as unknown on my phone. Of course, I thought you were selling something. And you are, are you not?"

The overly correct way he talked should have annoyed me.

It did. But it also didn't. Because it was kind of hot.

Damn him.

"That depends on your proposition. Warning, I will hang up if you insult me."

"That depends. Does ten thousand dollars a month sound insulting?"

Ten. Thousand. Dollars. A. Month.

My mouth went dry.

I forced myself to be cool. "That depends. What will I be required to do for that *significant* amount of money?"

"I require a fake girlfriend for an indefinite period. The amount of money reflects the fact that I'd need you to be flexible with your time for a few months. I might require you for anything up to six months."

A possible sixty thousand dollars? To be his fake girlfriend. But wait—

"Before you ask, I am not soliciting you for sex. For the last year, my mother and sister-in-law have become obsessed with finding me a wife. They've been throwing women at me and manipulating me into dates, and I am so beyond fucking exhausted by their attempts that I just need a break. If they think I'm seeing someone, it will get them off my back."

Wow. And I'd thought being paid to wait in line for a cronut was ridiculous. "Seriously? It's that bad?"

"You saw them at my niece's party. That was just the tip of the iceberg. I've been set up on more dates I didn't know I was walking into than I care to count. They have also sent women and their pets into my clinic with fake symptoms. They have encouraged women to buy a damn pet just to have an excuse to come to my clinic."

Laughter bubbled on my lips.

"It's not funny. It's harassment."

My laughter died at his tone and I felt a twinge of sympathy I didn't want to feel for him. "Can't you just tell them to back off?"

"They swallowed the 'marriage makes everything better' Kool-Aid a long time ago. There's no convincing them otherwise, despite—" He cut off abruptly. "Look, are you interested or not?"

"Ten thousand dollars a month to pretend to be your girlfriend?"

"What? You want more?"

"No! I just . . ." The whole proposal baffled me.

"Are you interested or not?" he repeated. "I have an early sur-gery in the morning and need to go to bed soon."

My lips twitched with laughter again. I so wanted to ruffle his uptight feathers.

Which was probably why agreeing to this was a bad idea. More-over, what sane person offered someone ten thousand dollars a month to fake-date them?

As if he heard the thought he grumbled, "Look, I know it sounds erratic to pay someone thousands of dollars to pretend to date them, but the money is . . . an inheritance that I can't . . . well . . . anyway, I just like the idea of spending it on something that seems wasteful but will actually benefit me and get them off my back."

"Sounds like you all need family therapy."

"We're fine. We love each other. But we also drive each other mad. Like most families."

That was very true.

But ten thousand dollars a month? While I'd never needed much in life, that would allow me to go on my road trip. I could make that money last and have the time of my life. Free as a bird. Moreover, I'd witnessed the intense matchmaking at his niece's birthday party. I remembered thinking how trapped I'd have felt in that situation too. Despite his grumpiness, I experienced a twinge of sympathy again.

Plus, ten thousand dollars.

"I'm interested."

"Fine. Come to my clinic tomorrow at noon."

Bossy! "I'm line sitting tomorrow and have no idea how long I'll be there."

"If you take this job, it will have priority over your others. Are we clear?"

Bristling, I huffed, "Well, I haven't accepted the job yet, so to-morrow I'm line sitting, and if I'm done at noon, I'll be there. If I'm not going to be done at noon, I'll text you and we'll arrange a meeting time. Okay? Bye-bye." I hung up before he could say anything that would absolutely change my mind about entertaining his proposal.

As I strode toward the bar, adrenaline surging through my body, excited to tell my friends about the proposition, my cell vibrated in my hand.

It was a text from the number I'd just dialed.

> Don't you know it's rude to hang up on a person?

I saved Rafe's number to my contacts and replied,

> I would've thought having a woman hang up on you was a refreshing change of pace.

My phone buzzed in my hand again just as I neared my friends' table.

> I'll pay you extra if you lose the smartass attitude.

Laughing, I quickly texted back.

> You couldn't afford it.

"She's grinning like the cat that got the cream." Roger hooted as I took my seat next to him.

"Well, tell us." Kendall leaned across the table. "What did he want?"

I stared at all three of them, still reeling from Rafe's proposal. "To change my life."

Chapter Four

THE VETERINARY CLINIC ON COLUMBUS AVENUE WASN'T AT all what I'd had in mind. I was certain I'd step into a cold modern space and instead I found myself in a clinic that, while modern, was warm and inviting.

A massive paw print was etched into the frosted front window, along with the words **WHITMAN VETERINARY CLINIC.** Inside the middling-sized reception area was curved bench seating along the window with a walnut base and a thick, padded blue cushioned top. The base of the bench matched the curved walnut reception desk opposite it, where a young man sitting behind the desk wore light blue scrubs. The flooring was a light-colored parquet, the wall behind the reception desk a stone tile, the reception desk counter a shiny quartz.

It was a fun twist on sophisticated yet inviting and . . . not what I expected.

One woman and her tiny Chihuahua waited on the bench.

"May I help you?" the baby-faced man in scrubs queried with a smile.

I stepped toward the desk, my heeled boots clicking loudly against the parquet flooring. "Yeah, I have an appointment with Dr. Whitman at noon. Star Meadows."

His eyes lit with recognition. "Yes, Dr. Whitman told me to expect you. An emergency appointment has come in"—he glanced at the woman and her Chihuahua—"but he'll be with you as soon as he can."

Nodding, I sat down at the opposite end of the bench.

The place didn't smell of animals, which meant Whitman's cleaning staff was *good*.

Pulling out my phone, I saw I had a text from Roger asking me if I was there yet. My friends were intrigued to see what else Rafe had to say for himself. I couldn't deny I was curious too at the thought of doing practically nothing and earning more than enough money to travel.

The young man got up and disappeared behind a door I hadn't even noticed. A brief glimpse inside revealed what appeared to be a small pharmacy. He stayed in there a few minutes. Though I had a reading app on my phone, I preferred my e-reader and pulled it out of my purse. I was a big fan of books and I'd read anything. Thriller, romance, mystery, historical fiction, nonfiction. One benefit of my job was being able to *inhale* books during my working week.

The sound of Rafe's resonant voice filtering down the hallway brought my head up, and my heart started beating alarmingly fast. The downside of this proposition was, of course, the way he made me feel.

When Rafe appeared in the reception, I felt hyperalert; every inch of me felt sensitive and *awake*. Goodness, he was tall. I kept forgetting how tall and broad-shouldered he was. His white coat almost strained across those shoulders. He wore a light blue button-down shirt underneath and he'd left one button open at his throat. My fingers itched to undo the next one.

Oh boy.

An older man walked at his side, holding a cat in a pet carrier. "Just once a day," Rafe instructed. "And bland food for the next week."

"Thank you, Dr. Whitman." The older man's lips pinched together in worry.

My heart fluttered as Rafe's gaze caught mine as he crossed the room to the reception desk. He gave me an almost imperceptible nod, that stoic, hard expression on his face, before he turned to the reception desk. The guy behind it had reappeared from the mystery room while I'd been engrossed in my historical fiction book about an Old Hollywood starlet. "Finn"—Rafe's voice caused a pleasant sensation in the pit of my stomach—"can you arrange an appointment for Millie and Mr. Danvers to see me in one week's time?"

"Of course." Finn smiled warmly at the older man. "And I have Millie's prescription ready for you."

Satisfied, Rafe patted Mr. Danvers on the shoulder and pivoted toward me. "I have an emergency appointment and then I'll be right with you."

"Sure." I shrugged, waving my e-reader. "I have something to keep me occupied."

His eyes narrowed on the device in what might have been curiosity, but it was difficult to tell with him. Rafe focused on the woman and her Chihuahua. Though he didn't smile, his tone was a hundred times warmer as he inquired, "Ms. Van Alstyne, what brings you and Gilbert to my office today?"

Gilbert? I eyed the tiny dog, who did *not* look like a Gilbert.

As if sensing my amusement, Rafe shot me a look out of the corner of his eye.

Gilbert? I mouthed.

He gave me a quelling look, though I could have sworn I saw a twinkle of humor in his gaze. However, since that seemed impossible, I decided I'd imagined it.

Ms. Van Alstyne was quietly spoken and I watched as Rafe lifted Gilbert into his arms, petting him gently and murmuring words of greeting as he also bent his head toward Gilbert's owner, listening patiently to her as they wandered out of the reception together.

Yup, the whole vet thing was definitely an issue for my libido.

A little while later, another patient and her dog entered the practice. I observed her interaction at the reception desk, hoping it wouldn't further delay my meeting with Rafe.

"Rocco and I have an appointment with Dr. Hayes," she relayed.

Dr. Hayes?

There was another vet here?

The young woman moved to take a seat on the bench, but her pit bull, Rocco, stopped her by pulling on his short leash to get to me.

I dropped my e-reader on my lap to scratch behind both his ears. "Hey, you," I murmured to him, grinning. "Aren't you just the most handsome guy?"

"Do you hear that, Rocco?" his owner cooed. "Another admirer."

Laughing, I released him so she could take a seat. "He's gorgeous."

She smiled. "Thanks. He's got some knee issues, so he's getting used to this place."

"Yeah, he doesn't seem bothered to be here at all."

"He likes Dr. Hayes."

It was on the tip of my tongue to ask who this mysterious Dr. Hayes was, but there was no need. Footsteps sounded down the hallway, growing louder, until a tall figure appeared where Rafe had disappeared with Gilbert. I raised an eyebrow at the sight of the good-looking blond dude wearing a set of green scrubs. He couldn't have been much older than me, putting him around Rafe's age. His gaze swept the reception, stopping on me with a slight frown, before returning to the woman and Rocco. As he approached the pit bull, however, his attention kept flickering to me.

"And how is Rocco today?" The man lowered to his haunches to pet the pit bull as he wagged his tail and made delighted chuffing sounds. I'd never seen a dog so happy to see his vet.

"Hi, Dr. Hayes," the woman said, beaming at him. I didn't blame her. He was even more gorgeous up close. "He's been struggling lately, so I thought I better bring him in for another checkup."

Dr. Hayes.

This was the other vet.

Oh.

Oh, I got it.

A small smile played on my lips.

Two young handsome vets running a clinic together on the Upper West Side. I bet they made a killing. Maybe Rafe wasn't so uptight that he didn't know how to use good looks to his advantage.

"Okay, Rocco, let's have a look at you." Dr. Hayes stood and his dark gaze came to me. "Are you being attended to?"

"She's here to see Dr. Whitman," Finn replied.

Interest gleamed in the vet's chocolate brown eyes. He gave me a brief, curious smile. "All right."

Then he was gone, leading Rocco and her admiring owner out of the reception area.

"Can I get you anything? Water, perhaps?" Finn asked.

"I'm okay, but thank you." I smiled widely, appreciative that he'd think to ask.

His cheeks turned a little red at the crests as he nodded and focused on his computer. Noting his blue scrubs, I wondered about them, considering Dr. Hayes wore green scrubs.

"Are you a vet too?"

Finn's mouth quirked up at the corners. "No. I'm a veterinary nurse."

"So as good as."

He preened, visibly pleased. "Well, I do a lot. There are two nurses here. Me and Rebecca. We do all the health checks and vaccinations, some of the more unpleasant tasks like . . . well"—his cheeks flushed—"stuff. And uh, nail clipping, dental checks. We do all that. Plus, we do all the reception work too."

"It sounds like this place couldn't run without you."

That obviously delighted him. "Are you sure I can't get you anything, Ms. Meadows?"

"Please call me Star. And I'm really okay."

Finn nodded. "Dr. Whitman shouldn't be much longer."

Thankfully, Finn was right. A few minutes later, Rafe appeared with Ms. Van Alstyne and Gilbert. They murmured together at the reception desk and then Rafe held the door open for her as she and her Chihuahua left the building.

Then I found myself under his keen regard. His gaze lowered down my body to where my floral skirt flowed over my legs and covered my boots. I stared back, trying not to squirm.

"This way," he announced abruptly, marching across the reception area.

Jumping up from my seat, I hurried to follow him, throwing Finn a small smile and ignoring how he stared after us wide-eyed.

My boots were loud on the floor as I rushed after Rafe. He led me down a narrow hallway that had two doors with signs that read **EXAM ROOM 1** and **EXAM ROOM 2**.

At the end of that hall, we stopped at one of three doors. Rafe held the door open and gestured me forward. He'd ushered me into what I could only presume was his office. There was a small window on the back wall that I assumed faced into the alleyway. Artificial lighting and the same walnut touches saved the room from being dreary. There were framed degrees on his wall, as well as a family photograph.

"Take a seat."

I did, watching him round his desk to sit in his dark brown leather chair. He leaned back in it, eyes hooked to mine. My breathing grew a little shallow.

"What are you reading?" he surprised me by asking.

It was then I realized I still clutched my e-reader in my hand. I stuffed it into my purse. "Uh, a book about an Old Hollywood starlet."

"Tragic?" he queried, as if he was genuinely interested.

"Parts of it." I smiled at him. "Do you want to start a book club?"

He sighed wearily. "I'd really like to discuss paying you a bonus to not have you make smart comments like that."

"I wasn't being smart." I really wasn't. "I'd love to start a book club."

"Someone give me patience," Rafe muttered before he sat forward, elbows on his desk. "Do we have a deal or not?"

"So is Dr. Hayes your partner here, or does he work for you?"

He scowled. "What does it matter?"

"It's very smart," I mused. "The two of you running this place."

"Why's that?"

I guffawed. "You know why."

"I do?"

"Look at you both. You must have every person inclined toward the male gender in New York lining up to bring their beloved pets to you."

"You met Owen." He sat back in his chair, eyeing me coldly. "Owen is my friend. We went through vet school together at Cornell. He's my employee. And if we're going to do this, he's completely off-limits to you."

Wow, he was a surly bastard. "Noted, Mr. Sunshine. Will you be telling Owen the truth about us . . . *if* we do this?"

Rafe's eyes narrowed. "That's none of your business."

Huh. "Well, it kind of will be, because I don't want to be the idiot pretending to like you in front of him if he already knows the truth."

That muscle in his jaw ticced. "Fine. I haven't decided if I'm telling him, but I will let you know if I do. Happy? Do we have a deal or not?"

"About the smart comments? Definitely not. About the fake dating thing, maybe. I need to know exactly what will be required of me. And I'll want it in a contract so you can't renege on payments."

Affronted, he denied, "I would never."

"Still . . ."

"Fine. I'll draw up a contract."

"Detailing . . . ?"

Rafe sighed again. "Like I said last night, my mother and sister-in-law are driving me up the wall with their matchmaking efforts. I'd like you to pretend to date me for up to the next six months. Then we'll pretend you dump me, breaking my heart, leaving me so devastated, I'll get at least another six months beyond that of reprieve from their hellish romantic machinations."

He said it so deadpan, I almost burst into laughter.

"You want me to pretend to date you for six months and then pretend to break your heart?"

"Yes."

"And just to be clear, you don't expect sex?"

His nostrils flared. "Of course I don't." Then something flickered in Rafe's gaze. "Though, I suppose, we might be required to occasionally show affection toward each other so that people believe we're in love."

Required to occasionally show affection toward each other? My lips twitched with the desperate need to laugh. "PG kissing and touching?"

Rafe cleared his throat, apparently uncomfortable. "I suppose."

"Oh, I'll need you to be perfectly clear in the contract about what it is we're doing here."

"Fine, PG kissing and touching will be required."

"Fine."

"Fine." He glowered at me. "Anything else?"

Laughter tickled my throat. "Hey, this is your party."

Rafe rolled his neck on his shoulders as if my mere presence stressed him. "Like I said last night, I'll need you to be flexible with your schedule to accommodate our venture."

"While I'm happy to prioritize this job over my others, I'll need to know our schedule beforehand so I know not to take jobs that will interfere with this. Do you have an app that keeps your schedule, appointments, social calendar?"

"I have one for work, but not my social calendar, as you call it."

"Then we'll download one we can share. Anytime you update it, I'll get a notification on my phone and vice versa."

His brows pulled together. "That sounds very efficient."

"*You* sound surprised."

"*You* don't seem like a person who would be very organized."

I gave him a tight smile. "Just because there's not a giant stick up my ass or because I don't plan my life to its every inch doesn't mean I'm not capable and organized. I have two jobs. I need to keep those straight."

"Fine." He nodded coldly.

"Fine."

"Fine." This time his voice held an edge as he hurried to order, "Don't say 'fine.'"

"You're the one who keeps saying 'fine.'"

He scowled.

I sighed. Boy, he was a barrel of laughs. So, so unbelievably beautiful to look at, but was it worth it to put up with his grim demeanor? *Remember the money.* "You'll really pay me ten thousand dollars a month?"

"For some freedom, I'd pay more."

The exhaustion in his eyes suddenly made me feel sympathy that I probably shouldn't have. "I can't believe your family would continue to do this to you if they truly knew what a strain it is on you." Then something occurred to me. "Is it . . . is there another reason you perhaps don't want to find a *lady* to settle down with?"

"Subtle," he said dryly. "And no, I'm not gay. If I were gay, they'd be foisting every eligible gay man on me. It's the fact that I'm thirty-three years old and alone that bothers them. I think they're afraid if they don't intervene now, I'll spend my life alone forever."

"And would you?"

"Of course."

Curious, I leaned forward. "You don't want a wife, a family?"

Rafe stared right through me. "Do we have a deal or not, Ms. Meadows?"

Okay, no personal questions. I considered him. "I won't be required to change who I am for this role? Change my appearance, my personality?"

He studied me in such a way that my thighs pressed tight together in reaction. His expression was irritatingly unreadable as our eyes met again. "No. Just be you. I rather like the idea of giving them what they want at the same time as what they'll never expect."

My neck prickled. "What does that mean?"

"They're expecting a society princess or a career woman." His lips quirked up at the corners. "I'm looking forward to seeing how they react to you."

Huh. My cheeks heated and an ache I didn't like bloomed in the middle of my chest. I thought . . . yeah; I thought I'd definitely just been insulted. While it was a relief to know I didn't have to pretend to be anything but myself, it reminded me that Rafe looked down his high and mighty nose at me. It gave me pause. "I have a few stipulations that I want written into the contract."

He gestured for me to go ahead.

I straightened in my seat. "You will not mock, berate, or humiliate me in front of your friends and family. I won't be anyone's punch line or punching bag."

Outraged, he fumed, "I would never."

"Your niece's party suggests otherwise. I overheard how you spoke about me to your sister-in-law."

Something like remorse flashed across his features before he rearranged them into an imperious mask. "I promise it won't happen again."

"And just now? Am I supposed to ignore the fact that you want to use me to needle your family? Like I'm . . . someone who would offend them?"

Both his eyebrows rose. "Ms. Meadows . . . I . . . that's not what . . . that's not how I intended it. I just meant that you'll be a surprising choice and it's not every day I get to surprise my family. They think I'm predictable."

"Oh." That ache dissipated at his sincerity. "Okay."

He shifted as if he was uncomfortable, and an awkward silence fell between us. Deciding we were better off sniping at each other than enduring this discomfiting weirdness, I announced, "Good. Now, in private, I don't expect you to be Mr. Warm and Fuzzy, but I also don't expect to be verbally abused."

"What on earth . . ." he grumbled in exasperation as he sank back into his chair. "When have I verbally abused you?"

"You called my Scottish brogue awful. That I butchered the accent."

"That wasn't verbal abuse, that was honesty."

I narrowed my eyes.

Rafe rolled his eyes. "Fine. I will keep my opinion on your Scottish brogue to myself." Then he muttered something under his breath about the ridiculousness of our conversation.

I wanted so badly to unwind him. Mess up his perfect hair, rip off a couple of buttons on his shirt and say something that would make him laugh, big and loud.

Those kinds of thoughts should have made me run for the exit.

Instead I summarized, "Six months, ten grand a month, fake dating, fake falling in love, fake breaking up, no sex, PG kissing and touching, and polite courteousness between us?"

"Yes."

"And how can you trust me?" I shrugged. "How do you know I'm not some horrible person who will infiltrate your life and try to con millions out of you? I know your father is kind of a big deal in the business world. Aren't millionaires usually paranoid about protecting themselves from con artists and strangers?"

He stared at me stonily for a second and then reached across the desk to where a tablet computer lay. He tapped on it and the screen lit up. After a few more taps on the screen, he turned it and pushed it across the desk toward me.

"Star Shine Meadows, twenty-eight years old, social security number, date of birth, born in Sacramento, California, parents Arlo and Dawn Meadows moved you around a lot, until you moved to New York City when you were twenty-one. You've had a plethora of jobs, mostly bartending and waitressing, until you got into line sitting and character costume acting a few years ago. You live on Staten Island."

I gaped at the email that detailed everything down to the high school I'd attended and the fact that I was in the drama club and graduated with a 3.8 GPA. Despite my grades, my parents had never encouraged me to attend college, and I hadn't liked the idea that college meant deciding my career path when I was only eighteen years old. The thought made me feel claustrophobic, so I'd gone the way of my parents and just taken jobs that fed and clothed me and kept a roof over my head.

"You had me investigated?"

"Of course." He shrugged. "Like you said, I can't invite someone into my life who might be shady. While your career is nonexistent, no one can say you don't work hard, and you have no record or nefarious history that my PI could dig up. Your credit check and demeanor reveal someone who is generally unmaterialistic. My gut tells me you're not really interested in my money beyond the ten thousand. The ten thousand a month is required for a specific purpose, am I right?"

"I want to travel."

He smirked. "See. For some odd reason, I believe you. So we're good to go."

Irked beyond measure that he'd investigated me, I demanded, "I want one of those."

He frowned. "One of what?"

"A file. A private investigation file into you."

"Easy." He scowled. "It's called Google."

"Will Google tell me what your high school GPA was?"

"4.0."

Of course it was.

"Anything else?"

"I can't believe you had me investigated."

"You just said yourself I'd be a fool to invite a stranger into my life without some background information. It's not like I did a deep dive. I just looked into the basics."

"Fine."

"Fine." He glowered. "Don't say 'fine.'"

"I will say 'fine' if I want." I stood up. "That's another thing to put in the contract. No bossing me around."

"I doubt anyone could truly boss you around."

I beamed at the compliment. "Thank you."

Rafe shook his head, standing from his chair. "You are very odd."

"I'll take that as a compliment too." I pulled open his office door before he could. "At least odd isn't boring."

"No one could ever accuse you of being boring, Ms. Meadows." I felt the heat of his stare at my back and glanced over my shoulder. My breath caught as the scent of his cologne tickled my senses. Those serious blue eyes of his held me captive.

"You should really call me Star," I replied, my voice softer, a little huskier than intended. "If you want your family to believe we're dating."

His eyes flickered to my lips and then back to hold mine. "Fine. Star it is."

"And I can call you Rafe?"

He nodded and then gestured me impatiently out of his office. "Let me show you out."

"But . . . don't you want to arrange our first . . . appointment?"

"I'll text you with the arrangements and we'll set up that app thing you were talking about."

"All right. Try to give me as much notice as possible."

He gave me a brief nod. "Text me your email and I'll send over the contract. Once that's signed, I'll need your bank details."

Wow. This was actually happening. To cover my sudden uncharacteristic burst of nerves, I muttered dryly, "I would have thought your PI would have dug up my email address at the very least."

"Funny. Should I prepare myself for this level of humor during our fake relationship?"

I grinned. "I don't know. Should I prepare myself for droll stick-up-the-ass responses to everything I say?"

Rafe groaned and brushed past me into the hall. "This is going to be a long six months."

Chapter Five

MUSIC FROM THE NEIGHBOR DIRECTLY BENEATH ME SWELLED
up through the floor, but luckily the guy was a mutual fan of the
Airborne Toxic Event, so I hummed along to "Faithless" as I made
an omelet for my late dinner. I had spent the last thirty-six hours line
sitting for theater tickets in the pouring rain and all I wanted to do
was grab a bite to eat that didn't have processed, artificial crap in it,
and then fall asleep on my Murphy bed.

While my apartment was bigger than any I'd rented in New
York, it was still a studio. My landlord had furnished the place with
a bed and two chairs, but I'd asked him to take those out because
Jude had a friend who was selling one of those fancy new Murphy
beds with the built-ins. I got it for a steal! It was the first time in my
adult life that I had shelves. I'd only been in the apartment a year
and I'd already filled every inch of them with books.

Books made a place feel cozy and lived in. So much so, I didn't
care it only took three steps to cover the entire length of my kitchen.

I switched off the cooktop after I'd plated up my omelet, grabbed
water, and settled down on my sofa to watch a show Kendall had

waxed lyrical over for years. I'd finally given in to her pleading to watch it and fired up my laptop.

Eleven and Mike had just met on the screen when my phone buzzed beside me. At the sight of Rafe's name, I experienced a flutter in my chest. That was normal, considering our unusual agreement, right? There was absolutely no other reason for my heart to skip a beat.

Pausing the show, I swiped my screen and hit the speaker button. "Howdy doo-dee," I answered.

"Tell me that is not how you answer the phone," Rafe commented wearily.

I grinned. "For you, I'll make sure it always is."

"May I request that you don't?"

Seriously, I was smiling so hard my cheeks hurt. "Oh, I don't know. I quite like the reaction I got."

"You are exasperating."

"Did you say I'm exhilarating?"

"*Exasperating*," he repeated, exasperated.

"Exasperating, exhilarating, tomayto, tomahto."

"Why is it when I call you, I immediately forget why I called?"

Chuckling, I shoved away my nearly empty plate and relaxed against my sofa. "Because I'm dazzling."

"Someone likes herself."

"Of course I do. Don't you like yourself?"

Rafe was quiet a moment and then when he spoke, his tone was tighter, more formal. "I'm calling to arrange our first date. My plan is to pretend with my family that I'm busy this next month, so that when I announce we're dating, they'll think we've been dating all this time."

"Does that mean we won't start this thing for a month?"

"Exactly. That should give you plenty of time to figure out your schedule, right?"

"Yeah, that's great." So why did I feel disappointed I wouldn't see him for the next month? It made no sense! The man was a pain in the ass.

"It means that our actual first fake date will be at our monthly family dinner because they'll think we've been dating for weeks."

Wow. Talk about throwing us both to the lions. "Don't you think we should practice or something before we just dive right in with the family?"

"I'll come over to your place the day before the family dinner to tell you what you need to know. My parents live in Harrison, so we'll also have the drive to go over everything again. We'll make sure you know the things about my family that you would know if we'd been dating for a month."

It all sounded a little too laid-back, even for me. I mean, I was a fly-by-the-seat-of-my-pants kind of gal, but I felt like a deception on this level required research, test runs, spending more time together to be comfortable enough that we appeared as if we'd been dating for a month.

I nibbled on my bottom lip and then suggested, "Shouldn't we meet up before then?"

"Why?"

I rolled my eyes, trying not to be offended by his obvious lack of interest in spending any more time with me than he needed to. "So that we become more comfortable with one another?"

"Star, you yelled across a busy street that I'd left peanut butter and jelly in your bedsheets. To me. A man you'd met once. I don't think a person could be more comfortable with another person than you are with anyone you meet."

I burst out laughing at his droll tone. "Okay, I'll give you that. I sometimes forget about boundaries."

Something like amusement hummed in his voice as he replied, "That is a very diplomatic way of putting it."

"How would you put it?"

"You don't want to know."

"Hmm, you're probably right."

"So, according to my calendar"—he was abruptly all business again—"next month's family dinner is May fourteenth. I'll drop by your apartment the Saturday before. I work Saturday mornings, so if you can clear your schedule for late afternoon, I can drop by then."

I typed it into my calendar. "Will I text you my address?"

Rafe cleared his throat. "I have it."

Right. Because he'd investigated me. "Of course. How is Bob?"

"Excuse me?"

"Your PI guy. Aren't they all called Bob?"

"You are the strangest person I have ever met."

"Then you haven't lived much. Also, I'm sending you a link right now to a calendar app we can share. I'll set everything up. You just download it, okay?"

"Right. Thank you. So . . . I guess I'll see you in four weeks."

I felt that strangely deflated sensation again, but ignored it. This—Rafe—was a job. A very well-paying job. Nothing more. "Okay. I'll see you then."

"This was productive. Good night."

So brusque and formal. I shook my head. "Try unbuttoning the second button over the next few weeks, okay?"

"What—"

"Talk soon." I hung up before our conversation turned antagonistic again.

Rafe texted a few minutes later to tell me he'd downloaded the app, so I set everything up until we could both see our shared calendar. Amusement filled me as I considered setting dates like *Rafe's Surgery—Operation Remove Stick from Ass*, but I wasn't sure that'd go over so well.

My amusement died, however, as I came out of a text with Rafe and my attention lingered on the conversation with Dawn, my mom. I tapped on it, noting the text message I'd sent a week ago that had still gone unanswered. That wasn't unusual. My parents were self-proclaimed hippies. The only reason they had cell phones was because it was almost impossible to navigate modern society without one. Plus, it was the easiest way for us to stay in contact, what with them in Colorado and me in New York.

Not that they were good at the keeping-in-contact thing.

With a heavy sigh, I tapped out of the conversation and got ready for bed.

After I'd cleaned up, changed into my PJs, and lowered the Murphy bed, I sank into it and my eyelids slammed shut. The music from downstairs had quieted and so the last sound in my ears before sleep took me was that of Rafe Whitman's low, resonant voice.

Chapter Six

THERE WERE MANY TIMES OVER THE NEXT FOUR WEEKS WHEN I almost talked myself out of the job with Rafe Whitman. I was used to dressing up as characters and pretending to be someone else; however, it hadn't really occurred to me how different it would be to deceive an entire group of people for an extended period.

When I thought too hard on that, on how nice Philippa Whitman had been to me and how I was going to lie to her and her family, I almost chickened out.

Jude would encourage my doubts, still adamantly against the whole thing. Kendall would remind me that if Rafe wasn't concerned about lying to his own family, then I shouldn't have a problem with it. She said, and I quote, "You're defending his right to live his life however he pleases, and that is an ethos we all live by." Roger wasn't so lofty in his encouragement. He merely reminded me about the ten thousand dollars a month and, I wouldn't lie, for the first time in my life the green stuff swayed me.

I just . . . I guess I was more restless than I'd thought. Something was missing in my life and I was positive it was traveling. The ability to just pick up and leave and wander the country, free of commitment. It had to be that.

So, for once, money was important.

I just had to live with the fact that I had fallen to its temptations.

Something that I now reminded myself as I wiped my hands across my jeans and waited for Rafe to appear in my doorway. I'd just buzzed him in so we could go over everything I needed to know about his family before dinner tomorrow.

Hearing footsteps in the hallway, I straightened, bracing myself to see him for the first time in a month. We'd shared a few texts to clarify days and times, as Rafe updated our shared calendar with events he wanted me to attend with him over the next few months.

Then he was there.

Taller and broader than I remembered as he filled my entire doorway.

I'd also, apparently, forgotten how gorgeous he was with his thick dark hair and denim-blue eyes. My breath caught in my throat as I attempted not to ogle him. He wore black suit pants and a dark green cashmere sweater that molded to his powerful physique. The sleeves were pushed up to just below his elbow, revealing corded forearms. He was like a Marvel hero out of costume. "Hi," I croaked. "Come in."

Rafe entered the apartment, closing the door behind him, and his attention never left me. His gaze drifted down my body to my bare feet. My toenails were pink and glittery and my big toes had daisy flowers stickered onto the nails. He quirked an eyebrow and dragged his gaze back up in a way that caused goose bumps to prickle down my bare arms. Rafe seemed to linger on my bare midriff before our eyes met.

"Is this the kind of thing you're planning to wear tomorrow?"

I wore an off-the-shoulder white peasant blouse with buttons down the front, puff sleeves, and a cropped hemline. Not sure if he liked or disliked it, I shrugged. "Well, I was thinking I'd wear shoes, if it's all right with you."

His lips twitched as he nodded and then looked around my small apartment. A frown marred his brow, deepening the more he studied it. "This place is tiny."

I snorted at the observation. "Yeah."

Rafe looked back at me. "I can only imagine what you're being charged for this place. Rental costs are a travesty."

"Do you rent in the city?" I was curious. "Should I know where you live?"

"Yes." He nodded and gazed around. "Where should we sit to discuss?"

Way to avoid giving me his address. What did he think I'd do? Gather my gang of ne'er-do-wells and break into his apartment during the night to steal the family jewels?

I gestured to my sofa. "May I offer you a drink?" Jeez, now I sounded formal. We would never be able to convince his family we'd been dating for a month if we continued like this.

As if the same thing had occurred to him, he scowled. "Yes, please. Coffee, black, if you have it."

He took his coffee black. Not surprising. "Have a seat."

Yet as I made coffee, one black and one with milky sugary goodness in it, Rafe didn't take a seat. He stood before my sofa, staring at my bookshelves. "You have quite the eclectic taste in literature," he commented.

"I have quite the eclectic taste in all things." I brought the coffees over. "I like what I like, no matter what it is. Do you read a lot?"

"I used to." He lowered down onto my sofa, making it look tiny. "Now I don't have as much time to read as I'd like."

Sitting down beside him, I ignored the way his cologne teased my senses. "What genres do you enjoy?"

"Right. You need to know this stuff." He turned to me.

Truthfully, I'd genuinely wanted to know, but whatever. "Right."

"I enjoy crime, mystery, thrillers."

"Do you like nonfiction? Autobiographies? I love autobiographies."

"Not really." Rafe frowned and shifted uncomfortably. "I'm not much of a people person."

Why was that personality trait suddenly adorable when he admitted to it?

"I'm a total people person. Love people. They're so freaking weird."

Humor lit his eyes. "Yes, they are."

"So you prefer animals, huh? To people, I mean?"

Nodding, he replied quietly, "Animals are a lot more straightforward than humans. And if you love them, their loyalty is unwavering."

Oh wow.

Our gazes held, his so blue and deep. Tightness constricted in my chest.

Rafe wrenched his gaze away, taking a quick sip of coffee. "I've lived in New York my whole life, attended a private high school in Manhattan, went on to Columbia for my undergraduate degree and then Cornell for my veterinary license. I worked as a vet in a couple of clinics before I opened my own and hired Owen, who, as I said, I met at Cornell. That was two years ago.

"My father, as I'm sure you already know, is Gregory Whitman. He started his shipping company Mercurious in the mideighties, and it has become one of the biggest homegrown shipping companies in the country. Not the biggest in the grand scheme of things, but extremely successful. My father expected all of his children to go into the family business, and only my brother decided to. Hugo is the new CEO of Mercurious now that my father's technically retired—though he likes to be kept informed on everything as if he still works there—and Hugo spends almost all of his time working, although he has a wife and child at home. My sister, Gigi—Georgina—is five years younger than me, and she is a software engineer for one of the biggest tech companies on the planet. She's a genius, and she's always gone her own way." His lips curled into a genuine smile, and my heart raced a little harder at the sight. "You'll understand when you meet her. I have an inkling you two will get along."

That was good to know. "Your mom?"

"Grew up in Connecticut, upper-middle-class family, graduated from Brown, met my father in her senior year of college, and got married instead of pursuing the teaching career she'd had in mind. Neither of them expected my father's business to take off the way it did, but she'd grown up in a world that made her the perfect partner in navigating New York society. My father credits her with creating connections that launched Mercurious."

"That's awesome."

He shrugged. "She seems satisfied with her life."

His tepid response confused me. "Do you have a good relationship with your parents? I mean, beyond the fact that your mother has driven you to hire someone to pretend to be your girlfriend."

Rafe's lips pursed. "I'm not sure that is information even someone I'm dating would have at this point."

"Are all rich people as guarded as you?"

"Yes."

I bit back a smile. "Okay then. Anything else I should know? Grandparents?"

"My dad was raised by a single mom. Nana. She passed away ten years ago."

Seeing the flash of pain in his eyes, I had to stop myself from reaching out to touch him. "I'm so sorry."

"Thank you." He shifted uncomfortably. "My mom's parents, my gran and grandpa, retired to Key Largo. We see them once a year at Christmas. We're not as close to them as we were to my nana, so they won't factor in this ruse."

"Oh. Okay. Anything else?"

"Pippa. Phillipa."

"Your sister-in-law and mom's partner in crime?"

"The very one. Hugo met Pippa at Harvard. She'd graduated from Harvard Law School and worked a year at a fancy law firm in the city when my brother proposed and asked her to give it up to be his partner. But what he really meant was to be his society wife and mother to his children. And she gave up everything to do it. They've been together for seventeen years."

Hearing the obvious disbelief in his voice, I suggested, "She must have wanted that life or she wouldn't have given up practicing law for it."

"She's obviously so bored that she now dedicates her time to trying to find me a wife. This was a woman who wanted to work her way up to being a criminal court judge and now spends her days managing their social calendar and sending eligible women to my clinic. Pippa wanted to be a hands-on mother, but she had to hire a nanny because she's constantly involved in some charitable event or another that rich people host to make themselves feel better for having more than their fair share of the world's wealth. Pippa is bright, kind, and capable. Don't you, as a woman, think she should pursue a career, do something productive with her talents?"

Wow. His words stung. In insulting his sister-in-law, he was also insulting me because I knew he didn't think my jobs counted as something worthwhile. "Why is striving to be an excellent mother and running charitable events not ambitious? Why can't giving her intelligence and kindness and capability to her children and others count as something useful?"

"I'm surprised. You strike me as a feminist, but this isn't very feminist of you."

I stiffened. "Of course it is. True feminism is supporting each other in whatever endeavors we pursue. So being a stay-at-home mom isn't any less important than someone who goes to work every day in an office. If *someone* wants to turn their nose up at Pippa for choosing that path in life, then *they're* not a true feminist.

"Equality for all is something I will always fight for, and a woman should never feel guilted or forced into or out of a career or the life she wants. But I also won't tear someone down for *choosing* to live their life the way they want to live it. The problem with our society is that we're so fixed on either outdated ideals or pushing for progress that we forget to just allow people to be who they want to be. Why the hell, as long as it isn't hurting anyone, can we not just allow people to live their lives the way they want to and stop pressuring them to live the way anyone else dictates they should? Isn't that why we're here, right now? Because in your world 'being thirty-three and a bachelor is concerning'? Which is bullshit, and we both know it." I drew in a sharp breath, needing it after my rambling tirade.

He was silent so long I didn't think he'd respond. I studied him, the way the muscle in his jaw flexed as he stared at me as if he'd never seen me before.

"You're right," he agreed quietly, shocking me. "You're absolutely right. I . . . I'm focusing my frustration with Pippa on the wrong things. Of course I'm proud of how well she's raising Charmaine. I shouldn't have said what I said."

Rafe continued to stare, his eyes washing over my face in a way that made my breath quicken.

"Well . . ." I let out shaky laughter, trying to defuse the sudden tension between us, "Wonders never cease. You admitted you were wrong."

"I happen to do that on occasion, but don't get used to it."

I smiled, looking away. "I won't."

"I guess we've covered all we need to for now. You know my niece is eight years old."

"It seems like you and Charmaine are close?"

Rafe's expression warmed. "She's a sweetheart. And, uh, my brother works a lot, so I try to be there for her when I can."

Don't make me like you, Whitman.

After another moment of tension-filled silence as we stared at each other, Rafe abruptly stood. "I'll collect you tomorrow at three thirty. We do dinner a little early on a Sunday."

We were done? *Okay*, then. "That's fine."

As I closed the door on him, I considered that he hadn't bothered to ask me anything about myself beyond what his PI had already told me. His lack of interest in me stung. It was also kind of rude.

He lost some points for that.

Which was good.

Because I seriously did not want to feel anything remotely positive toward the brooding pain in the ass.

Chapter Seven

I SWEAR I HAD PLENTY OF TIME TO GET READY FOR RAFE PICK-
ing me up for the dinner at his parents' house. It was a rare Sunday
off work, so I thought I'd do some grocery shopping in the morning,
clean my apartment after that, and then read for a while before I had
to get ready.

But it was almost time for Rafe to arrive and I was still half naked in front of my laptop. It was perched on my kitchen counter and
Roger's, Kendall's, and Jude's faces peered out from the screen.

"This has to be it. This is my lucky dress. I was wearing this
when I scored free coffee at Blue Bean, when I met that guy at that
art gallery thing and had the best sex of my life, *and* I got half off the
dress in the first place." I huffed out the last part, feeling sweaty and
not at all ready to meet my fake boyfriend's fancy parents.

"There was nothing wrong with the other six," Jude retorted.
"And why does it matter? I thought this guy wanted you to just be
you during all this?"

"He does. But I'd put effort into dressing for a boyfriend's
parents."

"You've never met a boyfriend's parents in your life," Roger teased.

"Uh, she hasn't had a boyfriend since she was a kid," Kendall corrected him. "Just a series of casual love affairs, like that *guy* from that art gallery *thing*."

I just laughed at her teasing because it was true. I was the biggest commitment-phobe I knew. Why was I freaking out about what I was going to wear to meet Rafe's parents? Like this was real. I was acting out of character.

I slumped with my dress half on. "You're right. I should wear what I want."

"And I just lost thirty minutes of my life for nothing," Jude grumbled.

Kendall slapped him on the arm. "Shut up."

"It's true!" I yanked up the short sleeves of my blue dress. "I've wasted your time and mine. This is a job. I should wear whatever I would wear for any other job. Now I'm a sweaty mess for no good reason."

"You are not," Roger assured me. "You look beautiful, and this dress is perfect."

It was a comfortable but inexpensive short-sleeved maxi dress, fitted at the waist, with a tiered skirt that wasn't overly voluminous like some of my other dresses. It was blue and white polka dot and I could dress it up or down. I quickly slipped on my espadrilles that had an ankle strap, not ties (tie espadrilles were a pain in the butt).

"Jewelry?" I asked my friends.

"Ooh, what about those earrings—the white ones with all the dangling petals?" Kendall suggested.

"Yes!" I pulled my jewelry box out from under my sofa bed and found the earrings. Grabbing a mix of white, blue, and gold bangles, I shoved a bundle on my wrists so I jingled as I walked.

Fluffing my hair, I stood in front of the laptop. "Okay, I'm good?"

"Beautiful!"

"Gorgeous."

"Yeah, I'd do you."

I beamed at my friends. "You guys are the best. Thank you for putting up with me. As you were!"

"Text me when you get there and when you get home," Roger ordered before I could end the video chat. His tone was stern. "I'm still not convinced this guy isn't a serial killer."

"Fair," I agreed. "I'll text you. I promise. Love you all!"

"Love you."

"Love ya, babes."

"Yeah, yeah, you too."

I grinned and closed my laptop just as my door buzzed.

I'D TOLD RAFE TO WAIT FOR ME, BUT HE'D INSISTED ON COM-ing up to my door to collect me. It was kind of an old-fashioned gentlemanly gesture.

I would not admit to liking that facet of his personality at all.

Or that I got no small amount of pleasure out of the way his eyes drifted over my body when I opened the door. There was a flicker of something that could have been mistaken for a positive reaction. Almost as if he liked what he saw.

However, he quickly wiped the reaction from his features and gruffly gestured for me to follow him, so I probably imagined that brief flare of appreciation.

Outside my building, parked on my street, and drawing attention from people passing by, was the coolest car I'd ever seen. I knew very little about cars, but I'd seen enough old movies to know it had to be an American classic. Whoever had restored it did it lovingly. I was gawking at the impressive silver-blue shininess, wondering who it belonged to, when Rafe walked right up and unlocked it.

He opened the passenger door for me. "Ready?"

Mute with shock, I hurried across the sidewalk and slid into the car ass first. I lifted my skirt so it didn't get caught in the door, flashing my legs as I pulled in my feet. Looking up at Rafe, I saw his gaze lingering on my bare skin for a split second before he slammed the door shut.

I blinked against the abrupt motion and then turned to take in my surroundings.

Holy shit.

I was almost afraid to put my hands on the seats—they were a perfect ivory leather. Even the interior of the door was lined in ivory leather with chrome detailing. The steering wheel protruded from the dash and was much thinner than modern steering wheels. It was finished in a tan leather. The dashboard was a trip back in time. No computer system, no fancy-schmancy stuff. Just cool chrome-covered dials and a speedometer.

Rafe got into the driver's side. His seat was pushed back farther than mine to accommodate his long legs.

He didn't say a word about the fact that he'd turned up in the coolest car ever, so cool that even I, who was not "into cars," thought it was the coolest car ever. I thought Rafe would show up in a practical SUV. Or worse, a supercar.

Not this. It was like sitting next to Danny Zuko without all the hair oil.

A few seconds later, the car growled to life and we were gliding down the street, turning heads.

"What kind of car is this?"

Rafe's hands were light and relaxed on the steering wheel. I noticed how long and graceful his fingers were, in contrast to his large masculine knuckles. A tingle between my legs startled me, and I wrenched my gaze from his seductive limbs.

"It's a 1965 Pontiac Catalina."

Definitely an American classic. "Where did you get it?" I was endlessly curious since the car and Rafe seemed like contradictory beings. If a car could count as a being. I was pretty sure car enthusiasts everywhere thought that they could.

My fake date flicked me a look before focusing on the road. "I restored it."

I think my jaw hit my lap. "You? You restored a 1965 Pontiac?"

"Catalina," he murmured, as if that part was very important. Maybe it was. I wouldn't know. "When I was sixteen, my father offered to buy me a car like he did my brother before me. We lived in New York, used a town car most of the time, so we didn't have need of one, but we also had our summer home in Harrison—now my parents' full-time home—and my brother used his car during the summer months. But I'd been obsessed with classic cars since my grandfather bought me a set of mini classics to play with when I was six years old. So I told my father that I wanted to buy a 1965 Pontiac Catalina." The corner of his mouth kicked up. "Dad told me that a fully restored Pontiac Catalina would cost more than what he had in mind, so I would need to buy one that required a lot of work. I think he thought I'd balk and just ask for a new car. Instead, I asked him to buy me a piece-of-junk Pontiac."

"And you turned it into this?" I was in awe.

Rafe chuckled, his fingers lovingly stroking the steering wheel.

"Eventually. It took a long time. Dad ended up buying me a Mustang for the summers. And I spent all of my free time trying to restore this baby. When Dad retired a few years ago, we finished her together. I've only been driving her for a year. I keep her in a garage in the city."

"You spent sixteen years restoring a car?"

He frowned. "Yes, so? I've been busy."

"No, I don't mean it like that. I meant . . . wow. I don't think I've committed myself to anything for that long. That's impressive. And

I like that your dad helped. You'll always have those memories." I reached out to touch the dashboard. "So . . . Was she—or he—just a shell when you bought her?"

"You like cars?"

"No." I snorted. "But this one is the coolest freaking car I've ever seen."

That's when Rafe Whitman smiled at me for the very first time. I swear my heart and clit swelled in unison.

"Yeah?" He looked boyishly pleased about my interest in his car. It was such a sexy look and I hated that I thought he was sexy. "Well, *she* was a shell. Part of the reason it took so long to restore her was because sourcing original parts is not easy. For a start, someone had taken out the engine. It took time, but I finally tracked down a 421-cubic-inch two-plus-two V8 engine. The 1965 was the only model that featured that type of engine. She's got a four-speed synchro-mesh manual transmission with the Hurst shifter," he relayed as he stroked said shifter. Who knew talking about cars could be so sexual? Or maybe it was just Rafe talking about cars.

"The chrome work, the paint work?"

His expression was wry. "We learned what we could about restoring her and got a lot of help from my dad's old mechanic friend at a garage in Harrison, but the bodywork . . . I left that to the professionals."

"She really is a beauty. Not at all what I expected you to drive."

Just like that, his frown returned. "What did you expect me to drive?"

I shrugged. "Something practical."

I knew immediately it was the wrong thing to say because the atmosphere inside the coolest car ever suddenly did not match the car's vibe.

"So, do you remember everything from yesterday?" Rafe's tone was formal, detached again.

Apparently, the "practical" comment offended him. After the things he'd said to me?

You'd think someone who could dish out the honesty could take it in return.

We spent the rest of the journey upstate going over information about his family. He added things he hadn't told me yesterday, but he was right. It was all fresh in my mind for meeting them.

Something occurred to me, however, once we were in Harrison. We'd driven down leafy, tree-lined streets and had just turned onto a street separated into entrance and exit by an island of beautiful, perfectly trimmed trees. "Uh, we haven't discussed how we supposedly got together after meeting at Pippa's?"

"I told my family I got your number from the company you work for. That I lied and told them I wanted to hire you. My mother found it pretty romantic," he said dryly.

I chuckled, the tension releasing a little now that he was being more affable. "Okay. And where did we go on our first date?"

"I took you to Konbanwa, my favorite sushi restaurant in Manhattan."

I grimaced. "I hate sushi."

"Seriously?"

"Don't act so surprised . . ." I faded off as I noted the enormous homes we passed. Rafe took a left down another tree-lined road, passing a few more large houses on either side of a traffic circle with a large tree in the middle. He drove off the circle and toward a low stone wall with white gates. He picked up a key fob from the center dash and clicked it. The gate swung open and we drove onto the circular brick-paved driveway of a stunning house nestled among the aspens.

"Holy . . ."

It was a two-story red brick with white trim and . . . it was sprawling.

I swallowed hard.

Rafe parked his Pontiac behind a Porsche. There was a fancy white SUV in front of the Porsche. "Don't act so surprised . . . ?" He reminded me I'd been in the middle of responding to him about sushi.

"Oh, yeah." I looked away from the mammoth house to him. "That I don't like sushi."

He shrugged. "Then we'll say that. Though it's a travesty."

"That I don't like raw fish in my mouth?"

Rafe wrinkled his nose adorably. "Well, when you put it like that . . ."

I grinned, ignoring the nervous butterflies in my belly. "And our subsequent dates?"

"Movies, dinner, walks in Central Park. The usual."

"I really feel like we should have practiced this more."

"We'll be fine. Just be yourself." Something wicked glimmered in his eyes. "That will be interesting for all involved."

Chapter Eight

AT FIRST, I DIDN'T NOTICE ANY SPECIFIC DETAILS ABOUT HIS family home because Rafe had taken hold of my hand to lead me. He didn't just clasp my hand either. He linked our fingers together and gave me a squeeze of reassurance that shocked me.

My skin tingled, little sparks of feeling shooting up my arm. And that was all I could concentrate on until I was forced otherwise by the introduction to his family.

That was when I realized the Whitman house was exactly how I'd imagined inside. Vaulted ceilings, a modern farmhouse vibe, and lots of gigantic windows overlooking the sprawling backyard that had total privacy from the woodlands beyond. From what I could see outside the windows, the backyard had terraced levels that led down onto a lawn, a tennis court, and a massive pool.

Oh, how the other half lived.

Thankfully, I was not easily intimidated and I didn't believe that having money made a person superior to me. My uncharacteristic nervousness as I met Rafe's family was all about our deception. I kept reminding myself of the money and the road trip to freedom it would afford me.

It might have been better if the Whitmans weren't nice, but they welcomed me into their vast home with a friendliness I'm not sure I was expecting considering how unfriendly Rafe was.

His mother, Jennifer Whitman (who insisted I call her Jen), embraced me as if I were a long-lost family member. "I'm so happy to meet you," she greeted me with genuine enthusiasm, holding my biceps as she studied my face. The joy in her eyes brightened. "And you're so beautiful." I could almost sense her visualizing how pretty my children with Rafe could be, and I suddenly understood what might have driven Rafe to hire me.

I tried not to laugh in hysterical terror and grinned. "Look who's talking. I can see where Rafe gets his good looks."

She chuckled at Rafe. "I like her already."

Gregory Whitman, or Greg, was reserved in a way that reminded me so much of his son. And while I hadn't been lying that Jen Whitman was a beauty, Rafe definitely got his looks from his father. That dark hair against those true-blue eyes and all the chiseled angles of his face were definitely inherited from Greg Whitman.

Greg welcomed me with a small smile and a handshake, and I hadn't felt like I was under a microscope when he looked at me. I could not say the same for his brother, Hugo, whose gaze bored into me as we were introduced. The brothers didn't look at all alike. Hugo had his mom's brownish-auburn coloring and dark eyes, and he was shorter. While fit, he didn't have Rafe's broad shoulders or impressive biceps.

Pippa Whitman, Hugo's wife, I had, of course, met before, and while friendly, I could tell she was uncomfortable with my presence from her strained smile. Whether because she'd hired me or because she didn't like me "dating" Rafe, I didn't know. Their daughter,

Charmaine, remembered me as Merida and wanted me to come play with her. Pippa had to explain to her I was Uncle Rafe's date and not *her* playdate.

Last but definitely not least was the vibrant youngest Whitman. Georgina "Gigi" Whitman had purple hair, oversized gold wire-rimmed glasses, and about a million piercings along the rim of her left ear. She was beautiful, entirely her own person, and I felt an affinity toward her before even a word was spoken.

While Jen insisted everyone follow her to a less formal sitting area at the back of the house, just off the kitchen, Gigi wound her arm through mine. "So is it true you're a professional character actor and line sitter?"

"It is. Is it true you're some kind of tech genius?"

"It is." She grinned at me, eyes the same color as Rafe's glittering with amusement. "I've never met a professional character actor or line sitter before. I'm fascinated."

"It's not that interesting."

She scoffed. "Of course it is. They're not exactly orthodox professions. You met my brother dressed as a Disney character. Dating you is the most interesting thing he's ever done in his life."

I frowned because that didn't seem fair. "Not true. He spent sixteen years restoring a 1965 Pontiac. That's interesting."

"Don't get me wrong, I love my brother. And you're right. He's always gone his own way, which is great. He and I have that in common. But romantically, he's always played it safe."

"And I'm unsafe?" I quirked an eyebrow.

Gigi laughed. "I don't know. I guess we'll find out."

I'D EXPECTED IN A HOUSE THIS BIG THAT THERE WOULD BE staff—a cook, maybe. But Greg and Jen did all the cooking. Jen had prepared all the sides and salads, while Greg worked the most impressive grill I'd ever seen in the most impressive outdoor kitchen I'd ever encountered. It was bigger and fancier than my indoor kitchen and situated on the top-level terrace right off their large interior farmhouse-style kitchen. We were all seated around an outdoor dining table. The food looked amazing and I said so to the Whitmans, who took my praise with pleased thanks.

They were so nice, in fact, that (despite the gleam I'd seen in Jen's eyes earlier) I found it hard to imagine her hounding Rafe to settle down. But it had to be true or I wouldn't be there.

At first I just ate and listened to them all talk over each other about work and life and the city. There was history in their words and familiarity in the scene. I knew this gathering was not unusual. That they made the effort to come together for family dinners. Pippa grilled Gigi about when she was bringing a date to the next one, and Gigi evaded the question. Charmaine thought this was hilarious and teased her aunt. Greg asked Hugo questions about the business, while Jen yo-yoed between inquiries about Rafe's work and our dating life.

This was like a scene from a movie or a TV show. *This* was what the traditional family looked like, right?

I wouldn't know.

Neither would Roger or Jude. Kendall was the only one of us who'd grown up with a "traditional" family, but I'd never met them. As a kid, I'd also never been invited over to a friend's house for dinner. Ever. This was my first experience of a family dinner.

"So, Star, Rafe tells us you met at Charmaine's birthday party?" Jen sat at one end of the table, Greg at the other. I was on Jen's right with Rafe on mine. Hugo was on Rafe's right, and Gigi, Pippa, and Charmaine sat opposite us.

"Yeah. I was Merida."

"And I really thought you were her," Charmaine piped up wearily.

I gave her an apologetic smile. "I'm sorry, sweetie."

"That's okay. I do miss the accent, though."

I shot Rafe an "aha, I told you so" look and he rolled his eyes in a way that made me stifle laughter.

"Rafe also told us you've been dating for a month?"

"Yeah." I nudged him playfully while still looking at Jen. "I'm still deciding whether I like him."

Rafe grunted at my teasing while his mother laughed. "Good girl, keep him on his toes."

"I hear Rafe took you to Konbanwa for your first date." Pippa leaned across the table. "It's very difficult to get reservations there last minute."

I guessed I was supposed to be impressed by that, so I widened my eyes and nodded with an "ooh, really" expression on my face.

"Star hates sushi, so I'm afraid it was lost on her," Rafe told them before taking a big bite of his burger.

His Adam's apple bobbed as he swallowed. He had a very masculine throat.

"You don't like sushi?"

I wrenched my stare from Rafe to his sister-in-law. "Why is everyone so surprised I don't like raw fish in my mouth?"

Gigi choked on a swallow of her drink while Greg and Jen shared a chuckle.

"Sushi is a wonder and we're going to persuade you of that," Pippa declared with a determined tilt to her chin.

She could try, but she would fail.

"It's surprising you got a second date if you took her for sushi on your first," Gigi teased her brother.

Rafe shrugged, deadpan. "What can I say? I'm irresistible."

I was beginning to worry that something about him actually was.

"So you're a Disney princess?" Hugo broke the fun moment between Rafe and his sister. There was just enough hint of disdain in Hugo's tone to pick up on, even though I didn't think I was meant to.

"A character actor," I corrected him, leaning around Rafe to give his brother one of my "kill 'em with kindness" smiles. "And a line sitter."

"Line sitting? Yes, Rafe mentioned as much. Tell us about that?" Jen peered at me, seemingly genuinely curious.

"People pay me to wait in line for things that they don't have time to wait for. Theater tickets, sneakers, phones, games, restaurant launch tickets . . . the list goes on."

"People actually pay you to do this?" Greg was just as bemused by it as Rafe.

I nodded. "You'd be amazed."

"What is the world coming to?" he murmured to himself, again, like Rafe.

"What's the longest you've ever waited in line?" Gigi queried.

"Four days."

"You've waited in line four days?" Rafe frowned at me.

Surprised by the displeased look on his face, I shrugged uncertainly. "Yes. It was in winter too. Thank God for tents."

Jen's frown mirrored Rafe's. "What was the wait for?"

"*Hamilton* tickets."

"My goodness. That can't be safe or healthy." She gave Rafe an admonishing look, as if it were his fault that I'd waited in line four days for tickets.

"I was paid extremely well," I told her. "Seriously. It was worth the four days."

"Mom's right, it's not safe." Rafe's brows were so furrowed they almost made one line. I could imagine his brain turning and wondered what problem he was trying to solve. Unfortunately, I had the strangest feeling the problem was me.

"Star. That's an unusual name." Jen broke the sudden tension. "In fact, your full name is even more so."

"What's your full name?" Gigi quizzed me from across the table.

"Star Shine Meadows," Jen answered for me.

Gigi grinned. "Isn't that pretty?"

I swore I heard Hugo snort, but I ignored it.

If you grew up faced with enough derision, you kind of became immune to it. "Thanks." I smiled at Gigi. "My parents are very bohemian."

Jen raised an eyebrow. "Oh? How so?"

The entire family seemed to lean in to hear my answer. I looked up at Rafe and he gave me an almost imperceptible shrug, as if to say *Tell them whatever you want.*

He really didn't care.

In fact, I had a feeling he wanted me to shock them.

Okay, then.

I looked back at Jen. "They're artists. Dawn is a silversmith and makes jewelry and belt buckles and all sorts of things. Arlo is a mixed media artist and he sells his work online and in local galleries. They move around a lot, so they've sold their stuff all over."

"Dawn and Arlo? Those are your parents?" Pippa inquired.

"Yeah, they don't subscribe to traditional terms, so I'm not allowed to call them Mom and Dad." I shrugged.

Rafe stiffened beside me.

Jen shared a glance with Greg, and I didn't follow her gaze because I wasn't sure I wanted to see his expression. She gave me a small smile that didn't reach her eyes. "How interesting."

"You moved around a lot?" Gigi frowned.

I nodded. "Yeah. They moved us every four years or so."

"That must have been hard on your education," Hugo murmured dryly, as if he already knew about my background. He probably did.

"She graduated with a 3.8 GPA," Rafe answered for me, giving his brother a hard look.

"Despite all the moving?" Jen's smile returned. "Well, I knew you had to be very smart. Rafe has always liked smart girls."

"Mom," Rafe murmured with a scowl.

"What? It's true. You know, he took the class valedictorian to prom, even though the prettiest girl in school asked him to go with her."

"Looks aren't everything," I reminded her.

"Of course," Jen hurried to say. "Exactly. It's just . . . boys don't tend to have that foresight, but my Rafe has always been wise."

"A good thing too, Mom," Gigi interjected. "The prettiest girl in Rafe's year was Cheryl Wharton, and she'd drown her own sister if she thought it would help her get ahead in life."

Rafe covered a laugh by coughing into his fist.

My lips twisted, but Jen spoke before I could. "Now, Georgina, the Whartons are friends of this family and we don't speak ill of our friends."

Gigi rolled her eyes. "Oh, let's be real. They're our frenemies."

"What on earth are frenemies?"

"It's 'friends' and 'enemies' put together," I supplied helpfully.

"Oh." She frowned at Gigi. But then she amended, "Okay, they're our frenemies, but we still should be polite about them because of the friend part."

I tried to hide a grin as I glanced up at Rafe to find him watching me. There was a gleam of amusement in his eyes that made my cheeks feel hot.

"What were we talking about?" Jen mused.

"Star," Hugo reminded her. "College. Star didn't go to college. Right, Star?"

At the disdainful and almost accusatory tone, Greg Whitman said Hugo's name in sharp warning.

Like always, I ignored the indignation that kind of judgmental attitude inspired. "I was raised by parents who didn't believe that you needed a college education to succeed. A lot of college graduates end up doing the kinds of jobs I'm doing now, anyway. Unless they specialize, a degree doesn't mean what it used to mean."

"That is very true," Greg agreed, "but that is why grad school is important. Look at Rafe. Look at Gigi."

Not Hugo, because he'd taken over his father's company.

And Greg seemed proud of Rafe and Gigi for the paths they'd taken. I would have assumed it bothered him that his children didn't want to join the family business, but I guess having his eldest take over was good enough.

"You didn't want grad school? A career?" Jen probed.

I shook my head. "The thought of constraining myself to school for another four to eight years filled *me* with dread. I itched to get out there and live my own life. I decided against college."

"College isn't for everyone," Gigi offered kindly, giving her mom a pointed look.

Jen smiled weakly. I wondered if my shine was fading as they got to know me. Familiar disappointment hung behind me like a shadow.

"Wasn't moving around a lot difficult?" Pippa placed a hand on Charmaine's head, and her daughter bussed into her touch like a kitten. Was there ever a time when Dawn offered me such natural, casual affection? "I couldn't imagine dragging our daughter all over the country her entire childhood."

"You know what, it made me grow up independent," I replied a little too brightly. I could feel Rafe studying me as I continued, "I'm well traveled and I met lots of new kids. Dawn and Arlo would take off for weeks at a time to meet old friends in another state or sell their art, and it taught me to look after myself."

Jen seemed outright horrified. "They left you alone? How old were you?"

There was that knot in my chest again. "Uh, I guess they started doing that when I was ten, eleven."

"Oh dear," I heard Pippa mutter.

Heat flared in my cheeks and I brushed off the strained atmosphere as they exchanged uneasy glances. "Hey, that's nothing." I laughed, though it sounded false even to my ears. "When I was a baby, they once put me in a sink in a bathroom supply store for a joke and then forgot about me. It made the newspaper. They kept the clipping."

No one laughed.

Because I guess it wasn't funny.

A knot tightened in my chest and I looked at Rafe, desperate for him to change the subject.

Whatever he saw in my face made him clear his throat. "Gigi, why didn't you bring the intern you're banging to dinner?"

Hugo choked on the food he'd just put in his mouth.

"Rafe," Pippa scolded, shooting her daughter a meaningful look.

Charmaine stared between them, confused. "What does 'banging' mean?"

Rafe had the decency to look sheepish as he lied and said it was a form of dancing. That knot in my chest eased and if he'd looked at me in that moment, he might have seen more than gratitude in my gaze.

Gigi glowered at her brother. "You're awful."

He grinned at her, a slight dimple I'd never noticed before creasing his left cheek, and an explosion of tingles awoke between my legs.

Whoa.

The man had the sexiest smile ever. Of course he did. Maybe that was why he didn't smile a lot, because of its arousing effect? Or he was just a grumpy bastard. One or the other.

"What intern?" Greg's tone was light but his expression was rigid.

"He's legal," she assured her father, shooting Rafe another death glare. "He's twenty-three and it's nothing. That's why I didn't bring him to dinner. But thanks."

Rafe's lips twitched with laughter before he mouthed *I'm sorry*.

"You owe me," she muttered back before stabbing her salad with her fork as if she was imagining stabbing Rafe instead.

"If it isn't serious, then I suggest you end it." Jen gave her daughter a smile that didn't reach her eyes. "Life is too short to be fooling around."

Gigi cut her brother another dark look.

"Although those relationships can certainly lead to more. Who knows?" I attempted to save her.

"Yes." Jen considered this and then asked me, "Have your parents been married long?"

Rafe relaxed back in his seat, but his biceps seemed to deliberately brush mine as if reminding me he was there.

"They're not married."

"No?" Jen was visibly perturbed. "Why not?"

"They believe that marriage and monogamy are the foolish trappings of an unimaginative, delusional, and uptight hierarchal society." I said the words by heart; I'd heard them so many times. "They're devoted to each other, but they also had several lovers when I was growing up. I called them my aunts and uncles." I added the last because it was true, but also because I enjoyed people's reactions to this facet of our family history.

Utter silence.

That was the reaction at the Whitman family dinner.

Jen peered at me, and I could tell I'd lost her. Was I like my parents? Would I insist her darling son share me with other men? She gave Rafe a pointed look and I could almost hear her telling him *No, she will not do.*

And for some reason, that knot in my chest made me agitated enough to add fuel to the fire. "Oh, I think more and more people are coming around to that way of thinking. My three best friends are in a polyamorous relationship."

More silence and gaping awkwardly at each other.

"What's a polmoros relationship?" Charmaine asked, mispronouncing the word.

And I blanched, having forgotten an eight-year-old was at the table. I gave Pippa an apologetic look.

She gave me a strained *it's okay* smile and distracted Charmaine with a quiet question of her own.

It was later, when Pippa had taken Charmaine for a walk around the grounds after dinner and the rest of us had moved down a terrace to a large comfortable outdoor corner sofa and chairs, that Hugo peered at me. "Your friends are really in a polyamorous relationship? A functioning one?"

I heard the judgment in his voice and stiffened. "Yes. And I don't know any three people who are happier."

"I hope you don't think you'll be dragging my brother into a situation like that?"

"Hugo," Greg admonished.

Gigi threw a peanut at him.

Jen remained silent, watching.

Rafe . . . well, Rafe shocked me once more.

Sitting next to me on the sofa, he shifted close enough that our bodies pressed together, the heat of him licking up my side as he slid his arm around my shoulders and drew me against him. "Oh, Star already knows I'm not a man who shares."

And while my reaction appalled the feminist in me, my cavewoman brain kicked in and I felt an aroused squeeze low in my belly at the claiming.

Oh boy.

At that moment, it started to dawn on me that I was in trouble and couldn't forget it was all pretend between us.

Chapter Nine

THE WHITMANS BID ME A FRIENDLY GOODBYE, BUT IT WAS FAR
less warm than my reception, except for Gigi, who took my hands in
hers. "Please come back. You're the most interesting person anyone
has brought home in a while. I think you're going to be so good for
Rafe."

Guilt flared to life. These were nice people. Hugo was kind of
an ass, but I had a feeling he was just doing the overprotective big
brother thing. Greg was difficult to read, but Jen, I think, just knew
what she wanted for her son, and someone like me wasn't it. That
made her an overprotective mom, and that was better than the mom
I had. Now that I'd met Rafe's family, it felt wrong to deceive them.

"My mom will come around once she thinks this is real. Right
now, she's not sure, but in a few weeks, believe me, she'll already
start planning the wedding," Rafe muttered in my ear as he held my
hand and walked me back to the car with his family watching.

"Seriously?"

"Yes. So wipe the guilt out of your eyes."

I hadn't realized I'd been so obvious.

Once we were in the car and I'd waved to them all as Rafe pulled away, I commented, "Your dad didn't seem shocked by what I had to say at all."

"Oh, he was shocked. He's just good at hiding it. Besides, it's my mom who's on my case to get married. My dad could not care less."

"Why is your mom so insistent you marry?"

"She wants me to have the life she had. She and my dad adore each other. They've had their ups and downs like anyone, but they've had a good life. Her life is the example she thinks we should all live by. Mom can't see past it."

"She thinks because marriage made *her* so happy that it's the answer to *all* happiness?"

"Exactly."

We were silent for a few minutes and then Rafe's hands squeezed the steering wheel and released. He did that a few times before he spoke. "I want to apologize for not asking about your family."

Rafe's look was quick but piercing before he focused on the road.

"When I came to your apartment to go over my family background, it was . . . it was rude and self-involved to forget to ask you about yours. I'm not usually . . ." He sighed heavily. "I got wrapped up trying to maintain a professional distance between us, but a decent person would have asked."

"It's okay," I assured him, finding his apology adorable. "This job is about you."

"Technically, it's about us. We're pretending to date. And I should have known that about your mom and dad before it came out at my parents' table."

"It's fine."

Rafe nodded, but the tension remained between us, and I wasn't sure why.

Then he asked, "Do you really believe all that stuff about your parents and your upbringing? That it was all for the best and made you independent?"

There was that fisted knot in my chest again. I sighed, staring out the passenger-side window, watching the world fly by. "It definitely made me independent, but would I recommend it? No." I smiled ruefully as all the memories of my childhood flooded through me. They were tinged with one powerful emotion.

Loneliness.

"My childhood sucked," I admitted quietly. The only other people I'd ever confessed that to were Roger, Jude, and Kendall.

"I'm sorry," he commiserated.

"My parents should never have had a child. I don't even like them very much. Is that awful?"

Rafe shook his head. "Not at all. *They're* awful for neglecting you like that."

My smile strained as a familiar hurt stole its hands around that knot in my chest. "Yeah, well . . . they got one thing right."

"What's that?"

"Freedom *is* everything and you should never tie yourself completely down to one place and one person. Glad I'm here to help make sure that doesn't happen to you."

Rafe's frown deepened, but he didn't respond. Silence fell between us and after a while I reached over to turn the dial on the radio up to allow Tom Grennan's growly voice to fill the car.

Chapter Ten

PUSHING INSIDE THE PUB, I LET MY EYES ADJUST TO THE DIM
light and then swept the joint for my "date." The sound of wood
scraping against wood drew my attention and there he was, unfold-
ing his large body from a wooden chair, his napkin falling to the
table in front of him. As I wound through the tables in the small
restaurant area, I smiled at the sight of him pulling out my chair
for me.

"Thanks," I murmured as I sat and Rafe deftly tucked me
back in.

No one had ever pulled out my chair before.

It was so gentlemanly.

I must have been gawking at him in wonder, because Rafe
frowned as he sat back down. "What?"

"Nothing." I swept my hair off one shoulder to allow a little air
on my hot skin, and Rafe's eyes followed the movement. His gaze
lingered on my bare throat and he might as well have been staring
at my breasts for the way it made me feel. *Ignore it.* "What do you
think?"

His eyes came back to mine. "Of what?"

At his seemingly perpetually bored tone, my lips twitched. "This place. It doesn't look like much, but they do the best burgers."

"So I've heard." Rafe shrugged. "My friend Alfie lives on the island. He's in a band and they've played here a few times. I haven't eaten here, though."

Now I was truly gaping at him. "Your friend is in a band? That has played here?"

"Yes. Is there something wrong with that?"

"No." I shook my head. "I've just . . . I've probably heard them play." Where on earth had he met this friend that did not sound like the kind of friend he'd meet via his family?

As if he heard the question, Rafe lifted the menu to peruse it as he offered, "I met him at vet school. He dropped out, but we stayed friends."

"Cool." Rafe had friends. First Owen, now Alfie. That was nice. I didn't want him to be a truly unhappy bachelor with no social life who worked constantly.

But then I supposed that was what I was there to find out. After I divulged some illuminating history at his parents' dinner table, Rafe realized I was previously correct. We should have taken time to get to know each other better before we pretended to be a couple in front of other people. Luckily, we'd gotten away with it with his family, but his mom and Pippa were insisting on his presence at a charity event next Saturday evening and Pippa had attempted to set him up on a date.

I tried not to feel insulted by that since this wasn't real between us, but it was difficult not to take it personally that she didn't want me dating her brother-in-law. Rafe had told her he was bringing me and now, a week after the family dinner, he wanted to meet me to "get to know me" and vice versa.

Since I was definitely getting more out of our bargain considering

I'd only had to attend one date since he'd begun paying me, I, of course, cleared my schedule to meet him at my favorite cheeseburger place. Rafe had insisted on coming to Staten Island instead of making me trudge into the city, and that was really thoughtful.

Speaking of trudging . . . "Did you get a cab here? I didn't see the Pontiac parked outside."

The left side of his mouth curled up. "I don't leave my baby lying around in strange places."

For some absurd reason, those words in his rumbly voice caused a clench deep in my lower belly.

I cleared my throat. "Makes sense. Did you cab it?"

"No. I got the subway, then the ferry and the bus."

"You did public transport?"

His lips pinched together for a few seconds as he kept his gaze on his menu. "Yes, imagine that: the rich boy worked out how to get on a bus."

Wincing, I sucked in a breath. "Sorry."

He looked up from the menu, his expression indecipherable. "I won't pretend my family isn't wealthy, Star. I'm not ashamed of it. But I'm also not a frivolous person and I try to be as aware of my privilege as possible. If I don't need to take expensive cabs everywhere, then I won't."

I nodded and was about to apologize again when I realized that I'd never jumped to conclusions about people before I met Rafe. That wasn't me. I was not a judgmental person. The dynamic between me and Rafe was different and, honestly, I wasn't going to take all the blame for it. "I rarely judge people. It's not in my nature, considering I've been judged my whole life. But I think you put me on the defense when we first met and it comes naturally to react to anything you say in that way. I'll stop, though. I promise."

Rafe studied me for so long I thought he might just get up and walk out. Then he said, "As I mentioned before, I was in a horrible mood when we met." He sighed heavily. "I've been in a horrible mood for months. And you're right. I might not understand your choices of profession, or like them, for that matter, but they are your choices and it's not my place to judge. I'll stop too."

Not exactly a groveling apology, but it would do. Yet I couldn't just graciously accept it, could I? It bothered me that he was so against my jobs, and I didn't know why it bothered me. It shouldn't! "What is so wrong with my jobs?"

He cut me a look and then lifted his menu. "What's good here?"

"Don't avoid." I shoved his menu down. "And the bacon cheese-burger."

"Hey, are you guys ready to order?" A gorgeous young woman in a tight polo shirt and an even tighter short black skirt stopped at our table. Her fabulous long legs were bare and she wore cute high-top sneakers because she didn't need high heels to make her legs look like they went on forever. I glanced at Rafe. It wouldn't be the first time I was out for a meal with a guy and he'd ogled the server.

Rafe didn't even look up from the menu. He asked me first, "What are you having?"

"Bacon cheeseburger," I answered, handing her my menu. "And a soda water and lime."

"Make that two and just water. Thank you." He gave her his menu.

As if just noticing him, the server ran her eyes down Rafe's body and then shot me a *nice one, sister* look before she walked away.

Rafe sat back in his seat, eyeing me suddenly like a sleepy tiger. He was unfairly attractive. I swear heat bloomed beneath my cheeks with no warning whenever he looked at me. "So . . . where do we start with this getting-to-know-you stuff?"

I snorted. "We could start with you not avoiding my question. Why do you dislike my jobs?"

He stared impassively at me. "I really don't want to fight."

"Why will this turn into a fight?"

"Because my opinion will more than likely offend you."

My mind whirred around the possible reasons for his disdain. As if mere disdain weren't enough. "Well, now I need to know."

"Fine."

"Fine."

His eyes narrowed. "Fine."

I swallowed another "fine" and gave him a *well, what are you waiting for?* gesture.

"You're an intelligent woman, and I think you could do so much more with your life."

I hadn't expected that. "Oh." Then something occurred to me. "You didn't know I was intelligent at Charmaine's party and you were a . . . unpleasant about my job then too."

"I was in a mood," he repeated. "Though you were correct that day. A bad mood was no excuse to expect my rudeness to be acceptable. I don't think anyone has ever lectured me in such a cheerful way before, let alone actually been in the right."

I slumped back in my seat. "Wonders never cease."

"Don't make me take it back."

Biting my lip and the laughter that trembled on it, I nodded for him to continue.

"While I heard you when you said you bring joy to people's lives with the character acting—and I can see that—I still think you can do more. As for the line sitting, I think the entire thing is ridiculous, that people are ridiculous and greedy and lazy, but worst of all, I don't think it's safe for you. I don't like it."

To be fair, Roger didn't like it when I had to line sit for days in a tent. In fact, he'd even joined me when he could, so I wasn't alone. I carried pepper spray and a rape whistle, but I usually didn't sleep much during the overnight waits. "Okay . . . maybe you're not wrong about the safety issues. But you should know that my friend Roger usually stays with me when he can during those."

Rafe's eyes narrowed.

"As to your other points, maybe line sitting is a little ridiculous, but it's not always because people are lazy. Lots of people just don't have the time. They're overworked and stressed, and these things that I wait in line for, for them, are the things that bring a little joy to their lives. And they deserve that joy. If I can provide that for them and make money doing it, I don't see what's so wrong about that."

Those sexy denim-blue eyes studied me, sweeping over my features, as if tallying every little detail he found. Then he shocked me by replying, "You have a way of humbling me I'm not sure I like."

I shifted uncomfortably. "Humbling you?"

"You see people with a glass-half-full attitude and yet, from what I've gleaned, you didn't have the best upbringing. I had a wonderful upbringing and yet—"

"You see people with a glass-half-empty attitude," I finished quietly.

Rafe's lips twisted and he nodded slowly. "I don't know how that happens. Human beings are strange."

"It takes effort, Rafe. I have to *choose* to see the world that way. Every day. But I think my life is better for it."

"I still don't like your jobs." He shrugged unapologetically. "I think there's more out there for you."

A little bite of hurt cut through the warmth I'd felt growing between us. "Why aren't I okay the way I am?"

For the first time, the hardness left his features entirely as his face slackened with remorse. "I didn't mean it that way. I just . . . I don't like the idea of someone as smart as you *scraping* by."

My tone was steely. "I'm not scraping by. I'm happy. I'm not overworked or overwhelmed, sitting in some office, hating my work and turning into someone who sees the world with that glass-half-empty kind of attitude. Just because my life doesn't fit into your idea of what a life should be doesn't mean it's bad. Haven't we had this conversation before? You're acting exactly like your mom and Pippa with you and this whole dating nonsense."

That damn muscle in his jaw flexed as his gaze bored intensely into mine. Then he swallowed. "There you go . . . humbling me again."

At his dry tone, I relaxed. "I think it's a good thing I came into your life, Rafferty Whitman. If only because you're about to taste the best damn bacon cheeseburger you've ever had."

Like sunshine bursting through a cloud, Rafe grinned at me. There was that little dimple.

His smile gave me butterflies.

And those winged creatures in my stomach were a warning I was way in over my head.

A little while later, after I'd watched Rafe take a man-sized bite out of his burger, he swallowed, then wiped his lips with his napkin. "You're right. That's a great burger . . . but I know of a better one."

"Hush." I leaned across the table, smiling. "That's blasphemy here."

His eyes gleamed with amusement. "It's also true. There's a gourmet burger place in Harrison and I know that sounds pretentious, but trust me, when you taste their burgers, you'll agree with me." He said it like it was a foregone conclusion that I would. Taste them, that is. "What other kind of food do you like?"

Realizing he was diving into our getting-to-know-you stuff, which was the entire point of our lunch, I shrugged. "Most foods, except for raw fish and offal. I'm also allergic to strawberries, which is ironic considering my hair."

Rafe's lips twitched around a fry as he eyed my hair.

"You?"

He shrugged. "I'll try anything once. Don't like oysters, pesto, dates, raisins, and watermelon. What *is* the point of a watermelon?"

At his boyishly perturbed question, I chuckled. "I'm actually not sure, but I quite like it. It's refreshing."

"It's just water."

Laughing, I shrugged, giving him that. "Favorite food?"

"My mom makes this steak dinner with these amazing potatoes and fried eggs. It's my favorite."

Not fancy at all. I liked that. "Sounds good."

"Yours?"

"I'm a big fan of pizza." I shrugged. "My tastes are simple."

We discussed music, movies, and books, and I vowed to make Rafe find more time for himself. He hadn't been to the movies in a year, and the last book he read was six months ago. His clinic had totally taken up all of his free time, but I had a feeling he'd allowed it. After all, he was here with me right now. He'd made the time. So he could make the time to do other things. To leave space for the things that brought him joy.

"Is your job the reason for your glass-half-empty attitude? I know you love animals, but is the job more demanding than you expected it to be?"

"I love being a vet." Sincerity shone in his eyes. "Starting my clinic has meant longer hours, but Owen has been great. And soon we might hire a third vet."

"That's good. You've made it work in a short amount of time."

Humor sparked in his eyes. "Maybe you were on to something about me and Owen."

I chuckled. "The hot vets. That's probably what you should have called the clinic."

He rolled his eyes, but I saw the corner of his mouth tug upward.

"Why did you become a vet? It seems a little random, considering the family business."

Rafe shrugged. "It's as simple as I love animals. We had a ton of pets growing up. Our last family dog passed away a year after Gigi moved out, so my parents never bothered to get another dog. I miss him. The house doesn't feel the same without the sounds of paws clicking on the floor and barking out in the backyard." I could see the fond memories in his eyes. "And while I sometimes keep my clients' pets at my apartment with me overnight so I can monitor them, I just don't have the time to keep a dog of my own."

"You could make it work. He or she could spend the day at the clinic with you."

Rafe considered this. "I have thought about it. I just . . . I don't want to take on such a tremendous responsibility while we're still building the clinic into something."

I understood, but I hoped he'd get a dog someday. It was obvious how much he missed having a furry friend in his life by the tinge of longing in his tone when he was talking about it. "I've never had a pet."

"Never?"

"Nope. After Dawn and Arlo realized what a responsibility a kid was, they weren't interested in adding any more responsibility onto their plates. Thankfully, for all animal kind." I grinned.

Rafe didn't smile back. A hard glint entered his gaze. "You said you were used to being judged. What did you mean by that?"

It was a little too heavy a discussion for our get-to-know-you, so I answered with a light tone, "My parents flaunted their nontraditional values, and their love of pot, and sent me to school in clothes no one else was wearing. They were investigated a couple of times by social services, and I was bullied at every school I attended. While I had a few casual friendships, none of the parents of the kids I became friendly with wanted anything to do with me because of my parents. It got a little better in high school, but"—I shrugged—"I still never felt like I belonged."

Seeing the sympathy in Rafe's expression made my stomach knot. "Star, I'm sorry you went through that."

"I'm fine," I told him breezily. "I have a very thick skin because of it. Thankfully for you, or I might never have agreed to this."

I'd meant it as a joke, but Rafe looked stricken. "If I acted like some jackass bully, I am very sorry."

Oh wow. I swallowed hard at how sincere he sounded. "You didn't. You weren't particularly nice, but it wasn't as bad as that, and you've apologized already. Let's just move on."

Rafe stared at me as if he were trying to read every line in my body.

"Dessert?" I broke the strained silence.

My shoulders slumped with relief when he agreed. "Today's my cheat day, so why not?"

"Cheat day?"

He shrugged. "I only have one day a week when I can eat junk food. The rest of the week, I treat food as fuel and my body as a machine that needs the right kind of fuel to function."

My eyes swept over his impressive arms and shoulders, and I cleared my throat. "I can see that. You don't expect that from me, right?"

Rafe's lips twitched. "Why would I think I had any right over what you do with your body?"

"Good answer, Whitman."

We'd just decided to share dessert when a male voice called out my name.

I turned in my chair as a figure approached us, and, as the lights above us illuminated him, I smiled. "Hey, Misha."

Good-looking and rangy, Misha reminded me of a cowboy even though he was born and raised on Staten Island. His lean but strong physique was outfitted in his usual uniform of plaid shirt tucked into jeans, ending in cowboy boots.

He leaned down to press a kiss to the corner of my mouth, a little too close to my lips to be honest, considering it would appear to the casual observer that I was on a date. I noted his gaze flick to Rafe before he looked at me with a grin. "Damn, you get more beautiful every day."

Did I mention Misha was the biggest flirt in the world? I rolled my eyes. "How many women have you said that to today?"

"Just you." He winked and settled his hand on my shoulder as he stared at Rafe. "Hey, man."

Rafe stared up at him without smiling. "Hey."

"This is Rafe." I hurried to introduce them. "Rafe, this is my friend Misha."

When Rafe said no more but just stared stonily at him, Misha lost some of his cockiness and removed his hand from my shoulder. "Anyway, nice to see you, Star. Call me sometime."

I murmured a noncommittal "Have a good one" because I had no intention of calling him, and turned back to Rafe.

He was still annoyingly expressionless. *"Friend?"*

"We casually dated."

Rafe curled his lip at the thought.

I frowned. "What?"

"Nothing . . ." He contemplated me. Then he said, "I suppose we should discuss past relationships. That's something couples do and something we would know. My mom has already asked me to divulge information about your past relationships after you came across as a commitment-phobe at dinner."

There was censure in his tone and I suddenly realized that from his point of view, I'd screwed up. I was supposed to be deceiving his family into believing this was a serious relationship. "Shit. I'm sorry."

He nodded. "It's fine. Like I said before, it's fixable."

"I've never been in a serious relationship. Maybe we should lie about that too."

Rafe contemplated this. "Never?"

"I'm not a serious-relationship person. I told you . . . I don't like the idea of being tied down. Metaphorically speaking."

His gaze was curious. "And physically speaking?"

I shrugged mysteriously. That was for my lovers to know. "Do I need to make up a past fake relationship too? Rafe?"

Whatever thoughts were in his head cleared as his eyes unglazed and he sat back with a little cough. "What?"

"Fake relationship from the past?"

"Um . . . right. His name was Misha." He flicked a hand in the direction Misha had walked away. "You dated for three years and broke up because he dressed like a cowboy and cheated on you."

Amusement built inside me. "I have to add the cowboy thing?"

"Frankly, Pippa would see *that* as enough reason for you to break up with him."

I threw my head back in laughter and when I finally stopped, I found him staring at me in a way that made my breath catch. "A lot of women like the cowboy thing, you know."

"You?" he asked with an intensity that made the electricity spark between us.

"Been there, done that," I assured him.

"Dessert?" The server's voice cut through the sudden tension at our table.

Rafe met her eyes but didn't linger on her pretty face as he ordered. "A slice of the chocolate fudge cake. Two forks, please."

"Sure thing."

Feeling suddenly agitated and not wanting to deep dive into why, I quizzed him, "What about you?"

"What about me?"

"Past relationships?"

"I've been in four serious relationships."

My eyes widened. "Four *serious* relationships?"

"I don't do casual well."

Yeah, somehow, with how intense he was, that didn't surprise me. It disappointed me and I didn't want to analyze that either, but it made sense. "Not a one-night-stand kind of guy, huh?"

"I had plenty of those in college. I'm past that now. It's empty."

"I've actually never had a one-night stand."

He frowned. "You just said you only do casual dating."

"Yeah, 'dating' being the operative word. I've had lovers. Not boyfriends. But also not one-night stands."

"I guess 'lovers' is a nicer term than 'booty calls.'"

If he expected me to bite, he would be dissatisfied. "It's definitely the more mature term."

"And do these lovers have other lovers while you're with them?" He scowled.

"I hope not. I still like to be safe. But you can never really know, so it's important to look after your sexual health. I get tested when a casual relationship ends."

"You're very frank."

"Sex isn't something we should be ashamed to talk about. Speaking of . . . we never discussed whether we have to . . . abstain from sexual relationships with other people during this." I refused to acknowledge the burn of jealousy at the thought of Rafe having sex with another woman. It was one reason I should probably get laid if the opportunity arose.

Rafe's expression blanked. "We can't take the chance anyone might see you with someone else, and it gets back to my family. Same for me."

"This is a big city. I doubt they'd know."

"I wouldn't put it past Pippa to set our family PI on you."

"What?" I gaped.

He shrugged like that wasn't crazy. "Anyway, I can't stop you if you decide otherwise, but I would appreciate it if you didn't. If I can make peace with the idea of being friendly with my right hand for six months, I'm hoping you'll be okay with using some of your new earnings to buy a vibrator."

There was a bite to his words and I knew he'd meant to shock, perhaps even offend me. But I was too busy imagining him getting friendly with his right hand and pissed off that it made me hot from the tips of my toes to the top of my head. I smirked at him and just as he took a casual sip of his water, I replied, "Friendly right hand, huh? How thoughtful of you to provide some imagery for me to use to get off to during those long six months."

Rafe choked on the water he'd just sipped, spluttering, and shooting daggers at me with his eyes as he swiped my clean napkin to mop up his chin and splattered shirt.

My eyes, I'm sure, gleamed with challenge. It would take a lot more than a few provocative words to shock me.

Chapter Eleven

"WHAT IS THIS CHARITY FOR, AND HOW DOES IT ALL WORK?" I
walked at Rafe's side as we followed a stream of elegantly dressed
people into the hotel ballroom.

Rafe picked me up in a hired town car, but he'd come right up to
my apartment to collect me, where I'd waited nervously for his reaction to my appearance.

Unfortunately, his reaction wasn't worth the nerves because the
expressionless pain in the ass just gave me an abrupt nod and then
urged me out of my apartment. All while I tried not to drool over the
sight of him in a tux.

Because he was a drool-worthy sight.

Those broad shoulders and that tapered waist in a fitted tux . . .
hello, James Bond next generation.

For all his reaction told me, I looked adequate.

Men.

Why did I even care?

I'd never cared what a guy thought of my appearance before, and that was no lie! I wore what I wore, I liked what I liked, and they either did too or they could stuff it.

It pissed me off that Rafe Whitman, of all people, could get under my skin like this. I tried to tell myself it was merely because he'd given me a lot of money to buy a nice dress, and I hoped that I'd struck the balance between staying true to myself and what was required of me.

The hair and dress were me; the shoes and makeup were not. I rarely wore a lot of makeup except for mascara, but I'd allowed Kendall to do my whole face up and I had to admit she'd done a great job. While a lot of women around me had their hair in fancy updos, I'd left mine loose in waves down my back.

On my feet were spiked gold stilettos with ankle straps. I wasn't used to walking in anything without a wedge, so I clung onto Rafe's arm for more than just the deception.

"It's a benefit for a domestic children's charity. My mother is on the board of directors and Pippa started getting involved with it when she married Hugo. They fund everything from food for children in dire poverty, resources for group homes, scholarships, clothing . . . you name it, they provide where they can. The tickets to these things cost a small fortune, but that's because the profit goes to the charity. This is also an auction. People donate items of worth that they're willing to part with, and all the profits go to the charity."

"Wow, that's wonderful. Think of all the lives your mom has impacted doing this." I stared at the decorated ballroom. It looked like it was set up for the fanciest wedding reception I'd ever attended.

Rafe's arm tightened in mine and he replied, "I do. I've thought about it more after what you said to me at lunch. She's done a lot of good with her life."

I beamed up at him, pleased that my opinion had opened his eyes to that fact. "Including being a good mom." It was a guess, but I had a feeling I was right.

"She is a wonderful mom. She'd be the best mom if she hadn't forced me to do this." He gestured between us.

I laughed. "Of course. I almost forgot about that one little negative."

Though it didn't feel like a negative to me. While I was definitely out of my comfort zone with this group of guests, I'd never really minded being out of my comfort zone. I guess because I'd been thrown out of it so many times in my youth that I was used to it.

"You made it."

We turned at the familiar voice. Jen Whitman hurried over to us, shimmering in a silver gown that had an elegant thirties vibe. Jen clasped Rafe's cheek in her hand, adoration for her son beaming out of her. "You look so handsome. Thank you for coming. Your brother and sister couldn't attend, so I appreciate you making the effort."

"You look beautiful, Mom." He kissed her cheek.

I melted a little.

Jen's eyes glittered with emotion at her son's sweet words before she turned to me, a friendly smile on her face. It did, however, lack the overt warmth of our first meeting. Guess I'd really messed up with my commitment-phobic comments. "Nice to see you, Star." Her gaze flickered over my dress and I wasn't sure she spoke the truth when she said, "You look lovely."

"Thank you. And you really do look beautiful. So chic."

Her expression softened at my sincerity. "Well, thank you. You're very kind." She looked up at Rafe. "Now I have lots to do, so I apologize if you see little of me this evening, but enjoy yourself."

"Don't worry about us. Go do your thing," Rafe assured her.

"Wish me luck." She hurried away in her high heels as if they were sneakers. How did she do that?

Thinking of her lukewarm reaction to me, I gave Rafe an apologetic look. "I'll need to make it clear to her I'm committed to you or she's going to foist other women on you again."

"She'll come around. Let's find our table." He placed his hand on my lower back to lead me across the room to the table chart, and I swear my butt tingled at his fingers' proximity. My breath catching at the sensation, I tried to shake it off. You'd think a guy had never put his hand on my lower back before.

"Do you feel guilty?" I asked to distract myself.

"'Guilty'?" Rafe frowned down at me.

"About . . ." I gestured between us, not wanting to say the words out loud in case someone heard us.

Understanding dawned in his eyes. "Us."

"Yes."

"Of course I do. I almost called you a million times to cancel this . . . but then Pippa sent another woman to my clinic this week as a setup and I was reminded *why* we're doing this."

Indignation flared through me. I'd known she'd tried to steer him to someone else after our dinner, but to try to set him up again when she knew he and I were dating? Well, fake-dating, but she didn't know that! "Wow. She really doesn't like me."

I felt his gaze on my cheek, but I pretended to be focused on peering past another guest to look at the seating chart. "It doesn't matter if she likes you. All that matters is she thinks *I* like you. A lot."

Did that mean he didn't like me? Not romantically. But not even in a platonic way? I knew I wasn't everyone's cup of tea. No one could be. Yet . . . it was never nice to think someone didn't like you. Even if I was determined to never try to make someone like me if they didn't, I had to ignore a flare of hurt. I pointed to the chart. "Table four."

"Sounds about right." His hand pressed deeper into my back, and I followed his guide. People greeted him and he said hello, but he didn't stop to chat, and by the curious looks sent my way, I was glad for it.

"Is it considered rude not to stop and chat?"

"Probably." He held out my chair for me.

I snorted because he sounded like he could not care less, and I had to admit that I liked that about him.

We were the first people at the table. I stared at the opulent centerpiece of white lilies and roses. At the shiny, fancy silverware and gleaming white plates with silver edges. "I've never seen a table like this."

Rafe glanced over it all, bemused.

"I guess you're used to it."

His gaze met mine. "I suppose I am. Does it seem ridiculous to you?"

Since he sounded genuinely interested, I shrugged. "Not for a cause. If this is what it takes to lure wealthy people out to donate money to something worthwhile, then why not?"

He smiled wryly. "Yes, my mother is excellent at that."

I chuckled and turned in my seat to watch the guests flow into the room. A lot of people hadn't taken their seats yet as they caught up with each other.

"I come to these events for my family. Otherwise, this kind of socializing wouldn't be my choice."

Turning to study his too-handsome face, I smiled. "Would any kind of socializing be?"

He gave me a dark but amused look. "You're funny."

I had to hold back more laughter and sought to change the subject. "Are you on call tonight?"

"No. Owen is."

"So how does that work? How do people get in contact with you if they have a pet emergency?"

"We each have a separate cell and our patients' owners have an emergency contact number that forwards to those cells. I switched mine off tonight, so only Owen will receive the calls."

"Do you get a lot of emergency calls?"

"Yes." He sighed. "Our patient list is fairly small in big-picture terms, but we're already pushed at this point."

"Which is why you're considering a third vet?"

"Exactly."

"You should do it if you can." I touched his knee without thinking, and his gaze dropped to my hand. I pulled back, thinking his look meant I shouldn't touch him. Though I was a tactile person, I'd learned to read people to make sure they were comfortable with my casual touches. "You don't want to burn out."

His gaze rose to mine and he said matter-of-factly, "You can touch me. It makes this whole thing more believable if you do."

I swallowed around the sudden sensation of my racing heart. "Right." Needing to break our intense eye contact, I turned to observe the room, noting that more people were heading to their seats. Then I spotted Pippa talking to two women who looked like they could be mother and daughter.

Rafe groaned beside me.

"What?"

"Pippa."

"What about her?"

Rafe leaned into me, his breath tickling my cheek as he murmured, "Those women she's talking to . . . the younger one is the person she tried to set me up with for this event."

I turned my head slightly, bringing our faces just inches apart. "It sounds like Pippa is worse than your mom."

"In some ways, she is. I don't think she even knows why she's so set on seeing me settled." His attention moved from his sister-in-law to me, and his eyes narrowed as he realized how close we were. But he didn't move back. Instead, he searched my eyes.

My heartbeat sprinted, and I was almost afraid to breathe.

Needing to break that tension again, I wrenched my gaze from his and found Pippa shooting us quick glances. "What do you think *she'd* do if I yelled at her across the room about leaving peanut butter and jelly in my sheets?"

Rafe's answer was to move away, but only because he'd thrown his head back in laughter.

Butterflies raged to life as pleasure washed over me at the sight. He grinned at me, mischief dancing in his eyes.

"See, now you've made me want to do it."

He chuckled. "Part of me wants you to, but I doubt she or my mother would forgive you."

"Shame." I turned in my seat to face the table. "If I weren't so darn set on making a good impression, I could have some fun."

"Be yourself," Rafe surprised me by saying. "Just the kind of self who is committed to me. That's all I want them to see."

Before long, our table had filled, and Rafe introduced me to the people he knew. There was a couple he'd never met before and so we made quick introductions. Otherwise, the table was so big we didn't really have to make conversation with them. In fact, Rafe made it clear to me he didn't want to by constantly leaning in to murmur in my ear. He asked if I was enjoying myself, if my food was okay, what I thought of the music, what I'd usually be doing on a Saturday night. By the time the meal was over and the auction was soon to start, we'd turned toward each other in our seats, our knees touching as we talked about our weeks.

I told Rafe about the birthday party I worked the night before for an eleven-year-old boy who was a *Lord of the Rings* fan. His parents hired me as Arwen, and a colleague I'd worked with only once before was Gandalf. The kid had spent most of the night coming on to me.

"An eleven-year-old. What is happening to our youth?"

Rafe grinned at the story, and I swear I was getting addicted to his smiles now that he was regularly bestowing them upon me. "Sounds like he had an elf fetish."

"An elf fetish!" I exclaimed, without thinking about where I was. "Of course! Still, a fetish at eleven . . ."

That made his shoulders shake with laughter.

I smacked his arm playfully. "Hey, you weren't the object of the fetish."

"Are you talking about a foot fetish?" the woman next to me at the table—Andrea, I think her name was—leaned in to ask, her eyes wide.

Laughter trembled on my lips, but I contained it. "Um—"

"Because I just had to switch podiatrists because of that. I swear my feet aroused the woman."

Rafe coughed into his fist, and I knew he was covering laughter.

I poked his thigh under the table. "How awful."

He grabbed the offending finger and forced open my hand to tickle my palm. Bastard! I squirmed in my seat, trying to keep a straight face as this poor woman told me about her struggle to find a new podiatrist.

Her husband, thankfully, pulled her attention away and I turned on Rafe, tugging my hand from his. "You're the devil."

Laughter gleamed in his eyes, and I couldn't help but grin at him. I'd never expected to see this playful boyish side of him.

"You know, I had a patient yesterday who I'm pretty sure had a hand fetish. Kept licking the hell out of mine," he informed me with such deadpan seriousness that I cackle-laughed.

Not elegant. Not classy.

And he grinned at me like he didn't give a damn it was neither.

"You two look like you're having fun."

We turned to find Pippa standing behind us.

"You look beautiful, Pippa," I commented sincerely.

Her pale blue gown was stunning against her ivory skin and dark hair.

"Thank you. You look very pretty as well." Her attention turned to Rafe. "There is someone I'd like you to meet. Do you have a second?"

Rafe's entire demeanor changed. "Who is it?"

His sister-in-law's eyes narrowed. "A friend."

"Why do you want us to meet?"

She sighed. "Rafe, do you have to be so rude?"

"It's not rude. What you're doing is rude." He stared stonily at her now and as she flushed, I suddenly realized what was going on.

She was trying to steal him away to introduce him to a woman she wanted to set him up with.

While he was supposed to be here. On a date with me.

Wow.

Even *I* thought that was rude.

Not sure why I felt so agitated by that, I decided to take a break from their family stare-down. "If you'll both excuse me, I need to use the restroom."

"Oh, of course." Pippa stepped aside.

Rafe caught my hand as I stood, and I forced myself to meet his gaze. "Do you know where it is?"

I gave him a smile that didn't quite reach my eyes and tugged on my hand. "I think I'll find it easily enough."

The champagne they'd been serving at the table had gone to my head, and I felt a little rush as I tried to stroll through the fairly busy dance floor without going over on my stilettos.

There was a line outside the ladies' restroom, so it took a while, and the whole time I wondered if Pippa had talked Rafe into meeting this woman she thought was better for him than me. I knew it was ridiculous to be annoyed or hurt considering we were fake-dating, but Pippa didn't know that. What she was doing *was* rude.

Maybe she was doing it because I wasn't like the women who normally circulated around Rafe. Or maybe she was doing it because of my comments about commitment at the dinner table.

Either way, she was mistreating me, but she either thought I was too stupid to realize it or just didn't care if I did.

While I'd never thought about being in a serious relationship before and was actually terrified by the thought, I considered what my real reaction would be to that if what Rafe and I had wasn't a deception.

And so I walked out of that restroom on a mission.

I scanned the room as I entered it and found Rafe still at our table and Pippa across the room, talking to some guy. I marched over to her and she caught sight of me in her peripheral. Perhaps seeing the determined look on my face, she muttered something to the man and stepped away to meet me.

"Star, is everything all right?"

"May we have a word? In private?"

Her brows drew together. "Now isn't the best time—"

"It'll just take a second." I walked away, hoping she'd follow.

Thankfully, when I stopped outside the ballroom entrance, where we had more privacy, I found that Pippa had followed me.

"Is everything—"

"I know what you're doing." I cut her off again, giving her a smile to soften my tone and coming words. "Trying to set Rafe up with other women. He told me. And I know that's what you were trying to do right now."

She sighed. "Star—"

"I'm serious about Rafe." I tried not to flush at the lie. "We're in a relationship. A committed one. You trying to set him up with other women while he's seeing me is not only rude, but it's unkind to me. And you don't strike me as a cruel person."

Pippa blanched. "Oh . . . Star . . . I . . . you're right. I'm very sorry. I . . . just wasn't sure after our dinner if you were serious about Rafe. But now that I know you are, I promise I'll back off."

I nodded. "Thank you. I'd appreciate it."

Her eyes gleamed with remorse. "I really am very sorry."

Guilt flooded me. Ugh. I'd said what I said for Rafe's sake. The whole point of our deception was to get his sister-in-law and mother off his back. That didn't mean it wasn't horrible, making Pippa feel bad when I was the one lying to her. Reaching out, I took her hand and squeezed it in silent apology. Though to her, it would seem like reassurance. "I know. We're good. Let's just move on."

She gave me a tight smile. "Okay. Thank you."

"Enjoy the rest of your night."

I left her at the entrance and strode back into the ballroom, seeking Rafe. He'd turned in his chair. A frown marred his brow. But it melted as our gazes locked.

Then, as I crossed the room toward him, his eyes drifted down my body.

Rafe had given me a bonus to buy suitable clothes to attend events with him. I'd found a designer dress on Fifth Avenue that was exactly my style. A bohemian-print maxi dress in black and copper, with billowing sleeves that tightened at the wrists. It had a nipped-in waist with a high neckline to offset the fact that there was a daring slit up one side of the full skirt.

Rafe's gaze lingered on my bare leg as it flashed in and out of the layers of skirt as I walked toward him.

By the time I reached our table again, I was flushed from his perusal.

He didn't move, meaning I had to brush up against him to sit down. When our eyes met, his were hooded. We stared at one another, the rest of the room, the music, the chatter fading around us.

Then finally, Rafe broke the silence. "What did you say to Pippa?"

I looked away. "I just told her politely that you and I are serious and she needed to back off from setting you up with other women."

His silence made me look at him.

There was that unreadable expression on his face again.

"Shouldn't I have?"

Rafe cleared his throat. "No, you did the right thing. I appreciate it. Thank you."

"I felt like a lying asshole," I murmured, guilt-ridden.

He placed a hand on my knee under the table, drawing my gaze to his. If he moved his fingers, he'd push the slit of the dress open and touch bare skin. "Hey, you're not the liar. I am. *You* don't need to feel guilty about this. This decision was mine."

"And mine to agree to it."

His hand squeezed reflexively. "Do you . . . want to stop?"

I want your hand to slide northward.

There.

I'd admitted it.

At least to myself.

In knowing I was this attracted to Rafe, I should have told him yes, that I wanted to end this now before it got messy.

So why couldn't I bring myself to say those words?

Instead, I shook my head.

Rafe's shoulders relaxed and he took his hand off my knee. "Good. And seriously, thank you. Having her off my back helps me a lot."

I scanned the room for Pippa again. She was always talking to someone different. "Where's Hugo?"

Rafe followed my gaze. "Business trip."

"You know, I think she might be fixated on you to avoid fixating on the fact that her husband doesn't seem to be around a lot."

He leaned toward me but his eyes were on his sister-in-law. "You're probably right."

"Was your dad away a lot?"

"Yes, and no. He somehow always made time for his family. My dad is an excellent delegator. I think that's how he got the balance right."

"But Hugo isn't the same?"

Rafe pursed his lips. "No. He's more of a control freak than our father. Takes too much upon himself . . . I think he's so determined to make the company work, to prove to our family that he can, that he forgets the most important lesson our father taught us: family always comes first. Maybe I've forgotten too."

Seeing the guilt that matched my own, I leaned into him. "Rafe, we can stop this. I wouldn't be put out if you changed your mind. I would understand completely, in fact."

He sighed, his gaze still on Pippa. "They never need to know. And it just . . . gives me some space."

Did it really, though? He didn't have to dodge the weekly matchmaking efforts of his mom and sister-in-law, but he did have to make an effort to pretend to date me.

I looked over at Pippa, wondering what was really behind all of this. Pippa glanced over at us and I glanced away, not wanting her to think we were talking about her. In looking away from her, I found myself staring into Rafe's eyes.

His face was close.

Too close.

Or just close enough, depending on how you looked at it.

His eyes searched mine and I ignored the blood rushing in my ears as I closed the distance between us and gently brushed my lips over his.

My mouth tingled from the brief touch as I pulled away.

Rafe scowled hard at my mouth . . . but I honestly wasn't sure if it was because I'd kissed him or because I'd barely kissed him. "What was that?" His voice was rough.

I shrugged and lied. "Just playing my part."

A loud banging made me jerk in my seat and I turned toward the front of the ballroom, where a small stage was set up. Jen stood in front of a lectern with a gavel in her hand. "Honored guests, it's time for the auction to begin."

Nice timing, I thought, as the auction distracted us from the barely-there kiss that somehow, despite its barely-there status, haunted my lips more than any kiss ever had.

Chapter Twelve

Let me know whenever you're in the city
and I'll come meet you for coffee. Gxx

I stared at the text from Gigi, chewing on my lip in thought. After another Sunday dinner with Rafe's family, I'd exchanged numbers with his little sister. Rafe was right. She and I got along great despite our vastly different upbringings. She was disarming and lacking in all pretension. I liked her a lot. But I also felt horrible pursuing a friendship with her when she falsely thought I was her brother's girlfriend.

I'd said so to Rafe as we left his parents' house for the city.

"Oh." He'd frowned. "I thought I told you. Gigi knows the truth."

"About our deal?"

He'd nodded with a shrug, eyes on the road. "If anyone understands why I'm doing this, it's my little sister. And she was all excited about our so-called relationship and since she's the one person in my family who just wants me to be happy, no matter what, I couldn't lie to her. This whole thing is harder than I'd thought it would be."

"I wish you'd told me."

"I have now, and if Gigi wants a genuine friendship with you, there's no rule saying you can't pursue that."

Except that I wasn't a casual, fair-weather type of friend. If I decided someone was in my life, they were *in* my life through the good and bad. Wouldn't it be weird maintaining a friendship with Gigi once this whole thing with Rafe was over? Shouldn't I keep her at a distance?

The problem was, these two Whitmans were getting under my skin.

The more I spent time with Rafe's family, the guiltier I felt. Jen had warmed up to me again at dinner, and even Greg was a little more loquacious this time around. Hugo wasn't there, but Pippa and Charmaine were.

The deeper I got in with Rafe's family, the worse my remorse was going to be. While I'd thought Rafe an unfeeling moody bastard the first few weeks I'd known him, I now suspected that Rafe actually felt things more deeply than most people and that was his problem. The longer this went on, the greater his guilt would grow too.

Yet Gigi knew the truth and understood it, so . . . maybe there was no harm in being friends?

> I have a line-sitting job on Tuesday that should only last a couple of hours. Text you when I'm done?

Gigi responded with a bunch of celebratory emojis and **Can't wait!** She was kind of adorable.

• • •

IT WAS AN UNSEASONABLY HOT JUNE MORNING AND I SWEAR
there was a pool of sweat underneath my wig as I hurried down the
street toward the subway from what had been the job from hell. I
was a sunshine-and-roses kind of person, but even I didn't know
how to handle a four-year-old who screamed bloody murder every
time I got near her.

People in New York were used to seeing all kinds of things walk
past them, so no one blinked an eye at the woman in the brown wig
and gold Belle dress. Yes, I had been hired for a four-year-old's
birthday party to host it as Belle from *Beauty and the Beast* because
it was the four-year-old's favorite movie. After that experience, however, I was thinking it was not the four-year-old's favorite movie but
the four-year-old's *mom's* favorite movie.

That kid was terrified of me from the moment I walked in
dressed in costume.

It wasn't like I hadn't experienced kids crying before.

My theory was that those kids instinctually knew they were being lied to, and their little warning instincts were telling them to run
for cover. There was nothing wrong with that. Good instincts to
have. But I'd never had a child scream until she almost passed out.
Every time I told her mom that I should leave because I was distress-
ing her kid (and eventually all the other kids), the mom got angry
and belligerent.

I rarely felt frazzled.

But I was *frazzled.*

My cell blared in my matching gold purse just as I was about to
walk down the subway steps. Instead, I moved off to the side, duck-
ing into the doorway of a nearby building, and pulled out my cell.

Rafe's name flashed on the screen.

Familiar butterflies woke up in my belly and I ignored them as always. "Hey," I answered a little breathlessly. The cheap fabric of the dress was sticking under my arms and I was desperate to get to Brooklyn to the offices of We Bring Them to Life. Before every gig, I stopped in there for my costume change and then went back afterward to drop off the costume so they could have it dry-cleaned. The only time I ever went home in costume was if the event ran past our company's office hours.

"Hey, have I caught you at a bad time?" Rafe asked.

"No. Just finished up the job from hell, but I'll tell you all about it later."

"You okay?"

My heart raced at the genuine concern in his voice. "I'm good. Promise. What's up?"

"We have an issue. I forgot Pippa has a friend who lives in my building and she told Pippa that she's never seen you come over. I wondered if you'd come over tomorrow night. According to our schedule, you're not in the city tomorrow, so I'll send a cab."

I'd begun updating our shared app with my work schedule so Rafe would know exactly when I was free for our ruse. "That's a forty-minute cab ride. Longer if traffic is busy," I reminded him.

"I'm paying."

It was part of the job, I guessed. "Of course, I'll be there."

"Don't eat. I'll cook."

Of course he could cook. "Okay."

"You're not allergic to dogs, are you?"

"No, why?"

"I'll have a guest tomorrow night. One of my patients. He's a big friendly giant, though."

I smiled at the thought. "I love dogs."

"Good. You're free tomorrow from five, right? I'll send the cab around five thirty."

"Sounds good. See you then."

. . .

RAFE TIMED MY ARRIVAL PERFECTLY.

I knew this because as we stepped into the elevator of his building, the doors opened to reveal an elegant woman around Pippa's age.

"Rafe." She stepped out, her gaze darting between us. "N-nice to see you."

"You too, Octavia. This is my girlfriend, Star."

I smiled. "Nice to meet you."

"Star. Right. Nice to meet you too."

Rafe placed a hand on my lower back as his other shot out to keep the elevator doors open. "Have a good night."

I let him lead me into the elevator as Octavia threw us one last look. As she walked away, she fumbled for her purse. The doors closed and Rafe shot me a disbelieving look. "She is calling my sister-in-law right this second."

Laughter trembled on my lips. "Why are they so obsessed with you?"

"I have no idea." He sighed heavily.

"You knew she would be here at this time?"

"Octavia always has some event to go to and she leaves the building at exactly six thirty."

We stepped out of the elevator onto polished floors that were immaculate. Rafe's building was on West 63rd Street and was modern, clean, and obviously expensive. My sandals sounded noisily on the floor as Rafe led me down a wide hallway to a blue door with his apartment number on it.

The kitchen was to the right as we stepped into a small foyer. It was a modern kitchen, small but top of the line, and it was open to the dining/living room. My attention was drawn past Rafe's furnishings to the wall of glass that led out onto a small balcony that overlooked the Hudson River.

"Wow."

His apartment was small compared to Pippa and Hugo's, but it had a view over the Hudson.

I didn't even want to think what this place was costing him.

"Yeah, the view is great." Rafe understood my awe, but he didn't linger over it. Instead, he strode past me into the living room and squatted down to his haunches before the Great Dane the view had distracted me from. He was a puppy by the looks of his size. "Hey, buddy. Told you I wouldn't be long." He smoothed his big hand over the dog's head, and the dog tried to swipe a lick of Rafe's wrist.

"Who do we have here?" I smiled as I approached slowly.

The Dane finally noticed me and his ears perked up, but only his head moved toward me.

"This is Hector. He got neutered today and his owner wanted me to keep him overnight for observation." The whole time he talked, Rafe smoothed his hands down Hector's head and back. "Finn and Rebecca take turns doing the night shifts for this kind of thing, but now and then, if the animal is up to it, I'll bring them home with me for the night. Hector's doing good, but he's tired and still drowsy."

I reached out to let Hector sniff my fingers and he licked them, which I took as an okay to pet him. He bussed into my touch as I scratched behind his ears and told him he was such a handsome, gorgeous boy. Hector lapped up my attention, staring at me with open adoration, and I felt a brief pang of longing in my chest. "I think dogs are my soul mates."

"How so?"

I looked up at Rafe and found him watching me with a softness in his eyes that made my breath catch. It took me a second to remember my train of thought. Wrenching my gaze from his and back to Hector helped. "Well, they're just so open and full of love. Aggressive dogs are generally made, not born, right?"

"Correct."

"And if you treat them well, feed them, take care of them, provide them with affection, dogs love with an unfaltering loyalty that puts us humans to shame."

"And they're your soul mates?"

Realizing what he thought I meant by that, I shrugged with a small laugh. "I just mean that I admire their openness and sense of loyalty. I try to be the same." Standing up, I gazed around his apartment to change the subject. "This is very stylish, Mr. Whitman."

It was true. Unlike my eclectic collection of stuff, Rafe's living room and small dining area looked like something out of a fancy magazine. Plush chaise sofa, end tables, modern table lamps and decor. A flat screen was mounted on the wall. A hallway to the left of that wall clearly led to the bathroom and bedrooms.

"Want a tour?"

"I am nosy." I grinned in the affirmative.

His eyes brightened with amusement, and he led me down that hallway.

It turned out the apartment was one bedroom with a decent-sized and exquisitely designed bathroom. The bedroom, like the living room, had bifold doors that led onto a balcony overlooking the Hudson.

"You have nice taste," I told him honestly. It wasn't my taste but it was good taste.

His lips twisted as he led me back into the living area, where Hector was now asleep on his dog bed. "My mom furnished it. I don't have the time or the patience for that stuff."

"I thought it had an experienced touch."

"Take a seat." He gestured to the couch. "You want a drink while I cook?"

"What do you have?"

"Beer, wine, water."

"I'll have a beer."

A few minutes later, I was sipping on the chilled bottle of beer he'd pulled out of his fridge while he sipped on one as he cooked a pasta dish. I'd kicked off my sandals and made myself at home, curled up on his couch. Rafe moved around his kitchen at ease, seeming more relaxed than I'd ever seen him.

"You seem like you're in a good mood?"

Rafe looked up from chopping and shrugged with a small smile. "Pippa hasn't sent anyone into my clinic since the charity auction. Mom hasn't called to set me up on a date with another friend's daughter or tried to psychoanalyze why I'm alone or tried to dig deep into my past relationships and where they all went wrong. She actually asks me about my work now rather than about my personal life. It's nice."

"I'm glad this is working out how you hoped."

He met my gaze. "Oh, it's definitely working out better than I'd hoped."

I stared at him. What did that mean?

Rafe gave me this sexy, mysterious smile before he returned to chopping up vegetables and asked me how I felt about anchovies.

Chapter Thirteen

How is today's line sitting?

Dramatic. Some girl tried to jump in front of a bunch of us and I thought the others were going to kill her.

And how did that end?

I talked everyone down with some crude jokes and candy bars. We're all friends now.

Wednesday 12:48 pm

Of course that's how it ended with you in the mix.

Wednesday 12:49 pm

Well I am awesome. How's your day going?

Wednesday 12:50 pm

Up and down. Had to put a patient to sleep this morning and an hour later had a successful surgery with another patient. Just how it goes.

Wednesday 12:51 pm

I'm sorry you had a sad morning. Do you need anything? I can walk out of this line if you need me to bring you anything.

Wednesday 12:51 pm

Thank you, I appreciate it. But it's unfortunately something I've gotten used to doing.

Wednesday 12:52 pm

I'm here if you need anything.

Wednesday 12:53 pm

Thanks.

At two minutes past two, just as I was nearing the front of the line to buy the new Nike sneakers my client wanted, my phone rang. I smiled at the sight of Rafe's name and wasn't surprised considering I'd received a text to inform me my package had been delivered to his clinic.

"Hey."

"Hey." His voice was low, a little hoarse. He cleared his throat. "You sent me things."

I grinned at how confused he sounded. "I did send you things." In fact, I'd found a place near his clinic that did all kinds of gift baskets. I'd called them up and they'd put together a small basket that included craft beer from a place upstate, packets of different nuts, a cheese board, and gourmet chips. "I want you to go home tonight and relax with some beer and some snacks, and just try to let today go. Because you might be used to it, but that doesn't mean it doesn't affect you."

Rafe was quiet so long I had a horrible moment when I thought I might have crossed some invisible line between us. But then he spoke. "Thank you, Star. I really appreciate it."

I smiled down at my feet, those damn butterflies flapping around in my belly. "You're welcome."

"No one has ever sent me craft beer before." There was a teasing note to his words.

I grinned harder. "Or gourmet chips, I'd bet."

"Or gourmet chips."

Biting my lip against a giddy, overwhelming feeling, I tried to physically shake it off with a shrug. "It was nothing."

Rafe's voice was gravelly as he promised, "It's not nothing to me."

My impulse was to tell him I knew a few very explicit ways he could thank me, but I remembered at the last second he wasn't actually my lover. He was my fake boyfriend. "Uh . . . well, I'm glad if it cheered you up a little. My line is moving, so . . ."

"So I'll let you go." Was that laughter in his voice? "I'll pick you up on Saturday."

"Right. See you then." I hung up, shaking my head at myself and muttering, "You were the one that sent the damn basket."

The problem was that Rafe had started texting me daily and we'd begun swapping little anecdotes about our days. It was confusing to me. Hence the sending of the basket, which had led to him getting that sexy, grateful tone in his voice that had led to my body forgetting the facts.

Rafe Whitman was off-limits for so many reasons.

Only last night, on a call with Kendall, she seemed to need assurance this was just a business deal. When I asked why, she told me she was worried Rafe might fall for commitment-phobic me.

"Let's face it, Star, you're very lovable and almost all the guys you've been in a casual thing with have fallen in love with you and gotten their hearts broken."

I didn't want to break anyone's heart.

So I had to find a way to rid myself of this impossible attraction to Rafe Whitman.

SATURDAY HAD BEEN SCHEDULED INTO OUR APP FROM AL-most the beginning of our ruse. Rafe's family's friends were celebrating the wife's sixtieth birthday. They lived in Harrison, near Rafe's parents' house. It had rained most of the week, making line sitting extra fun, but today upstate, the sun was shining. Since it was a garden party, I'd chosen to wear a slimline sleeveless maxi dress with a halter neck. The design of the dress left my back bare to the top of my ass. It turned a pretty summer dress into something a little sexier. I'd piled my hair into a messy knot at my nape and was wearing the biggest hoop earrings known to humanity, lots of bracelets that jingled as I walked, and gladiator sandals so I could be comfy. They also took the edge off the sexiness of the dress.

Rafe picked me up in his Pontiac and I was a little ashamed of myself at how excited I was to be back in the car. So materialistic of me! I couldn't help myself. His car was freaking cool.

As he opened the passenger door for me and I slipped by him, he sucked in his breath so harshly I heard it. I glanced at him over my shoulder and found his eyes glued to my lower back. "What?" I strained to see what had caught his attention. "Is my underwear showing?"

Squeezing his eyes closed as if he were in pain, Rafe gave a shake of his head. "No. Get in."

I narrowed my eyes at his sharp tone but slid into the car. I'd barely gotten my legs in when he slammed the door shut and rounded the hood.

What the hell?

Really? We were back to Mr. Grumpy Whitman? He'd seemed fine five minutes ago.

As soon as he was in the car, I spoke calmly though my words were blunt. "What has crawled up His Majesty's ass today?"

His teeth clenched as he side-eyed me and gritted out, "Nothing."

That might have been all he'd said for the entire journey if I hadn't pestered him with questions about this family friend's birthday party. The questioning had the desired effect of loosening him up. The friends, the Van Beeks, had known Jen and Greg Whitman for thirty years. I didn't think my parents had ever held on to friends for longer than a few years before they moved on to the next place.

The Van Beeks' home was just as impressive as the Whitmans', and they clearly knew many people, because their huge garden was teeming with folks. As we walked around the front and to the backyard, Rafe placed his hand on the bare skin of my lower back and I shivered at the brush of his palm against my skin.

"You cold?" He frowned down at me.

"Nope." I couldn't look at him.

I stared at the yard instead. It was similar to the Whitmans', minus the tennis court. Today it was laid out with tables decorated in linen and silverware. A string quartet played off to the side beneath a beautiful oak tree, and it wasn't my imagination that they were doing classical versions of current pop songs. To our left, a little farther from the main action, was a large tent with an open awning and inside it appeared to be a full working kitchen, staff, and buffet setup. Servers passed with trays of champagne, and I noted they were coming and going from a bar next to the kitchen.

Wow.

These people did not do parties like other people.

"Rafe, Star, thank God!" Gigi hurried over to us, beautiful in a fifties-style summer dress. Her feet were noticeably bare, and I saw for the first time the tattoo of vines and flowers that wove along the edge of her right foot and crawled up the side of her ankle. It was beautiful.

Rafe leaned down to kiss his sister's cheek and murmured in amusement, "Where are your shoes?"

"Oh, they were crippling my feet." Gigi hugged me tight. "I kicked them off somewhere. Who knows where?"

"I'd have done the same." And I would have. "Your tattoo is awesome."

"Thank you! And look at you. You were smart and chose sexy-comfort." Gigi eyed my feet and then swept her gaze upward. "You look unbearably beautiful. I'm not sure we can still be friends."

I rolled my eyes. "You couldn't live without me now." Gigi and I had met up a few times for coffee while I was in the city, and I had to admit I was falling a little in platonic love with Rafe's sister. She reminded me a lot of Kendall and I couldn't wait for them to meet.

"This is true." Gigi gave Rafe a meaningful look. "You should really do something about that."

Rafe scowled at his sister while I frowned in confusion. "What does that mean?"

"Ooh, there's Sharon. I haven't spoken to her in ages. Catch up with you later!" Gigi dashed away with all the energy of an eight-year-old.

"What did she mean?" I looked up at Rafe.

He shook his head. "No idea."

Then his hand slid onto my back again and my brain fritzed. It was all I could think about as we walked through the party, nodding hello to people we passed. Rafe led us to a small cluster of guests who stood near a makeshift dance floor. Jen and Greg were among them.

The sounds of children's laughter and screams met my ears and I followed them to the pool where kids were in their swimsuits goofing around. I smiled at that, because the sight of them took a little of the stuffiness out of the party. I spotted Charmaine among the group and knew that Pippa, and possibly Hugo, had to be around somewhere.

Jen saw us first, her eyes lighting up as we approached. Rafe's parents greeted us warmly, and the whole time he didn't remove his hand from my back. He gestured to the couple that stood with his parents. "Star, this is Emily and Matthew Van Beek. Emily, Matthew, this is my girlfriend, Star."

I shook hands with the couple, who seemed friendly, and wished

Emily a happy birthday. I tried to concentrate on the conversation, but as they asked if it was true Rafe and I met at Charmaine's birthday party, Rafe's hand lifted from my back . . . and then I felt his touch between my shoulder blades. He trailed his fingertips lightly down my spine. Slowly, sensually.

My breasts swelled at the unexpected touch, my nipples hardening. Panicked, I didn't answer Emily right away.

Someone coughed and then Rafe spoke. "We did meet at Charmaine's party." He trailed his fingers back up my spine.

The bastard.

I didn't dare look down to see if my nipples were poking through the thin fabric of my dress. I couldn't wear a bra, so all I had on was boob tape.

What was he doing to me?

"So you're friends with Pippa?" Emily smiled.

Trying not to frown, I wondered why if they were such close friends of the Whitmans they didn't know how we'd met.

"Yes," Jen answered for me.

Greg eyed her with a frown.

"Well, now we are." I stared in confusion at Jen. "But, no, I was at the party working. I'm a costume character actor."

Matthew looked curious. "What does that entail?"

Rafe started drawing little circles on my lower back. I sucked in a breath and tried to subtly nudge him. If he felt the nudge, he didn't stop. It was extremely distracting!

And arousing.

"I, uh . . ." What the hell did Matthew ask?

"Star dresses up as cultural icons. Disney characters, movie characters, et cetera," Rafe supplied for me.

"Oh." Emily shot Jen a visible *what on earth?* look.

I stiffened.

Rafe must have felt it, because his hand opened on my back and slid around to my hip to squeeze me in reassurance. "She's also a professional line sitter."

"Do I even want to ask?" Emily chuckled.

"And is that your career?" Matthew was clearly trying to figure me out.

"Those are my jobs. I don't really believe in the idea of a career."

Emily guffawed. "Well, I never."

"I mean for myself. Of course, I believe in careers. We need doctors, lawyers, vets . . . I get it. Just not for me."

When Jen glanced away as if I'd embarrassed her, I felt my stomach knot.

"Aren't you unusual, dear?" Emily observed, and I knew it wasn't a compliment.

Ugh.

These were the Whitmans' friends?

"Star *is* unusual." Rafe glowered at Emily. "Unlike most people, she's kind to everyone, considerate, lacking in pretension, free-spirited, and the best fucking sex I've ever had." Rafe gave them all a tight grin. "Now, where is the bar?"

While I was pretty sure I stood there gaping like someone had just hooked me on a fishing line, Greg struggled not to laugh as he pointed out the bar to us. The rest of his companions stared at Rafe as if he were a stranger who'd trespassed upon their party.

Thankfully, my legs worked as Rafe guided me away from his parents and their friends, muttering under his breath about "these fucking people." Laughter rose inside me as I hurried to keep up, then he stopped at the bar. He ordered two cold beers and then led me away from the party beneath the shade of another massive oak. "Here." He handed me a beer.

I choked on a snort before blurting out, "The best fucking sex you've ever had?"

Rafe studied my face for a second and then burst into laughter.

I was so shocked by this I could only gawk at him.

When his laughter trailed off, he grinned that sexy, boyishly wicked smile of his that made me want to rip his clothes off and turn that "best fucking sex" comment into reality. "They were rude and judgmental."

I glanced over at where his parents now stood alone, talking to each other in what seemed like hushed tones. "You've come a long way, Whitman."

Fingers, cold from the bottle of beer, touched my bare back again and I jumped a little as I turned back to him. Rafe caressed the skin, right in the middle of my spine, almost in a soothing motion. Something like remorse glimmered in his eyes. "If that's how I acted when we met, then I'm sorry, Star. I was a prick."

Who was this guy?

What was going on here? With the affectionate, sensual touches and apologies and sticking up for me? "Rafe . . ."

"Rafe Whitman, as I live and breathe."

The woman's voice changed Rafe's demeanor in a blink. His hand fell away from my body, his expression blanked, and he straightened, stiff and composed.

I followed his gaze to the woman who approached us with a smirk playing on her full lips. She was a level of sexy that would have made me insecure if I were the type of woman who allowed herself to feel small. Seriously, she was built like a Kardashian, and you could see every line of her sleek curves in the pale pink body-contouring dress she wore. It was sleeveless, with a scoop neck, and the hemline ended just below her knees. Her pale pink pumps matched. Her whole look was conservative but outrageously sexy, which was something I hadn't known anyone could pull off.

Her dark eyes flickered to me for a second before dismissing me.

She forced herself between us to lay a hand on Rafe's chest as she leaned up to kiss his cheek.

Rafe, thankfully, didn't lean into the kiss.

When she pulled back, she stayed close, hand still on his chest.

I wanted to rip that hand right off him.

The flare of jealousy was startling.

Rafe glanced down at her perfectly manicured hand like it was bird poop and instead of relief, I felt my protective instincts awaken.

He stepped out of her touch and toward me, sliding his arm around me to draw me against him. I snuggled into him, my bangles jingling on my wrist as I rested my hand where hers had been, as if to erase her touch. "Camille, how are you?"

Camille observed our embrace and her smile turned pained before she covered it with one filled with triumph. "I'm well. Just got promoted to junior vice president at the bank."

"Congratulations," Rafe said tonelessly.

Who was this sexy corporate woman?

She lost some of her confidence at his less-than-enthusiastic response. A sad tenderness replaced it. "You look great, Rafferty." Her gaze came to me when he said nothing, and she reluctantly held out her hand. "I'm Camille Westmoreland. Rafe and I used to date."

I pulled on my best acting skills and didn't react to that or the way Rafe tensed even more at her announcement. "Star." I shook her hand. "Rafe's girlfriend."

"And I always thought Rafe had a type," she murmured, dragging her eyes down my body in obvious disbelief. Or maybe even disdain.

"Camille," Rafe warned.

She shook her head like he was a misbehaving child who'd disappointed her. "You know where I am when you decide to get serious about your life."

My jaw actually dropped.

Camille sauntered off, generous hips swaying almost hypnotically. Looking up at Rafe, I spluttered, "Th-these people . . . Rafe, please tell me they are not all like this?"

"They're not all like this. But they do think life should be lived a certain way. I told you that. That's why you're here in the first place."

For some reason, I did not want to be reminded of that right now. "Used to date?"

"I don't want to talk about it." He finished his beer and grabbed my hand. "Let's find something to eat."

An hour later, Rafe was no less brooding. We'd had a stilted conversation with Pippa and Hugo for a while. Pippa had spent the whole time bobbing up and down trying to see past people to the pool, muttering about how no one was watching the kids, until finally she stalked off to do that herself. Hugo was barely there anyway. It was obvious his mind was elsewhere, and when Pippa walked away, he used it as an excuse to disappear into the house.

Gigi returned to us and navigated introductions with other guests who were mutual friends. Thankfully, not everyone was as passive-aggressively rude as the Van Beeks and Camille Westmoreland. In fact, most of the guests were very nice and I would have been having a good time if Rafe hadn't reformed to the guy I'd met at Charmaine's birthday party.

"What is wrong with you?" Gigi grumbled when another couple left after Rafe grunted answers at their casual questions.

"Nothing."

His sister looked at me, and I gestured subtly with my head. Getting my hint, she excused herself and I stepped into Rafe's personal space. His nostrils flared at my sudden proximity.

"So . . . used to date?" I tried again.

"I told you—"

"Why are you so sore about it?"

"I'm not sore about it. I'm pissed that she approached me the way she did when she can see you're my date. It's typical Camille."

"Then you are giving her too much power."

He frowned. "What?"

"Whatever she did, if you really are over it, why are you allowing her to ruin your day?"

"She was rude to you."

"Yet when the Van Beeks were rude, you made me laugh about it. C'mon, you can be honest with me, you know. I might be the only one other than Gigi who you can be honest with at this point." I pressed a fingertip into his chest, the gesture teasing. Finding solid muscle teased me in a different way. I dropped my hand. "So?"

Rafe exhaled heavily, but the tension in his shoulders loosened as he held my gaze. "Camille was my last relationship. We broke up two years ago. Dated for four years and she cheated on me with a famous actor and dumped me."

My lips parted in shock. "She what?"

"Oh, that's not the worst part. When he dumped her, I came home to our apartment to find her there, cooking dinner like nothing had happened. She expected me to take her back."

"She did not?" I gaped at the outrageous arrogance.

"She did. So *I* moved out. Now and then we show up at the same events because of mutual acquaintances and even if she has a date, she tries to convince me we'll end up together."

And he was still bothered about this? Did that mean he still cared about her? A burn flared in my chest, and to my horror, I realized it was jealousy. "You don't want her back? You can't forgive her?"

Rafe's gaze searched mine. "I was blind to her for a long time. I couldn't see past her intelligence, confidence, her ambition—"

"Her rockin' bod," I added.

"Maybe that too." His smile slipped as he swallowed hard. "But I see past all that now. To what's important. She was self-involved and she could be unkind. I used to ignore all the catty, judgmental comments she made about other people, writing them off as a consequence of her drive and ambition. Now I think she was never that confident. Who needs to tear down other people to be truly confident, right? But I couldn't see that then. I just saw her intelligence and determination and I was attracted to her for it. Looking back, I'm not proud of the guy who admired her. That's not the guy I thought I was."

"You know, there's nothing wrong with admiring ambition. I don't judge people for that. In fact, contrary to popular belief, I'm the most ambitious person I know."

He quirked an interested eyebrow.

I grinned. "Everyone has ambitions. To be a doctor, a lawyer, an astronaut, a vet, a successful businessperson, a good mother, a good father . . . *My* ambition is to live a life that makes me truly happy. And I reckon that's probably the most ambitious anyone can be in this world."

Rafe's eyes lightened, and the look he gave me made my heart race.

So much so, I sought to change the subject. "So you're over her?" Why did I need the words?

He continued to stare at me with a brooding intensity. "Oh, I am definitely over Camille."

Relief filled me and I swear, someone else took over my body. Perhaps the green-eyed monster. Because the next thing I knew, I'd grabbed hold of his lapel and pulled him down to me as I lifted onto my tiptoes and covered his mouth with mine. It was supposed to be a quick but hard kiss. However, Rafe brought our mouths back together with his hand on my nape. His other hand pressed deep into my back as he took over the kiss.

I gasped at the touch of his tongue to mine, and the sound seemed to ignite Rafe. He deepened the kiss and I met him in it. My tongue to his. His kiss was hungry, desperate almost, and it set every inch of me on fire. It wasn't pretty or romantic. It was blatantly sexual and it consumed me with the need to get him very, very naked and inside me.

"Uh, guys, get a room." Gigi's voice cut through the moment like a bucket of cold water.

I jerked back, remembering where we were, and Rafe's hand flexed around my nape as if to stop me from moving away. My lips tingled as we breathed hard, gazing at each other in stupefaction.

Hottest kiss of my life.

Rafe appeared dazed enough for me to believe maybe it was for him too.

But this wasn't supposed to be real. We both needed to remember that. So I grinned mischievously. "Well played, Whitman. I hope the ex saw that." I stepped out of his touch and glanced at Gigi, who smiled knowingly at us.

At Rafe's silence, I forced myself to look at him.

The glint of hard determination in his eyes made my heart pound.

Oh boy.

"I need another beer."

WHILE I DIDN'T KNOW HOW TO ACT AROUND RAFE AFTER THE most spectacular kiss anyone had ever given me, he'd returned to Mr. Relaxed. In fact, he was in a damn good mood. I couldn't analyze that without freaking out.

When it came time to leave, Jen got me alone and apologized if the Van Beeks had offended me. I told her I wasn't easily offended, but I was grateful that she'd acknowledged her friend's rude behavior.

Rafe had stuck to his one-beer rule because he was driving, but after our kiss, I'd had a few more, and between that and too much sun, I was feeling a little tipsy. I commandeered the radio in the car and switched it to a rock station. Making myself at home, I'd kicked off my gladiator sandals and put my feet on the dash, tapping my hands on my knees as I sang along to the Eagles.

We slowed in traffic, and I glanced at Rafe, only to find him staring at my legs. My dress had fallen with gravity, baring me from the knee down.

"Sorry." I lowered my legs, thinking he minded my feet on his pretty car. "I wasn't thinking."

His gaze flew to mine. "It's fine."

I didn't put my feet back up on the dash.

The music changed to Queen, and Rafe reached over and turned down the volume. "Do you think I'm a prick for dating Camille?"

Shocked by his question—a question that suggested he cared about my opinion—I struggled to find the right words.

His expression turned guarded. "You do."

"No." I hurried to assure him as I straightened in my seat. "I already told you that. Look, we've all dated people we wished we hadn't."

"She cheated because I didn't love her. She'd tell me she loved me and I couldn't say it back."

"Wow. You dated her for four years without saying 'I love you'?"

He shrugged. "I was focused on setting up my clinic and I had little free time and Camille was ambitious, so she understood. I thought I wanted someone like that. Someone who didn't mind if I didn't show up for dinner that night. Someone who didn't mind if I couldn't say 'I love you.' Turns out she minded."

I quizzed him, "Now you don't want someone like that?"

He didn't answer. Instead, he asked, "Have you ever been in love, Star?"

I had not expected such a question. Squirming with discomfort, I looked out at the passing scenery as the traffic eased and we picked up speed. "No. You?"

"I thought once, maybe, but now I don't think so."

There was that burn in my chest again. I looked back at him. "Who was the maybe once?"

"My first serious girlfriend. High school sweethearts. She's the only girl I ever said the words to. It ended because that's all we were meant to be."

"I think the kind of romantic love people grow up searching for—that monogamy and commitment to one person—I'm not sure it really exists."

"I am." He surprised me again. "My parents are prime examples that it exists."

"Then they must be the exception to the rule. My parents love each other, but they couldn't stay loyal to each other. That's how their relationship has survived. And look at Roger, Kendall, and Jude. They have the best relationship I've ever seen, but they required that third person to make it that way."

Rafe's lip curled at the corner. "I think in their case, they're the exception to the rule. Few people could make a polyamorous relationship work. I know I could never share like that."

"But they share each other. It's not like both guys are just with Kendall. They're with each other too."

"Still couldn't do it. I know I'd feel more for one person because that's the way I'm built. And I'd get jealous as hell watching her with some other guy or girl. Wouldn't you?"

I thought of my unexpected jealousy over Camille and answered honestly, "Maybe."

"Hmm."

At his "hmm" I studied him. "What?"

He flicked me a look. "Nothing."

"You're full of a lot of nothings today."

Rafe grinned at that, and I sighed at my answering butterflies. Damn this man and my attraction to him.

Suddenly, his cell phone blared and he cursed. "That's my emergency cell." He pulled up the center console with one hand, eyes on the road, and I reached in for the phone before he could.

"Dr. Whitman's phone," I answered, and he shot me a grateful look. I switched it to speaker.

"Hi, this is Amber Schuler, Rocky's owner," a panicked woman's voice said down the line.

Rafe nodded at me and I inquired, "How can I help you, Amber?"

"My niece left a candy bar sitting out and Rocky ate it. It's milk chocolate and it was a lot."

He scowled, glancing at his watch, and murmured, "Ask her when."

"When did Rocky eat the chocolate?"

"About five minutes ago. I got to him too late."

"Ms. Schuler, this is Rafe." He raised his voice, and I held the phone closer to him.

"Dr. Whitman," she breathed in obvious relief. "What do I do?"

"I can give Rocky an injection to make him sick, Ms. Schuler, if you can get him to the clinic in a half hour."

"I can do that. Absolutely, we'll be there."

"See you then."

As I hung up, Rafe asked, "Are you okay with a pit stop?"

"Of course," I said, more than a little in awe. Because his ability to calm down his patient's owner with just the sound of his voice was a very, very attractive quality indeed.

Chapter Fourteen

IT TURNED OUT NOT ONLY DID RAFE HAVE TO GIVE ROCKY AN
injection to make him vomit, but we had to wait two hours after the
little guy vomited up all the chocolate to make sure he was doing
okay. By the time Amber walked out of the clinic with Rocky in her
arms, it was past midnight.

Rafe shut the door behind her and looked down at me where I'd
curled up on the bench in the waiting room, exchanging texts with
Roger, who was out with Kendall at our local bar.

Hair a little mussed, his shirt unbuttoned, tie loose, Rafe the
tired vet was a little too sexy for my own good. I attempted to avoid
staring at the mouth that had devoured mine so well this afternoon.
"You okay?"

"Yeah." He slumped down next to me and leaned his elbows on
his knees, head hanging. "Long day."

I sat up and nudged his thigh. "You should go home, get some
sleep."

Rafe looked sharply at me. "What about you?"

"I should get going."

He sat up, turning into me. "You're not traveling home at this
time. No. No way."

His bossiness was adorable. "Well, that's a problem for you, because I am."

"No, you'll stay with me." He stood up and held out a hand. "C'mon. I'll sleep on the couch."

"I'm not putting you out of your bed. Rafe, I'll grab a cab if it makes you feel better."

"It doesn't." He dropped his hand and gave me a wearied, beleaguered stare. "Please, Star. I'll just worry."

Something warm and surprising and scary spread in a heat across my chest as I stood. "All right. I wouldn't want you to worry. But I'm taking the couch."

He turned, shaking his head, but I saw the hint of a smile on his face as he pulled open the door and gestured me out first. "It's not in my programming to allow such a thing to occur."

Sometimes I loved the way he talked. Grinning to myself, I shrugged. "Fair enough. If you want me to take the bed, I'll take the bed."

STARING DOWN AT RAFE'S BED, I REALIZED IT WAS MUCH EASier to be blasé about the whole thing when I wasn't standing in his bedroom, staring at the space where he laid his well-formed body every night, and breathing in his scent. The smell of his cologne lingered in the air and I bet it was all over his pillows too.

"Here."

I turned at his voice to find Rafe holding out a perfectly folded T-shirt.

"For you to sleep in," he clarified.

"Oh." I took it, trying not to touch him. "Right, thanks."

The easiness that existed between us as we drove to his apartment and parked his car in a neighboring garage had dissipated as soon as we stepped inside his home. Suddenly, I became very aware of the fact that it was late at night and we were alone at his place after sharing the world's best kiss.

By the awkward tension, I'd say it was quite possible Rafe was thinking the same thing.

"I'll let you change first." He gestured to the bathroom. "I don't have a spare toothbrush but there's mouthwash."

"Great." I smiled at him, but the exchange felt strained.

He frowned. "Can I get you anything else?"

"No, this is great." *Stop saying "great."* "I'll just . . ." I nodded toward the bathroom and then scooted around him to disappear inside. Locking the door behind me, I leaned against it, shaking my head. What the hell was wrong with me?

Pushing off the door with a frustrated sigh, I took care of business, gave myself a quick wash with what Rafe had available, scrubbed my face clean, and changed into Rafe's T-shirt. I opened the bathroom door and called out, "Hey, do you mind if I use your hairbrush?"

"Go ahead," he called back from the living room.

I unpinned the curls, making a pile of bobby pins on the corner of his countertop, reminding myself to collect those in the morning.

It hit me again that I was staying overnight in Rafe's apartment.

As I fluffed out my hair and brushed out the tangles, I noted the flush high on my cheeks and that familiar gleam in my eyes. My nipples poked through the borrowed T-shirt that smelled of Rafe and hit me midthigh. I was turned on. By the mere thought of being alone with him in his apartment.

This was not a normal reaction to someone.

"Fuck," I muttered.

Swallowing hard, I scooted out of the bedroom, with my dress and shoes folded in my hands, fully intending to avoid him.

But he was standing right outside the door.

"Oh." I startled to a stop as my eyes wandered, with a mind of their own, down his body and back up again. He wore a T-shirt and plaid pajama pants. The T-shirt hung loose around his middle but strained around those impressive biceps and broad shoulders.

Oh boy.

My eyes flew to his face and my skin grew even hotter at the way he stared at my legs. I think even my legs blushed. "I'm going to go to bed now," I announced with false cheer, backing into said bedroom. I fake-yawned. "Oh, tired. Long day. So tired. Night-night." Abruptly, I closed the door in his face. My heart raced in my chest, the blood rushing in my ears.

Then, in an amused rumble that made me want to open the door again, I heard "Good night, Star."

IT WAS UNCLEAR WHAT WOKE ME UP, BUT I STARTLED AWAKE and, for a split second, panicked at finding myself in an unfamiliar bed. The scent of Rafe on the pillows, however, caused my memory to flood back and I remembered crawling into his bed after the awkward good night. Somehow, I must have fallen asleep. It might have had something to do with the fact that the man owned a bed made of clouds. Seriously, the comfiest bed in the freaking world.

I rolled over and picked up my cell. Its battery was low but it was still alive, and the time on the screen told me it was almost dawn.

I had two choices available to me.

I could (a) try to fall back asleep and enjoy a few more hours in the comfiest cloud bed, then wake up and pretend everything was normal between us. Or (b) get up quietly, dress, and sneak out of his apartment before he woke up.

Before I could even let myself process why, I got out of Rafe's bed.

Channeling my inner ninja, I changed into my dress and tied on my sandals. Grabbing my cell and purse, I carefully opened the bedroom door, wincing at the slight squeak of its hinge. Tiptoeing out, I came to a stop at the sight of Rafe sleeping on his couch. He'd kicked the covers off, and he slept on his stomach, the right side of his face squished into a pillow. His lashes looked longer and even thicker in sleep. His T-shirt had pulled up on one side, revealing his strong lower back.

It took me a second to realize I was holding my breath at the sight of his masculine beauty.

Yup.

As if I couldn't help myself, I tiptoed over to him and dared to lean in. My lips brushed his warm cheek and I inhaled the scent of him. Something ferocious overwhelmed me.

Longing.

The kind of intense longing I hadn't felt since I was a kid and I wanted parents who paid attention to me and were overprotective. Who loved me more than they loved anything.

I definitely needed to get the hell out of there.

Jerking back, mind roiling with confusion, I hurried quietly away from him and spotted the notepad on his phone table. Quickly writing him a note, explaining I had an impromptu job to get up for (a lie), I told him I'd see him later.

Then I left.

"YOU JUST LEFT?" ROGER'S EYEBROWS WERE VERY, VERY HIGH, and I didn't know why.

"Yeah. So?"

Hours later, curled up on Roger's couch, I'd caught my best friend up on the garden party, emergency call, and subsequent overnighter.

"Has he called you?"

I shifted in discomfort. "Yeah, but I was busy, so I didn't pick up. He texted me."

"And?"

"He was just checking I got home okay." Truth.

"You replied, right?"

"Of course I did."

"So you snuck out?"

"I left."

"You snuck out."

"Potayto, potahto."

"You really like him," Roger surmised in astonishment.

He wasn't the only one astonished by that assessment. "Uh, I do not. I admit I'm attracted to him, but only on a very basic level."

"Liar. If it was just attraction and you didn't like him, you wouldn't have snuck out. The Star I know would have hung around and made him breakfast."

"We didn't sleep together. I crashed at his place."

"You still wouldn't have given a crap about waking up in his bed if you didn't like him. Instead, you snuck out of there like it scared you to face him."

Frustration burst out of me. "Okay, so what if I did? I'm trying to maintain a professional distance with the guy."

Roger wrinkled his nose. "I'm confused. What would be wrong if you liked each other and dated for real?"

Like he didn't know. "Oh please, Roger, we both know once Rafe slept with me, the shine would start to wear off Star Shine Meadows."

"What the fuck does that mean?" Roger scowled fiercely.

"I don't belong in his world." As if that weren't already obvious. "He'd get bored of our differences pretty damn quick."

"When have you ever cared about that shit?"

I shook my head, not wanting to get into it. "It's beside the point. Rafe Whitman is Mr. Commitment Guy. I won't hurt him or me by starting something that I intend to finish within a few weeks."

"If that's the case, there would be no harm in dating him if you think he's going to get bored with you in a few weeks anyway."

My pulse was racing too hard for such a seemingly harmless discussion. "You're talking in circles and I'm done with this conversation."

Roger held up his hands in surrender, but his gaze was far too deep and searching. "I'll stop, but I want to end this by saying I've never seen you this agitated over a guy before, and I think it means something. You always said rules weren't for you, so why are you making these steadfast rules against being in a committed relationship with someone?"

"Because . . . I don't have it in me. Monogamy is not in my DNA." My friend opened his mouth to speak, but I held up a hand. "Please, Roger. Can we just hang out? I've been so busy lately that I feel like we haven't just hung out and chilled together. Especially alone." Jude and Kendall were in Brooklyn for an art showing that Roger didn't feel like attending.

"Okay." He grinned at me as he got up. "Let me order some pizza and we'll put on a movie. There's a new rom-com on Netflix that I've been dying to watch, but Jude keeps nay-saying."

I chuckled. "Sounds like an awesome plan."

As Roger called for takeout and set up the movie at the same time, I tried not to look at my phone, at my text string with Rafe. I attempted not to think about him at all. The harder I tried, the worse it got. The whole time we ate and watched that movie, I thought about the way he'd defended me to his parents' friends, how at ease he seemed when it was just the two of us, and of course, I couldn't get that scorching kiss off my mind either.

Chapter Fifteen

I'D SPENT THE LAST FEW FOURTH OF JULY WEEKENDS WITH MY
friends. Roger and Kendall usually hosted a party on the roof of
their apartment building. Jude begrudgingly went along with it, so I
wouldn't really call *him* a host.

This year was the first time I couldn't attend their party, and
Jude and Kendall were a little upset I'd prioritized work over them.
I knew that because they'd said it to my face. Roger had told them to
give me a break, and I had a feeling I knew why he was so cool about
my absence.

I couldn't make their party because I'd promised Rafe I'd attend
a weekend party at his parents' house. He said they hosted it every
year and it would look strange if he didn't attend with his girlfriend.

The thought of maintaining our ruse for an entire weekend had
me a little nervous, but I promised myself I could handle it. What I
couldn't handle was opening my apartment door to Rafe that Saturday morning and him staring at me as if he hadn't seen me in a year,
only for him to say in gravelly tones, "You look beautiful."

Before I could think of a response to the unexpected compliment, he took hold of my small suitcase. "I'll take this down to the car."

I checked myself in my full-length mirror before I left the apartment. During the shopping trip with Kendall, I'd been pleased that I'd bought clothes I knew I'd wear when my deal with Rafe ended. My current dress was one I'd bought at Anthropologie. It was blue with a pale pink print, strapless with a sweetheart neckline, and it fell to my ankles from beneath my boobs in a handkerchief hem. Kendall told me to wear my hair up because she said I had great collarbones and shoulders, whatever that meant, and this dress showed off all of that. The dress itself wasn't overly bohemian, but I had a gold bracelet around my left biceps. I wore a gold crystal and floral headpiece, and I decorated almost every one of my fingers with a slender gold ring of a unique style. My ears were bare because, hey, I was wearing what amounted to a crown, and earrings would be overkill. My reflection told me I'd deliberately chosen to be exactly myself today, to remind me, to remind Rafe of who I was.

I was not East Coast society chic.

I was Star Shine Meadows and I enjoyed dressing like I was a half-fae princess.

Yet Rafe had taken one look and said, "You look beautiful."

And he'd meant it?

What the actual heck?

Butterflies roiled in my belly as I grabbed my purse and stepped out of my apartment to lock up. That small suitcase Rafe carried downstairs was filled with two more outfits, just like this one. Not that it mattered, apparently, because Rafe didn't seem to care.

Warm air hit me as I stepped outside. It was only ten in the morning, but heavy heat already pressed against my skin, which meant we could look forward to a scorcher this afternoon. My mind quickly abandoned any thought of the weather as I took in Rafe leaning against his Pontiac.

In all the "You look beautiful" stuff, I hadn't processed what he was wearing. Surprising, since he was something to see, leaning against his car, his arms crossed over his chest, wearing a lightweight cotton shirt in a blue that probably brought out his eyes, but I wouldn't know because he was wearing cool-as-hell sunglasses. The shirt definitely brought out his muscles. It was fitted. He'd rolled the sleeves up to his elbows, and he wore it loose over his light gray dress pants. A few buttons were left undone at the collar, showing off his strong, tan throat.

Holy hotness, Superman.

Dammit.

As if he knew exactly what I was thinking, Rafe's lips curled upward slightly in an arrogant smirk that was also too hot for my own good. I couldn't see his eyes behind his sunglasses, which reminded me to pull mine out of my purse as I approached him. It gave me a reason to stop ogling him.

He stepped away from the car, but only to open the passenger-side door.

Always the gentleman.

"Thanks," I murmured.

As I moved to get into the car, Rafe touched my lower back and brought his lips so close to my ear I felt them brush my skin. "Did I mention you look beautiful?"

Goose bumps prickled my arms as I glanced up at him in surprise. He'd pulled his head up, but his body crowded mine and, while I couldn't see his eyes, I could have sworn he was smoldering at me.

What was going on? "Um . . . thanks?"

Rafe grinned as if my response was hilarious, and a riot of butterflies exploded in my belly. I must have gaped too long, because he chuckled, "Are you getting in or are we celebrating the Fourth on your sidewalk?"

"Oh, right. Fourth. Party. House. Harrison." I dove into the car, my mind reeling.

Was . . . Rafe Whitman flirting with me?

But why? There was no one around to see it. It was just us.

Confused, I didn't speak as he got into the car and pulled out onto the street. Once we were off the island, we hit pretty heavy midmorning traffic heading upstate. Looked like we weren't the only ones leaving the city for the weekend celebrations.

I'd slipped my sunglasses on and kept shooting side glances out of the corner of them. Rafe handled stick with a confidence that was mesmerizing. The muscles in his forearms flexed now and then with his movements. It was unfair that every inch of him was beautiful. I mean, I hadn't seen *every* inch, but usually people had some kind of flaw, right? That was what made them interesting. Rafe should be boring, he was that physically perfect. But he was anything but boring. Besides, it wasn't like he'd been blessed with the body of a superhero. The man actually got up at five every weekday to work out at the gym in his building. He even had a trainer. When I'd asked him why he enjoyed working out, he said not only did the actual workout take his mind off everything else going on in his life, but he always felt great after it. Energized.

I wondered how that energy would translate into the bedroom.

Dammit.

I ripped my gaze from his freaking forearm at the realization that his limb was turning me on. *Bad fake girlfriend.* I shook my head at myself.

"You okay over there? You're very quiet this morning," Rafe observed. "Do you need water? There's a cooler on the back seat with bottles of water and fruit juice. I've got snacks too. There are some breakfast bars, but there are also fresh bagels from the place around the corner from my building. I didn't know if you'd eat before we left."

Glancing over my shoulder, I spotted the cooler and a net grocery bag brimming with food. On top of it was a white bakery box.

Complimentary and considerate.

Seriously, what was going on with him?

"Do you want a bagel?" I asked. "I can hold it for you."

"Yeah?"

"Sure."

"Then, yeah, I've only had a protein shake this morning and I'm starving."

Nodding, I took off my seat belt to lean into the back.

"Be careful," Rafe murmured.

As I wedged myself between the front seats, the car suddenly swerved.

"Sorry, shit," Rafe growled. "Asshole came out of nowhere. You okay?"

I'd grabbed onto the back of the front seats, my nails digging into Rafe's perfect ivory leather. My heart lurched—not gonna lie—but I was okay. I told him so. Then I returned to trying to reach for water and food.

I thought I heard Rafe mutter something about his "own personal hell."

Frowning, I grabbed the bagels once I had the water and shimmied back into the front seat. "What?" I straightened out my dress, glad my boobs hadn't popped free with all the movement.

"What?" he repeated back at me.

"You said something."

"Nope."

"Hmm." I didn't push it. Instead, I pulled my seat belt back on, placed the water in cup holders, and then opened the bagel box. "Breakfast bagels. Yum." They'd already cut each of them in half for easier eating on the go. Probably a bagel no-no anywhere else, but I appreciated the practicality. I handed Rafe half of his.

Feeding him while he drove and then making sure he was watered felt awfully girlfriendy, but I tried not to think about it, just as I tried not to think about his odd behavior. Although the grumpy, brooding man I'd met three months ago had gradually disappeared over the weeks, this was different. He was different. And I didn't understand why.

To steer my thoughts elsewhere, I asked Rafe about his week, and he told me that poor Finn had expressed a cavapoo's anal glands the day before and the secretion had sprayed all over his face. I'd cackled at Rafe's boyishly wicked enjoyment of it, but I'd also felt truly bad for Finn. Honestly. I knew my amusement suggested otherwise, but poor Finn.

"We've all been there. He's gotta learn." Rafe shook his head, still grinning.

The conversation lulled me back into a comfortable place and I told Rafe about my week. Thursday had been my best day because I had a four-year-old's party at a preschool and I'd dressed as Elsa from *Frozen* while a colleague dressed as Anna.

"The kids were so cute and excited. I love it when they really believe I'm the character. Their wonder and awe makes my week." I beamed, thinking about the little birthday girl and how she'd clung to my sparkly blue skirts the entire time, smiling up at me like I was an angel. It made my chest throb just thinking about it.

"I bet you make a gorgeous Elsa," Rafe commented, shooting me a quick look. "The kids must have been in heaven."

What. The. Actual. Heck?

"Are you practicing right now?" I blurted out.

I could have sworn he restrained a smile, but he kept his head turned toward the road. "Practicing?"

"The compliments. The flirty compliments."

His mouth definitely tugged upward. "Okay."

Okay? That wasn't an answer! "Is that a yes? No? What?"

Rafe shrugged. "Sure."

Sure to yes or no or what? I spluttered, "Are you being deliberately infuriating?"

This time, he turned his head to grin at me before looking back at the road. "Am I?"

"Who are you, and what have you done with Rafe Whitman?"

"Are *you* feeling okay?" He blindly reached toward me as if he wanted to touch my forehead.

I slapped his hand away, laughter in my voice. "There's nothing wrong with *me*."

Rafe chuckled as he returned his hand to the wheel. "That is very true."

A tingle burst to life between my legs at the flirty rumble in those words, and I squirmed in my seat.

Yeah . . . I was very, very confused.

WHEN WE FIRST ARRIVED AT HIS PARENTS' HOUSE, RAFE CON-tinued to be affectionate and sweet, but now we had an audience. Guests had only just started arriving for the weekend house party, and Rafe kissed me on the mouth in front of his family before he told me he was taking our luggage to our rooms.

"Oh, *room*, darling," Jen corrected. "As in singular. We don't expect you two to pretend like you don't share a bed. And frankly, I needed the other rooms for guests."

Rafe stared at his mother, a frown between his brows. "You always put Camille and me in separate rooms. It drove her up the wall."

Jen shrugged. "That's because I didn't like *her*."

Gigi hooted. "Momma Jen keeping it real with some honesty. I love it!"

Jen rolled her eyes at her daughter's antics, but I could see the amusement there.

Then Gigi wrapped her arm around my shoulders and hugged me to her. "Looks like someone approves, gorgeous."

My cheeks flushed and I'm sure they thought it was humble modesty. But it wasn't. The heat was part guilt and part *holy shit, I'm stuck sharing a room with Rafe for the weekend.*

As if she had read my mind, Gigi whispered in my ear, "Don't feel guilty. Trust me, Rafe deserves this reprieve from my mom's matchmaking insanity." Gigi and I had spoken privately about it, and she'd told me that what I'd witnessed at Charmaine's birthday party was nothing compared to what she'd watched her brother endure. She'd once been out for coffee with him and he'd received five calls in an hour from women his mom and Pippa had given his number to.

I nodded at Gigi, giving her a small smile of thanks.

Then I looked over at Rafe. His smirk was cocky before he left the room with our luggage.

Was he . . .

No.

He couldn't be.

Right?

GIGI COMMANDEERED ME AS SOON AS WE JOINED THE PARTY, dragging me away from Rafe to ask me advice on how to deal with a friend who'd just lost her job and had started ghosting Gigi. I advised her to go see her friend to make sure she was okay. Sometimes low feelings made us push people away. After that, our conversation moved easily to more friend talk, guy talk, work, tattoos, and more. Before I knew it, so much time had passed, Rafe came to collect me.

"I need you by my side for this," he grumbled, pulling me away from his sister.

"I'm sorry. I didn't mean to get caught up."

He gave my waist a squeeze. "It's fine. In fact, I can't remember the last time I brought a woman home who got on so well with Gigi or any of my family, for that matter."

Huh.

I was not going to overanalyze that.

Within the next hour of the garden/pool party, Rafe had returned to Mr. Monosyllabic. But only, I realized, around the guests he didn't know. He kept me close with his arm around my waist as his mom introduced us to new friends and acquaintances and we said hello to old friends. Rafe was visibly more relaxed around the people he knew.

Something had slowly occurred to me over the last few weeks. We'd moved away from a conversation with a couple Pippa and Hugo had invited. During the exchange, Rafe had tightened his hold on me and barely said a word as the husband droned on about insurance for small businesses like Rafe's.

Getting nowhere with him, the man finally gave up and made an excuse for him and his wife to leave.

As soon as they were gone, Rafe released a sigh as if he was deflating, grabbed my hand, and glowered his way through the guests. He picked up two bottles of beer from the bar and kept walking until the music and murmur of conversation was just a hum in the background. We stopped in the shade of trees in the woodland behind his parents' property.

As I took the beer Rafe held out to me, I leaned against the nearest tree. "Is it shyness?"

Rafe pushed his sunglasses into his hair and frowned at me in question as he took a swig of cold beer.

"You're different around people you don't know."

His frown deepened. "I'm not shy. I'm just not comfortable making small talk with strangers. Never have been. Don't ask me why, I don't know. It's just the way I am."

Something like tenderness filled me. I considered him. "So if you're uncomfortable talking to strangers, how did you ever get a date?"

Rafe shrugged. "My lack of loquaciousness never seemed to bother the women I've dated."

My gaze dragged over him and his masculine beauty. "Of course it didn't."

"What does that mean?"

I snorted, gesturing to him with my free hand. "Look at you. You don't look like a vet, Rafe. You look like the model they hire to play the vet for the hot guy career calendar."

A tinge of red crested high on his cheeks as his eyes narrowed on me. Then his gaze swept down, lingering on my breasts, before traveling downward and back up again.

I was being smoldered at by Rafe Whitman and every inch of me loved it.

He was wearing too many clothes and so was I.

Shit.

"Anyway, lack of loquaciousness or not, I'm starting to think I've never really had a good radar for picking women who don't have ulterior motives," he mused sullenly.

I studied him in all his brooding. "What does that mean?"

He shrugged. "Most of my relationships have ended because my girlfriends turned out to be different people from what I'd been led to believe. And the hell of it is, my family always seemed to pick up on it before I did. Maybe that's why I never caught one of them chatting away with Gigi like they're long-lost friends." Rafe's gaze turned hot and intense again as he stared into my eyes, as if daring me to acknowledge the insinuation that I was a better fit than his previous girlfriends.

Heart racing, I pushed off the tree, then took a long swig of the beer before I said, "Shouldn't we get back?"

"Dying to know which Birkin bag should be in your closet or what the best insurance provider for it is?" Rafe drawled wryly.

Chuckling, I forced myself to relax. "Hey, these are your people. And they're not all like that. Most of them talk about their kids, which is nice. I like how much they care about them."

Rafe was quiet for a moment before he surprised me. "I know things aren't great with your parents, but you are in contact, right?"

I stiffened. "I texted my mom two months ago and she never got back to me. Worried, I tried my dad and he finally texted last week to let me know they were all good. Alive and stuff."

"I'm sorry."

"My mom is too uninvolved and yours is too involved. What a pair we make."

But Rafe didn't want to make light of my parents' shittiness. Anger and concern lit his eyes. "It's their loss, Star. It's their big fucking loss because they're missing out on someone very special."

My breath caught.

Rafe Whitman had just told me I was very special.

His expression darkened to something surprising. Arousing. "Star—"

"We should get back to the party," I practically squeaked as I pivoted away from him and toward the house. What was going on? Why was he suddenly acting like he wanted me? I couldn't handle it. "We can't make your family and friends believe we're dating if they're not around to see it."

A few seconds later, I heard Rafe's footsteps behind me, and then he was at my side, his hand on my back. "That's very true."

I waited for more flirt.

None came.

Great.

We were back on the same page. Hopefully.

So why was my heart racing a mile an hour as Rafe guided me

back to the party? We put our empty beer bottles on the bar and grabbed two fresh, cold ones. We nodded at people we'd already said hello to and then stopped to watch Gigi cannonball into the pool with the kids.

I grinned as she reached the surface, screaming, "I am the awesomest!"

"I love your sister," I told him in all honesty.

Rafe grunted at that.

"Get in here!" Gigi caught sight of us.

"I don't have a suit," I called back to her.

"You can have one of mine!"

Considering I was packing more curves than Gigi, I doubted anything of hers would fit me.

"C'mon, Star!"

"No!" Rafe called back.

Gigi made a face. "Why not?"

"Because she's busy." The bastard made sure of that by pulling me into him with one arm around my waist and bending his head to cover my mouth with his. I gasped at the sudden kiss, and he used the opportunity to slide his tongue over mine. Gigi's whistle was a reminder that we were in public and I had no choice but to lean into him and kiss him right back.

Absolutely no choice.

Honestly.

It had nothing to do with the fact that Rafe Whitman kissed like it was the last kiss he'd ever give.

Clapping broke through the hazy, lusty spell he'd cast over me, and I was the first to pull away. His arm tightened around me as if he didn't want me to go, and he glared at my now swollen mouth.

"Rafe," I murmured. "We have an audience."

He turned his head to look and sure enough, some guests were clapping and hooting at the show we'd put on, while others frowned in disapproval.

As if remembering himself, Rafe released me. I eased away and he licked his lips, eyes on my mouth. "Just . . . making sure they're buying it."

"Right," I murmured before taking a long pull of my beer.

Chapter Sixteen

BY THE TIME NIGHT FELL AND EVERYONE WAS LEAVING OR
making their way to a guest room, the tension between Rafe and me
was at breaking point. I constantly had to remind myself what a bad
idea it would be to cross the line with him, and he didn't make it
easy. He was casually flirtatious, complimentary, and considerate
without even thinking about it.

Thankfully, he hadn't kissed me like that again, but Jen had
caught me on the way to the bathroom later to thank me for making
her son so happy. Didn't that make me feel like the worst human being ever.

I was not a broody person, but Rafe must have been rubbing off
on me because I was definitely brooding by the time he led me to the
bedroom we were to share.

The room was large, with a massive bed and a bay window overlooking the backyard. Rafe told me it was his room growing up, but
there was no hint of a teenage boy here. Obviously his mother had
redecorated it into a grown-up guest room. When I'd stared at the
bed, apprehensive, he'd offered to sleep on the floor.

"No," I'd assured him, trying to pretend I was unaffected by the idea of proximity. "It's a gigantic bed. I'm sure we can share it without breaching each other's personal space."

Therefore, we'd readied for bed in tense silence and I wished like hell I'd brought one of my many oversized ratty T-shirts to sleep in, rather than the cute strappy summer nightie I'd brought thinking I'd be hot and *alone*.

Rafe took one look at me and glanced away quickly.

We'd gotten into bed together, my heartbeat pounding in my ears, and we'd lain down with space enough for another person (maybe even two) between us.

"Night, then," I'd tried to say, but it came out a hoarse whisper.

Rafe had exhaled and answered gruffly, "Night."

Then he switched off the light, and it plunged us into a darkness that seemed to weigh down on me.

I was aware of every breath he took, every minuscule shift of his body.

I imagined him rolling over onto me and kissing me like he'd kissed me out in the garden that day, and I could almost feel his hands on me.

Skin burning hot, I rolled onto my side, curled into a ball, and squeezed my eyes shut.

SLEEP MUST HAVE EVENTUALLY TAKEN ME, BECAUSE IT WAS hard heat and a masculine scent that wound into my consciousness and yanked me awake.

My eyes flew open and I stared at the bedside table and the curtained window beyond it. Dim light lit the room from the sunlight pouring through the cracks above and at the sides of the drawn curtains.

A heavy weight lay over my body and I glanced down without

moving my head and found Rafe's hand on my stomach, his arm resting over my waist.

The hard heat that had awoken me was him.

He was burrowed into me, his chest to my back. I could feel the rise and fall of his breathing and the soft exhalation of it in my hair. He was asleep.

But his body was not.

·I sucked in a breath as I registered the erection digging into my ass.

Arousal flushed through me like a wildfire, my nipples tightening as my breasts swelled against the fabric of my nightie. A rush of wet tingled between my thighs and I couldn't quite catch my breath. I was almost dizzy with the sensation. In fact, I think I lost complete control over my body, because my hips moved of their own accord so that my ass ground against Rafe. A moan fell out of me before I could stop it.

Rafe tensed.

I stiffened.

Then the hand on my stomach curled into a fist, taking the fabric of my nightie with it.

"Star?" Rafe's voice was hoarse with sleep. Then he groaned in realization and whispered, "Shit. Sorry."

But before he could move away, I lifted my ass again, feeling his cock press deeper, and this time I shivered with need.

"Fuck." Rafe released me, but only to roll me onto my back and brace himself over me.

My thighs parted as I gaped up at him in a heady, lust-filled fog. Sometime during the night, he'd taken his shirt off and Holy Hotness . . .

He was so beautiful.

Right now, his every feature was granite hard with hunger for me. "Star?"

I urged my hips up to make contact with his arousal. My eyelids fluttered as I moaned and Rafe let out another hoarse curse. Then he shifted between my legs, holding himself above me as his cock nudged near my clit. The friction was just a tease, but sensation sparked down my thighs and deep in my belly.

"Rafe," I gasped, my breathing quick and shallow.

"Jesus." He bent his head, pressing his face into the crook of my neck, his hot breath scattering goose bumps down my chest. His hips moved against mine as I arched into him.

The coil of tension tightening inside me squeezed sharply and my eyes flew open in wonder as I realized I might come like this. "Rafe."

Hearing the urgency in my voice, he lifted his head from my neck and gazed down at me with determination as he moved his hips faster, harder against me. We were dry-humping like two teenagers, and it was the sexiest thing that had ever happened to me.

Rafe yanked down one side of my nightie and his hips stuttered at the sight of my bare breast. "You're so fucking beautiful. I swear it's going to kill me." Then his hot mouth covered my taut nipple and I cried out, my back arching to push into him.

Patience snapped, Rafe's hand slipped between us, and I'd just felt the first spectacular press of his thumb on my clit when three bangs on the bedroom door broke us out of the spell.

"Morning, sleepyheads!" Gigi shouted through the door. "Mom told me to come wake you, so I'd start getting ready if I were you or she'll come up here herself."

Gigi, Rafe's sister, had just interrupted us having almost-sex in his old bed in his parents' house, parents whom we were *deceiving* by pretending to date. And Rafe was paying me to do that. Rafe who didn't do casual sex.

Cold reality flooded me, and Rafe cursed at my expression. "Star—"

"Off." I pushed him and he rolled off me with a disgruntled and very loud groan.

"Star—"

"Nope." I jumped out of bed, my heart hammering, my clit throbbing with unsatisfied desire. He'd blue-beaned me! Angry at that and at myself and at the sexy fucking sight of him half naked with his big cock stretching his pajama bottoms, I whisper-yelled, "That was not supposed to happen and it will never happen again!"

Rafe scrubbed his hands down his face. "Star—"

"Stop saying my name. I'm going to take a shower and when I get out here, we are never speaking of this again."

He pushed up to sitting, his brow furrowed, and he looked as if he was in pain. I thought maybe it was the hard-on he was rocking, but then he shocked me by saying, "I'm sorry. I didn't mean to push you into anything—"

"No." I stopped him, even more horrified by that than what had happened. "Rafe. No. I was right there with you. I just . . . it's a mistake. We're not . . . and I'm not." Frustrated with myself, I shrugged wearily. "Let's just pretend it didn't happen."

A hard glint replaced his concerned expression. "Go shower first."

Telling myself I was relieved, I grabbed my bag and marched into his bathroom.

It was only as I was showering and trying not to think about our awesome fooling around that I realized he'd never actually agreed to pretend it hadn't happened.

Chapter Seventeen

THE RIDE BACK TO THE CITY WAS NOT FUN.

Icy silence filled the car, and for once it wasn't Rafe's fault. Before meeting him, I rarely brooded. But he had me doing it twice in one weekend. Even Gigi and his mom had given Rafe concerned looks before we left. I knew in that moment I was doing a crappy job convincing them Rafe was in a happy serious relationship, but I couldn't pretend.

Rafe needed to know that the flirting and the affection and the sex were things that should never occur between us!

I tried to tell myself my silence was all about making a statement, putting professional distance between us.

Yet I was brooding.

Because . . . I *liked* Rafe.

However, I knew there was no place in my life for him.

Nor for me in his.

I think I might have sighed in relief when the Pontiac pulled up to my building, because Rafe gave me a sharp look. Ignoring it, I said, "I'll get my luggage."

Rafe was already out of the car, grabbing my suitcase from the back seat. When I reached him on the sidewalk, I couldn't meet his eyes. "I'll take it from here."

"I'll carry it up for you."

At his flat tone, I finally dared to meet his eyes. Dark clouds had blown in on the Fourth of July weekend as if sensing the turn in my mood. Consequently, Rafe was not wearing sunglasses and he was not hiding his displeasure.

"I can carry my own luggage."

"Star—"

"Rafe, give me my suitcase." I held out a hand.

He pushed his jaw out to the side in agitation but abruptly held the handle out to me.

I took it carefully so I didn't touch him. "Thanks. You'll call me about the details for our next event?"

Rafe studied me for a few seconds, his eyes searching. Whatever he found made him look away, and he nodded with a short, abrupt bob of his head. "Yeah, I'll call you."

"Drive safe."

When I reached my building entrance and looked back, Rafe still stood there, hands in his pockets, watching me with a granite look I would have assumed was anger just a few months ago.

Now I knew better.

Feeling guilty, confused, irritated, I quickly whirled around and hurried inside my building.

I WAS A HOT MESS.

While it had been me who drew the line in the sand between me and my fake boyfriend, I found myself pissed and hurt when I didn't hear from Rafe all week. I'd gotten used to his daily texts and check-ins. No one, not even Roger, checked in with me like that. Rafe's sudden absence from my life was a reminder to never allow myself to get used to someone.

I knew it wasn't fair to be pissed at him.

I'd made it clear I wanted us to forget what had happened and maintain some professionalism.

But I wasn't feeling very rational at the moment.

I wasn't feeling very me.

Stuck in my head, I wasn't great company, and my friends remarked on it and voiced their concern. I begged off with a lie about a bad period, which wasn't completely false for the first few days because my period had arrived the night I returned from Harrison.

Unfortunately, by day ten of radio silence from Rafe, I had no such excuse.

I was sad and angry and . . . hurt.

That he could evoke such a response was just one more reason to steer clear of the guy.

Even Gigi texted me to check in. But not her brother.

However, on day eleven, Rafe finally texted, but only to tell me he didn't need me to come to family dinner with him that Sunday.

His text had made my mood worse, so I'd called my friends to meet me at a bar in our neighborhood that had a dance floor. Kendall and I danced my blues away while Roger and Jude sat in a corner talking, and I woke up the next morning with the hangover from hell.

Deciding I'd done enough moping over Rafe Whitman, I called All on the Line and We Bring Them to Life and filled my schedule to the brim over the next week.

I did not add my schedule to the shared app with Rafe, considering I was pretty sure he'd fired me.

· · ·

THEN, ON DAY FIFTEEN, MY PHONE BEEPED WHILE I WAS WAIT-
ing in line for a new gaming system.

> You haven't updated the app with your
> schedule. Please do so. Your presence is
> still required this Friday night for Pippa
> and Hugo's anniversary dinner.

I'd stared at the text from Rafe, stunned. Not because he'd returned to bossy formality, but because apparently I wasn't fired.

And I'd lined up a line-sitting job that might go into Friday night.
Shit.

What was I to do?

If I quit, I'd lose all that money to go traveling. To take off. To
be free. To not care if a sexy vet texted me on the daily. But could I
face him when I was this hurt and angry?

I consoled myself with the knowledge that once I had all the
money he intended to pay me, this would be over and I'd never have
to see his too-handsome face again.

I'd just have to give the line-sitting job back.

My fingers flew over my phone screen. **Just text me the details.**

A minute later:

> I'll send a cab to pick you up at six. Dinner
> is at seven. I'll meet you there.

Wow. Now he couldn't even be bothered to pick me up himself.
Asshole.

Chapter Eighteen

RAFE WAS WAITING OUTSIDE PIPPA AND HUGO'S BUILDING when the cab he'd oh so politely sent me pulled up. He'd foregone a suit jacket and wore a white shirt, gray pants, and a waistcoat that matched the pants. The waistcoat delineated his trim waist and flat stomach.

I'd forgotten how tall he was.

Butterflies, mostly nervous ones, fluttered to life as I got out of the prepaid cab after tipping the driver. A warm breeze blew over my bare legs as I crossed the sidewalk to meet Rafe. I'd chosen to wear a short summer dress with my favorite wedged heels. Looking at Rafe, I wondered if I was underdressed for the event but then reminded myself I didn't care.

Rafe didn't seem to care either, because he barely looked at me as he opened the apartment door. "Shall we?" He gestured me in first.

His familiar scent hit me with such impact, a tight knot took up residence in my chest again. Rafe's coldness was as hurtful as his absence, and I hated he had that power over my emotions.

The building receptionist nodded at Rafe, and he pressed a button on the nearest elevator. Tension crackled, but not the sexy kind.

We stepped in and hit the button for his brother's floor, which was near the top.

The elevator glided slowly upward and my hurt built up too until I blurted out dully, "I'm surprised you texted. I thought I'd been given the heave-ho."

We both stared at the elevator doors as Rafe replied, just as tonelessly, "I would tell you if you were no longer required."

His words cut deeper than I could believe. Tears stung my eyes, but I blinked them back. I tried to swallow past the emotion.

"Anyway, Pippa sent a friend to the clinic the morning before I texted you, so she obviously took your lack of presence at the last family dinner as proof you and I are on the downward spiral."

So he'd just needed Pippa off his back.

"Right."

I felt Rafe look at me now. "Are you . . . well?"

I huffed bitterly, not able to hide it. "Yeah."

"Star—"

That anger that had been building up, that I'd tried so hard to push down, suddenly blew out of me as I whipped around to face him. "You don't get what you want from me, so you just cut me out? No calls, no texts, and I was more than likely fired until Pippa started her shit again, right?"

Rafe gazed down at me, his eyes searching, but I couldn't discern what was going on behind them. "It isn't like that. I didn't mean for it to seem like I cut you out. You made it obvious you wanted to maintain some professionalism."

"I didn't know that meant we'd stop treating each other with kindness." The elevator slowed to a stop and I realized I was blaming him for something that wasn't his fault. It was mine. For having allowed the professional distance to be breached. For allowing my-self to think that Rafe Whitman actually cared about *me*. "Don't worry about it, Whitman. You're not the first person in my life to just disappear when they feel like it. Pretty used to it, in fact."

His face slackened. "Star—"

The elevator doors opened and I stepped out into the hallway. Rafe followed, taking hold of my elbow to slow me. "Star, wait—"

"Rafe, there you are!"

We both looked up to see Pippa waving at us from her apartment door. Rafe sighed in exasperation and released my elbow, but only to take hold of my hand. I tried not to tense as he squeezed it and led me over to his sister-in-law.

She eyed me in surprise. "You came." Her gaze drifted down my blue summer dress before she looked up at Rafe. "Shame on you for not telling Star about the dress code."

"Dress code?" I replied flatly.

She gestured to her black cocktail dress. "Formal wear." She eyed Rafe suddenly. "Though I see you forgot your dinner jacket."

"I didn't forget." Rafe gestured to the door. "Are you going to let us in or lecture us on things that don't matter?"

Pippa frowned. "You better not be in a mood at my party, Rafe." She shot me a frown like his mood was my fault and then led us inside.

I'd forgotten how big their apartment was.

"Star—" Rafe bent to my ear, but Pippa cut him off, telling us to hurry because everyone else was already seated.

From there, we were introduced to the couples sitting at the long dinner table. Jen and Greg were there, of course, and I felt a pang of sadness and guilt when I saw how happy Jen was to see me. Gigi wasn't in attendance because she was working overtime on a project she'd mentioned to me in her texts.

At first I thought everyone was coupled up, but as conversation filled the table while staff served us a three-course meal, it became apparent that two of the women were flying solo.

They were both in their early thirties and were stylish, attractive career women. Miriam, the redhead, was a book editor for a large publishing house, and Elle was a buyer for a fashion house.

Elle, I noted, kept shooting Rafe longing looks, but I doubted Rafe noticed, because I could feel him studying me.

I spent most of the meal making small talk with the couple on my left.

After dinner, everyone moved to the lounge for drinks and I excused myself to use the bathroom. My hands shook as I washed them, and I looked at myself in the mirror and didn't recognize the woman staring back. The last time I'd allowed a guy to make me feel horrible was when I'd lost my virginity to Matt Remner and he'd dumped me two days later for my friend Ashley. I'd cried myself sick until Dawn got impatient with me and told me it was my fault for believing Matt should be monogamous. She said human beings were not monogamous creatures and I only had myself to blame for my hurt feelings, considering she and Arlo had taught me monogamy was a fairy tale.

She was right. But as a sixteen-year-old girl with her first big crush, and parents who had never loved her the way she needed, I'd wanted to believe in the idea of one special person. That Matt thought I was so special, he only wanted me.

But Matt Remner had proven my parents correct.

I'd never let a guy make me feel bad about myself again.

Or hurt me like that.

Until now.

"Stupid, stupid woman," I whispered harshly to myself.

Pulling myself together, I returned to the living room and halted in the doorway to search for Rafe.

My heart skipped an unpleasant little beat when I found him.

He stood in the corner by the balcony doors, his back to me as he bent his head to talk with Elle. Their bodies were close and she was laughing and flirtatiously touching his arm.

He didn't stop her.

So I guess this was his way of saying I wasn't required any longer?

Jealousy and hurt burned through my chest.

Hugo suddenly appeared at my side, expression grim. "That is the look of a woman realizing she doesn't fit with my brother."

Hoping I'd misunderstood, I asked, "Excuse me?"

Hugo gestured with his drink toward Rafe. "Elle. Now *she* fits, doesn't she?"

I'd known all along that Hugo was the Whitman truly unhappy to see Rafe with me. Yet it was still shocking to have him say it to my face. Remaining composed, I shrugged. "What do you care?"

"My brother needs a partner who understands him. Who understands his world. Like Pippa understands mine. Like Elle would understand. Unlike you, a woman-child who was barely raised and disdains success."

I flinched inwardly at his insults. "You don't know a thing about me."

"That's what would concern me if I didn't know my brother will grow bored with your pretty face and settle where he should." He gestured again in Rafe and Elle's direction.

"Your brother isn't you," I spat, angrier at his words than I ever thought I could be.

"What does that mean?" Hugo narrowed his eyes.

"It means don't tell me what Rafe needs based on what *you* need. Rafe isn't you."

Hugo stepped toward me with indignation in his eyes, and I felt a flare of alarm a second before Rafe's voice cut between us. "Problem here?"

Relieved by the sight of him towering over us, I took a deep breath. Rafe glowered ferociously at his brother.

Hugo gave him a smarmy smile and I wondered how two brothers could be so different. "No problem. Just a friendly chat."

Rafe slid his eyes to me, brow furrowed with concern.

"I'd like to leave," I told him truthfully.

His expression darkened as he turned back to his brother and demanded quietly, "What did you say to her?"

"Nothing she didn't already know." Hugo patted him on the arm. "Now relax, little brother, and don't even think about causing a scene." He slid past us like the snake he was and crossed the room to where Pippa chatted with Jen.

Rafe glared after him and then looked at me. Those eyes searched my face again.

Then, as if making a decision, he took hold of my hand and marched out of the room and down the long narrow hallway that led to what I assumed were the bedrooms. "Rafe?"

He didn't answer, and I hurried in my wedged heels to keep up with his long strides. His grip on my hand was unyielding.

We reached a set of double doors and Rafe opened one of them, pulled me inside, and shut the door behind us. I barely gaped at the luxurious primary suite because Rafe pulled me through a walk-in closet and into the fanciest bathroom I'd ever seen in my life. I skittered to a stop in the middle of the room as Rafe shut the door behind us and locked it.

Those butterflies roared to life in my belly again.

Rafe scowled down at me, hands on his hips, his breathing a little too fast.

"What are you doing?" I demanded. "We shouldn't be in here."

"We need to talk privately."

"About what?"

Rafe stared at me like I'd lost my mind. "About whatever the fuck Hugo just said to you, but more importantly, about what you said to me in the elevator."

Fear made my heart beat faster. "I don't want to do this."

"Tough," he snapped. "We're doing it."

"Fine. You were flirting with Elle, and Hugo was just pointing out the obvious."

"I wasn't flirting with Elle." Rafe stepped toward me, eyes narrowed. "And what was the obvious?"

"That you and I don't fit." I shrugged like I didn't care. "He seemed pretty eager to make sure I knew it, so I guess we fooled him into thinking this was real between us. Good job, partner."

"It seemed pretty real between us at my parents' house that morning." Rafe took another step toward me.

I braced myself against his proximity. "I thought our friendship was real, but like I said, when you didn't get what you wanted . . ." I made a scissor gesture with my fingers.

Rafe looked pissed. "I did not cut you out. I was following your lead. You barely said a word the entire ride back to your place."

"Because I was trying to return us to friends, to where we'd been before we almost had sex. I wasn't trying to throw you away!"

His head jerked back at my words.

Words that revealed too much.

Remorse filled his expression as he reached for me, but I retreated. Rafe curled his hand into a fist and lowered it to his side. His voice dropped to a low gravel. "I didn't mean to make it seem like I was throwing you away. I was trying . . ." He squeezed his eyes shut for a second, and when he opened them they blazed with emotions that made my breath catch. "I hoped that if I pulled back, you'd see you missed me. Like I missed you."

I gaped at him in shock. "What?"

He closed the distance between us, cupping my face gently in his hands. "I don't want to fake this anymore when for me . . . this is very real, Star."

"So you were playing games with me?" I whispered.

"No. No, I wasn't trying to play games with you. You're just so closed off to the idea of anything real that I didn't know how else to get you to see that we have something. I thought if you missed me, it might change your mind." Guilt flashed over his face. "But it was the wrong move with you and I'm so fucking sorry. I'm sorry if I hurt you. You are the last person I want to hurt." He brought his forehead to mine, his hands sliding down my face to my neck and down to grasp my upper arms. "Star, I want this to be real between us."

Blood rushed in my ears as a confusing mix of elation and anxiety whipped through me. "Casual?"

He lifted his head to give me a weirdly sexy admonishing look. "What do you think?"

"I-I-I think you know I don't do relationships and that this is a bad idea. I can't commit to anyone."

"Or . . . you just don't want to be disappointed by other people's lack of commitment to you."

I tried to pull away from him as I whisper-yelled, "Don't psychoanalyze me, Rafe Whitman!"

His lips twitched. "I think you need a little psychoanalyzing, Star Shine Meadows."

"You're infuriating!"

"You're perfect," he answered seriously.

Warmth pushed through my earlier hurt at the tenderness in his eyes. "Rafe—"

His mouth cut me off as it crashed down over mine.

I moaned in surprise and then hunger as his tongue licked mine. His arms wrapped around me, crushing me to his hard chest, and in an instant, my skin was aflame with need for him.

Damn the man!

Rafe groaned as I met him kiss for desperate kiss and suddenly my feet were off the ground and Rafe's hands were gripping my thighs as we moved backward. Then just as suddenly my ass was on the bathroom counter and my legs wrapped around Rafe's hips as his hungry kisses intensified.

When his lips finally left mine, it was to trail magical kisses along my jaw to my ear. His voice was guttural. "I'm sorry if I hurt you, but know I missed you so fucking much."

That should have been the cold splash of water I needed to extract myself from the situation, but Rafe's mouth returned to mine for another head-spinning, scorching kiss. He was hard and we were grinding on each other like out-of-control teens. My hands explored his taut body over the soft material of his shirt and waistcoat and I desperately wanted to rip everything off him but was distracted from doing so when Rafe suddenly broke our kiss.

I panted for breath, my body trembling with need as I stared up at his lust-darkened eyes.

Then I gasped as his hands slid under my dress, coasting up my thighs as he held my gaze. His fingers curled into my underwear, and I let out another moan of excitement as he roughly yanked my panties down. "Rafe?" I was ten percent scandalized and ninety percent thrilled as hell.

He gave me a wicked smile and pulled my ass along the counter until I was almost hanging off it, and then pushed my thighs apart. He lowered to his knees and I whimpered in anticipation.

"We shouldn't here . . ." I declared with zero real objection.

Rafe smoothed his hands along my inner thighs, gazing up at me with that cocky smirk. "I've fantasized about doing this to you for weeks. And someone should go down on their woman in this bathroom, because we sure as fuck know Hugo won't."

I let out a cackle of laughter, slapping a hand over my mouth to quiet it, but there was no need. Rafe's tongue touched me, and as he licked his way up to my clit, I groaned as sensation spiked down all four limbs. Arousal tightened in exquisite need low in my belly as my heart pounded in my ears.

Rafe Whitman's dark head was buried beneath my thighs, and he was feasting on me.

His fingers dug into my thighs as he expertly licked and sucked at my clit. To tease me, he'd take a break from there to push his tongue inside me, then when I was growing desperate, he'd return to where I needed him at that bundle of tormented nerves. My body tightened, my thighs closing in on him, my chest heaving and shuddering as the tension spiraled tighter and tighter toward explosion.

"Rafe!" I reached for his head, my fingers threading through his silky thick hair and curling tight. He growled at the tug on it and thrust his fingers inside me, the sensation of fullness overwhelming. That was all I needed, apparently. The tension shattered inside me and I couldn't have stopped my cry of release even if his family had been outside the door listening. I shuddered and shook against his mouth as he lapped up every drop of my orgasm.

Then he was on his feet and I was in his arms, his face buried in the crook of my neck as he held me tighter than anyone had ever held me. His hands soothed down my back as mine caressed his and we shook against each other.

I felt safe.

I felt sated and safer than I'd felt in a long time.

Tears burned my eyes and I swallowed them back as that familiar fear filled me, trying to singe away the beauty of the moment.

Rafe lifted his face from my throat and cupped my cheeks in his big hands. He kissed my lips lightly. When he gently helped me back into my underwear, his touch affectionate, caring, like I was precious to him, I wanted to cry again.

"What about you?" I asked to distract myself.

"Oh, that was for me too, trust me."

"Rafe . . . I don't . . . I'm not sure—"

He pressed his thumb to my lips. "Don't decide right now. Promise me you'll think about it."

I couldn't deny him that, so I nodded.

Rafe released my lips, curled his hand around my nape, and then brushed the gentlest, most tender kiss against my forehead.

A different kind of ache filled that hollow in my chest.

I was so freaking screwed.

Chapter Nineteen

ONCE RAFE AND I MADE OURSELVES PRESENTABLE, WE RE-turned to the party hand in hand and I tried to look composed. However, my body still throbbed with arousal and my mind spun, unsure of what to do with Rafe's proposal.

I didn't want to be the person who panicked at the thought of giving Rafe a chance. However, giving him a chance meant making myself responsible for someone else's feelings. What if I disappointed him? What if I truly couldn't remain monogamous?

Rafe deposited me beside his mom and dad and another couple. "Wait here. I'll be just a second." His expression was reassuring before he stalked across the room. To confront his brother.

Oh boy.

Jen sweetly put her arm around me and gave me a little squeeze. "Everything okay?"

I knew my smile didn't reach my eyes. "I didn't dress appropriately," I lied. Like I actually cared.

Yet Jen bought the lie and tutted, "Oh, don't be silly, sweetheart.

You look beautiful, you always do. I like that you have your own sense of style."

One more reason to give in to the idea of something real with Rafe was his family. Except for Hugo, the rest of the Whitmans were pretty darn lovable and I wouldn't have to feel guilty about lying to them anymore.

I thanked her and tried to look inconspicuously at Rafe, who followed Hugo out of the room.

Greg appeared at my side as Jen turned away to engage their friends in conversation again. "Are you having a nice time, Star?"

"Uh, yeah, thanks. You?"

He nodded, but his gaze moved to where Hugo and Rafe had disappeared and he sighed. "Jen and I raised two very different sons."

Understatement.

"And I know Hugo can appear . . ." He gave me a wry smile. "Well, he can act like an ass."

I tried to cover my chuckle and failed.

"But he isn't, underneath it all. There is a good man there."

Hmm, I'd have to see it to believe it.

"Even so, I'm sorry if he said something to make you feel uncomfortable tonight."

My eyes flew to Greg's, and I knew he'd witnessed our confrontation.

Greg's expression hardened. "Rafe won't stand for it. And I want you to know that I won't either. You are welcome in this family and we're over the moon that you make our son so happy."

Wow.

It was the most Greg Whitman had said to me in the months I'd been fake-dating Rafe.

Pressure, crushing pressure, weighed heavily on my shoulders, and I tried to control my breathing so his father didn't witness my anxiety. My voice hoarse, I forced out the words "Thank you. That means a lot."

He patted my shoulder as Rafe reappeared, looking more pissed off than when he'd left the room. Greg gently nudged me toward him. "Looks like he could use you right about now."

With a grim smile, I bridged the distance between me and Rafe, who slid an arm around my waist. "You okay?" My gaze met Elle's as I turned with him to walk back to his parents.

She stared at us in obvious disappointment, and I felt a confusing thrill of triumph that was very unlike me. I was not a jealous or possessive type at all.

Really.

Usually.

Rafe's hand tensed on my hip. "I think it's time to go."

Shit. Shit. Shit.

I didn't want to be the reason for a rift between Hugo and Rafe. This family was awesome and I would not be a problem for them.

"Don't even think about using this as an excuse to say no to me," Rafe warned, and I gaped at him. How the hell did he know what I was thinking? His mouth curled at the corners. "I've gotten to know you pretty well, Ms. Meadows, and I know how your mind works."

"Stop reading my mind, Mr. Whitman. It's creepy," I murmured.

He laughed, and warmth flooded me. I really loved that I could turn his frown upside down. Once we stopped at his parents, he waited for them to turn from their conversation with the couple whose name I'd forgotten as soon as Pippa said it at dinner because I'd been preoccupied with Rafe. "Mom, Dad, we're leaving."

"It's a little early to leave." Jen pursed her lips.

"I have an early surgery tomorrow."

"Oh. Of course, then."

Greg eyed his son. "All okay?"

Rafe's expression hardened and I was curious to know just what Hugo had said to him.

I asked as soon as we left the apartment.

"The same stupid nonsense he said to you. Prick." Rafe hit the button on the elevator and turned to me angrily. "But he will never, ever accost you like that again. He's been warned, and I don't give second warnings."

My stomach roiled nervously. "Rafe, I don't want to cause conflict between you and your brother."

We got in the elevator and each leaned against the opposite side as if subconsciously preparing for battle. As the elevator descended, I held his fierce gaze.

"I already told you, you're not. Hugo and I have disagreed our whole adult lives and I don't see that changing anytime soon."

"I'm sorry." I still didn't like the idea that I would be another thing for them to disagree over. The Whitmans were such a beautiful family, and they deserved to be happy.

"You're not the one who needs to be sorry."

My skin flushed in remembrance of what had happened less than an hour ago in his brother and sister-in-law's bathroom. "I think you've already apologized, and very thoroughly."

Rafe's gaze was hot as he dragged it down my body and back up again. "You have no idea how much I want to be inside you right now."

Arousal flooded deep in my belly so abruptly at his words that I sucked in a surprised breath.

His nostrils flared at my reaction.

"We could go back to your place," I whispered.

Rafe squeezed his eyes closed as if he were in pain, and he dropped his head with a groan.

"What?"

When he raised his eyes, he let out a slow exhalation. "I can't. Not until I know where we stand."

Oh boy, he really was Mr. Commitment.

I had never met a guy quite like Rafe Whitman.

Weeks ago, he'd told me he'd had one-night stands but he was over that phase, and obviously he'd spoken the truth. I commented as much.

Rafe shook his head. "If it were just a blinding attraction, I'd fuck you right here in this elevator."

And now my nipples were hard.

"But it isn't. I have real feelings for you. So I can't do the casual thing. I'd just be asking to get hurt."

I couldn't believe as I stood there gaping at this intensely deep man who was being open and vulnerable with me that he was the same guy who'd been so closed off when we met. Unfortunately, despite all the good things his words said about him and his intentions toward me, I felt that crushing pressure on my chest increase in intensity. It almost killed my arousal.

Before I could find the words to respond to him, my cell rang in my purse and I fumbled to shut it off, only to see Arlo's name flashing on the screen. "It's my father," I told Rafe, giving him an apologetic look. "He never calls."

If the interruption frustrated him, he hid it well. "You better answer, then."

The elevator doors opened just as I picked up the call. "Arlo?"

"Hey, Star Shine." Arlo's lazy drawl filled me with a flood of emotions because apparently Rafe had opened a floodgate tonight. "Need a big-ass favor."

Great.

"Oh, yeah?" I gritted my teeth. Four months had passed since I had an actual conversation with my parents. I hadn't seen either of them in two years, and the first call I get was for a favor? Of course it was!

"Yeah. Kinda last minute, but I'm going in for a coronary bypass thing in two days and the doc says I need someone to be there to take me home and look after me for a couple of weeks. You know I hate asking anyone for shit, but Dawn just took off on some girls' road trip. Shoulda seen it coming since you know she can't deal with hospitals and sick people. So yeah, I kinda need you to come take care of me, Star Shine."

I stopped in the middle of the sidewalk and I must have had a look of horror on my face, because Rafe bent his head to mine in concern. "Coronary bypass surgery?"

Rafe's brows knitted together.

"Yeah, yeah." Arlo was dismissive, as if it were no big deal that he was going in for major heart surgery. If he was having major heart surgery, then they must have known for a while that he had heart issues and neither he nor Dawn had told me. "I've got, like, some choked-up arteries in there or something. You know, heart disease." Again, he said it as if it were nothing.

Shaking my head in bewilderment, I snapped, "You're just calling me about this now?"

"Oh, look, I can't deal with stress right now, so don't give me shit. Just tell me if you can come or not."

Again, I gritted my teeth against my irritation. "Of course I'll be there. I'll fly out tomorrow. You're still in Boulder, right?"

"'Course. We wouldn't go somewhere else without telling you that."

I barely contained my snort. "I'll see you tomorrow."

"Thanks, Star Shine. You're with it." Arlo hung up.

Pulling my phone away from my ear, I couldn't quite believe what had just happened.

"Everything okay?" Rafe smoothed a hand down my back.

I looked up at him. Felt his strong, comforting presence. It was as if my body were being pulled in two different directions. Part of me wanted to rest my head on his chest and tell him how much I thought my parents really sucked. The other part of me wanted to run as far away from him as I could get so I could go back to pretending like Dawn and Arlo weren't so bad. Instead, I told him everything Arlo had relayed.

"Jesus, okay, well, we need to get you a flight." Rafe pulled out his phone.

"I can do that." I touched his arm to stop him. "Seriously, I can take care of this."

He searched my face. "You sure? You look like you just got punched a dozen times in the gut."

I did feel that way, so . . . "It's just Dawn." I threw my hands up in disbelief. "Who goes on a freaking girls' road trip when their partner of thirty-three years is scheduled for major surgery?" No. No decent person did that!

I was calling her!

I scrolled angrily through my contacts and hit her number.

And got her voice mail.

"Fuck!"

"Hey, hey." Rafe took me by my shoulders, forcing me to meet his calm gaze. "It's okay. You got this. You are capable and strong and you can do this. Just tell me what I can do to help."

I wanted to tell him he could give me some space and time . . . but I was terrified I'd hurt him. He was the last person I wanted to hurt. "A cab. I need a cab so I can go home and get everything organized."

Rafe frowned. "Can I do anything else?"

Reaching up onto my tiptoes, I pressed a brief kiss to his warm mouth. "I'm good."

Deciding to let me have that, Rafe, like a magician, waved down a cab in a few seconds. As it pulled up to the sidewalk, he kissed me a little longer, a little harder than I'd kissed him. "Call me if you need me. And can you text me your parents' address?"

"Why?"

"Just so I have it. In case of an emergency."

"Okay. Thank you." I opened the cab door and then turned back to him because he deserved . . . more. "About us . . . I . . ."

"Don't." Rafe shook his head. "No pressure. Not while you have this on your mind."

Did he have to be so freaking perfect? There was a small piece of me that desperately needed him to act like the cold asshole I'd met at his niece's party, so I could just forget about him.

"Let me know when you get home," he demanded as I got into the cab.

I nodded, my mind reeling.

What a strange damn night.

Chapter Twenty

ROGER WAS WORRIED ABOUT ME. HE'D CALLED A BUNCH OF times since I'd told him about Arlo and when he couldn't get out of a studio session to take me to the airport, he insisted that Jude escort me. Because Roger was worried, Jude was too.

"I want you to tell us if your asshole father is making your life miserable, because I'm not afraid to come down there and break a heart patient's nose," Jude had demanded as we pulled up to Newark Airport.

No amount of reassurance seemed to help appease my friends, and they weren't the only ones. Rafe had texted me last night and called me first thing this morning. He'd asked for my flight numbers and my parents' address and so I'd texted them over without thinking about it because I had a million things to do in a brief span of time.

I'd promised to let everyone know once I landed, so I did that in the cab as we drove from Denver International Airport.

I hadn't known what I was expecting to find in Arlo, but he answered the door to the small ranch house, seeming in good spirits.

My parents' small home was on the outskirts of the city in a neighborhood where the properties all sat on generous plots of land surrounded by mountains and trees. The extra land made room for Dawn's workshop and Arlo's studio to the back of the property. For two people who said they didn't hold on to material things, they both made decent money with their art, and making money from art was just about the hardest thing a person could do careerwise.

Arlo greeted me with a hug and gestured me into the house.

It was a mess.

And it smelled.

I wrinkled my nose in distaste. There were half-empty take-out containers littered on the coffee table, dirty dishes covering every inch of the kitchen counters. A sewage smell suggested something was growing mold somewhere.

When I lived with them, I took care of housekeeping. Neither of my parents were neat freaks, but Dawn liked things clean at least. Arlo, apparently, did not.

"When did you say Dawn left?"

Arlo rubbed the nape of his neck, appearing sheepish. "Uh . . . well, yeah, she actually took off about two weeks ago, but I thought she would be back in time for the surgery."

I shook my head at my selfish mother and my helpless father.

Dropping my bags, I put my hands to my hips. "First things first. This place needs cleaning."

"Oh, I'm not allowed to do anything strenuous. I've barely even lifted a paintbrush," Arlo drawled.

I studied him, noting the dark circles under his eyes. I'd gotten my strawberry-blond hair and my nose from Arlo, but that was it. He was tall and loose-limbed, his hair long and tied back in a ponytail, and his goatee needed a trim. Arlo was a very good-looking guy and laid-back (most of the time), so I got what Dawn had seen in him. But I was all Dawn except for the hair and nose. My mom and

I almost shared the same face except for that button nose I'd inherited from Arlo.

As if he'd read my mind, he smiled at me with fondness. "You look more and more like Dawn every time I see you."

"Great," I murmured dryly, looking around at the pit I had to clean. "So . . . she's not coming back?"

"Not for a few weeks. You know Dawn. I can't tie that woman's free spirit down."

This wasn't free spirit. Her actions were downright selfish and unkind. "So . . ." I studied Arlo and noted that beyond the dark circles, he looked a little thin. "Why do you need coronary bypass surgery?"

"I had a heart thing a few weeks back, just before Dawn left."

My own heart thumped hard in my chest. "A heart attack?"

"Yeah, one of those." He shrugged like it was no big deal and wandered into the kitchen. "You need a drink? I usually have beer to offer, but Doc said I can't have any before the surgery."

"Arlo." I sighed impatiently. "Why did you have a heart attack? You generally eat well and you do yoga with Dawn nearly every day."

He shrugged again. "It's some kinda blockage in one of my arteries. They don't think it was a lifestyle thing that caused it. They think it's some kinda scarring of the heart tissue that's happened over years, so they gotta do this to divert the blood flow or something."

An awful realization hit me. "Is this for life? You mentioned heart disease."

"Yeah, but they think I got a good chance of living life normally because of my lifestyle. Usually folks need to change their diet, up their exercise, but they said with a few exceptions, like cutting out the beer and pot, I'm doing all right as I am. I'll miss the fucking pot but I like life more, so I'll do it, I s'pose."

I needed to talk to his doctor because I couldn't trust Arlo's lackadaisical response to absolutely everything in life. "Okay. What time do we need to be at the hospital tomorrow?"

"We gotta be in Denver at two o'clock. I'm just in there for prepping, you know. Surgery isn't until the day after. Luckily, Dawn talked me into health insurance a while back or I'd be fucked. You got health insurance, kid? I know it's copping to the man to hand over cash for that shit, but turns out anything could happen and it's saving me a shit ton of dough."

"I've got health insurance." It wasn't the greatest health insurance in the world, but it was something.

Arlo picked up dirty socks off the couch, threw them across the room, and sat down with a grin. "That's cool. So tell me what you've been up to, Star Shine. You still waitressing at that drag show?"

I closed my eyes, asking every deity in our universe for patience. "That was six years ago, Arlo."

"It was? Well, you know me and time don't get along great. What you up to these days? Oh, wait." He suddenly got up again. "I got to show you the commission I just did. It'll blow your fucking mind. This guy right here"—he pointed his thumbs toward himself—"is like a fine wine. I get better with age." He chortled as I reluctantly followed him through the house and out back toward his studio.

Patience.

I just needed a little patience.

AS HARD AS I TRIED TO GET IN CONTACT WITH DAWN, I COULD not get hold of the woman. Arlo was in surgery for four hours, and they were some of the most nerve-racking hours of my life. He was a further four days in the hospital and then on Friday I took him home.

It had been an emotional and stressful week at my parents' house. I dreamed of memories from my childhood, things I hadn't thought about in years. The sight of Dawn's clothing reminded me of her perpetual absence. Even when she was present, she was never really there. My bosses at All on the Line and We Bring Them to Life called asking if I knew when I'd have availability again and had warned me subtly that I'd start losing the best jobs or my spot completely on their roster if I couldn't give them a return date. I'd told them I'd be back in two weeks and hoped that was true. Mostly because I didn't think I could take Arlo for any longer than that. I'd scrubbed the house from top to bottom, done all the laundry that had piled up, and restocked the groceries. Arlo didn't even notice, which was fine because, hello, heart surgery. However, Arlo the Patient was the worst version of my father anyone could encounter, and my desperation to get hold of Dawn grew by the second. Guilt filled me every time I wished I were anywhere but there because Arlo had just had major surgery and I should *want* to be there to look after him.

"You didn't season this," Arlo grumbled that Saturday morning as he ate the scrambled eggs I'd cooked.

"I just followed doctor's orders. Want more?"

He shot me a disgusted look. "Why the fuck would I want more of this shit?" Trying not to flinch, I reached for his plate and he slapped my arm away. "What the hell are you doing?"

My skin stung right along with my feelings. "I thought you didn't want it."

"I'm eating it, aren't I? Stupid girl."

"Hey." I said it with a gentle sharpness. "Hit me again and I walk, okay?"

Arlo scowled. "Mellow out, kid, and stop being such a downer. You can't stress me out. Doc said so."

I walked out of the bedroom before I gave in to the urge to strangle him.

Then the doorbell rang.

Even though I knew if it was Dawn, she'd have walked right in, I couldn't help but wish it were her, anyway.

To my shock, the person standing on the doorstep was someone unexpected.

It was Rafe.

He'd called me and texted throughout the week, just enough to let me know he was thinking about me, but not too much to put pressure on me.

Yet there he was.

Considerate, caring, sexy Rafe Whitman. In Boulder, Colorado. For me.

"Rafe?"

He gave me a small smile and I felt instantly calm. "Hey."

"I'M NOT HERE FOR ANYTHING," RAFE ASSURED ME THAT NIGHT as he lay stretched out on the guest bed I slept in. "I'm just here for you."

Deciding to put my confusion about us aside for now, I wearily climbed into the bed and accepted his invitation to snuggle into him. Resting my head over Rafe's heart, I sighed heavily.

It had been a *day*.

While Arlo was happy to meet Rafe, to have someone new for company, his good mood didn't last. Rafe chatted with him for a while and Arlo, who pretended to be a lover of animals our whole life even though he'd never taken care of an animal ever, thought Rafe being a vet was the shit. But as soon as he found out who Rafe's family was, he started lecturing him on the evil of big business and corporations.

To his credit, Rafe calmly listened and didn't react.

He did react, however, every time Arlo snapped impatiently at me. I could see Rafe's expression growing darker as the day wore on, and I shook my head at him in a silent request to let it go.

He did.

Until I'd reached out to take Arlo's dinner tray and he curled his hand around my wrist and shoved me away with enough force that I had to correct my balance.

Rafe had shot out of his chair, and Arlo's gaze flew up and widened as if he had suddenly realized Rafe was a big guy. But Rafe didn't yell. He just stared stonily at Arlo and warned, "Never do that again."

Arlo actually gulped and looked at me like a little boy who'd done wrong. "Sorry, Star Shine," he'd murmured, and pushed the tray toward me.

"Your dad is a piece of work," Rafe opined tightly as we lay on the bed hours later. He trailed his fingertips down my bare arm and my eyelids drooped tiredly. "Has he always treated you like that? The physical stuff too?"

I tensed at the fury I heard buried beneath his words. "No. I promise. He's never been the greatest at remembering I exist, but when he does, he's usually casually affectionate and kind. You're witnessing the worst version of him. I'm sorry."

"You don't have to apologize."

When he'd arrived this morning, Rafe had explained he just wanted to be there for me to keep me company for the weekend. Owen was covering his Saturday appointments. Neither Roger, Kendall, nor Jude could get away this weekend, though Roger was planning to fly out on Tuesday to spend a few days with me. Rafe hadn't liked that I didn't have anyone with me for support, so he'd jumped on a plane.

Even lying in his brawny arms, I couldn't think about what his presence here meant without freaking out.

Instead, I confessed my guilt over wanting to be anywhere else. Tears burned in my eyes. "I'm a terrible daughter. An awful human being."

Rafe tightened his hold on me. "You are not. Arlo isn't making this easy on you and I can't even imagine how you're feeling about your mom."

"I hate her right now," I admitted.

"That's understandable."

"I hate being here." My whispered confession rang out between us. "There's a reason I don't visit my parents a lot. It just . . . hurts."

Rafe's voice was gruff. "You want to talk about it?"

I couldn't. I shook my head and closed my eyes. For years, I'd shoved down the ugly emotions I felt about my childhood, determined they would not ruin my spirit or my glass-half-full attitude toward life. If I spoke about it, if I popped the lid off that bottle and let the genie out, who knew what kind of mess it would leave me in?

Rafe's chest moved up and down in a big sigh, but he didn't push me.

"Talk to me about *your* family," I implored.

"My family?"

"Yeah. What it was like growing up as a Whitman? To have siblings? I always wanted a brother or sister."

"Okay . . . Uh . . . Did I ever tell you about the time Gigi catfished me?"

Laughter, and the relief of amusement, glowed through me. "No."

"She was only ten. I was eighteen and somehow she found out about my crush on an older woman."

I grinned harder. "Go on."

"I'd just broken up with my high school sweetheart and I'd decided that younger women weren't for me." Mirth trembled in his voice. "I set my sights on this younger friend of my mom's, but she was still a good fifteen years older than me. Newly divorced and I was convinced she was giving me the eye."

I was convinced she probably was.

"Anyway, I'd told a few of my friends that I was going to sleep with her before I left for college. And out of nowhere, she starts private messaging me. So I think I'm in. Thankfully, I said nothing overtly sexual to her in those messages, because when I turned up at our rendezvous point, Gigi was there on her bike to confess I'd been messaging her all along. She blackmailed me into taking her for ice cream every week for the rest of the summer. She said if I didn't, she'd send a file of the private messages to my parents."

Shaking with laughter at her ingeniousness, I quizzed him, "What happened next?"

"I bought her goddamn ice cream every week and lied to my friends about what happened."

"You never got your older woman?"

"Well . . . I got a different one at college."

A flash of irrational jealousy scored through me, but I ignored it. I was too exhausted to deal with it and the myriad of emotions bubbling inside me. "Tell me another story."

"Uh . . . let's see . . . there was the time Hugo and I decided we wanted to be David Attenborough and took off to live in the wild while we were on vacation in Oregon. My dad sent search and rescue after us."

Grinning, I patted his stomach. "Yes, tell me that story."

"Hugo was about twelve, I'd just turned nine . . ."

Rafe's voice and arms wrapped me in a cocoon of safety as I listened sleepily to a story that proved at one point he and Hugo had been the best of friends. My heart felt easy knowing Rafe had had a childhood filled with sibling friendship, and parents who loved them so much they were mindless with fear when the boys took off into a dangerous wilderness. My eyelids grew heavy as his voice soothed me, and soon I was deep asleep.

Chapter Twenty-One

THE CLOSENESS I'D EXPERIENCED WITH RAFE THAT NIGHT ALL went to hell the next day.

It started when I woke up in his arms. Unlike the Fourth of July weekend, this time we were asleep on our sides facing one another, my cheek pressed against Rafe's chest. He had an arm stretched out above us on the pillows and the other wrapped around my waist. Our legs tangled in each other's.

We were both still fully clothed.

My first thought:

I feel so safe and wanted.

My second thought:

I want to wake up in this man's arms every day for the rest of my life.

My third thought wasn't so much a thought as much as it was a fearful instruction from the back of my mind to get the hell out of this situation with Rafe as quickly as possible.

That crushing pressure returned to my chest and I shoved none too gently out of his arms to roll away from him. Rafe grunted as he woke up.

"Hey, what time is it?" he sleepily asked.

"I don't know." I couldn't look at him as I grabbed clean clothes and underwear. "I'll check. You don't want to miss your flight." I hurried from the room, checked in on Arlo to find him asleep, and dove into the bathroom before Rafe could fully rouse himself.

By the time I emerged, sleep-rumpled Rafe had disappeared. He'd changed his clothes and sat in the living room waiting for me. "Bathroom's free," I announced as I wandered into the kitchen to start breakfast for Arlo.

"I washed at the kitchen sink."

"When is your flight?" I opened the refrigerator, staring blindly inside because I had no idea what I was looking for.

"Star."

"Do you want breakfast before you go?"

"What I want is for you to turn around and look at me."

Flinching at his hard tone, I reluctantly faced him and found him standing in the kitchen, staring at me with a slightly panicked glimmer in his eyes.

"What the hell is going on?"

What was going on was that I'd fallen asleep to this man telling me stories about a normal, happy childhood only to wake up feeling *extremely* attached to him when those stories actually only highlighted our *extreme* differences.

Rafe Whitman wanted what his parents had.

I couldn't give it to him. While I was many things, I wasn't a person who strung someone along.

A choking sensation filled my throat, but I forced past it and let the words out. "I appreciate you coming here, but I can't do this with you. I'm sorry."

He took a deep breath, his expression pained. And then he asked, "Why?"

"I'm not good for you. I can't give you what you want."

"In what way?"

"In every way!" I yelled now in frustration because it should be obvious and I just wanted this over with, and him gone. For good.

"Well, I'm sorry, that doesn't cut it. I need to know why."

"Because you want me to commit to you and I don't have that in me!"

"How do you know that if you won't try?"

"I just know!" I gestured around the house. "Look around, Rafe! I'm coming from a totally different place than you and I'm just going to let you down!"

"Bullshit!" he yelled back now. "You're not afraid of letting me down. You are terrified of *me* letting *you* down like the assholes who raised you!"

"Don't psychoanalyze me again!"

"Get your head out of your ass and maybe I won't have to!"

"Stop yelling at me!" Tears flooded my eyes. "Just . . . stop."

Remorse filled Rafe's expression and he took a step toward me.

"Don't." I held up a hand to ward him off. "Please."

The horrifying disappointment and hurt on his face made me want to die inside. "Star . . . don't do this."

I couldn't look at him. "You need to go."

"Star—"

"I asked you to leave."

Rafe let out a shuddering breath. "If he were well enough, I'd kick Arlo's ass. He messed you up good. They both did." Face clouded with anger, Rafe walked away, crossed the room to where he'd left his overnight bag, grabbed it, and marched out the door.

He slammed it so hard behind him, I jumped.

Suddenly that crushing pressure disappeared, but the hollowness it left behind was worse. "Fuck!" I sobbed, fisting my hands in front of me, wishing I had something I could tear apart.

"Star Shine!" Arlo called from his room.

My heart lurched. "Shit." I wiped at my tears, trying to scrub away the evidence of what had just happened.

"Star Shine!"

"I'm coming!" Shaking my whole body as if to shake off Rafe, I let out a shuddering sigh and hurried into my father's bedroom.

Arlo sat up in bed, his expression contemplative.

"Hungry?" I asked from the doorway as if my entire body weren't trembling with adrenaline.

"C'mere."

Reluctantly I crossed the room and sat in the chair next to his bed. "What's up?"

His blue eyes searched my face and I noted that he really needed a shave and his goatee trimmed, and I should offer to help him do that. "Your friend leave?"

How much had he heard? "Yeah."

"You know, I've got money saved. I'm thinking I'm going to hire someone to come out and make my meals and stuff for the next few weeks."

Anger followed my shock at this announcement. "Isn't Dawn coming back at all?"

Sadness slackened Arlo's features. "No, it's not her vibe. I think I've been angry about that and taking it out on you. Sorry about that."

Wonders never ceased. "Why isn't she here?"

"Dawn hates being around sick people."

"But you're not people. You're the man she's spent thirty-three years with."

Instead of responding to that, Arlo twisted his lips. "Your friend doesn't think much of me, huh?"

"What do you mean?"

"I heard him before he slammed out of here like the fuzz was on his tail."

I shifted uncomfortably in my seat. "He meant nothing by it."

"I don't care. You know I've never cared what anyone but Dawn thinks of me."

Not even me.

"He might not be wrong, though."

"What?" I gawked.

"Your friend. He might not be wrong that you've got this all up-side down in your mind about, you know . . . relationships and stuff."

I must have been in some alternate universe, because surely my so-called father wasn't trying to talk to me about my love life. "What?"

He snorted. "You think you're Dawn. But you're not. You might look alike, but that's where the similarities end. I love Dawn, you know that. But she abandoned me when I needed her and you didn't do that. Far as I can tell from all your stories of your life in New York, you're loyal to your friends too. You're there for them like you've been there for me."

"That's different," I murmured, though I was still reeling from his confession that he felt abandoned by Dawn.

"It's not so different." He sighed and rested his head on his pillow as he stared up at the ceiling. "All that talk about being commitment-free all these years was just bullshit on my part. I said it because that's what Dawn wanted to hear. She was the one who couldn't be monogamous, who wanted our relationship to last but needed other lovers in her life to make it work. I didn't want to share her." He sounded suddenly belligerent as his eyes flew to my shocked ones. "I love her. I could have lived happily without ever touching another woman, just Dawn. But I had to show her I was cool with the sharing thing, so I did it."

Did he realize how incredibly immature that sounded?

"Arlo, are you telling me all these years you've wanted to be in a committed relationship with my mother?"

"Don't call her that." He winced.

I rolled my eyes. "Well?"

"Yeah, I told you that, didn't I? I didn't want to share, but I wanted to keep her, so I did everything she asked, the way she wanted!" His voice rose with his growing anger, and I worried about his heart. "And in the end, I still don't have her. Look around, Star Shine, where the hell is the woman? Things get heavy and she fucking bolts."

Compassion mingled with the pain I felt over the scene with Rafe. "I'm sorry."

"But look who is here." He pointed at me. "*You* showed up. Even though you've got a life, your work, a man, you showed up for me."

"He's not my man." I glared down at my feet.

"But he could be, if that's what you want. Look at me, Star Shine."

I raised my gaze to him.

He gave me a small smile. "I don't know you all that well."

What a horribly sad thing for a father to say to his daughter.

"But I do know from what I've seen over the years, from what I see of the woman in front of me, that you are *not* Dawn. You're not her. You won't hurt your man like she hurt me."

I STAYED ONE MORE WEEK WITH ARLO.

In that time we interviewed a few nurses and we hired a woman named Maggie, who Arlo outrageously flirted with. She dealt with him with steely-eyed professionalism, and I liked her matter-of-fact attitude. I felt confident I was leaving Arlo in excellent hands.

It had not been an easy week. The first open conversation I'd ever had with Arlo hadn't mended all my wounds. In fact, once I had time to think about it, I was pissed at him.

I was pissed at both my parents for providing me with a crappy emotional upbringing and for giving me all these hang-ups about trust, commitment, and relationships. I was even angrier that it turned out to be hypocritical bullshit.

Rafe didn't call.

However, I heard his voice in my head all the same.

"You're not afraid of letting me down. You are terrified of me letting you down like the assholes who raised you!"

Too smart for his own good.

Roger picked me up from the airport and I cried in my friend's arms, finally letting the last few months of emotions out.

"You need to call Rafe," Roger insisted. "You need to tell him you've changed your mind and you want to try something real with him."

I shook my head. "It's done. I'm done messing with his head."

"You're making a mistake," my friend warned me.

I stared at him dully. "Then it's my mistake to make."

Chapter Twenty-Two

THE SOUNDS OF HONKING, ENGINES, THE GRATING DRILL OF
a jackhammer, conversation, and rock music blaring from the phone
of the person waiting in line in front of me wouldn't fade into the
background as I tried to read a book. Early August in New York
could be hot, and today was one of those days. It was humid, and the
air was filled with the scent of traffic fumes and something unpleasant blowing up from the subway grate a few feet from me.

Gone was my glass-half-full attitude and it was all because of the
freaking hollow ache in my chest that wouldn't go away. I was sad.
Lonely. And it didn't seem as if those feelings were going away anytime soon. I'd returned to New York and fallen right back into routine, minus my job for Rafe.

I hadn't seen or heard from him in two weeks, and I missed him
and I was pissed that I missed him.

Unable to bear any connection to his world, I'd ignored Gigi's
texts. She'd finally stopped reaching out, which just made me feel
like the worst human ever.

So there I was, my usually sunny disposition in the toilet. My
hair stuck to my neck, my sundress to my skin, and my feet were

covered in soot from the traffic from just standing there, waiting in line for free tickets to the opening launch of a new restaurant. Yeah, someone was paying me to wait for free tickets.

"I bet the food stinks," I muttered to myself.

A woman passed me with a huge to-go cup of coffee in her hand and despite the heat, I eyed her enviously. My last coffee had been three hours ago, and I needed an energy boost.

Someone tapped me on the shoulder and I turned to find a young couple at my back. The line stretched out all the way down the sidewalk behind them. "Yeah?"

The guy leaned into me. "So . . . uh . . . what are we waiting for?"

I scowled. "You don't know what you're waiting in line for?"

They shook their heads.

Rolling my eyes, I turned back around. "Morons."

"Did you just call someone a moron? How very un-Star-like." My head whipped up to the side at the familiar voice.

And there he was.

Rafe.

What?

His denim-blue eyes shone as he squinted against the sunlight. I drank in every inch of him like the thirsty, thirsty woman I was. He wore a green T-shirt, dark blue jeans, and a crisp pair of navy Converse that appeared as if they'd never been worn. In his hands were two tall cups of coffee. He held one out to me. "Thought you might need a pick-me-up, and apparently if you're calling people morons, I was right."

Mouth hanging open in surprise and confusion, I took the coffee on autopilot as he stepped right up next to me, his arm brushing mine. "So, what *are* we waiting for?"

Rafe was here.

Waiting in line with me.

"What are you doing here? How did you find me?"

His eyes searched my face as if committing every detail to memory. "Roger called me. And he told me where to find you."

Betrayed by my best friend.

I narrowed my eyes and shook my fist as I hissed, "Roger."

Rafe pivoted his body toward mine and spoke with laughter in his voice. "Did you just *actually* shake your fist like a cartoon character?"

"Maybe." I took an angry sip of coffee and watched the way Rafe stared at me as if I were the most *wonderful* human who ever lived. It was messing with my head! "Stop it."

"Stop what?"

"Looking at me like that."

"Like what?"

"Like you . . . like you like what you see."

"I can't help it. I do like what I see." He shrugged casually. "So much so that when Roger called me, I kicked my ass for letting this sit between us for two weeks." Rafe eyed me in all seriousness now. "I don't want to give up on this. On you. I had to come here and try one last time to convince you to give us a chance. No strings, no casual sex. A real relationship. If you agree to this, it's knowing that we're in a monogamous relationship that we're committed to making work. If you can't do that, I have to walk away. For good. Because I can't do casual with you. And before you decide, Roger told me about your unusually unsunny disposition these days. Think about every scowl you've worn in place of that beautiful smile, every person you've called a moron instead of seeing the best in said moron. You miss me. Like I miss you. If you think *you're* in a bad mood, you can only imagine what I've been like. For the sake of Owen and everyone who has to deal with me on a daily basis, please think carefully before making your decision."

His words filled the hollowness in my chest. But . . . "We're too different. You'll get sick of me."

Rafe's brows drew together. "I want you because you're you, differences and all. I already told you I like you just as you are."

My pulse raced so hard I could feel it throbbing in my neck. Yes,
I was still afraid of committing myself to Rafe, but I think he'd been
right at my parents' house. I think *I* was more afraid of trusting *him*.
Yet the thought of watching him walk away for good after two weeks
of absolute misery without him . . .

You know, I'd always thought I was a pretty brave person. Now
was the time to prove that to myself. "What about the money? I can't
take money from you, Rafe, if we're dating for real."

He swallowed hard, his breathing a little shallow as he stepped
toward me. "I wouldn't expect you to. Frankly, it would be highly
inappropriate."

I snort-laughed as giddiness bubbled up inside me. "Yeah. That
means I'll have to give it *all* back to you."

His frown was instantaneous. "What? No."

"Yes. I haven't spent any of it, so I'm returning it. I couldn't keep
it now. It would be this, well, *weird* thing between us."

Rafe contemplated this and sighed. "I get it. Okay."

"You'll take the money back?"

His big hand came to rest on my hip and the weight of his touch
gave me a thrill of excitement. "You're agreeing to a real relationship
with me?"

Despite the fear that still hovered in the background, the sounds
of New York no longer chafed. They were familiar and wonderful.
The scent of exhaust fumes didn't bother me, and the grate smell had
disappeared in lieu of Rafe's cologne. My dress didn't cling; instead
it felt sexy against my sweat-damp skin. I tried to suppress a shaky
smile, but its trembling beam broke through. "I'll date you for real."

I caught a brief glimpse of his smile before I was hauled up
against him, my mouth crushed beneath his. He kissed me so pas-
sionately the people behind us started hooting and whistling.

Rafe reluctantly broke the kiss and I panted for breath. If my skin had been hot in the summer heat before, it was now ablaze.

"Well fuck me," I muttered, dazed.

"Oh, I intend to," he murmured back, and I flushed at the same time I laughed.

"Hate to put the brakes on that." I smoothed my free hand over his chest, looking forward to exploring him when he was naked. "But I really do still have to wait in line."

"I have the next hour free. I'll wait with you."

"Really?" My eyes lit up at an hour with Rafe. "But it's hot out here."

"It is, but so are you, so it's worth it."

I tried to bite my lip to stop the goofy, dreamy smile curling my mouth, but I could tell by the way Rafe's expression heated that I hadn't succeeded. The line moved a little, so I turned and we moved forward with our free arms wrapped around each other's waists.

I was standing in line with Rafe Whitman, whom I was now officially dating.

Why did I suddenly feel like a sixteen-year-old girl dating her first big crush?

Hopefully this time, Rafe didn't squash me like Matt had.

Batting the negative thoughts away, I took a sip of my coffee. "This is nice so far."

Rafe smiled down at me. "Yeah." Then he gestured to the line. "What are we waiting for?"

"Free tickets to a new restaurant launch."

He stared down at me, expressionless, for a few seconds. Then he said, "*Free* tickets?"

I held back my laughter. "Yup."

"Someone is paying you to wait in line for something that is free?"

"Yes."

"Doesn't that defeat the purpose of it being free?"

"Depends on how much they're paying me," I cracked.

"Well?" He raised an eyebrow.

Chuckling, I nodded. "It definitely defeats the purpose of it being free."

Rafe shook his head and muttered, "People are ludicrous."

"Maybe the person paying me just has FOMO."

He grimaced. "Is that some kind of medical problem?"

I threw my head back in laughter and let myself sink into him as my giggles petered out. Rafe's arm tightened around me and as I looked up at him, I found him grinning down at me.

"I'm guessing not."

"Maybe it is in some countries," I joked.

"Whatever it is, they need to take a good long look at their life. Paying someone to wait in a goddamn line for free tickets," he muttered in exasperation before he took a sip of his coffee.

I got a sudden flashback to the last time he'd been present when I was line sitting.

"Hey, remember that time you got peanut butter and jelly on my bedsheets?" I teased.

Rafe went with the subject change, bending his head to whisper in my ear. "I remember you shouting that *lie* across the plaza, yes. And I remember thinking you were incredibly annoying, but also that I'd really like to lick peanut butter off your nipples."

I choked on air at his unexpected confession as my body fully reacted. Rafe Whitman definitely knew how to surprise me. Hotter than hades now, I turned to him, our faces close as we stared into each other's eyes. Sexual tension stretched between us like a taut wire on the verge of snapping. "Are you just saying that to mess with me, or did you really think that?"

His eyes were bright with a gorgeous mix of amusement and desire. "Yes. I might have even thought about it while I was alone that night."

There was a real threat of me ripping his clothes off right then and there, so I tried to break some of the tension with a fake frown. "You thought I was incredibly annoying?"

Laughing, Rafe straightened and shrugged. "First time we met, I was in such a shitty mood that I shouldn't have taken out on you, so I'm sorry."

"Apology accepted already."

"But I thought you were being fake with the whole optimistic life-is-sunshine-and-roses attitude." Seeing the look on my face, he reached out to smooth his thumb over my cheek. "I know it's real now. It was just hard for me to believe that anyone could reach your age and still see the world and everyone in it the way that you do."

"So I annoyed you at first?"

He shrugged apologetically. "Even though you tried really hard to like me, I know I annoyed you too."

"But I did try."

Rafe chuckled. "I annoyed you."

"I wanted to mess up your hair, throw away your ties, and spill coffee all over you so badly," I admitted.

His shoulders shook with laughter, and then he smoldered at me again. "Minus the coffee spillage, I am happy for you to do all those things to me when we're alone."

Seriously, my body was currently one hundred percent ready to discover every inch of his, and it was giving me brain fog. I had a feeling if he stayed any longer, I'd give in to temptation and walk away from this job. "Okay, if you're just going to keep saying naughty things to me when I can't do anything about it, you're going to have to leave."

He grinned, but at my grim expression, his smile dropped. "You're not serious?"

I leaned into him. "It is hot right now and yet I am visibly turned on, in public, so you should probably go."

His eyes dropped to my chest and I saw a faint flush across his cheeks as he swallowed hard.

Yup. Time for him to go. "I'll call you later."

"You're not seriously kicking me out of line?" He stepped into me. "I'll stop."

"It's too late. All I can think about with you standing here is sex."

His eyes danced with smug pleasure.

I shook my head, laughing. "We'll meet later."

"When? Where?" he demanded impatiently.

Suddenly, an idea sprang to mind. Rafe and I were great in our little bubble when my commitment phobia didn't rear its ugly head. We were even halfway to great among his family. But he'd never met *my* family. My real family. Roger, Jude, and Kendall. Who were in a polyamorous relationship, which was something Rafe did not understand. If we were going to work, I had to know that he could be friends with my friends even though they had stepped outside a box society deemed "normal." And I really needed to know that before sex made me even more attached to the guy. "My friends and I are going out tonight in our neighborhood. Come with us."

"You want our first actual date to be with your friends?"

"They're my family here, Rafe. I've met yours and I want you to meet mine."

As if he understood what I wasn't saying, he nodded contemplatively. "Okay. What time?"

"Around eight. I'll text you the address."

"Sounds like a plan. But I'm not going anywhere. I still have a whole forty-five minutes to make you think about nothing but sex."

Cruel, cruel man. "Don't make me," I warned him.

He frowned. "Make you what?"

"Embarrass you into leaving."

"I can't be embarrassed."

Oh really. I reared back from him in mock horror and cried, "You want to do what to me?"

Rafe's expression flattened. "Star—"

"In your grandmother's bed?" I yelled.

He squeezed his eyes closed as people turned in line to look and the couple behind us choked on their laughter.

"You want me to wear her nightie?"

Rafe glowered at me, shaking his head. "You're evil."

Laughter trembled around my reply. "And what are the carrots for?"

Without a word, he marched away and I almost peed myself, I was laughing so hard. Yes, it was immature, but I loved messing with him. I also almost missed the vibration of my phone in my purse. It was a text from Rafe.

> Make no mistake, you will pay for that. I'll see you tonight.

Chuckling to myself, I texted back.

> Will I at least enjoy my punishment?

> Yes.

I cackle-laughed at his one-word response and half marveled, half panicked over the fact that one person could affect my mood so much. The day had started out miserable and yet now I was excited. Scared. But lighter. Freer. All because of Rafferty "Rafe" Whitman.

Chapter Twenty-Three

THIS NIGHT WAS GOING BETTER THAN I COULD HAVE HOPED.

I was taken aback by how nervous I was for my friends to meet Rafe. They'd teased me mercilessly about my obvious agitation as we waited for Rafe to arrive at River's Bar.

About fifteen minutes into our wait, Jude suddenly blurted, "Holy fuck."

We'd followed his gaze to find Rafe walking through the crowded bar toward us, head above a lot of people, seeming even taller with those broad, broad shoulders. Women and men turned their heads to watch him stroll by.

"Well, isn't he something?" Roger had murmured in my ear.

I hadn't responded. I was too busy nervously grinning from ear to ear because I was so stupidly happy to see Rafe and scared he and my friends would clash. I'd squeezed out of the booth to greet him and Rafe had reached out before he'd even drawn to a stop to take hold of my waist. He'd tugged me to him and I'd practically fallen into the sexy but quick kiss he'd given me.

Roger, Jude, and Kendall had gaped up at us as if we were a fascinating TV show. However, Roger, as always, was the first to pull himself together. He'd warmly shaken Rafe's hand and while Rafe was stiff and quiet, I could tell he was trying. I'd already warned my friends that he was not the greatest at meeting new people.

With a beer in hand, though, it wasn't long before he was engaged in conversation with Roger about music production. Rafe seemed genuinely interested, and I could tell by the delighted gleam in Roger's eyes that my best friend was enamored with him.

It was going great!

Until Jude announced loudly, "You know the three of us are in a relationship, right?"

I tensed.

Rafe stared blankly at Jude, and I knew him well enough now to know that he was weighing his words. "Star told me months ago, yes."

"Does it bother you?"

"Why would it bother me?"

"You strike me as a traditionalist."

Rafe shrugged. "If you're happy, it's none of my business."

I'd positioned Rafe between me and Roger, and my side was pressed to Rafe's, so he knew I was there, I was listening, and I would jump in if needed. Sensing my tension, Rafe, still looking at Jude, slid a hand over my knee and squeezed it in reassurance.

"So if Star came to you and said she wanted to add another person into your relationship, you'd be cool with that?" Jude pressed.

"No," Rafe replied calmly. "You guys might be happy with your relationship, and that's great, but that doesn't mean it works for everyone."

"You wouldn't do it for Star?"

"I'd do pretty much anything for her . . . but share her. She already knows that."

My breath caught at the "I'd do pretty much anything for her" part.

Thankfully, Jude liked that a lot and stopped being a pain in the ass.

However, I guess the tension never quite left my body, because about twenty minutes later, Kendall got up and rounded the booth to approach me. She took hold of my hand and yanked on it. "C'mon, I love this song."

She wanted me to leave Rafe alone with Roger and Jude? I shook my head.

"Please." Kendall gave me big eyes.

Rafe nudged me. "Go dance if you want."

I studied his face, trying to gauge whether he was okay for me to leave him. "Sure?"

His lips twitched as if what I'd said was funny. "Yes."

Reluctantly, I let Kendall pull me up and lead me over to the dance floor. She tugged me to her as she danced and shouted over the music, "I had to get you out of there. You were helicopter moming him!"

Offended, I spluttered, "N-no, I wasn't!"

Kendall snorted. "You were practically glued to his side, glaring at Roger and Jude in case they said anything out of turn. I've never seen you this off-kilter or protective of a guy before. It's hilarious!"

She was right. I wanted to look over my shoulder so badly to make sure the guys were still including Rafe in the conversation.

As if she'd read my thoughts, Kendall glanced at our table. "They're chatting. It's all good. Now relax. You need to relax, Star!" She leaned in so I could hear her say more quietly, more seriously, "It'll never work if you don't trust it to work."

Her words hit me so hard, I stopped swaying my hips to the beat of the music. Feeling more emotional than I could remember feeling in a long while, I asked her, "Do you think I can do this?"

Kendall leaned in again. "I think I've never seen you look at anyone the way you look at him. I think for you, there's no one but him and so I know you can do this."

There's no one but him.

Wow.

Was she right?

I thought about the last few months.

Had I even looked at another guy?

Nope.

I had not.

Double wow.

"This is an amazing thing for you, so just enjoy yourself, okay?" She threw her hands up with a whoop and danced.

Laughing at her energy, I shook off my worries, my overwrought emotions, and let the music take over.

We were on song two when I was spinning, hands in the air, my hips popping from side to side to the beat, and my gaze hit our table. Specifically, Rafe. My breath caught. He wasn't engaged in conversation with the boys. All three of them were watching us. Well, Rafe was watching me.

A shiver skated down my spine at his hooded expression.

I spun slowly away from that magnetic stare and Kendall leaned in to say, "Holy shit, the way he's looking at you. Every so-inclined person in this place wishes they were you right now."

I laughed, feeling the thrill of my feminine power.

One of my favorite dance songs came on next, "No Lie" by Dua Lipa and Sean Paul. Kendall and I shared a high five because we both loved the track and then started moving with even more energy. It was a sexy freaking song and the chorus was the perfect rhythm of beats to pop your hips to.

I was so lost in the music, the feel of hands on my hips startled me, as did the heat at my back. But just as quickly, the scent of his cologne relaxed me, and I turned my head to the side and up to find Rafe. He moved his body into me, my ass to his crotch; his fingers tightened on my hips, and then he swayed his hips to the rhythm of the song.

Rafe Whitman was sexy-dancing with me.

I sucked in a breath, overtaken by the sensual spell he cast over me. The man could dance. He had rhythm. That said very good things about what he could do with that rhythm in bed.

His lips brushed the side of my neck as his fingers squeezed my hips with every sway to the left. His chest rose and fell and I could feel his breathing grow fast and shallow in line with mine. My nipples were taut beneath my bra, a pulse throbbed between my legs, and I was half convinced that if I didn't get him alone soon I'd have sex with him right there on the dance floor.

He kissed my neck again and then trailed his lips up toward my ear. "Do you have any idea how sexy you are?" Rafe's question was hoarse with need. "Or how much I want you?"

My mouth felt dry with thirst for him and I whirled in his arms, my hands resting on his chest as he gripped my hips again. Those denim-blue eyes were dark beneath the dim lights of the bar, but I could see the harshness etched into his features. The harshness of need. I shivered, fevered, my pulse racing so fast, I felt a little mindless. "We need to go back to my apartment. Right now."

Rafe's nostrils flared. "Let's go."

I'D BARELY GOTTEN MY APARTMENT DOOR OPEN WHEN HE was on me. Rafe's kisses were fervid, deep, so damn sexual every part of me was electrified. We practically fell inside and I slammed the door shut with my foot because my hands were occupied beneath Rafe's T-shirt.

His skin was overheated and smooth, and I loved following the dips and curves of his muscular abs.

He groaned into my mouth as we stumbled backward toward my bed. Rafe tried to fumble with the complicated ties on the back of my dress and I broke out of the kiss to shake my head. "No time." I needed him in me now.

I'd love to say that our first time was slow and tender, but there were months of pent-up sexual tension bursting at the seams between us. When I fell onto my bed and Rafe came down over me, so big and masculine and clearly wanting me, I just needed to be filled by him. To satisfy the hunger that had yawned between us for weeks.

Rafe was on board with that.

I pulled up the skirt of my dress as Rafe fell between my legs, and I bent my knees to hug his hips with my inner thighs. He held my sultry gaze as his fingers slipped beneath my underwear to try me. That flame in his eyes burned brighter at finding me wet. He grunted, and then he tore the lacy undies down my legs. I kicked them free, thighs spreading for him again.

The sound of Rafe pulling down the zipper on his jeans caused another flip of arousal deep in my belly. "Hurry," I gasped, up on my elbows to watch him as he yanked his wallet out of the back pocket of his jeans. He pushed them and his underwear just far enough down to release himself. "Oh." A thick, throbbing erection of above-average size strained toward his stomach as he yanked a condom out of his wallet.

Watching him roll it on, I started to second-guess whether he would fit even as I squirmed with anticipation.

"Of course you're hung like a horse," I commented breathlessly. "You never do anything in half measures."

Rafe fought his laughter as he crawled back over me and pinned my wrists to the bed. I moaned at the sensation of being held down as he nudged between my legs. No man had ever made me feel so fragile and feminine as Rafe did, but I found I actually liked the sensation in bed. I liked our differences a lot.

His amusement disappeared at my obvious arousal, and he pushed inside, holding my gaze.

My desire for him eased his way considerably, but I still felt an exquisite burn of pressure as he slowly filled me.

"Fuck." He squeezed his eyes closed as if he was in pain. "You feel amazing."

Then he retreated and the friction was delicious. "Rafe," I gasped. "Faster, harder."

He took direction extremely well.

His grip on my wrists tightened as he bowed his head into my neck and began to thrust.

My thighs squeezed against his hips, the friction of his jeans against my bare skin erotic beyond bearing, as that coiling tension inside me sprang so tight with only a few drives of his cock inside me. I came on a loud, shocked cry of sensation as my inner muscles clenched and unclenched around him.

"Star, Star, fuck," he panted, and then he stiffened seconds before he groaned in release, his hips shuddering between my thighs.

My inner muscles continued to flutter around him as I stared up at the ceiling in disbelief.

I'd come too quickly, but I'd come hard.

Still, it wasn't enough. It wasn't nearly enough.

"I want you again," I whispered.

Rafe released my wrists and I lowered my arms to slip my hands under his T-shirt, finding his skin fevered and slightly damp. He lifted his head, bracing himself on his hands to hold his body off me, and he slowly slid out. I moaned, and his expression turned searing.

"Give me a minute. And then we're doing it right the second time."

I smiled saucily. "The first time felt pretty damn right to me."

He grinned before pressing a sweet kiss to my lips. Then he said, "I have fantasized about kissing every inch of your body for weeks. We didn't even get our clothes off."

"It was still hot."

"I think the last time I came that fast I was a teenager," he joked. "So yeah, it was hot." He rolled off me. I sat up to watch him cross the room and disappear into my bathroom to deal with the condom. When he returned, I took in his mussed hair and flushed skin and desperately wanted to see all of him naked. I pushed off the bed, the skirts of my dress falling down, and as I stood, I realized I hadn't even taken off my shoes.

Rafe watched me prowl toward him with a hooded gaze that promised he was about to devour me. I shivered, quite happy to be devoured. But first things first.

"Take your clothes off," I ordered quietly as I stopped so there was enough space between us that I could enjoy the entire show.

Rafe obliged. He whipped his T-shirt off first. Then his shoes and socks. His eyes never left mine as he pushed his jeans and boxers down his legs. He was hard again as he kicked himself free of his clothes. Standing before me, completely unabashed by his nakedness, he allowed me to look my fill. I took a moment to sear the sight of him into my memory. Such a broad chest and shoulders, so defined and muscular and masculine. Thick thighs and well-formed calves. Long, long legs.

My heart raced at the sight of him. I'd never dated a guy who looked after his body quite like Rafe looked after his, and while I'd never considered myself a shallow person, I was most definitely delighted by the fruits of his labor.

"Now it's your turn."

I shook. Not with sexual nerves. I liked sex and had few hang-ups about it. Besides, we'd already popped the lid on that. No, I shook with nerves because taking it slow allowed my mind to slow. To remember that this wasn't just some guy I was attracted to and using to scratch an itch.

This was Rafe.

And I wanted what we had to be something more.

For the first time since my first time, I wanted to make love.

Wow.

Big night.

With trembling fingers, I untied the ties of my dress, the ones Rafe had trouble with earlier, and let it fall to the floor. I stepped out of it in only my underwear and my wedged heels. Rafe's eyes mapped every inch of me. He swallowed hard. I deliberately turned around as I bent over to take off my shoes and Rafe groaned loudly. When I straightened, I held his eyes as I unclipped my bra and let it drop. Finally, I took out the pins holding my hair up, dropping them to the floor without a care, as I shook my hair until it fell down my back.

I was totally naked and vulnerable to him.

Rafe took his time studying me. His cock strained harder toward him, and there was that sexy but also adorable flush high on his cheeks. When his blue eyes met mine, I inhaled sharply at the raw need in them.

"My fantasy doesn't even begin to live up to the reality of you," he confessed in that low, rumbling voice. "I've never laid eyes on anything so beautiful."

Tears burned my eyes. "Rafe . . ." I didn't know what to say. How did a person respond to the most epic compliment ever given? And who would have thought that brooding guy I'd met all those months ago could be such a romantic? "You're beautiful too."

He didn't seem to know what to do with that, so he just smiled. "Can I touch you?"

He swallowed hard again. "You don't have to ask."

"I . . . I want to touch you without you touching me."

"So, basically, you want to torture me?"

I laughed softly. "Not intentionally." I approached him slowly and as his eyes fell to my breasts, his breathing increased. His fists clenched at his sides. I stopped before him and reached out to press my palms to his pecs. Rafe took in a deep breath as our eyes met. I'd never had any man look at me the way he looked at me. Like he might die if he didn't touch me. Yet he didn't reach for me.

He gave me this.

Lightly trailing my fingertips over his skin, I memorized the contours of his chest, my thumbs stroking over his hard nipples. My touch made his abdominal muscles flex in response. I brushed my lips over a nipple and he shuddered, so I licked it and he lifted his arms before he remembered himself and lowered them again.

I teased his other nipple as my hands coasted up his chest and along his strong shoulders and down his arms. Then I kissed lower, soft, wet kisses down his six-pack.

Rafe's breathing was loud and shallow now. "Star . . ."

I followed his happy trail with my mouth, avoiding his arousal as it strained up for some lovin'. Smiling to myself, I lowered to my knees, feeling the sharp V-cut of his hips and smoothing my hands down his lightly furred thighs until I was eye level with his cock.

"Star—fuck!" he grunted as his scorching hardness passed between my lips, and I felt his thighs tense under my fingertips. My tongue trailed along a vein on the underside of his cock and his breathing stuttered before seeming to stop entirely when I sucked, bobbing my head so my mouth slid excruciatingly slowly up and down his length.

Rafe still didn't touch me.

I looked up at him, and I could tell he was losing it. A war clearly written on his face. He wanted this but— "You have to stop or I'm going to come," he choked out.

I released him with a smug smile. "That's kind of the point."

Rafe shook his head, clearly dazed. "No, I want to be inside you when I come again."

Deciding that teasing him any further was cruel, I kissed my way up his body. Then I tilted my head back as I leaned my naked body against his, his arousal digging into my stomach. "Your turn."

He took my hand with a nod and then walked around me, leading me back to the bed. Rafe sat down on the edge and then reached for my waist. For a second, he paused, smoothing his rough hands along my curves as he drank me in. Then he arranged me on his lap so I straddled him, my knees just touching the bed on either side of him.

He kissed me.

Rafe's kiss was slow, exploring, our tongues tangling in a mimic of what our bodies wanted to do. I crushed my breasts to his hard chest, needing to be closer, needing friction, needing the kiss to be impossibly deeper. Rafe held me tight, his hands smoothing down my back and over the rise of my ass as we devoured each other's mouths.

He broke the kiss, his gaze lowering to my breasts, and then he cupped me in his big, beautiful hands. I arched my back, my nipples pebbling, eager for his touch. When his thumbs brushed them, I shuddered, a sigh escaping from between my lips. My breasts were supersensitive, which I'd only recently discovered wasn't something all women experienced. Kendall said hers weren't particularly effective at getting her off, but I loved having my breasts touched. Having Rafe touch them was a fantasy come true.

My hips squirmed with need as he rolled my nipples between his fingers and thumbs, his gaze fascinated, as if my response thrilled him. Then he bent his head and covered my right nipple with his mouth, and I cried out as sensation scored down my belly and my clit pulsed.

Rafe growled as if he could feel every inch of my reaction, and his other hand dipped between us, his thumb finding the bundle of nerves at the apex of my thighs. I jerked at his touch, on sensory overload as he tugged ruthlessly at my nipple, scraping his teeth over it before licking and sucking.

The tension coiled tight in my womb and I dug my fingers into his strong shoulders as he moved his mouth to my left breast and treated my other nipple to the same.

I shattered, crying out his name as I came, shuddering on his lap as he laved and licked at my breasts until every inch of me was wrung out with the orgasm.

"Wallet," he breathed harshly against my chest.

It took me a second for the word to compute and then I searched around for it frantically. Thankfully, it was still on the bed by my pillow. Rafe turned to follow my gaze and stretched out to get it without dislodging me. He gripped my ass to keep me in place and his fingers slipped, making me shiver.

He grabbed his wallet and shot me a fiery look.

Then he was kissing me again, this time harder, more demanding, as he blindly took out a condom. We broke the kiss in order for him to tear the wrapper and then I was lifting my hips in anticipation as he rolled it on. The man had barely secured himself when I rose up over him, guided his tip in, then slammed down.

We moaned against each other's lips before our mouths met fully. Our kiss was desperate, needful as I rose again and came down. I clung to his shoulders, flooded with feeling. The overwhelming fullness of him inside me, the hard grip he had on my ass while his other hand squeezed and molded my breast with just the right amount of pressure. I leaned back, breaking the kiss, but only so his cock thrust into me at the most delicious angle. Only so I could watch him. I moved slowly, building toward an exquisite orgasm.

My eyes never left Rafe's handsome face as I moved, feeling sexy and powerful beneath his gleaming gaze, watching the way his nostrils flared as he lingered on my breasts and the way his eyes dropped to watch me ride him. He gripped me tight, urging me on; his jaw clenched as the heat between us increased and a light sheen of sweat coated our skin.

All I cared about in that moment was being this deeply connected to Rafe. And the growing pleasure low in my belly, the sound of our uncontrolled breaths and my mews of pleasure, the intoxicating scent of sex.

Our eyes met and I moved on him, holding his gaze. There wasn't just passion and need in his eyes. There was tenderness and awe.

We were making love.

That knowledge was my undoing. My orgasm came upon me suddenly and I came around him, my stomach muscles rippling with the release, my inner muscles squeezing him tight.

"Fuck." Rafe's hold turned almost bruising. Then he arched his neck and groaned long and hard as I felt him throb inside me.

Eventually he let out a sharp exhalation, opening his eyes, chest rising and falling quickly as he stared at me as if he'd seen nothing like me before.

Suffice to say, making love to Rafe Whitman was the best damn thing I'd ever experienced. By the look of wonder in his eyes, it was the best damn sex of his life too.

I pressed a soft kiss to his lips and whispered, "What now?"

He wrapped his arms around me, crushing me to him, and the movement made us both draw in a breath because he was still inside me. "I'd like to stay the night."

No guy had ever stayed the night. "What if I snore?"

"You don't. I would have heard you that night at my apartment. But even if you did, I'd still like to stay the night."

A happy smile prodded my lips, one I tried to hide but couldn't, and Rafe's eyes glinted warmly. "Okay. You're staying the night."

After we'd cleaned up, we'd gotten into my bed and I felt all of sixteen again, watching his big body slide under my duvet. As soon as I got in, Rafe pulled me to him. He was a cuddler.

I'd never been cuddled in my sleep before, so I wasn't sure how I'd handle it, but I found it was just like that night at my parents' house except better. I enjoyed falling asleep with my head on his chest, feeling his heartbeat beneath my ear. I liked how warm and safe and wanted he made me feel.

Even better, I enjoyed waking up just before dawn to the feel of his tongue on my clit, to the orgasm that shattered me into full consciousness before he thrust inside me and brought me to my second orgasm.

It was by far not my last of the day.

Chapter Twenty-Four

REAL-DATING RAFE WHITMAN WAS VERY DIFFERENT FROM
fake-dating Rafe Whitman. Obviously, the fan-freaking-tastic sex
was one of the big differences, but his playful boyishness was another. I loved that side of him. Over the next few weeks, I spent a lot
of time at Rafe's apartment. Mostly because I knew he needed to be
close to his clinic for his patients and also because it was easier for
me to get to jobs from his place than mine. During those overnight
stays, I discovered that Rafe, along with all the veggies in his fridge
and freezer, had a drawer dedicated to candy bars. Snickers, to be
exact. There was just a drawer filled with Snickers. I couldn't help
but bite back a smile at his adorable defensiveness as he explained
that he allowed himself a Snickers bar twice a week and he just liked
to make sure he was stocked up. I was at once impressed with his
willpower and amused by his need to have a stockpile. The man as-
serted so much self-control that he needed to know that when he
wanted to let loose, he had what he needed to do that.

I wondered if that was part of my appeal for him. That he knew whenever he needed to, he could just let loose with me. The thought made me smile.

Another quirk of Rafe's was to set two alarms. The first to wake him up, though he'd doze off again, and the second to get him out of bed. He said he didn't like the feeling of having to jump out of bed as soon as he'd awakened, that his body needed time to accept that it was morning. Worried it bothered me, he told me he'd just set the one alarm, but I didn't care. I liked knowing these things about him. Like Rafe's commitment to working out. Even if we'd spent half the night making love, he'd still get up at five in the morning to hit the gym in his building. He'd leave me sleeping in his bed and I'd only get up for the day once he'd returned.

One morning he'd come back and I was already awake and the sight of him all sweaty and flushed turned me on big-time. He'd kicked off his sneakers and grinned at me knowingly. "After I shower," he promised.

I shook my head. "I want you now."

A bead of sweat rolled down Rafe's temple. "I'm a mess."

"You're sexy as hell." I'd pushed the duvet off and my nightie up in invitation.

With an unreadable look on his face, Rafe strolled to me. "You want me like this?"

"Yeah."

"You sure about that?"

"Yeah."

Then the bastard braced himself over me and shook his head like a dog, spraying me with the fruits of his labor! I squealed, trying to cover myself, and his laughter spread warmth through me as he nuzzled into me. I was still giggling when he suddenly hauled me up into his arms like I was his bride and marched determinedly toward the bathroom.

"What are you doing?"

He grinned at me. "Now you need a shower too."

I squirmed in anticipation. "You're an evil genius."

"Now you're getting it."

"IF IT'S GOING SO GREAT BETWEEN YOU, WHY ARE YOU WOR-ried about what to wear again?" Jude grumbled.

My three best buddies stared at me from my laptop screen, their minimalist living room in the background. The reason I had them on a Zoom call was because Rafe and I had officially been dating for two weeks and this Sunday was my first dinner with his family as his real girlfriend.

I was genuinely nervous this time. It made little sense because I'd met his family, and they all, except for Gigi, thought we were actually dating from day one. Rafe and I had agreed that telling his parents the truth about our start would only hurt them and perhaps even put them off me entirely.

Even so, I had the nerves.

"Is that a no to this dress?"

"I like it," Roger replied.

"What about the violet-blue dress? The one with the little white flowers all over it? You look so pretty in that," Kendall opined.

Nodding, I shuffled out of the peach dress I currently wore and walked to my closet in my underwear. "What are you guys doing today?" I called over my shoulder.

"Not a lot. Might go out for a bite later," Roger answered.

A loud knock at my door signaled Rafe's arrival to pick me up. Shit. I walked out of my closet, dress in hand. "Come in!"

My boyfriend (*boyfriend!*) walked in and closed the door, his eyebrows lifting in appreciation to find me in my underwear.

"I'll be two seconds," I promised.

"Hey, Rafe!" Kendall called from the computer.

Rafe's chin jerked in surprise as his gaze flew to the laptop. He took in the sight of my three friends' faces on the screen, then scowled as he grunted a hello at them before walking out of shot into the kitchen. Tension visibly rode his shoulders. I pulled on the dress as my friends made overexaggerated grimaces at me.

"I'll call you guys later."

"You better." Kendall gave me big eyes, silently communicating *Tell us what the hell that was later.*

I said goodbye, closed the laptop, and looked over at Rafe, who leaned against my counter, unhappy eyes on me.

"Everything okay?" I fluffed my hair out from where strands were caught in the back of my dress.

His gaze shifted to the laptop and back to me. "Why were you in your underwear for that video call?"

Oh.

I stiffened. "Because they're my friends and they were helping me pick out a dress while we chatted."

"Do you strip to your underwear in front of people a lot?"

A flush of anger crawled up my neck. "No. They're my best friends. Not people."

Sensing my anger, Rafe sighed heavily and pushed off the counter. "I'm sorry. I . . . just . . . I don't like it."

"That I was in my underwear in front of my friends?"

"Two of whom are guys who are into women."

No. Nope. This wasn't happening. "They're my best friends. I won't change that friendship with them, not even for you. And it's no different from wearing a bikini in front of them."

"One, that's not what I'm saying. Two, underwear differs from a bikini. A bikini is something you wear in public, not standing alone in your apartment with just three people watching you. There are less sexual connotations with a bikini."

I glowered. "I can't believe you're trying to dictate who I show my body to. This is *my* body, Rafe. Not yours."

He nodded calmly as he approached me, and I braced myself, still flushed with agitation. "You're right. But would you be okay if I showed my body to another woman? Just me alone in my apartment with her? Even if I told you she and I were just friends?"

A different burn of emotion flashed across my chest and my jaw clenched when I realized it was possessiveness. No. I clearly did not like the thought of another woman seeing Rafe's body.

Shit.

That was new.

He had the decency not to look smug when he saw the answer on my face. "I know this makes me seem like a caveman asshole, but I'm not. I won't stop you from video calling people in your underwear, because you're right, it's your body. But I didn't like it. Because I'm not perfect, Star. People aren't perfect."

"Explain. Other than the sexual connotations, explain, and I'll try to understand."

"Do you really need me to? I know you don't like the thought of this if it was the other way around. Isn't that enough?"

"I'd like to think I'm a more rational being than that." I was frustrated that apparently I wasn't!

"So would I." He laughed unhappily. "But unfortunately, feelings don't always work the way you want them to." His eyes warmed. "I like that I'm the only one who gets to see you alone in your underwear. That I'm the only one who gets to see you naked. It's a privilege. I'm selfish. I like how I know things about you very few people know and that I'm the only one who gets that from you now."

"So it's emotional, not sexual?"

"Oh, it's both." He shrugged as if in apology.

I nodded slowly. "All right."

"All right . . . ?"

"I'll think about it." No promises. Even though I could see where Rafe was coming from and I, honestly, would probably hate it if he were to undress in front of another woman in the same scenario, I just couldn't set a precedent that meant changing the way I interacted with my friends. I had a close relationship with Roger, Jude, and Kendall. They were family, which was why I knew there was nothing sexual in it, so I wasn't sure I wanted to make that compromise for Rafe. Moreover, I had to wonder if the whole situation was different for him because his last serious girlfriend had cheated on him. It would make sense that betrayal had planted some insecurities in Rafe, and while I was sympathetic to that, I wouldn't allow it to dictate how I behaved in our relationship.

To my surprise, Rafe cupped my face in his hands, his thumbs sweeping my cheeks.

"You're not pissed?"

He shook his head with a small smile. "You wouldn't be you if that wasn't your response."

Rafe was right. Just like me, he wasn't perfect. There were things about him I didn't understand, just like I knew there were things about me he didn't understand. But I found I liked our differences. And I liked that he could surprise me.

I just liked *him*. A lot. "I really like you."

Rafe's eyes darkened as they dropped to my mouth. "I really like you too."

WHATEVER TENSION HAD BUILT BETWEEN US IN MY APART-ment had dissipated by the time we were in his Pontiac, driving to his parents' in Harrison. I'd told Jude about Rafe's restoration job on his car because Jude liked old cars, so Rafe had waited patiently while I snapped some pics to send before we took off.

Five minutes after I sent them, Jude had sent a text in response.

> I approve.

I grinned because I wondered if he was talking about more than the car.

I'd shot texts off to my friends to assure them all was well with me and Rafe, and then a text from Gigi lit up my screen. A few days after Rafe and I became official, I called her to apologize for blowing her off, but she was lovely and understanding and we were all good. She was excited to see us at lunch.

When we arrived, Gigi proved that by running and throwing herself into my arms. "I'm so happy," she whispered into my hair. "You're exactly what he needs."

Her acceptance meant a lot to me, and I squeezed her hard in response.

We spent most of the afternoon on the shaded lower terrace, enjoying the warm weather. September was approaching and with it the cooler weather would come and, Rafe warned, more invitations to events. Their social circle was returning from their summer vacations, and there was always some party or function going on somewhere during the fall. Thankfully, Rafe's schedule meant he couldn't accept invitations to everything, but family obligation required him to attend some. And he wanted me with him.

If I could make it through those events *pretending* to be his girlfriend, I was pretty sure I could do it as his real one.

Whatever nerves I'd felt soon disappeared too as I fell into a familiar rhythm with his family. Hugo barely looked at me, but everyone else (even Pippa) was great. At one point, I sat next to Jen on the lower terrace, Rafe sat opposite us, and Charmaine, who'd been in the pool only seconds before, ran up and slapped Rafe on the arm. "You're it, Uncle Rafe!"

Without hesitation, he grinned and jumped out of his chair. She screamed in delight and took off, and butterflies whooshed to life in my belly as I watched him chase her around the lawn. When he finally caught her, he swung her up into his arms as if she weighed nothing, and her little-girl giggles filled the air.

Hot damn.

I suddenly was finding it a little hard to breathe.

"I like that."

Jen's voice broke me out of Rafe's spell. "What?"

She searched my face and her intensity reminded me of Rafe in those few seconds. Tenderness softened her expression. "I like the way you look at my son. He's happier than I can remember seeing him in a long time."

In the last few weeks, I'd determinedly not allowed myself to think about the future. I was afraid I'd freak out and blow it with Rafe. Therefore, I focused on our present. However, in that moment, I fought the overwhelming urge to burst into inexplicable tears.

As if his mom sensed the emotions roiling inside me, she grabbed my hand and squeezed it as if in reassurance.

Not long later, we were back up on the upper terrace digging into the amazing spread Jen and Pippa had set out. I'd asked every time I'd attended if I could help, but they always shooed me from the kitchen.

"Any line sitting jobs this week, Star?" Gigi inquired across the table. The idea of my job apparently fascinated Rafe's little sister, because she texted me every week to ask what I was waiting in line for.

I nodded around a mouthful of pasta and waited to swallow before answering. "A few. One of them is to get an autographed copy of a book. The bestselling thriller writer Pauline Hartcliffe is signing at the Strand. I'm going to get myself a copy too."

"How do you manage the commute?" Pippa frowned at me. "You spend most of your time in the city. All that back-and-forth must be exhausting and expensive. You should consider moving to Manhattan."

Yeah, 'cause we could all afford city living.

"Pippa, I don't know if you know this, but Manhattan isn't exactly affordable." Gigi took the words right out of my mouth.

Rafe's sister-in-law appeared uncomfortable as she pursed her lips and shifted in her seat. "Right."

If Rafe and I were going to do this for real, I had to make it clear I wasn't ashamed of my jobs or my lack of money. "My apartment on Staten Island has everything I need. And I get a lot of reading done during the commute."

"Rafe did say you love books." Jen smiled conspiratorially. "I'm a big reader too. Who's your favorite author?"

Before I could answer, Hugo interrupted. "Is that really your grand life plan? To work crappy-paying jobs, paying crappy rent for a crappy apartment? What happens when you're old and physically can't wait in line or people don't want an old woman dressing up as a Disney princess? Do you have a retirement plan?"

"Hugo." Greg heaved a sigh, cutting his elder son a dark look. "If you can't be civil, leave."

I tensed, my fingers curling tightly around my fork, but I smiled brightly at Greg. "It's fine, really."

Hugo grimaced. "Look, I'm sorry if it came out like that, but my question is relevant."

"It's also none of your damn business." Rafe stared stonily at his brother. Then his gaze shifted to Pippa. "And Star's commute won't be an issue in a while, anyway."

I looked at him with a puckered brow. "It won't?"

He met my gaze and shrugged. "In a while we'll probably move in together and since my place is bigger, I just assumed . . ." He frowned at my slackened expression. "Or not. We can move into your place. Shit, yeah, we can live there. I know you like being close to your friends."

Rafe had completely misunderstood my expression.

I didn't care about living on the Upper West Side.

I cared that he wanted us to move in together. That for him, it was just a given that we were on that path. "Live together?" I murmured.

His eyes searched mine. Then he said, "We practically do anyway. Right?"

Instead of the panic I thought I'd feel, I was excited. Living with Rafe meant I'd get to go to bed every night in his arms (because he was definitely a cuddler) and wake up beside him every morning. I could suddenly envision myself on his couch, reading a book while he watched a wildlife documentary. It was all very domesticated.

And weirdly thrilling.

"Your place would make the most sense," I agreed quietly. "You're close to the clinic and I work in the city most days."

Rafe's lips curled at the corners as his eyes lit with relief. "Yeah?"

I nodded, trying not to grin like the Cheshire Cat. "Though we'll need to install some bookshelves."

His hand slid under the table to squeeze my thigh. "I think that can be arranged."

Heat tingled between my legs and he must have seen the arousal in my gaze, because he swallowed hard and removed his hand. His expression promised me *later*.

"Consider carefully." Hugo interrupted our moment. "The last woman you lived with was Camille."

Rafe cut his brother a look. "Star isn't Camille."

"No, she very much isn't," Jen agreed, casting Hugo a glare of warning.

He held up his hands in surrender and dropped his gaze to his plate.

"Well . . . okay then." Pippa's voice sounded high-pitched, drawing my attention.

Rafe's sister-in-law stared at me as if she'd never seen me before.

I'd understand what that look meant later when she announced over dessert, "Star, I don't know if Rafe told you, but I've started freelancing. As an attorney."

He hadn't, actually. "Oh wow, that's great."

"Yes, I'm very excited to get back to work. Anyway, I'm now the attorney for my best friend, Pamela, and she owns a very successful interior design firm in the city. She told me she's looking for a new assistant. Someone to run errands, book appointments, take inventory, host the clients when they come into the office. But she also wants someone with style and an interest in aesthetics and I can't think of anyone better than you. You have such a great way with people, you have your own style, and this could be something that leads to more. I can absolutely get you this job if you want it. For me, Pamela would overlook your lack of a college degree."

Rafe cleared his throat beside me and I found him frowning at his sister-in-law. It was obvious she hadn't run this past him, and I wondered if she'd just come up with this a few minutes ago. I smiled at Pippa as I replied, "Oh, that's such a kind thought, Pippa, but I've never done office work."

"Oh, this is different from normal office work. Besides, you're so smart, I know you'd be a quick learner."

"Star has a job. Two, in fact," Rafe told her, his tone almost a warning.

Pippa shrugged. "This would be full-time Monday to Friday, but the salary would probably be more than what you make from both jobs. Plus, it includes great health insurance and dental and I could assist you in choosing a private pension investment plan that would be great for your retirement."

As I glanced around the table, it felt as if everyone was waiting with bated breath for my response. I wasn't stupid. I knew that at some point soon I really needed to think about my plans for the future, but the thought of taking on a job that came with that many strings made me feel claustrophobic. It wasn't a job I could just walk away from without upsetting Rafe's family. "I—"

"Think about it. You can take the week and tell me next Friday."

"Next Friday?"

"Greg's birthday dinner."

Oh right. I'd forgotten Rafe had asked me to that. Greg, unlike his wife, didn't like a big fuss and just wanted his family with him at his favorite seafood restaurant up the coast. Rafe had also complained that the whole reason he needed to hire a third vet at the clinic was because his family was constantly filling up his weekends with social events.

"So next Friday. You can give me your answer then." Pippa pursued the subject determinedly.

"Okay. Thanks."

She nodded, satisfied, and when my gaze hit Jen, I caught her exchanging a pleased look with Greg.

Dammit.

As much as Rafe's parents might like me, maybe they wanted their son with someone who was serious about her career.

Not that I wasn't serious about my future. I was serious about my pursuit of happiness. But I just . . . I'd spent most of my life living under the beliefs my parents instilled in me. To be free of ties and obligations and to live life by the second.

Between discovering Arlo's hypocrisy, that both my parents paid for health insurance, and the realization that being in a committed relationship with Rafe didn't scare me, I found myself floundering. What *did* I want? Did I want to continue living my life day to day, never knowing how much money was coming in? Or did I want a job I knew I'd have until I retired? An actual career. One that would allow me to save for that rainy day in the future. What if I decided to have kids? It was a possibility. Unlike Arlo and Dawn, I liked kids!

As much as I hated the way he'd said it, Hugo was right. There would come a time when I would no longer be desirable as a Disney princess. That was the harsh reality of life.

But what about my plans to travel across the country?

Did I really want to do that, or had I only wanted to do that to escape having to think about my future?

It all made my brain hurt.

Chapter Twenty-Five

"YOU'RE QUIET OVER THERE," RAFE OBSERVED AS SOON AS
we got into his car to leave. "I hope Pippa didn't freak you out. You
know you can say no to her, right?"

"I know," I assured him. "It just took me by surprise. And . . .
honestly got me thinking a little."

"About what?" He dropped his hand from the ignition to turn to
me, giving me his full attention.

I loved that about him.

So I told him everything that was whirring around in my head.

He considered my words once I'd finished. "Is there something
you want to do with your life? A passion?"

A tightness fisted in my chest. "I don't know. Is that pathetic?
I'm twenty-eight."

"Yeah, you're really old," he teased as he reached out to cup my
cheek. "Hey, you have time to figure out what you want. But don't let
Pippa push you into something you don't want just because you're
confused right now."

"When we first met, I meant it when I told you my only ambition was to be happy."

"I know that. And as much as I didn't understand it, I admired your clarity. I still do."

"But everything I believed was built on the bullshit my parents passed on to me . . . and, honestly, I think now, looking back, that I've lived my life a certain way not just because of what they taught me but because of everything they didn't give me. I've felt abandoned most of my childhood, and I think I've just been doing everything I can to not find myself in that position again where I'd feel abandoned. So no ties. To anything. No career I could pour my heart into only to fail at it or have a boss fire me. No guy to commit to in case he didn't want to commit back." Tears burned in my eyes. "Until you."

Rafe's expression was so tender as he smoothed his thumb over my cheek. "That's a big epiphany, Star. It's a lot to deal with. But you know I'm here to talk things out. Or just to be here, whatever you need."

Those tears threatened to let loose. "It doesn't bother you that I don't know what I want beyond wanting to be happy?"

He shook his head, eyes dark with affection. "Just honored I get to be there to watch you find what it is you want."

God, I *liked* him. So much. "I really like you." I repeated my words from that morning.

Rafe stroked my cheek with his thumb one more time. "I really like you too. And I meant what I said. If you need to talk about your parents, your childhood, in order to process everything, I'm here," he repeated.

"I think I'd like that." A safe place to finally let go of all the pain I'd kept locked down for such a long time. Pain that flared to life every time my calls and texts to my parents went unanswered. I hadn't heard from Dawn in months. Arlo's nurse, Maggie, kept me updated on his progress via texts. But that was it.

My parents were the worst.

However, my boyfriend was the freaking best.

Feeling more settled by his faith and reassurance, I blinked back my tears and relaxed as I watched him pull out of his parents' driveway. About ten minutes later, however, he unexpectedly turned off the highway and drove down a narrow road into woodlands.

"Where are we going?"

He didn't speak until we'd parked in the dark of a small makeshift parking lot in the middle of the woods. It was almost pitch-black. There was no one else around. Rafe switched off the engine and turned to me. "I didn't want to sit outside my parents' house talking about important things. We both know they were probably watching us."

I studied him, searching for the reason we were here. "What important things?"

"Your parents. Talk to me about them. I know a little, but not a lot. It's important to me I know where you're coming from. I grew up in a home with parents who love each other and weren't afraid to be publicly affectionate. Don't get me wrong, they fought like all couples do, but we were pretty secure knowing that our parents loved each other and loved us even more. That's where I'm coming from."

"I love that you had that. That you have that," I replied sincerely. "But that's not just where you're coming from."

Rafe frowned. "What do you mean?"

"You hired me to pretend to be your girlfriend to get your mom and Pippa off your back. How bad must it have been? Really?"

Nodding slowly, Rafe sighed and unclipped his seat belt and relaxed into his seat. "Like Hugo mentioned, Camille was the last woman I lived with."

"She was your last relationship and she cheated on you. I remember."

"Yeah." He cleared his throat. "Like I told you, I never loved her and I know that's why she cheated, but it was still disappointing and hurtful."

"Of course it was."

"I'd been in several long-term relationships by that point and I was just exhausted waiting for it to feel like how it must feel between my parents. I decided I needed a break from dating to see if being alone was what I actually wanted."

Oh. Understanding dawned. My heart raced.

"When things ended with Camille, my mom and Pippa took my despondency to mean that I'd really loved her and that I was broken. Eighteen months after the fact and I still hadn't started dating anyone new. They got worried. They got impatient. Six months before you and I met, the matchmaking attempts started. It was just constant, Star. Every time I spoke to my mom, that was all she wanted to talk about. I told you about the women they sent to my clinic. They gave out my number without my permission, and I was at a breaking point. If I hadn't met you, I would have had an explosive argument with my mom that I couldn't take back. I know it doesn't sound like much, but when someone you love can only see one thing when they look at you, it . . . it . . . just . . . it was suffocating."

Sympathy for Rafe, and anger toward Jen and Pippa, filled me as I reached for his hand. "I'm sorry they made you feel that way."

He searched my face. "I'm not, because look what happened. I know I don't want to be alone now."

There went my pulse, pounding hard again.

"Tell me about Arlo and Dawn. Your childhood."

I took a deep breath and answered honestly, "I don't talk about it a lot because I've come a long way in finally letting go of a lot of that hurt, choosing to forgive them for my own sake, and I worry that talking about it will bring it all up again."

"It might come up again if you don't talk about it. I see you looking at your phone sometimes and I worry it's because Dawn hasn't texted you back."

Wow, he paid attention. "I do do that sometimes." I heaved another massive sigh. "But I have to let go. I know I do."

"Why? You mentioned weeks ago on our first date that they left you in a shop when you were a baby. Is that true?"

I nodded unhappily. "I knew pretty young that things weren't right. When I was around six, Arlo and Dawn were really good friends with this couple who were self-proclaimed hippies too. They had three kids, and when we visited, the mom was always sweet and attentive to me, as well as to her kids. I didn't know what it was they were doing at the time, but her husband and my parents would get high. She never did. She was always there, looking after us, and I used to think even then, why didn't my mom look after me? I'd see the way other parents were with their kids when we were out or when I was at school. I'd overhear them asking their kids a million questions, making sure they had what they needed, asking about their day. Arlo and Dawn forgot to pick me up so many times from first grade that social services were called."

"Jesus," Rafe sneered. "Assholes."

"Yup. Pretty much. Dawn didn't want 'the man' on her case, so she made an effort to make sure I got to school and back. But it wasn't just one thing." I shook my head sadly. "It was everything, Rafe. They left me to my own devices all the time. I raised myself." Tears burned my nose. "I had no one to comfort me when I was sad because they didn't like talking about sad things, and when Matt Remner broke my sixteen-year-old heart by dumping me after taking my virginity, Dawn got sick of hearing me crying in my bedroom."

Rafe's fist curled in his lap.

"She told me to suck it up. That it was my fault for believing people should be monogamous."

"You were sixteen and some asshole treated you like shit," he bit out. "She should have wanted to kick his ass."

"That's not Dawn."

Rafe shook his head, the muscle in his jaw twitching as he clenched and unclenched his teeth.

"Talk to me," I whispered, blood rushing in my ears. What did he really think about all of this? About me?

"I . . ." He stared into my eyes and my breath caught at the emotion there. "I hate that you were alone for so long. That kills me."

A tear escaped at his words and I swiped it away quickly, but another followed. "I'm not alone now." I gave him a watery smile.

"No. You're not." It was a promise.

My breath caught and a primal need I didn't quite understand ignited my blood. "I want you."

"Now?" He cocked an eyebrow.

"Ever had sex in your car?" I unclipped my seat belt.

"No." Rafe searched my eyes. "Are you sure you want this?"

"I need this. I need you." At the answering heat in his eyes, I felt a thrill tingle between my legs. "Front or back?"

Rafe gave a bark of delighted laughter, and I caught the innuendo. I rolled my eyes. "I meant the car."

"Well, that's a damn shame," he teased, laughter trembling in his words.

"Do you want to have sex in your car or not?"

His answer was to slide his seat as far back as it would go.

"Front it is." I giggled as I clambered over the center console and into his arms.

"You sure?" he asked again.

"I'm always sure with you."

Something intense flashed in his eyes and then Rafe kissed me as he always kissed me, with his entire self. I was his entire focus as his lips moved over mine. No one had ever kissed me like Rafe. Like I was his oxygen. His kisses were seriously addictive for that reason alone.

As his hands smoothed down my waist, he broke the kiss, but only to murmur against my mouth, "I *like* everything about you, Star Shine Meadows."

The way he said it made my breath catch. Because, seriously, it had almost the same impact as if he'd used the other L-word.

Half-elated, half-terrified, I kissed him with *my* whole being, and what should have been an awesome quickie in his car was a slow, languid lovemaking as I rode us both toward bliss.

Chapter Twenty-Six

"BROADCAST NEWS ANALYST."

I looked up from my notebook and made a face at Roger. "What?"

"Broadcast news analyst," he read from his phone before taking a sip of coffee.

Understanding dawned. "Did you just google a list of jobs and now you're reading them to me?"

Upon meeting for coffee with my best friend during a rare moment where our schedules aligned, I'd informed him I had a future to start thinking about and I wanted to make a list of careers that I might be happy to pursue.

Roger quirked an eyebrow. "It's easier than just sitting here staring into space, trying to think up careers."

"C'mon, isn't there something that comes to mind when you look at me?"

"Yes. Acting."

While that was sweet . . . "I mean a stable career."

"Then no. Everything I think of when it comes to you is arty and bohemian and absolutely unstable."

"I don't scream 'stable' to you?"

"I'm not falling into that trap."

"Roger." I threw my napkin at him. "I'm serious about this."

"Well, what about the offer from Rafe's sister? Interior design is arty."

"But I won't be interior designing. I'll be fetching."

"It could lead to more, though."

"You sound like Pippa."

Roger ignored that and scrolled through his phone. "What about . . . social media expert?"

"I'm only on social media to keep up with work. I am not making it an integral part of my business if I don't have to."

"Right. Um . . . public relations specialist. You are good with people."

"Hmm. Okay. I'll write that one down. But wait, won't I need a degree in public relations for that?"

"Yup."

I scanned my small list of careers that interested me. "I think I might need a degree for all of these."

Roger cleared his throat and I looked up to see him giving me a careful half smile.

"What is it?"

"I think whatever you choose might involve going back to school."

Horrified, I gaped. "At my age?"

"Because twenty-eight is so old." His teasing reminded me of Rafe. "Star, it's more than likely you're going to need a degree to pursue a career."

"How the hell am I supposed to afford to go back to school?"

He shrugged. "Loans."

My head hurt. Groaning, I dropped it into my hands and stared at my list. "I could kill my parents."

"Your parents?"

"Yeah, I would like to officially blame them for everything that is wrong with my life."

Roger chuckled. "About time you started blaming them for something."

In all seriousness, I said, "What am I going to do, Roger? And shouldn't I feel more panicked than I am? I'm only stressed because I feel like I should be more stressed."

"Why? You make enough money to pay your rent and buy food and clothes and books."

"But I work jobs that can't last forever."

"Star, I've never met anyone who lands on her feet like you. When you set your mind to something, you achieve it. Just because it hasn't been some fancy degree for a fancy career doesn't mean you haven't succeeded at your goals."

"What if I want a fancy career after all?"

"Then I know you'll do what you need to do to achieve that. And so do you. That is why you are not panicking. You have more faith in yourself than you know."

I loved my friends. "You're the best."

"I'm aware. I take it the next coffee is on you as payment for my wisdom?"

Grinning, and feeling far better about my pathetic little list, I stood to go get him a much deserved second coffee.

ROGER'S REMINDER WAS EVERYTHING I NEEDED TO GO ABOUT my daily life without a storm cloud hanging over my head.

Until Friday night.

. . .

ON FRIDAY MORNING, I'D COME INTO THE CITY FOR A JOB AT A
new bakery opening. The bakery owners wanted me dressed as a
giant cupcake, which wasn't exactly character acting, but they were
paying the same fee as everyone else, so I was ready to don that cupcake costume.

I'd dropped my bag with clothes and toiletries off at Rafe's apartment before he left for work and promised to be back at his place by
five.

Perhaps it was the perfect storm of events. A handful of interactions that all happened in one day in a way that affected my emotions
and my decision making.

The job as a costume character actor usually involved dressing
up as a character in popular culture and imitating them. There was
a skill and challenge to that, that I enjoyed.

Donning a cupcake costume to stand outside a bakery in Brooklyn, yelling things to entice customers inside, wasn't my usual gig,
but it seemed We Bring Them to Life was branching out for the sake
of dollars.

However, one of the co-owners of the bakery grinned at me in
excitement when I showed, and the buzz of energy among their
small staff got me juiced up for them. I was ready to sell the heck out
of some cupcakes. Then, said co-owner asked, "I take it you don't
have class this morning?"

"Class?"

"School."

"Oh, I'm not a student. You think I'm young enough to be a student?" I was thrilled. "I'm twenty-eight."

Her eyes bugged out of her head. "Oh. Oh, *okay* then." It was the
way she said it. She drawled it so rudely, I almost shoved the cupcake
costume at her.

Instead, I decided to be me and give her the benefit of the doubt. She was nervous because her business was launching today. So I laughed it off and put on that pink cupcake, telling myself I looked adorable instead of stupid.

People did laugh at the giant pink cupcake as they walked by, but it wasn't the usual laughing along with me when I did my costume character acting jobs. They thought I was ridiculous. I couldn't shrug that off like I usually could. Maybe it was that damn "*okay* then."

The universe wasn't finished with me, though.

The gig lasted until one o'clock when the bakery closed, and I handed over the costume and they didn't tip me. Not even with baked goods.

Charming.

Then I scurried back to Manhattan to switch places with a colleague who'd been standing in line for a game console since five a.m. He had another job to get to, so I'd offered to take his place in line and finish the job. Thankfully, by the time I got there, he wasn't too far from the front entrance of the store.

Once I'd taken his place, I pulled out a snack from my purse and was munching on my lunch and reading my e-reader when the conversation behind me seeped in. Turning to look, I saw a young guy and a woman standing talking to people in line. The woman had a professional camera around her neck and the guy was writing things down on a tablet as he asked questions.

They seemed to get what they needed from that person and then started moving down the line, talking to people. Then I overheard their key question. "Are you a professional line sitter?"

Oh.

I braced myself, and then they were right next to me.

"Hi, we're from *The Daily*, and we're doing a piece on professional line sitting. Are you a professional line sitter, or are you just waiting for the console?"

I opened my mouth to answer in the former but something stopped me. Probably my shitty morning and my desire not to be in the newspaper. "Sorry, just waiting on the console."

The guy slumped. "We have found no line sitters in this line. How is that possible?"

I winced in sympathy.

Then the woman, the photographer, shrugged. "It's a stupid fucking job, anyway."

This time, I just winced.

The guy huffed at his colleague. "Not the point. I'm trying to write an article here."

"About morons who can't get an actual job and the morons who pay them to wait on shit for them?" she sneered as they continued down the line.

I stared blindly at the back of the head of the person in front of me, trying not to let that nasty woman's words affect me.

But like I said.

Perfect storm.

I was more than relieved to walk into Rafe's apartment at five that night. In fact, as soon as he opened the door, I walked right into his arms. With zero hesitation, he swung the door shut and then wrapped his arms tight around me, pressing a kiss to my temple. "You okay?"

"Tough day." I sighed into him, breathing in his cologne and enjoying how safe he made me feel.

"You want to talk about it?"

"Maybe later." I pulled away, but only to push up onto my tip-toes to give him a quick kiss. "How was your day?"

His expression fell as he pressed his lips tight.

"Oh no. What happened?"

"My first surgery on a client's Maine Coon this morning went badly. As bad as it can go. We ran the tests to make sure she was strong enough and all her blood work and tests came back fine. But her heart gave out during surgery."

Tears burned my nose. "Rafe, I'm sorry." I hugged him again and his hold on me tightened. "My day was heaven in comparison."

He kissed my head again and gave me a quick squeeze before pulling back. "I'm all right. It comes with the territory."

"Doesn't mean it doesn't suck."

"Very true."

"Are you sure you're in the mood for this dinner?"

"I can't miss my dad's birthday."

"Right. What can I do to help?"

He reached for my hand. "Now that you ask, I've got something I want to show you."

Intrigued, I let him lead me into the bedroom. He stopped at the dresser on the opposite wall of the bed and pulled out the middle drawer. It was empty. "I cleared it out for you so you can keep some things here. Pajamas, underwear, et cetera." As if he hadn't dropped a relationship bomb, he strolled over to the large closet and opened the doors. "And I cleared some space here too for you. Obviously, later, when you move in, I'll clear out half." He shot me a smirk. "Or more if you need it. And . . ." He gestured for me to follow him into the bathroom, which I did barely breathing. Rafe stopped at the vanity and pulled open the drawer under the sink. One side of it was empty. "You can keep toiletries here too. Saves all the back and forth with overnight bags."

Rafe had cleared out two drawers and closet space for me.

I'd never had a drawer before.

I'd never had anyone who wanted me as a permanent fixture in their life in this way before. Roger, Jude, and Kendall didn't count. It was different.

Rafe wanted me in his space.

A lot.

And I wanted that, I realized. That crushing, overwhelming sensation in my chest wasn't panic this time. It was elation and terror that this might go away. That Rafe might go away.

I couldn't lose him.

Not now that I had him.

Wow. The realization stunned me.

"Is . . . are you okay?" Rafe suddenly looked unsure, and I hated that, because Rafe was not a man who ever looked uncertain about anything.

"I'm more than okay."

His grin was slow, sexy. "Yeah?"

I nodded, biting my lip to hold off a smile and failing. "Yeah."

Five seconds later, the man had me pressed up against the bathroom wall, kissing the living daylights out of me. My fingers curled into his shirt as my leg climbed his, trying to pull him closer. His erection ground into me and I gasped into his kiss.

Rafe suddenly broke it with a growl as his fingers dug into my waist with feeling. "We can't. No time."

"When we get back, I will show you my appreciation for the drawers and closet," I promised him.

"Never have I ever wanted a family dinner to be over before it was started as much as I want this one to be." He kissed me hard and then reluctantly released me.

The emotions, the need to dump those emotions into each other in a primal, physical way, hovered between us for the rest of the night.

Adding to the perfect storm.

IT HAPPENED AFTER WE LEFT THE RESTAURANT.

Greg Whitman's favorite restaurant was this tiny little seafood place in a port town near the Connecticut border. It had been a great night despite the shitty day and heavy unspoken emotion and sexual tension hanging between me and Rafe.

Pippa and Hugo's nanny stayed home to watch Charmaine, so it was an adults-only evening. Jen had driven everyone but me and Rafe to the restaurant, which meant she and Rafe weren't drinking, but the rest of us indulged in some wine.

Some more so than others.

"Some" being Hugo.

He'd made a couple of muttered comments throughout the evening after I'd spoken on whatever subject we were discussing, and I'd pressed a hand to Rafe's thigh every time he tensed at my side in reaction. My boyfriend had already had the worst day, and I didn't want him to allow himself to be goaded by his brother when he wasn't feeling himself.

Other than those moments, dinner was excellent. There was lots of laughter and storytelling. They loved having me as an audience to share family memories with, and I enjoyed being able to give them the chance to reminisce.

Pippa had asked about the job with her friend Pamela before our meal arrived, but Gigi had saved me from answering by interrupting to ask me another question. I knew it was deliberate when Gigi did it the second time Pippa asked, and I decided I pretty much adored Rafe's little sister.

The subject didn't come up again.

It was all good.

Until it wasn't.

We'd left the restaurant, Jen and Gigi talking over each other, and we all walked the short distance down the street to a small parking lot where Rafe had parked the Pontiac next to Jen and Greg's Range Rover.

"I think this was the best family dinner we've had in a long time," Greg announced.

"Happy birthday, Dad," Rafe said again, patting him affectionately on the shoulder.

Hugo, however, snorted. "Family?" He waved a hand at me, swaying a little, and I noted his bleary, red eyes. He was not sober. "She's not family. She's a fucking temporary joke my little brother is playing on us."

Shocked silence filled the lot and dread roiled in my gut as I slowly turned to Rafe.

"Hugo—" Greg started, but Rafe put a hand on his dad's shoulder, stopping him.

Rafe glowered at his brother and Pippa looked uneasy at Hugo's side. "What the hell is your problem?"

"I'm just saying what we're all thinking. She's a joke!" He gestured to me again. "Look, she's not good enough for this family. Pippa offered her a decent job and she turned her nose up at it and do you know why? Because she's a gold digger, bro. She's counting on your money to see her through. So you need to get your mind off your dick and recognize she's lazy, hippie trash—"

He never had time to finish his insults because Rafe bridged the distance between them and swung his fist so hard into his brother's face, Hugo hit the ground like someone had dropped an anvil on him. Gigi, Jen, and Pippa cried out, falling backward out of the way. I gasped, blood rushing in my ears as Rafe bent over his brother, gripping his chin, fist still primed. "You speak about Star like that again and I will fucking end you. Do you get me?"

Jen cried out again, but Greg wrapped his arms around Rafe and yanked him away. "That's enough, son, that's enough."

"Oh my God," I murmured, shaking from head to toe as Rafe shrugged off his dad's hold and turned to me, fury blazing in his eyes. Hugo groaned on the ground and turned his head to spit out blood.

"Let's go." Rafe grabbed my hand and pulled me toward the car.

"Rafe!" Jen called after him.

"Son," Greg tried too.

But Rafe wasn't listening to anyone.

We pulled out of the lot, Rafe staring stonily ahead while I shared a quick glance of worry with Gigi as we passed.

The initial shock of the event waned enough for my panic to rise.

Hugo had said some horrible things about me and I understood Rafe's passionate reaction, especially after the day he'd had . . . but I couldn't be the cause of discord among them.

I couldn't cause a rift within the Whitman family.

A family that was the antithesis of mine.

Who loved each other through everything.

And I think beneath Hugo's asshole remarks was a genuine desire to protect Rafe.

He thought that someone like me, with no direction, no ambition, was using his brother.

"Babe," I whispered.

Rafe glanced at me, and I caught the sorrow in his eyes before he turned back to the road. "Star, I am so sorry." His voice was guttural with the apology.

I reached over to squeeze his leg. "You don't need to apologize to me."

"What he said . . ." His hands squeezed around the steering wheel and I noted the swelling on the knuckles of his right hand. Shit. We'd need to get ice on that pronto.

"He was drunk."

"No one, I don't care who they are, will ever get away with speaking about you like that, drunk or sober."

"He's just trying to protect you."

Rafe shot me a bewildered look. "You're defending him?"

"No. Yes." I sighed heavily. "He shouldn't have said what he said, but I think he is just trying to protect you."

"He doesn't know you. He hasn't even tried to get to know you. You don't fit into a perfect little traditional box, so to him you don't make sense. What he doesn't realize is that you don't need to make sense to him. You need to make sense to me, and you fucking do."

At his renewed agitation, I smoothed my hand over his leg. "It's okay."

"It's not okay."

His phone rang from inside his jacket.

"That'll be your family."

"Fuck my family."

I sucked in a breath. "Rafe, you don't mean that."

He exhaled slowly. "No, I don't. But I can't talk to them right now. I need time. Space. *We* need time and space from them." He nodded like that was the answer.

For me, it most definitely wasn't.

I would not be responsible for driving a wedge between him and his family.

Not now, not ever.

RAFE LEFT FOR THE GYM EARLY THE NEXT MORNING, LIKE AL-ways, but I didn't fall back asleep like always. Instead, I got up, made a coffee, and stared blindly at the phone in my hand for a while.

Everything that had happened yesterday played over and over in my mind.

The derisive bakery owner.

The disdainful journalist.

Rafe needing my comfort.

Rafe giving me two drawers in his apartment.

The unspoken words hanging between us.

Hugo's vitriol because he thought I wanted to live a lazy life leeching off Rafe. All because he thought I lacked drive and ambition.

Seriousness.

About Rafe. About our future.

And Rafe wanted space from his family because of their lack of acceptance of me.

I couldn't let that happen.

Yet I also couldn't let go of Rafe.

I didn't think I ever could now.

Pippa's cell number stared up at me from my phone. I still had it from playing Merida at Charmaine's birthday party. Hitting the number, I held the phone to my ear, my heart thudding wildly in my chest.

"Philippa Whitman speaking," she answered sharply.

"Pippa. It's Star."

Silence, then a stilted "Good morning, Star."

"I wondered . . . I wondered if the job with your friend was still available?"

More silence and then what I thought might be an exhalation of relief. "Yes, most definitely."

"Then I'd like the chance to work with her."

"Wonderful. You and I should meet first thing Monday so I can give you all the background information, and I'll give Pamela your number so she can call you to arrange everything. You've . . . This is the right decision, Star."

"I just . . . I *am* serious about Rafe. About our future."

"I know. And Star, while I do not agree with how Rafe handled the situation last night, please know that I am sorry for what was said."

"*You* have nothing to apologize for." That would be her husband.

"Right." She seemed to hear my unspoken words. "Well, I'll text you the time and place for Monday. I'm very excited for you. For all of us. This should . . . I think this will help."

I knew exactly what she meant because it was exactly why I'd called her.

"Me too." I hung up and threw my phone on the couch. Wandering over to Rafe's balcony, I opened the doors and stepped out, the chilly September morning air waking up goose bumps on my bare arms and legs. Bracing myself against the balcony, I stared out at the Hudson.

Uncertainty rode me.

But only until I heard Rafe returning. The door behind me slid open and then the hot, slightly damp heat of him hit my back as he braced his hands on the balcony next to mine and rested his chin on my shoulder.

I relaxed into him, and he slid his arms around my waist to hold me tight to him. We didn't say a word as we just stared out at the sun spilling across the water, listening to the city already noisy with life.

Just like that, my uncertainty melted away.

For some people, I'd do anything.

Rafe, as it turned out, was now top of that list.

Chapter Twenty-Seven

> You free for lunch tomorrow? X

My thumbs hovered over my phone screen as I stared holes through Kendall's text. Though we'd shared texts and a quick phone call here and there, I hadn't seen my friends in two weeks. And I wasn't free tomorrow. Dammit.

Sighing, I quickly texted back, **Pamela is taking me to a client's house tomorrow, sorry. Rain check? Xx**.

"That was a big sigh," Rafe commented as he curled a hand around my foot and switched out of one app and into another on his TV.

We were sharing blissful alone time. No family, no friends, no work. Just him and me, hanging out on his couch on a Sunday, doing nothing. It was awesome.

You know, except for the fact that we should have been at his parents' house for dinner. Rafe had successfully distracted me from bringing up the subject that morning with multiple orgasms, and who was I to argue with that? Yet now the day was stretching on.

We'd had lunch, we'd talked about our weeks, and still the topic was avoided.

Enough was enough. I prodded his hip with my big toe. "Have you talked to your brother yet?"

His hand tightened around my ankle. "Nope." He brushed his thumb over my sole and I yanked my foot back at the tickle. Rafe shot me a boyish grin before settling on a showing of *Planet Earth II*.

"Avoider," I muttered.

His amusement died. "I have nothing to say to him until he apologizes to you. *If* he apologizes to you, I will apologize for hitting him."

I'd tried to feel out Pippa and Gigi about it, but Pippa, like her brother-in-law, avoided the subject, and Gigi just didn't have a clue. She did, however, note her full support of Rafe for smacking Hugo in the nose for the awful things he'd said about me. Gigi's voice had trembled when she said that, and I understood in that moment that she cared about me too, and Hugo had not only hurt me and Rafe, he'd hurt her.

It was humbling. And unsettling. Just another reason I was determined to get the Whitmans back together.

Before I could push Rafe a little more about Hugo, my phone rang. I glanced down, thinking it would be Kendall, and instead froze at the sight of the name blinking across my screen.

Dawn

What the ever-loving . . . I answered, feeling anxious. "Dawn?"

Rafe's attention whipped from the screen to me.

My mom, I mouthed just as she hissed out, "Did you know about this?"

Stunned at her tone, I jerked my chin in surprise. "Dawn? What?"

"Did. You. Know. About. This?" she repeated like I was stupid.

Irritated that after months of not hearing a word from her, this was the attitude she treated me to, I snapped, "Well, it would be great if you told me what 'this' is!"

Rafe sat up straight, lips pressed together in a grim line.

"I need your address," Dawn demanded instead.

"My address? What is going on?"

"What is going on is that I came home from my girls' trip to find myself booted out of my own home. That's what's going on!"

My heart raced. "What? Why?"

"So you know nothing about this nurse Arlo is shacking up with?"

Maggie? No-nonsense Maggie? "What?"

"You don't know." Dawn sighed heavily. "Arlo hired a nurse to help him out and she helped him out all right. Right out of his mind and into his bed. Now you know I don't care about Arlo having his flings. I'd be a hypocrite if I did. But this isn't a fling. He ended it with me. I'm out. She's in." Her voice cracked. "After decades to-gether, the man dumped me. Says they're in love." A sob echoed down the line and although I felt a pang of sympathy for her, I couldn't forget that she'd abandoned me, abandoned Arlo.

So the thought foremost in my mind was *Way to go, Arlo*. De-spite his crappy parenting skills, I was glad he'd found someone who cared about him back. It was typical of him to fall in love in just a few short weeks, but as long as he was happy, who was I to judge? It wasn't like I didn't know the feeling.

"Did you hear me, Star? I need a place to stay until I can figure out what to do with myself and my studio. The bastard has my stu-dio. You got a couch you can sleep on, don't you? It's just I need the bed. Bad back, you know."

Was she serious?

"Are you there? Look, Star, I don't have time to dillydally. I'm on a bus right now, heading your way."

"You're on a bus right now heading my way because you need somewhere to stay because Arlo dumped you for his nurse?" I repeated, for Rafe's sake.

Rafe's eyes widened.

"Is this a bad line or something or are you just tormenting me? I need your address."

"No."

"What?"

"No." I got up off the couch, my anger rushing out of me in a flood. "I haven't heard from you in months. My calls and texts have gone unanswered and for all I knew, you could have been dead. Arlo had heart surgery and you abandoned him, but what's new, since you abandoned me as soon as you popped me out. If Arlo is happy with someone who isn't a selfish asshole who tries to mask her selfishness beneath a facade of bohemian rebellion, then good for him. Go live your life free of us, Dawn. It's what you've always wanted, anyway. I'm done with you too." I hung up and spun around to stare at Rafe.

My phone shook in my trembling fingers and I was breathing a little too fast.

Rafe considered me carefully and slowly got to his feet. "Are you okay?"

I walked into his arms, face-planting on his chest and, like always, he wrapped me up tight. "I feel sick."

"Star—"

"But only because I hate being mean to anyone. She needed to hear what I had to say."

"She did," he murmured in agreement, his hands smoothing up and down my back in comfort. "You were amazing. I'm proud of you."

"Arlo left her. For Maggie."

"Wow. You sure you're okay?"

I pulled my head back to stare up at him. "I stopped trying to make that woman feel like family a long time ago. Yet somehow, every time she ignored a call or a text, it still hurt. But she'll never change, Rafe. She's not someone I can count on and I've realized that to be happy, I need to feel like I can count on the people in my life. So I'm good. Being done with her . . . it feels right. I feel free of her. She can't hurt me this way."

Cupping my face in his hands, Rafe bent his head to kiss me softly, lovingly. "If that's what you truly need, then you did the right thing. So proud of you, baby," he reiterated.

I grinned up at him, still a little wet-eyed, still feeling shaky from my confrontation, but not enough to stop myself from saying, "You will not follow my example with your brother. You and Hugo need to fix this."

He searched my face. "That is not your fault."

"It kind of is."

"Star—"

"Rafe. I can't be this issue between you two. Please."

"How are you not angrier at what he said?"

"I'm more hurt than angry. And I do know I deserve an apology. But hopefully that will come with time. For now, I just want you two talking again."

"I can't apologize to him." His gaze was fierce on mine. "If he doesn't apologize first to me, I'll always hold some resentment against him. We started disagreeing over things as soon as I told my family I wanted to be a vet instead of joining the family business. Hugo took it worse than my dad. The things we've disagreed over have been mostly stupid shit, other than the company. Until two weeks ago when, drunk or not, he *hurt* you. He crudely insulted a kind, sweet woman who means a great deal to me. That I won't let go."

The "means a great deal to me" elated me. We hadn't exchanged those three little words yet. I hadn't said them because I'd never said them to a guy before and it still freaked me out a little. Rafe hadn't said them yet and maybe *that* was why it still freaked me out a little.

Not to mention I was worried and frustrated that I'd made no progress in the reuniting of Rafe and Hugo Whitman.

PAMELA SMYTHE WAS TALENTED. I'D EXPECTED WHEN PIPPA had walked me into her friend's office two weeks ago that I'd find myself surrounded by modern, minimalist design, but what I discovered was a designer who really listened to her clients.

I'd checked out the big beautiful professional books in the reception area of the small firm that bound pages and pages of Pamela's designs. She could rock the industrial New York loft look and was a master at the maximalist style. The woman knew how to pull together colors and patterns that most people wouldn't think worked. Plus, she'd come up with some really cool and inventive storage solutions for small spaces, something she had to deal with a lot in New York City.

Was I thrilled to be the assistant to an interior designer? No. But I also didn't hate it.

I disliked my new wardrobe more than I disliked my new job.

Pippa had insisted that I needed to dress the part, and while I'd talked her out of the scary pencil skirts and blouses she'd tried to shove in my face on a forced shopping trip, I had compromised. Today, for instance, I wore wide-leg black pants and a violet-blue blouse with balloon sleeves. With my hair twisted up into a ponytail, I'd never looked more chic and I'd never looked less like myself.

When Rafe had stepped out of the shower that morning, I'd been dressed and ready to go since Pamela needed me at the office early for a meeting her would-be client had to squeeze in before work. Rafe had frozen at the sight of me, a towel around his waist, as his gaze drifted down my body and back up again.

Did I mention I was wearing heels? Not wedges. Heels.

At the inexplicable look that crossed his face, nervousness built in me. "Do I look okay? This is one of the outfits Pippa and I chose."

I swore I saw the man frown before he turned his back on me. "You look great, baby. You always do."

Pamela had noted my outfit with approval and my response was almost as lukewarm as Rafe's had been.

There was gratitude in me, I promise. I knew that without Pippa's connections, there was no way I'd have gotten this job. I was making more than what I'd made with my two jobs combined and I had great health insurance.

Yet I missed not knowing what the day would bring. I missed reading a handful of books a week. The conversations I had with strangers while I waited in line. The smiles on kids' faces when they thought their favorite Disney princess had really turned up to their party.

I missed my friends.

Now I scheduled Pamela's meetings and managed her calendar. I answered phone calls and emails and relayed messages to my boss. I'd even booked flights and accommodation for her because she was visiting a client out of state. Then there were the many coffee runs. The upside to that was the office was close to Rafe's clinic, and I often had time to swing by with coffee for him and his staff too.

The most interesting part of my job was the meetings with clients. Pamela liked me in on a lot of them to take notes, and I enjoyed watching her ask clever questions that helped her figure out her clients' tastes.

I reminded myself of the positives because I wasn't sure that the almost claustrophobic feeling that came over me every time I stepped into the office wasn't just me being a spoiled brat who needed to grow up.

By midmorning the coffee run came around and as I waited in

line for my boss's order and coffee for Rafe and his colleagues, I stared at my phone. I hadn't heard from Dawn, but I didn't expect to ever. Honestly, I was part convinced she had a narcissistic personality, because nothing was ever her fault. There was no miraculous numbness to the pain Dawn could inflict, but I felt free of her, finally, and I was holding on to that feeling.

Kendall, however, hadn't replied to my text yesterday, and that did bother me. It wasn't like her, so I'd shot her a text this morning asking if she was okay and she'd replied, **All good. Rain check, definitely.** But there were no kisses, and she usually left me kisses at the end.

Maybe I was just reading too much into an "x," but I worried I was neglecting my friendships in all the new changes I was making. Deciding I needed to make time for them this weekend, I texted back, **The three of us, this Sunday, lunch? Xx.**

Kendall responded immediately. **I'll ask the guys if they're free but I'm in xx.**

I relaxed at the return of the kisses and nodded to myself. Effort. I just needed to make an effort to see them.

Feeling lighter, I strolled into Rafe's clinic five minutes later with all the coffee and a big smile on my face. Finn's eyes lit up at the sight of me, and without even saying hello he announced, "I'll let Rafe know you're here." Then he hurried out of the reception area to do just that.

I dropped the coffees on the counter and turned to see a woman, maybe a few years older than me, dressed chicly in cigarette pants, a short-sleeved silk blouse, and stilettos that would break my ankles. Attached to the lead in her hand was the cutest Pomeranian I'd ever seen. "Can I say hello?" My eyes trained on the groomed-to-perfection white fur ball.

"Yes, she's friendly," the woman replied.

Lowering to my haunches, I held out my hand so the pom could sniff my fingers. She did so and, after a few seconds, gave my fingers a swipe with her little tongue. "Oh, hello there, aren't you beautiful?" I scratched gently behind her ears and she panted happily up at me. "What's her name?"

"Diana."

My lips twitched at the name. "Of course. Hello, Diana, aren't you just the cutest? Look at you," I cooed over her as she lapped up my attention.

"I see you've met Diana."

I was so busy with the dog that I hadn't heard Rafe approach. Looking up, I found him towering over me in a nice shirt and suit pants, white coat on. My sexy vet. I gave Diana one last scratch and stood up to greet him. "She's kind of irresistible."

"Hmm." He wore a small smile as he leaned in to brush his lips over mine. "You'd know all about that."

I grinned, pleased. Rafe pressed his hand to my lower back as he turned me to Diana's owner. "Ms. Prescott, this is my girlfriend, Star."

At first, I didn't understand why he was introducing me to a patient's owner until I saw the look on her face. She was not happy. In fact, she appeared as if she'd just eaten something really, really sour.

Ah.

This had to be one of the overzealous owners who had a crush on my boyfriend. Usually, I didn't allow myself to think of the people who walked into Rafe's life and drooled over him, but I hated the idea of someone flirting with him and making him uncomfortable. Especially a patient's owner.

I leaned into him. "Brought coffee."

"You're wonderful." We turned, giving the stony-faced Ms. Prescott our backs, to find Finn eyeing the coffee on his counter like a dog eyeing the food his humans had told him he couldn't have but had been stupid enough to leave lying in front of him.

Laughing to myself at the thought, I handed Finn his coffee. "There you go."

I gave Rafe his Americano, and he promised to get Owen's latte to him.

Finn groaned after taking a sip and met my gaze. "I love you."

Rafe sighed unhappily at my side. "You don't love my girlfriend, Finn, because then I'd have to fire you."

Finn's expression froze in horror.

Shoving Rafe, I tutted. He knew his vet nurse was sensitive. "You're awful. And now I have to go."

He flashed me a boyish grin before he bent his head to capture my mouth in a much deeper kiss. So deep, my knees actually trembled and I had to press a hand to his chest for support. When he broke the kiss, he murmured against my lips, "Thanks for the coffee."

I stroked his chest affectionately. "Anytime."

Though it was a sweet moment, one of many with Rafe, I couldn't help but feel a little melancholy as I strolled back to work. Because . . . why *hadn't* he told me he loved me yet?

Weren't we there?

He had to know that with my issues, I'd need him to say it first, whether or not that was fair.

There was no way I could hand my heart over to another person again who might crush it without being certain I had their heart in return.

But maybe it was the same for Rafe?

Dammit.

Or maybe this wasn't even about Rafe. Maybe my conversation with my mom the day before had affected me more than I knew. Maybe, maybe, maybe.

All I knew was that I hadn't felt like myself lately.

Chapter Twenty-Eight

THE FOLLOWING SATURDAY, RAFE WAS WORKING AT THE clinic and Pamela had asked me to accompany her to a client's apartment in Brooklyn. I wasn't supposed to work Saturdays, but with Rafe working, I decided it was worth it to do some overtime and try to learn as much about the interior design business as possible.

My efforts to reconcile Rafe with Hugo all week had stalled because Rafe had returned to the Mr. Grumpy Broody bastard I'd first met anytime I brought up his brother's name. Hence why I put my attempts on pause.

Instead, I spent the entire afternoon discussing white with Pamela's client. White everything. White walls, white floors, white furniture. White, white, white. In my head, I just kept screaming *why, why, why?* Pamela did her best to convince the client to add pops of color, but they were pretty sold on a life of stress and misery, trying to keep their entire apartment white. It was exhausting and depressing. I needed color in my life. If I had to decorate homes in nothing but white for the rest of my life, I'd be miserable. I knew it was an overexaggeration of the situation, but it was an unhappy afternoon for me.

Until I returned to Rafe's apartment that night and he surprised me with some news.

"Hugo called."

I waited with bated breath for him to say more, my relief desperate to be set free. "Okay?"

Rafe frowned. "He wants me at Mom and Dad's tomorrow. He wants to apologize and to talk."

I sagged with relief. "Rafe, that's great."

"We'll see."

"Rafe—"

"No. We'll see. I'm not just going to forgive him if his apology is disingenuous."

"Well, you'll find out tomorrow."

"You're coming, right?" He pulled me into his arms, bending to press his forehead to mine. "I want to see him apologize to your face . . . and also I just . . . I need you there."

Lunch with my friends was set for tomorrow and I now hadn't seen them in three weeks.

Shit.

However, I couldn't leave Rafe to face this alone when he'd asked me. When he'd told me he *needed* me. Squeezing his waist, I whispered, "Of course I'll be there."

RAFE LEFT HALF AN HOUR LATER TO PICK UP PIZZA FROM A place we liked down the street, and I took that opportunity to step out onto his balcony to call Roger to explain why I was canceling.

"I feel awful and I really miss you guys, but Rafe needs me to be there tomorrow," I rushed to say after explaining the situation.

"Star, I get it. Don't worry. We'll do lunch next weekend," Roger offered easily.

"You're sure you're not mad?"

"We do miss you, but sometimes timing is just the worst."

"I love you guys."

"We know. We love you too. Let me know how it goes tomorrow."

Even though Roger's words were right and what I needed to hear, I still got off that call feeling like things were out of whack with us.

Or maybe things were just out of whack with me.

"WHAT THE HELL ARE YOU WEARING?" RAFE SCOWLED AT ME.

I felt my cheeks heat at his snotty tone. "Uh, thanks."

He exhaled slowly, scrubbing a hand over his face. "I didn't mean it like that."

"Then how did you mean it?"

Gesturing to me, he shrugged. "We're going to my parents' house. There's no reason for you to don your office costume."

Costume?

I looked down at the forest-green wide-leg pants and cream blouse with ruffled neck. Instead of heels, I wore my wedges. "I just thought it might be better if I show up like this."

"Better for whom?" Rafe crossed his bedroom and cupped my face in his hands. "Baby, I want you to be you."

But being me had caused a rift with his family.

I didn't even know who I was these days.

Right?

I could be this person in the fancy chic clothes.

Right?

"I'm comfortable," I lied.

Frustration hardened my boyfriend's features and he released me. "Okay. Let's go."

IT FELT LIKE FOREVER SINCE WE'D BEEN TO JEN AND GREG'S home. It was now the end of September and chilly enough that I wore a sweater over my blouse. Soon, the many trees surrounding their sprawling home would change colors. At some point during my relationship with Rafe, I'd gotten used to the Whitmans' home. It would never be the kind of house I could live in, but it had begun to symbolize familial familiarity. Today was the first day since that first dinner that I felt uncomfortable there.

Even with my hand clasped tight in Rafe's as we strolled up the front walk.

"Are you okay?" I quietly asked.

He squeezed my hand. "I'm good. You?"

"Nervous," I admitted.

"I hate that," he sighed. "I hate that my fucking brother has made you nervous to come to my parents' house."

"Rafe—"

"It's fine. I'm fine." He squeezed my hand again. "Let's just get this over with."

As soon as we walked into the house, Jen and Greg hurried into the foyer to meet us. Their smiles were strained as they greeted us. Immediately, Greg said to Rafe, "Hugo's in my office. Come with me, son."

Jen looped her arm through mine. "I've got Star," she reassured Rafe.

Still, he looked at me for confirmation. "I'm okay."

Rafe nodded but gave his mom a penetrating look, which she answered with a nod of her own. Then Greg led him out of sight.

Jen's gaze took me in as she turned me in her arms, and something like surprise lit her expression. "You look different, sweetheart. Good, but different."

"Oh. Pippa helped me pick out a wardrobe for work."

Jen seemed bemused by that as she eyed me. "Did she? You'll need to tell me all about it. I've missed you. And on that note"—she cupped my face disarmingly similarly to Rafe—"please know that I am so sorry for the way my son spoke to you. That was not okay, and I was very upset at him and hurt on your behalf."

God, Rafe's mom was *nice*. "Thanks, Jen. But I'm all right, honestly. I'm more worried about Rafe and Hugo. I don't want them to fall apart over this. I . . . I don't have a family like yours." My eyes burned from the tears I forced back. "You have such a nice family and I don't want to mess that up."

"Oh, Star." Her eyes glimmered with emotion. "This is not your fault, and you'll soon understand why. And thank you. I want you to know that I am so glad Rafe found you. I always hoped he'd end up with someone kind and warm, and my wish was granted many times over with you. You make him so happy."

My heart lurched in my chest. "Really?"

She beamed. "Really. Now come. Gigi has missed you and we both want to hear all about this new job. The most important thing being, do you like it?"

What had been a genuine smile on my face strained a little, but I followed her through the house, intent on reassuring her that all was well in Star Shine Meadows's world.

WHILE GIGI, JEN, PIPPA, AND CHARMAINE DID A GOOD JOB trying to distract me from the hour-long conversation happening in Greg's office, I couldn't stop my mind from wandering toward that room. Why was this taking so long? What was going on?

The mystery and intrigue only heightened when Rafe appeared on his own and asked me to come talk with him in private. He led me all the way upstairs to his old bedroom without saying a word.

"What's with the suspense?" I tried to tease as he closed the door behind us.

Rafe didn't smile. My pulse raced.

He sighed heavily, wearily, worry puckering his brow, and that shut me up.

Gesturing to the bed, we both sat down on its edge, our bodies turned toward one another. What the hell was going on?

"I wanted to explain everything to you first before Hugo makes his apology to you. I have his and my father's permission to share what's been going on, so you have some context."

Oh crap. "Okay."

Rafe squeezed his eyes closed and then opened them on another sigh. It was like he was trying to expel the tension out of his body with those exhales. "Hugo has been stressed for months, which is probably why he's been acting more of an ass than usual."

"Stressed about what?"

"Things have been difficult in the shipping industry over the past few years and Hugo hasn't been successful in trying to keep the business out of danger."

Oh no. My expression fell. "Rafe . . . I . . . what does that mean?"

"We're vulnerable. Mercurious is vulnerable. We're losing too many contracts because of new domestic shipping regulations. A Chinese company with a lot more clout than us wants to buy us out, and Hugo thinks he might have to sell. Our trust funds are safe, I'm okay financially, and my parents' retirement fund is safe, but in Hugo's mind, that isn't enough. He was carrying the weight of that. Stupid. Because all that matters is that my family wouldn't be living in the gutter, which we'd be far from doing. His priorities . . ." Rafe shook his head. "Hugo has a different idea of poverty than the rest of us."

"I see." I bet he did.

"Yeah. Anyway, I don't think it was just about losing his, *our*, wealth."

"He didn't want to fail your dad," I surmised. "He didn't want to be the one at the helm when all your dad's hard work sank."

Rafe looked so sad. "Exactly."

"Poor Hugo." I never thought I'd say that.

My boyfriend shook his head in amazement. "You are . . . where did you come from?"

Warmth spread across my chest as I reached for his hand. "What happens now?"

"He finally confessed everything to my dad, but my dad, being my dad, already knew the company was in trouble. He was just waiting for Hugo to come to him. I wish he hadn't. Hugo has been a bastard to everyone because of this stress. Including you."

"Does your dad have a solution?"

Rafe nodded. "Selling Mercurious. Dad thinks they can open it to bids. We won't get what it's worth because it's carrying some debt from the last few years, but a bigger company could integrate it into theirs and make bank, so we'll still make a lot of money off the sale. The hard part is negotiating terms for our employees and making sure they're taken care of. That's important to all of us."

Because they were good people. Even Hugo, apparently. "What will Hugo do after the sale?"

"Dad would like to broker a deal that keeps Hugo on in some capacity."

"Right. Is Hugo better for telling the truth?"

"Oh yeah. He apologized to me and I believe him. And he wants to apologize to you."

"He doesn't have to."

"Yes, he fucking does."

My lips twitched at Rafe's stern pronouncement. "All right."

. . .

OUR DRIVE HOME WAS SUBDUED. JUST LIKE DINNER.

While Hugo had apologized profusely to me and said, despite his stress at work, there was no excuse for the things he'd called me, there was still a weight on his shoulders. It was visible. Perhaps the worst of it had lifted, but I sensed a deep sadness in him. I think his family did too, because the conversation was quiet and stilted.

Even Charmaine asked why we were all acting strange.

Once we returned to Rafe's apartment I half expected Rafe to collapse on the couch and brood, but he didn't.

He locked the door behind us, met my gaze with a heated look that surprised me, and took me by the hand. Heart racing, I let him lead me into the bedroom.

Rafe whipped off his sweater and threw it on the floor. I instinctively reached out to smooth my hands over his pecs and down his strong abs. Rafe took me by the wrists to stop me, but only so he could push the sweater off my shoulders and slip his fingers under the hem of my blouse to pull it up and off. When he dropped it to the floor, he muttered, "Good riddance."

"What—" My question was swallowed in his kiss. My breasts crushed to his chest. He held me in his arms and moved his mouth over mine in a long, slow, delicious kiss.

My emotions from the last few weeks had been sitting on a ledge and for some reason, the way Rafe kissed me tonight tipped those emotions over the edge. They fed into the kiss as I wound my arms around his neck and curled my fingers into his soft, thick hair. Our tongues stroked in lazy exploration.

Rafe moved me back in the bed's direction, and our lips didn't part until he lifted me and then dropped me on my back across the middle of the mattress.

I lay there, panting, wanting to be connected to him in every way

I could be. He kept me trapped in his gaze as he unbuttoned his suit pants. I drank in every inch of him as he pushed them and his underwear down, standing proudly naked in front of me.

After we'd each gotten our health checks completed, I started taking birth control, which meant we'd begun having sex without a condom. I'd never had sex without a condom, but there was something thrilling about it with Rafe. While I was pretty sure it felt physically better for Rafe, it felt better on an emotional level for me. I liked that there were no barriers between us.

Once he was beautifully naked, he reached out to unbutton my pants and slide the zipper down. I tingled in anticipation, my nipples hardening as he yanked the pants, along with my underwear, down my legs.

"Take off your bra."

I happily obliged, throwing it toward the floor.

Rafe had a way of looking at me like he was seeing me for the first time. I shivered at the stark longing and lust glittering in his denim-blue eyes. Leaning over me, he grazed his knuckles across my stomach, his eyes following his fingers as they trailed along the bottom of my belly. I sucked in my breath at the sensation. My nipples peaked and I squirmed, trying to move his hand lower.

Rafe's gaze only intensified. Then his hand flattened on my stomach, and he smoothed it upward slowly, heading between my breasts. His touch was exploring, but the possessive look in his eyes as he held my gaze made me shiver with unexpected pleasure.

Then he stroked my breasts softly, his thumbs brushing over my nipples. Rafe still held my eyes as he gently, torturously teased my breasts. "I love these."

I smiled smugly. "They love you back."

Rafe grinned. "I'm well aware."

"Cocky." My attention dropped to his thick arousal. "Seriously, seriously cocky."

He leaned over, his erection pushing insistently against my belly, and his lips whispered over mine. "Sometimes I'm at work and I'll catch your scent out of nowhere and I'll remember going down on you that morning or fucking you the night before and there I am. A grown man. At work. Hard for just the memory of you."

"Rafe," I gasped.

"Do you think about me?" He squeezed my breasts hard, sensation shooting between my legs. "Do I make you wet just thinking about me?"

"Yes," I answered truthfully. "At the most inopportune moments too."

At that, he grinned in delight. "Good."

Then he pushed my thighs open, and he thrust his cock against me. I groaned, feeling a flush of heat move up my body from deep and low in my belly.

My thighs parted wider. I needed him inside me. Fast. Hard.

But Rafe was in the mood to make love tonight.

He kissed me, and I wrapped my arms around his strong back, trying to draw him closer. His lips moved down my chin, trailing in soft caresses along my throat and breasts.

If Rafe was in the mood for lovemaking, then I wanted to give that back to him. A lot was going on with his family right now, and if sex with me could bring him comfort, then I'd give that my all.

"Will you lie on your back for me?" I whispered.

Rafe lifted his head at the request, eyes searching mine. Then he moved, shifting off me to lie on his back.

I moved to straddle him, rubbing against his erection while I trailed my fingers lightly down his abs. His hard stomach tightened under my touch, and there was an answering pulse between my legs. Rafe clasped my hips in his hands and I moaned as I slid over him.

I kissed him, wet and deep, as I rolled my hips languidly against his arousal. His groans filled my mouth, making it difficult to break away, but I wanted to explore. I kissed my way down his throat, my lips trailing kisses down his chest. Rafe's big hands stroked me— caressing my back, my breasts, my sides, my stomach, and coasting down to cup my ass. He squeezed it, and my hips rolled over him instinctively. I gasped his name and his fingers were almost bruising as he guided me over him again.

"Rafe," I whimpered. "Wait."

He loosened his grip on me in answer.

I returned my attention to his nipple and sucked it between my teeth. His cock jerked against me. Feeling him taut with tension as my mouth continued its downward path, tasting every inch of his sculpted stomach, I delighted in it. I enjoyed making him wild with need.

Speaking of. I slid farther down his body and took him into my mouth.

Rafe's groan filled the bedroom, and my lower belly clenched with desire.

I wrapped my hand around the base of him and fisted it while I sucked. I found my rhythm quickly, growing more and more turned on as Rafe's pleasure intensified. His chest heaved and his thighs were taut as his hips pumped upward, thrusting in and out of my mouth and fist.

"Star, baby." He gasped, and I squeezed my thighs together, desperate for my own relief. "Stop . . . baby . . . stop."

I lifted my head at his rough plea and straddled him. "You want inside me instead?"

"I *need* inside you instead." He dipped his fingers between my legs, feeling how ready I was. "And you need me too."

I did need him.

That was what was so scary.

I wrapped my hands around him, bringing him to my center,

and pushed down on him. He filled me up so full, so overwhelming, every time.

"Star." He grunted, face etched with pleasure-pain as he grabbed my hips, his fingers biting into my skin, and my eyes flew open at his touch. "You're so tight. You feel so fucking good every time." His words echoed my own thoughts. "How's that possible? How's it possible you feel this good?" He didn't want answers, he was just muttering in mindless arousal.

I slowly rode him.

There was nothing else in the world but Rafe's eyes gazing into mine, the feel of his fevered skin beneath my touch, his hands gripping my hips, guiding me up and down him, the sounds of my pants, his groans.

The tension coiled tighter and tighter inside me, but I forced myself to ride him slowly. To love him with my body. Rafe must have had the same thought because suddenly I was flipped onto my back.

"Babe," I gasped, the word swallowed in his deep, passionate kiss. I curled my fingers in his hair, kissing him back like I needed his kiss to breathe. A hand slipped between my legs. His thumb circled my clit, and I whimpered into his mouth. Rafe took over the kiss while I sighed and panted and murmured his name, my hips pushing into his touch.

My thighs trembled.

My stomach tightened.

Rafe's thumb slicked over me and took me right over the edge.

As my body succumbed to the powerful orgasm, Rafe scattered kisses down my body, stopping a while at my breasts to kiss and lick and suck. I was primed from that alone as he kissed his way down my stomach and then pushed open my thighs.

My back bowed off the bed as his tongue circled my clit. I watched him between my legs, his eyes on mine as he sucked on my clit, licked, thrust his tongue into me, all until I was a writhing, flushed puddle of want beneath him. Our neighbors beyond the bedroom wall probably heard my cry of release as my climax hit.

I'd barely recovered when Rafe crawled over me and pinned my hands above my head. Face etched with hard desire, he thrust inside me, and my inner muscles clamped around him greedily.

"Fuck!" Rafe pumped slow but hard, his fingers lacing with mine and holding me down so I was completely at his mercy. To my amazement, the pressure grew inside me again.

I moved my hips against his drives, and this seemed to lead to his complete loss of control.

Rafe released my hands and got onto his knees, gripping my thighs, opening them wider. And then he pounded into me. Holy shit. I teetered on the edge of another epic orgasm.

"Take everything." Rafe's words were guttural, rough, husky, sexy. "I'm yours, baby, take everything I have."

I came on a scream.

And I knew it was his words that pushed me over the edge.

Rafe's eyes widened as I squeezed around him, the orgasm hitting me fiercely and doing so for him too. He made a choked sound of awe and his hips stuttered, the muscles in his neck corded, and his teeth gritted. Then he collapsed over me as he throbbed with release inside me.

"Fuck, Star, fuck." His chest heaved and he released his bruising grip on my thighs to fall to my side. Then I was in his arms again as we tried to catch our breath.

"You understand, right?" Rafe asked in a quiet rumble after a few minutes had passed.

I lifted my head to meet his gaze. Because . . . understand what?

He saw my confusion and I thought I saw a flash of disappointment in his face, but if it had been there, he kissed me as if it hadn't.

"Rafe?" I whispered once our lips parted.

"Go to sleep, baby. It's been a long day."

Because it had been just that, I closed my eyes and decided to dwell only on the bliss of our spectacular lovemaking, and not on the sensation of dread that had been desperate to take over me for the last few weeks.

Chapter Twenty-Nine

RAFE'S KISS GOOD-BYE THAT MORNING HAD BEEN A QUICK
peck of the lips in his kitchen before I slipped out to make the early
meeting Pamela had with another client. The whole nine to five,
Monday to Friday, was a sham. For the last six weeks, since starting
with Pamela, I'd worked all kinds of hours.

I'd seen my friends once in that whole time, and I hadn't spoken
to any of them in a week because their texts were as dry and as
empty as Rafe's kiss.

Rafe was pulling away from me.

Taking on more hours at the clinic, while I took on more hours in
the office.

Sometimes we were like ships passing in the night, except we
stopped for sex. The sex was still awesome. But it seemed like it was
the only time we really connected. Like . . . it was the only thing
keeping us connected.

"A seven a.m. start again?" Rafe commented that morning upon
returning from the gym to find me stepping out of the shower.

"Yeah."

"You know you don't have to stay in this job if you don't want to," he'd remarked.

"It's fine." I'd shrugged.

"Do you even like it?"

"Yeah, it's fine."

His expression had hardened in that way that made my stomach twist and, without another word, he'd slipped past me into the bathroom.

What could I tell him? Pippa, Jen, even Gigi, they were so happy I was doing well in this job with Pamela. Things were better between Hugo and Rafe, and Hugo had made no snide comments toward me. In fact, he'd been perfectly pleasant. We were all getting along great.

Mercurious had gone to auction and the original company interested in purchasing it won, so the takeover would be underway soon. The Whitmans were at peace with it, which mattered more than anything else.

I couldn't rock the boat by quitting the job with Pamela.

Though it wouldn't matter about any of it if Rafe was losing interest in me. I was just so confused. When we made love, it didn't feel like he wasn't interested in me, but . . . we didn't talk anymore. I couldn't because I was afraid of what I might say and he . . . he just seemed frustrated with me all the time. Maybe the shine had worn off Star Shine Meadows after all.

I was lonely.

"What do you think? Star?"

A hand waved in front of my face and I blinked rapidly, coming out of my depressed musings to find Pippa staring at me across the small bistro table, wide-eyed. Pamela sat next to her, one elegant eyebrow raised in concern. We'd squeezed in a quick coffee break with Pippa this morning.

"What?" I stared at them and then shook my head. "Sorry. I was somewhere else."

Pippa waved off my daydreaming. "It's fine. We were just saying we think you should change your name."

I laughed softly. "Right."

"No. I'm serious," Pippa said, *seriously.*

My pulse increased as that knot of dread in my gut tightened. "Change my name?"

"Yes. Star just isn't a name that people take seriously. You're a professional now. You should have a strong name."

"Meadows is a little wishy-washy too," Pamela added.

"Oh, but that shouldn't be an issue." Pippa shrugged. "She'll be a Whitman soon enough."

"Really?" Pamela smiled at me. "Things are that serious between you and Rafferty?"

"Of course they are. Rafe is nothing if not a serial monogamist. He has an MO. Meets girl, practically has her living with him within the first few weeks, then actually living with him within a few months. He usually dates the same woman for several years and has never proposed, but he's getting on a bit and, this time around, I can see him popping the question soon."

Wait. What? Reeling, I practically wheezed out, "His MO?"

Pippa frowned. "Yes, Mr. Serial Monogamy."

So she was telling me that all the exciting rush of wanting to be with each other all the time wasn't because it was *me* Rafe was with. It was because that was just who Rafe was in a relationship?

I wasn't special? He hadn't embroiled me so deeply into his life because I differed from the women who had come before me? It was because it was his MO?

I sucked in a breath as I remembered our conversation in his car that night after family dinner. He'd reiterated that he'd never loved Camille or any of the women he'd dated. The only woman, outside of family members, he'd ever said "I love you" to was his high school sweetheart.

Never since.

He hadn't told me either.

Right.

Okay then.

Having no clue that my heart was cleaving in half before her, Pippa leaned toward me. "Now, what about Sarah?"

"Excuse me?" I still wasn't over the devastating implication that I was just a cycle in Rafe's relationship routine. That I *wouldn't* be the one he said those three little words to. Because surely he'd know by now. He'd have said the words by now.

"Sarah instead of Star. Sarah Whitman is a strong name. And of course you'll need to drop the middle name entirely."

"Oh God yes," Pamela agreed.

As I listened to Pippa and my boss prattle on about my name change, I envisioned myself as Cartoon Star, transforming from a cute ray of sunshine into a storm cloud, until eventually my cloud filled with so much water, it didn't rain . . . it just exploded until there was nothing left of Star Shine Meadows.

"DO YOU WANT TO TALK ABOUT IT?" RAFE ASKED ABRUPTLY AS we rode in the back of the taxi that was taking us to Brooklyn.

Rain pelted down outside as we made the journey to the engagement party we'd been invited to. It was hosted by Rafe's friend from college, Nick, and Nick was getting married to his best friend Josh. Rafe told me they were childhood friends who'd only recently realized they were so much more, and usually I'd be excited to talk to them and find out about their romantic story. However, I felt a strange kind of numb as we sat in our nice party clothes, approaching our destination.

"About what?" I watched the rain-slicked streets pass by.

"You've been quiet all night. In fact, you've been quiet for weeks."

I looked at him. Pot meet kettle. "You're one to talk."

Rafe frowned. "What does that mean?"

"Just that you've been quiet too. Distant."

He scowled. "*I've* been distant?"

"We're here," the cabdriver announced as he slowed to a stop outside the building.

Thankfully, we didn't have time to pick up our conversation because we bumped into Owen and his date, Nadine, inside the building's foyer. Owen had been dating Nadine for three weeks, and I'd bumped into her once at the clinic.

Rafe and Owen made small talk about work while I complimented Nadine on her earrings and she complimented me on the crippling stilettos I wore. Pippa had picked out a few new dresses for me to wear at fall events, and I'd donned one of them for this party. It was a green silk dress with a 1940s silhouette that was actually kinda cute. I didn't mind it as much as some of the other crap I wore lately.

It was October now, so I wore a light coat that I wore to the office most days.

Wow, just hearing myself say that sentence in my head was weird.

The next twenty minutes passed in no time as Rafe introduced me to Nick and Josh and about a million other people whose names I couldn't remember. They were a fun group, though, and I relaxed enough to enjoy myself. The couple lived in a large apartment, but it was traditional, with a separate living room, kitchen, bedrooms, and bathrooms. Soon, all the social spaces filled up with guests.

Including Rafe's ex-girlfriend Camille Westmoreland.

She hadn't approached us yet, but she'd lifted a glass of champagne in Rafe's direction.

"What is she doing here?" I frowned.

Rafe shrugged. "She became good friends with Nick when she and I were together."

Great.

A little while later, I excused myself to use the bathroom. There was a small line, so I had to wait. By the time I returned to where I'd left Rafe in the living room, maybe only ten minutes had passed.

Yet that was enough time for Camille to make her move.

I hadn't forgotten her catty comment the last time we'd met. How she would wait for Rafe to get serious about his life. Like *I* wasn't serious.

Apparently I still wasn't. I'd tried a new job, dressing the part, but Pippa still wanted me to change my name. It was actually unbelievable.

I reminded myself I was doing this for Rafe, for the Whitmans, and for me. I'd never felt about anyone the way I felt about Rafe, and I also longed to be a part of a family like his. It was a secret longing, one I didn't even know existed inside me until I met them and fell in love with the idea.

I'd twisted myself up like a pretzel to keep the dream going.

My so-called boyfriend, who was part of that dream, was standing laughing with his ex-girlfriend while she played with the lapel on his suit jacket. What happened to his disdain for her? Last time we met her he could barely utter two words because wasn't this the woman who cheated on him?

My pulse raced as I studied the way Rafe tilted his head toward her in a familiar way. It was to hear her better. She got close to speak into his ear, her hand flattening on his chest (my chest!), and Rafe smiled at whatever she said.

The last time we bumped into Camille, he had no time for her, and now that things were dicey between him and me, he was flirting with her?

Had he moved Camille into his life as quickly as he'd moved me? Would I be the next woman he dated for years without really being in love with and then dump me to move on to the next to see if she sparked that elusive feeling in him?

As if he sensed me, Rafe's eyes flew across the room and he saw me.

I stared at him in open disgust and turned on my heel. I needed a drink and the bar was in the kitchen.

Jealousy and hurt burned in my chest as I pushed my way to the kitchen counter where the hired bartenders mixed cocktails. I slapped a hand down on the counter to get their attention. "Whiskey, whatever you got, straight up."

A hand slid across my back and I jerked in surprise to find it was a stranger I'd pushed past to get to the bar. He leaned into me, his hand pressing deeper into my back. "Drowning your sorrows, gorgeous?"

"Yup, sure am." The bartender pushed the shot glass of whiskey toward me. "Thanks." I shoved a tip toward him as I took the glass and threw back the whiskey.

It burned like a motherfucker down my throat and then exploded in a cascade of heat across my chest. "Another."

"Make that two." The guy said. He still had his hand on my back. It felt icky and presumptuous, but I didn't shove him off. Rafe had let Camille put her hands all over him, after all. If I were the Star Shine Meadows of six months ago, I wouldn't have given a rat's ass if a handsome stranger came on to me while I was on a date with another man, because that Star had smart rules against monogamy!

"Friend of the groom or the groom?" I inquired.

The stranger laughed. "I work with Josh. I'm Brent."

"She doesn't care and get your hand off her."

I stiffened at Rafe's voice, and Brent and I turned to look up at my boyfriend, whose face was harsh with anger.

Brent dropped his hand, muttered something unintelligible under his breath, and hurried away.

Scaredy-cat.

"Whiskey," the bartender said.

I whirled around and threw back the second shot.

I felt Rafe's heat at my back and then his lips near my ear as he demanded, "What the hell are you doing?"

"I'm drinking." I shrugged without looking and silently ordered another whiskey from the bartender. But the bartender was looking at Rafe, and whatever he saw there made him turn away to serve someone else. I glared up at Rafe. "Are you just determined to ruin my night?"

His hand wrapped tight around my biceps. "Come with me."

Not wanting to make a scene at his friend's party, I bristled but allowed Rafe to lead me out of the kitchen. To my surprise, he led me out of the apartment.

"Where are we going?"

"Home."

Home?

Icy silence settled between us as Rafe dropped my hand to hit the button for the elevator. As we got on and it descended to the first floor, I felt an invisible pressure on my chest as the tension between us grew with our silence.

"Rafe?"

"We'll talk at home," he bit out, as he pulled out his phone. "I'm booking an Uber."

"So we're just not going to talk until we're back at the apartment?" I seethed as my panic increased.

Rafe cut me a dark look. "We're not doing this in public."

My stomach somersaulted. Right.

If I could have smooshed myself up closer to the passenger-side door of the Uber that arrived, I would have. Anything to be sitting as far away as possible from the man who was about to hurt me worse than anyone ever had.

I almost didn't get on the elevator in his building. A huge part of me just wanted to bolt instead of endure the coming conversation. However, a bigger part of me was so pissed at him for dragging this out and I wanted him to know it.

As soon as I walked into his apartment, I made a beeline for the bathroom so I could start packing my shit.

"What are you doing?" Rafe growled in irritation as he followed me in. I looked up at him in the reflection of the mirror and noted his eyes were on the toiletries I was shoving into my toiletries bag.

When I turned to face him he pierced me with a look of anger and disappointment that made me want to smack him across the face.

"No." I pointed at him. "You don't get to look at me like that."

"You let a stranger put his hand on you at the bar you were determined to get smashed at because you saw me talking to my ex? What? That qualifies you to flirt with someone else?"

I laughed at the ridiculousness of his statement.

Rafe's expression darkened and I didn't care if I'd never seen him look so angry.

"*I* let another man touch *me*? I did that?"

"Yes, and I want to know why!"

"Uh, how about because the first chance you got, you were all over your ex and she was all over you?"

"Bullshit."

"She was touching you!" I yelled. "Stroking your lapel and your chest and you were just letting her. What? Is it Humiliate Star Day?"

His chin jerked in shock. "I . . . I wasn't even aware of her doing that."

"Oh, so you're that comfortable with her now that you just didn't notice her petting you?" Tears burned my eyes. "Or remember that the last time we saw her, she told you she was pretty much waiting for you to dump me."

"Star—"

Weeks of pent-up fears and frustrations bubbled between us. "No, no, seriously. I get it. You flirting with her. Makes sense."

"I wasn't flirting with her."

"I know when you're flirting, and you were flirting." I laughed hollowly. "Jesus, Rafe, I'm a big girl. You can be honest with me. If you don't want me anymore, it's no skin off my nose. You can marry your perfect society princess and I can go back to casual fucking my way through Staten Island 'cause that's what I'm good for. I still have my favorite fuck buddies saved in my phone."

His eyes dropped to my toiletries bag as understanding dawned. Then Rafe took hold of my biceps, bending his head toward mine, face etched with fury. "Stop this."

"What do you care who fucks me now that Ms. Camille's back in your life?"

"She met someone," he hissed, eyes blazing into mine. "She's in love. For real this time. He was at the party. She was apologizing for what she said the last time we met. We cleared the air. She told me she'd never felt this way about a guy and I've never heard her speak like that, so I told her I was happy for her."

I should have deflated at his explanation. Should have apologized. Yet I felt like I was floating away, like my feet couldn't quite touch the ground no matter how hard I tried, and I was furious about it. And I was furious at Rafe because . . . he didn't love me.

If he loved me, I knew he would have told me by now.

I was pathetic for sticking around, hoping that at some point, he'd fall in love with me. But I couldn't make myself leave him. Just in case love hit him, eventually. Hope was pretty shitty like that.

"Yeah, well, good for her." I shrugged out of his grip.

"You're not going to apologize?"

"For what?" I retorted belligerently.

Rafe gaped at me as if he'd never seen me before and bit out, "Favorite fuck buddies saved in your phone?"

Lifting my shoulders in a lazy shrug, I replied nastily, "They're backups. In case of an emergency."

Hurt lit his eyes and then anger. Suddenly I found myself pressed up against the bathroom counter, his front to my back, and my eyes flew to his in the mirror above the sink.

"Delete them." His chest heaved with emotion. "Because you don't need any backups. I'm your fucking 'in case of emergency.'" Rafe saw the raw desire on my face, and whatever thread of control he'd been holding on to snapped. He pushed up my dress and yanked down my underwear, the cool air blowing between my legs.

My body had been teetering on the edge of confusing arousal from the moment we'd started to argue. Now, with a million unsaid worries and emotions flooding between us, my skin flushed hot with desperate need.

Rafe slipped his fingers between my legs to check, and his eyes darkened at finding me ready. He held me pressed to the sink with one hand while his other yanked at his zipper and shoved his pants and underwear just far enough down to free himself.

And then he filled me.

I gasped, my back arching as Rafe thrust in and out.

"This is yours, only yours," he promised harshly. His grip on my hips tightened as he held my gaze in the mirror. "And this is mine, only mine."

Lust-fogged and insecure, I enjoyed the possessive words. They egged me on as Rafe fucked me, fast, hard, claiming. I gasped out his name with each hard drive into me.

The tension coiling inside me had needed little seduction, and I was pulsing and squeezing around Rafe as my climax hit me like a lightning bolt.

Instead of giving in to his own orgasm, he spun me around and gripped my right thigh in his hand and entered me again. He covered my mouth with his and I held on as he took what he needed to take from me, kissing him through his thrusts and then through the orgasm that shuddered over him.

As our hearts slowed and reality returned, tears wet my eyes.

Rafe tensed at the sight of them, and he brushed my hair back from my face. "Did I hurt you?"

I shook my head. "Did I hurt you?"

His gaze lowered so I couldn't see his expression, and he gently pulled out. I had hurt him. Dammit. I leaned against the counter as he cleaned us both up. His tenderness made the tears leak free.

Rafe saw them, sighed, and leaned his forehead against mine. "I don't want to be a couple who hurt each other like that."

My tears fell faster and I held on to his arms. "I know. I'm sorry. I didn't mean to act like a jealous ass."

"I can see how it might have seemed to you, but Star, I've been cheated on and you have to know that I would never do that to you."

"I never used to be like this," I whispered. "I'm sorry about what I said. I don't have numbers in my phone." I repeated, "I never used to be like this."

Rafe tensed and then pleaded, "Baby, talk to me."

I wanted to. I wanted to tell him about Cartoon Star and that sensation of floating away. But I was so scared if I did, I would lose him.

Rafe's emergency cell buzzed from his back pocket, saving me from having to answer. Frustration darkened his face as he yanked it out to answer it. He shot me a look of apology as he talked to a patient's frantic owner.

I fixed my clothes as Rafe wandered out of the bathroom. When I came out, he was hanging up the phone.

"I have to go into the clinic."

"Okay."

"Will you stay here? I shouldn't be too long."

I was afraid if I stayed, he'd ask me to tell him what was wrong again. So . . . I lied and told him I'd promised to meet Roger on Staten Island the next morning, and I wanted to spend the night at my own apartment. He put me in a cab a few minutes later, but I knew as he'd kissed me goodbye that I'd disappointed him by leaving on a night I should have stayed. Should have waited for him to return to me.

I should have lain in his arms to reassure us both.

Chapter Thirty

TO MAKE MY LIE THE TRUTH, I CALLED ROGER THE NEXT MORN-
ing, hoping he'd be around for a much overdue catch-up.

But it wasn't Roger who picked up his cell. It was Kendall.

"Oh, hey, how are you?" I was happy to hear her voice.

Kendall, apparently, wasn't happy to hear mine. "Roger would never say this because Roger is too nice for his own good, but he's in the shower, so I'm going to say you calling right now is fate and a chance for me to say my piece."

My pulse leaped. "Kend—"

"You are not who I thought you were. The first serious guy you bring into your life, you drop your friends who have been like family to you. I'm hurt and Jude's pissed, but mostly I'm angry on Roger's behalf because he'd do anything for you. You're like his little sister."

Emotion clogged my throat. "I love him. I love you guys. I've—"

"You've just abandoned us because we don't fit in with your conservative new family, right? Or the fancy Upper West Side job and apartment. I mean . . . who the hell are you anymore, Star? I never thought I'd see the day when you compromised who you are, the people you apparently love, for some fucking guy. So until you can pull your head out of your ass, don't call us anymore."

Tears dripped down my cheeks. "What happened to loving someone, no matter who they decide to be?"

"If you had included us in this, it would be different. But you've clearly decided we don't fit. But I wonder, Star . . . do *you* fit? With him, with them? Are you even happy?"

At my silence, Kendall sighed wearily. "I miss my friend. If she comes back, I'll be here. We'll be here."

Then she hung up on me.

I fell to my side on my bed, curled up into a ball, and bawled like a baby. The last time I'd felt this alone, so untethered, I was still a kid, living with Arlo and Dawn.

ARE YOU DROPPING BY TONIGHT AFTER WORK?

I stared at the text from Rafe. After my disastrous call with Kendall, I didn't feel like seeing anyone. I texted Rafe to tell him I was staying at my apartment for the next few nights and he'd tried to call. But I didn't answer. I just texted him and lied, told him I couldn't talk because I was with Kendall.

He called the next day and I didn't answer.

Monday at work I'd answered his call, but only because I knew I could use work to get out of it quickly. I made up an excuse about having a client on Staten Island to meet the next day, so it just made sense that I stayed at my apartment again. Telling him I had a call coming in, I hung up before he could object.

Now it was Tuesday, and I was scrambling for more excuses to avoid him for a while.

> Can't. Roger asked me to come listen to a
> new demo.

Twenty minutes later, Rafe responded to my lie.

> Okay. I guess I'll just pick you up at your
> place for the wedding?

I blinked in confusion at his text for a second, and then I remembered. Shit.

Jen and Greg's friends were renewing their vows on a Wednesday of all days and the reception was on a yacht (in October!) of all things. I'd used one of my personal days so I could attend as Rafe's date because the couple in question were like an aunt and uncle, he'd said.

Shit.

Shit, shit, shit.

Well, I would have to face him sometime.

> Sure. What time?

Chapter Thirty-One

"I MISSED YOU," RAFE CONFESSED WHEN HE PICKED ME UP ON Wednesday morning.

I wished he'd told me he loved me instead.

The wall I put up was just instinctual. It was the wall I'd learned to build, brick by brick, against Arlo and Dawn. It kept the people who could hurt me behind a barrier between them and my heart, so they had no chance of crushing it.

When he kissed me hello, I barely kissed him back. While I answered his questions, I didn't encourage conversation. Instead, I sat in his cool car in a wedding outfit Pippa picked out. It was a golden-yellow pencil dress that restricted my movement, and I wanted to tear the skirt right up the side so I could walk easier in the matching stilettos. On my lap was a matching purse. On my head was a freaking matching hat.

I missed my flowy floral dresses and my wedges. I wanted to rip off the hat and replace it with a flower crown.

My lack of loquaciousness, the numbness that had settled into my bones, caused Rafe to brood. When that man was in brooding mode, his bad vibes could fill an entire auditorium. If I hadn't been locked inside my head, I probably would have suffocated beneath the ferocity of his brooding.

The beach and yacht club where the Whitmans' friends, the Taylors, were getting married was a ten-minute drive from Rafe's parents' home. A valet parked the car and I walked into the venue ahead of Rafe. He caught up with me and took a tight hold of my hand, tight enough to draw me out of my sullen stupor. Staring straight ahead, his expression was aloof, but I noted the grim lines around his mouth.

The crushing hold he had on my hand.

"Rafe, you're hurting me."

He didn't look at me, but his hand eased up on mine. Still, he didn't let go.

The ceremony was being held in the club's ballroom. Pippa waved us over to a row of chairs where she sat next to Hugo, Charmaine, Jen, Greg, and Gigi. As Rafe and I slid into the row, we exchanged hellos and pleasantries and told each other how nice we looked.

"You look perfect in that yellow. I'm so glad I convinced you to buy this outfit for today." Pippa preened, patting my shoulder.

Rafe, who still hadn't let go of my hand, tightened his fingers around mine at her words, and I had to jerk on him to get him to ease up again.

"WHO PEED IN RAFE'S CEREAL THIS MORNING?" GIGI GRI-maced an hour later as we stood on the upper deck of the large yacht docked in the marina.

I frowned innocently at her. "Excuse me?"

"Rafe." She gestured to where her brother had departed to get us drinks from the bar. "I haven't seen him this moody since before he met you. Did you guys fight?"

"Not that I'm aware of." I shrugged.

Gigi's brows pinched together. "Do you even care if he's in a shitty mood?"

"He's not in a bad mood," I denied.

"No one should be in a bad mood today," Pippa interrupted, appearing at our sides with Hugo and another couple, who looked vaguely familiar. I was pretty sure I'd already met them multiple times at other parties, but I had never been good with names. "Why Hugo and I never had our reception on a yacht, I do not know. It's fabulous."

"Yeah, maybe in September, but it's cold in October." Gigi wrapped her shawl tighter around her. "Where's Charmaine?"

"On the lower deck with the other kids watching a movie. There's a nanny looking after them." Pippa glanced behind her at the bar. "Oh, Hugo, Rafe is getting drinks. Could you help him?"

Once Hugo departed, Pippa drew me into a conversation with the couple (whose names I still couldn't remember), who were interested in hiring Pamela to redesign their summer house on Martha's Vineyard. Gigi, the traitor, made an excuse to leave and I was left there, nodding along as they talked on and on about their visions for the house. In fact, they were so decided in what they wanted, I think they were looking for a stylist, not an interior designer.

Rafe and Hugo had returned to our sides a while ago and they were still talking about their love for shiplap.

"We've only been married for three years, but I swear this house is the third person we needed to spice up our relationship," the woman joked. "We have so much fun talking about what we're going to do with it. It's safer than a third person." They all laughed except for me and Rafe.

Some devil that was desperate to break me out of my numbness opened my mouth for me. "Actually, a third person in a relationship can be a blessing."

The guy sneered. "Oh, really?"

"Yeah. My best friends are in a polyamorous relationship and they're the happiest people I know."

A stunned silence fell between us.

Pippa suddenly chuckled and swatted a hand in my direction. "Oh, Star, you and your sense of humor."

"Oh, she's joking?" The woman appeared relieved. "She's joking. You're joking."

I opened my mouth to tell her no, but Pippa beat me to it. "Of course she's joking. Star's best friends are me and Gigi, and we're definitely not in a polyamorous relationship."

Everyone but me, Rafe, and Hugo laughed.

Hugo cut his brother and me a worried look while Rafe glared at the floor.

Me . . . I fell silent.

In that moment, I felt like I'd betrayed Roger, Jude, and Kendall.

Thankfully, not too long later, the couple moved away to talk with someone else and Pippa asked me to chat with Pamela about taking them on as clients.

I said I would.

"And have you thought any more about the name change? Pamela and I still think it's a great idea."

Rafe stiffened at my side. "Name change?"

Pippa nodded, smiling brightly. "I had the wonderful idea of changing Star's name. We're thinking Sarah."

I looked at Rafe, who turned to stare at me in disbelief. "Name change?"

"To something more professional. Star is . . . well"—she touched my hand in apology—"is a good-time girl's name."

"Pippa," Hugo warned.

I'd always liked my name. It was the one thing my hippie parents gave me I liked. I took a massive chug of my champagne, and Rafe made a low growling noise before he abruptly marched away.

"Pippa," Hugo snapped at her.

"What?" She was wide-eyed. "What did I do?"

Giving them both a strained smile, I told them I'd go after Rafe, but it was a lie. Instead, I made my way to the lower deck and found the cabin where the kids were watching *Mulan*. Half of them looked bored and pissed off, pulling at fancy dresses and little ties. They had discarded suit jackets over the back of the corner sofa, and there were piles of junk food on the floor in the middle of the small TV room.

The nanny was snoozing in an armchair.

"Star!" Charmaine waved to me from her place between two boys. "Come watch *Mulan* with us."

I smiled affectionately at her, my gaze drifting to the little boy beside her who was currently tugging on his shirt collar. I tugged on the high neckline of my dress and felt the fabric tense as I tried to cross the room. Restricted.

That was how I felt.

Freaking restricted.

Hanging out with a bunch of kids who felt the same seemed like a far better option than hanging out on a boat, losing my identity bit by bit.

I SWEAR I DIDN'T SEE THE KID LEAVE THE CABIN, BUT TWENTY minutes into my hideout, a boy around ten or eleven threw open the door to the cabin and yelled, "Look what I got!"

My eyes grew wide as the kids launched themselves across the room in cries of excitement.

What he "got" was a rare Löwchen dog.

The one the bride had walked down the aisle using a pearl-decorated lead.

Holy crap, he'd stolen the Taylors' dog.

"Where did you get her? Or him?" I launched myself off the couch, scowling as I twisted my ankle in the stupid shoes because my stupid dress was too tight to move in. The hat was lying somewhere behind the couch because I'd let Charmaine take it off my head and throw it like a Frisbee.

The boy backed up at my tone. "This is my grandma's dog!"

He was related to the Taylors. That was fine, then, right? "Okay. Well, maybe we should return it to Grandma."

"No. She spends more time with this dog than her own family. Mom says so all the time." He jutted his chin out stubbornly. "Maybe it's time Tallulah took a swim."

"Oh no. No, no, let's talk about this." I gently pushed past the kids. They tried to clamber for the dog, so I pivoted and whistled loudly. "Hey, nanny, wake up!"

The young woman lying passed out on the armchair jolted awake. "I'm here, I'm alive, what?" She blinked blearily at me and then at the kids and swallowed hard. "Oh. I'm sorry. I'm awake. I promise."

"It's cool. Can you just handle them while I—" I turned to talk to the boy with the dog and found only empty space. "Where did he go?"

"He left," Charmaine supplied helpfully.

With Tallulah the dog. To take her for a swim.

"Oh shit." I kicked off my shoes and hurried from the room to a chorus of "Ooh!" and "She said a bad word!" I think I also heard Charmaine declare proudly, "That's my aunt Star."

Hurrying past several startled guests, I ran out of the covered lower deck and onto the port side.

There he was, running down the side of the yacht, Tallulah in hand, heading toward the stern.

With a noise of disbelief, I yanked up the stupid confining skirt of my dress and chased after him. "Hey, kid! Stop!"

He glanced back at me and then sped up. Musicians had set up shop on the back of the lower deck, and while they peered at the boy, they didn't stop playing. Even as they saw a strawberry blond in glaring yellow chase after him.

The little creep came to a stop and held the frightened, wide-eyed Tallulah over the side of the boat.

"Don't you dare!" I yelled.

I heard a gasp above us and looked up to find the bride, Pippa, Jen, and Rafe staring down at us.

"Michael Wallace Taylor, do not even think of throwing Lula overboard or I will cut you off! You'll never see a penny!" Mrs. Taylor shrieked in fury.

Rafe, stern-faced, pushed away from the balcony railing and disappeared, probably on his way down.

"Hey, Michael." I smiled coaxingly. "It looks like you'll get in big trouble if you do this, so joke's over, kid. Come on. Let's just get back to the party."

"Sure." He agreed with a wicked grin.

Then he let go of the dog.

Time seemed to hold suspended as I heard his grandmother's horrified cry.

The little creep even looked shocked he'd done it.

Then I heard the dog hit the water.

Oh, heck no!

Without thinking about it, I yanked down the side zipper on my dress and shimmied out of it, only to launch myself off the boat in my underwear.

Plunging into freezing cold October water stunned me momentarily, and it took me a minute to swim back to the surface. Gasping for breath, already chittering with the chill, I spotted Lula paddling around, barking her disapproval. Poor baby. I swam toward her.

"Hey, Lula." I approached her slowly, my legs kicking to stay afloat. I hoped this water was clean. "Come here, girl."

The dog paddled away from me.

"Lula!"

A massive splash drew my attention and I looked back to see Rafe powering through the water toward me. He looked pissed.

"She won't come to me!" I told him as he approached, but he didn't speak. He just swam past me, grabbed the dog, who yipped at him but otherwise allowed Rafe to hold her, and swam back with one arm, Lula in the other.

"You okay?" he barked at me.

"I'm fine. Cold."

He nodded, his face pale with the chill of the water. "Swim back with me."

Lula's momma was there at the first set of deck ladders, reaching down for the frightened, drenched dog. She cuddled Lula to her chest, not caring about her white wedding gown one bit as she cried relieved tears into her dog's head.

Her grandkid really was a pill.

Rafe reached for me. "You first."

I hauled myself up the ladders, water running down my body. I felt Rafe's hands on my hips guiding me up, and then Jen and Greg were there to pull me onto the deck. They covered me with a blanket, murmuring their concern.

Rafe pulled himself up onto the deck, and I noted he wore only his suit pants. He shot me a quick glance, saw that his parents had me in hand, and turned to Mrs. Taylor to examine Lula. After he checked her eyes and tried his best to listen to her pulse without a stethoscope, he patted Lula's head gently. "I hate to say this, Helena, but I think you should get her to your vet. She was dropped in, which means she went under before she paddled back to the surface and while she looks fine now, she could have inhaled enough water to cause breathing problems."

"Thank you, Rafe. Our vet makes house calls. I'll call her now to come to the marina." She patted his cheek and then looked at me. "And thank you, Star. Thank you so much for jumping in after her." She turned in Mr. Taylor's arms and the two of them disappeared down the side of the boat.

Rafe looked at me, hands on hips, eyes glowing with anger. "Even though it was stupid."

My back straightened. "Excuse me?"

"What were you trying to prove?" He clearly did not care that we had an audience.

"N-nothing," I spluttered. "What do you mean?"

"Jumping in after the dog! You could have drowned!"

"I can swim!" I yelled back.

Rafe's lips pinched together and then he suddenly seemed to realize where we were and that the guests were all watching us, including his family. "Let's talk about this later. We need to get cleaned up."

"Yes, I think we've had enough drama and embarrassment for one day." Pippa nodded, apparently affronted by the whole thing.

I just . . . I lost my shit.

"Oh, I embarrassed you by trying to save a dog?"

Pippa flinched in surprise. "Well, no, of course not—"

"I mean, first it's the way I dress, my friends, my name, my job . . . now it's the way I save animals!" I whirled on Rafe. "And you!" Tears flooded my eyes. "You just stand there . . ." I shook my head. Ironically, it was like the cold water had broken through my numbness. "I have tried to be what everyone wanted for you . . . but I thought love would feel different than this. Better. So if this is love,

Whitman, you can drown it in this goddamn marina. I am sick of trying to fit in when I was perfectly happy before I met you. I do love you, more than I knew I could love anyone. But I cannot choose you over me. You and I . . . I think we're done." Tears streamed down my face as I pulled out of Jen's hands, whispering a hoarse "sorry" under my breath as I grabbed the stupid yellow dress off the deck and stormed through our audience.

I'd barely made it onto the dock when I heard his booming deep voice call out, "Star, don't even think about taking another step!"

The heart-wrenching sobs I'd been holding back were desperate to burst forth, but I shoved them down to face him. Rafe marched onto the gangplank, face hard with determination, water still glistening on his naked torso. I wondered if he realized everyone had followed behind him to watch the show from the yacht. Including his entire family, again.

Dammit.

"We have an audience," I told him.

"I could give a flying fuck if people watch us. You do not"—he slowed to a halt in front of me, seeming uncaring that we were both soaking wet and it was October—"get to break up with me and run off without me having a say."

"You don't have to say anything." I couldn't meet his eyes. "It just didn't work out."

"You tell me you love me, but you're okay to just give up like this?"

My eyes flew to his in anger. "I have tried harder than anyone to make this work!"

"By not being yourself? Did I ask you to do any of that?"

"You didn't stop me."

"Because I didn't know what the hell was going on in your head. You said you didn't know what you wanted with your life, so I tried giving you space to try things out even if I didn't like how it was changing you. Believe me, I'd come to the end of my patience with this bullshit and had planned to confront you after the wedding."

What? I gawked at him in confusion. "Why stay with me then, if you didn't like the changes?"

"Because I love you!" He grabbed my arms in exasperation. "I think I've loved you since the moment you sent me that gift basket after my crappy morning at work. I love you and I don't want to lose you, Star."

Shock rendered me speechless for a second. Then I blurted out, "The basket was months ago. That was before we were . . . us."

He nodded slowly, searching my face with his familiar intensity.

"Why didn't you tell me?" My chest ached so badly. "I've been so afraid to walk away from all of this crap your sister-in-law has been putting me through—no, strike that—that *I've* been putting myself through because I didn't want to lose my chance with you. I kept hoping and waiting that you'd fall in love with me back."

Rafe sighed heavily and drew me closer. "I didn't want to scare you away. I didn't know you loved me back and it wasn't easy convincing you to commit to me in the first place, remember? I thought it was better to wait for you to tell me first."

Understanding dawned and I was suddenly exhausted. "So we're two morons who've been in love with each other for months but were too afraid to say it?"

He chuckled humorlessly. "Yeah, baby, looks like it."

I pressed my hands to his bare chest and leaned into him. "You really didn't speak up about the changes because you didn't know how *I* felt about them?"

Frustration darkened his expression. "Yeah. But I felt like I was losing you. You were so decided in being who you want to be, everyone else be damned, that I thought my input would just piss you off. I suspected you weren't happy, but you completely shut me out.

And that terrified me, Star. So I didn't push. I didn't want to push and lose you anyway."

"Even if I wasn't acting like the person you fell in love with?"

"In the most important ways, you will always be you, no matter how you dress or what job you have, and I would take any part of you over having nothing at all."

My tears set free and he kissed them from my cheeks.

"I've never felt about anyone the way I feel about you," he whispered against my lips, his breathing harsh. "I tried to show you how I felt without saying it. But I should have just said it. I love you, Star. You. The you you want to be. Never doubt it. Because, baby, my love for you is fucking immeasurable. If I'm honest, I'm not sure I will ever be fully comfortable with how much I love you."

An overwhelming sense of relief nearly took me out at the knees. "I get it." I reached up to clasp his face in my hands. "I tried to convince myself I was happy being someone I thought fit better with your family because I wanted us all to get along. Being a part of your family is important to me. I didn't want to drive a wedge between you and them. I didn't want that for you because I love you too much."

His hands tightened on me. "I love my family, but they don't get to decide who fits with me. *I* do. And the woman who fits me is perfectly named, wears dresses that make me want to *undress* her, is kind and honest with everyone around her, including herself, and her biggest ambition in life is to be happy. So if you're okay with it, I'd like her back now."

The last few weeks of pressure had crippled me more than I'd realized. It all welled up out of me as I sobbed, falling into Rafe. Between crying, I choked out the words "I love you so much."

We held each other, relief and the cold making us tremble together.

Rafe sighed against the top of my head. "I always believed every human being belongs to themself, and in all the important ways that matter, I still believe that. But I also think it's bullshit. Because I've never felt like I *belonged* more than when I'm with you."

"Me too." I nodded, completely understanding.

He gently pushed me away, but only to bend his head and take my mouth in a hungry kiss. I clung on, kissing him back even as I cried a well of relief and weeks of pent-up emotion. Tasting my tears, Rafe released my lips and gently wiped my cheeks with his thumbs. "Now let's get inside and get dry before we both catch a chill. And then I think we should go home."

"Home?"

Rafe nodded. "I don't want to spend another day without you. I hated the last few nights without you in the apartment."

"Are you asking me to move in with you?"

He grinned, holding me tighter to him. "Yes. What do you say?"

I smiled back, looping my arms around his neck. "I say yes, but you have to let me pay rent."

Rafe sighed. "Star—"

"Rafe. This is who I am."

"Okay. We'll work it out."

"Yeah . . ." Happiness filled me, and for the first time in weeks I felt the relief of being truly myself as I promised him, "We absolutely will."

Chapter Thirty-Two

"ARE YOU READY TO GO?" RAFE ASKED FROM THE DOORWAY.

I stood on the entrance of our living space staring at the new floor-to-ceiling shelving unit we'd spent yesterday building. Except for a space in the middle for Rafe's large TV, the wall was now filled with my books and knickknacks. Now that I had extra room, the knickknacks would soon be thrown over for more books.

The sight of all of my books together looked great. I'd gone to bed giddy about it and even as we ate the breakfast bagels Rafe put together, my eyes kept straying to the shelving unit. Rafe's once very polished apartment was starting to look more like home. More like ours. He hadn't complained when I'd draped my favorite hand-embroidered throw over his couch and added a couple of colorful cushions to the bed.

And when I'd been unpacking, I'd placed photos of me, Roger, Kendall, and Jude on the bed, wondering where I'd put them, only for Rafe to put them in pride of place on the TV sideboard. Now they were on the shelves along with photos of Rafe's family and a few selfies I'd taken with Rafe and then framed.

It had been a month since our infamous fight and declaration of love, but it could have been a year for how intrinsically woven into this apartment I now was. Rafe had made sure I knew this place was ours now. For the first time in my life, a physical space felt like home. Because of the person I shared it with.

"Are you okay?" he asked, stepping up behind me.

I leaned into his heat and smiled. "I'm great. The place looks great."

He slid his fingers through mine and gave a gentle tug. "It does."

Finally dragging my eyes off the shelves, I followed him out of the apartment. Once he'd locked up, Rafe threaded his fingers through mine again and we strolled hand in hand toward the elevator. Just as we got on, a voice called for us to hold it. Then our neighbor Mrs. Granville stepped in.

Her eyes lit up as I smiled at her greeting. "Oh, Star, it's you. How are you, sweetheart?"

Rafe's hand tightened in mine as the elevator descended. When I chanced a glance at him, his eyebrow was raised in question. Grinning, I looked back at Mrs. Granville. "I'm fantastic. How are you?"

"Well, I have to say, I tried that herbal tea you mentioned and I cannot believe it . . . but it works."

Pleased, I nodded. "I told you."

"Something so simple. And I took your advice about not eating before bedtime and taking a long walk each day, and it is working wonders."

I could sense Rafe's curiosity. "I'm so glad."

The older woman gave me a wry smile. "I've not been brave enough to try meditation yet, but I did see there's a yoga class here in the building, so I might try it."

"You should. I'll go with you," I offered impulsively.

"You'd do that?"

"Sure. We'll see if there's a class that works for both our schedules and go together."

"Well, that would be lovely." Mrs. Granville's gaze moved to Rafe. "You've found yourself a very thoughtful young lady."

Rafe nodded. "I have."

"I hear you're a vet."

"I am."

"My daughter is thinking of buying a puppy. I could recommend your veterinary services."

"I would welcome that. Thank you."

"Very good."

After getting off the elevator, we parted ways at the building's entrance and as soon as Mrs. Granville was out of sight, Rafe shook his head, chuckling to himself.

"What?" I asked, leaning into him as we walked toward the garage where he kept his car.

"I've lived in this building for two years and barely said a word to any of my neighbors. You've lived here a month and you're taking yoga with one of them. And what was the herbal tea thing about?"

"Oh, well, I got talking to Mrs. Granville in the lobby one day and she asked me in for coffee and she told me that she lost her husband nine months ago."

Rafe's smile fell. "I didn't know."

I rubbed his arm. "It's okay. She's had a tough time sleeping, so I just asked about her routine and it turns out she was doing all the wrong things. I suggested some herbal tea, to stop taking her meals so late in the evening, and to include some physical activity into her daily routine. It doesn't work for everyone, but I thought it might help."

"How did you know all that?"

"Because Roger went through a phase of not sleeping when his mom died. They were never close and it brought up a lot of stuff for him. So he tried everything and those things were the things that worked best."

Rafe squeezed my hand, his expression filled with affection that made me warm from the inside out. "Have I told you lately that I love you?"

I grinned. "Yes, but it never gets old, so you can keep saying it."

THE WHITMANS' HOUSE WAS FILLED WITH CONVERSATION, laughter, and the smell of good food cooking in the kitchen.

Like I said, it had been a month since my and Rafe's infamous fight and declaration of love at the yacht wedding. Apparently, we were the talk of the town for a while, but I could not care less. Neither could Rafe. We'd both agreed that, considering we were in love for real now, there was no point causing an upset with his family and telling them the truth about our original arrangement. It would just hurt his parents, and Pippa would never understand.

Rafe and I were settling back into the couple we were before I let myself get caught up in trying to *make* myself a part of his family. In the end, the only person who was truly disgruntled I'd decided to be myself again was Pippa. And Pamela, because I quit. I'd just finished working out my notice, and I'd returned to character costume acting and line sitting until I figured out what it was that I really wanted to do.

For now, I was happy, and that was enough.

I grinned at Roger as he finished telling Rafe's family one of his many funny stories from working as a music producer. "I would tell you my funniest, but that will have to wait until we have adult ears only in the room." He smiled at Charmaine, who looked so serious about this pronouncement.

"I can have adult ears!" she insisted.

"Oh, you have to grow into them, sweetie," Roger replied.

She argued with him because she was her mother's daughter and I felt eyes burning into my face. Looking up, I found Rafe leaning against the doorway to the family room, soft gaze on me. I beamed at him.

His expression grew even warmer, more tender.

Everyone I cared about was in this room, and it made me content, which made Rafe Whitman happy.

If we were going to do this for real, I'd wanted his family to know who I really was, and so did he. He also wanted them to know that I wasn't going anywhere. So I'd asked if my family could come to family dinner so they could meet them. Roger, Kendall, and Jude.

Despite the horrible conversation I'd had with Kendall weeks ago, they forgave me immediately as soon as I apologized and explained what had been going on in my head. Even Jude let it go and we all knew he could be a grudge holder.

They'd also agreed to have dinner with Rafe's family.

While they'd been visibly shocked at the size of his parents' sprawling home when they drove up, they weren't intimidated by money. Jude was a little quiet, but that was only because he was like Rafe when it came to meeting new people.

I'd introduced the three of them as my family to the Whitmans, and while Pippa was visibly uncomfortable (though trying her best not to be), Jen, Greg, Gigi, and even Hugo were warm and welcoming to them.

It was going better than I could have ever hoped.

Rafe jerked his head subtly in a "c'mere" gesture, and I got up and crossed the room to him.

"What's up?" I took hold of his hand.

"I want to show you something."

That something was apparently in his old bedroom. Rafe closed the door behind us and guided me over to the bed. He stopped me at the foot of it, his hands on my biceps. He studied my expression, his hands sliding slowly down my arms. The silky fabric of the sleeves smoothed his way.

"Have I told you I like your dress?" His eyes danced with humor.

That was probably because I was wearing a silk cotton hippie dress in autumn colors. It had massive bell sleeves and an exaggerated skirt with a slit up the side. I'd paired it with cowboy boots I'd left at the front door.

"I'm glad, but I like it even if you don't like it."

"Good to know." Then he commented with a slight question in his tone, "You look happy?"

"I'm pretty blissed out," I promised him.

"That's all it takes? Bookshelves at home, you in that dress, your friends here with my family? You're easy to please."

"Don't forget *doing* you every day. That makes me happy."

"Doing me?" He grinned, stepping close to press me to him. "I can see I'm going to be the romantic between the two of us."

"Doing you isn't romantic? Not even the way I did you last night?" I cocked an eyebrow.

I might have gone down on him when a movie we were watching got sexy. Rafe burst out laughing. "It was very romantic for me, thank you."

"Hey." I glanced around his room. "Did you ever have sex in here with your high school sweetie?"

"No. This was our summer place and she always vacationed in Europe with her family."

"So . . . you've never had sex in this room?"

"Well." Wicked humor gleamed in his eyes. "I did dry-hump this one woman and it was hot."

Knowing he was talking about me, I grinned. "That sounds like a very romantic story." I slipped my hands under his sweater and he sucked in a breath. "But you know what would be even more romantic?"

"What's that?" His voice was gruff, eyes low-lidded.

"Making love in this bed. Right now."

"Your friends and my family are downstairs."

"Hasn't stopped you before," I reminded him.

He nudged me against the bed. "Well, if one of them walks in on us, we're paying for their therapy."

"Not if it's Jude or Kendall. They'll love it."

Rafe groaned. "Don't tell me that."

I laughed and lowered myself to his bed. "C'mon, take off your pants and make love to your girlfriend in your parents' house while they're all downstairs." I reached beneath my skirts and whipped off my underwear, dangling the lacy bit of material between my fingers like a prize. "I'm ready to make love."

Rafe's shoulders shook with laughter. "Yes, I'm definitely the more romantic of the two of us."

"What? I said 'make love.'" I yanked him by a belt loop toward me. "Now quickly, before someone comes to check on us."

"You're right, this is so romantic," he replied dryly as he unzipped his pants. "A quickie on my childhood bed."

"You cannot possibly be complaining about getting some in the middle of the day?" I looped my arms around his neck as he came down over me.

"I'm just saying call it what it is." He kissed me tenderly as he slipped his hand between my legs. Finding me ready, he guided himself inside me and I arched into his slow glide, wrapping my legs around his waist.

Holding his gaze, I clasped his face in my hands, my breath

hitching every time he retreated and returned to me. While beautiful tension coiled tight, tighter and tighter, low in my belly, an overwhelming feeling of awe flooded over me.

I'd never felt so connected to anyone in my entire life.

I'd never pictured anyone, not even my friends, in every conceivable version of my future, right until my last day. Until Rafe. I couldn't imagine that journey without him now.

"I love you," I murmured against his lips as he moved inside me.

His features hardened as his thrusts deepened, and his voice was gruff as he replied, "I love you too."

No one interrupted, thankfully. We took our time. And my orgasm was even more spectacular for it. If the time it took for Rafe to stop shuddering was evidence, his was good too.

He pressed his face to my throat, trying to catch his breath, and I rubbed my hand on his back, beneath his sweater in soothing circles. "See. Totally romantic."

I felt his smile against my skin and grinned up at the ceiling.

Epilogue

> Got engaged, Star Shine. Popped
> the question to Maggie last night.
> She said yes.

I looked down at the reply from Arlo. We hadn't spoken since I'd called him to ask if what Dawn had told me was true. It was, of course, and I'd told him I was happy for him if he was happy. He was. But even then I hadn't expected this response to my text checking in.

Arlo and Dawn had never gotten married, so it surprised me Arlo was into that.

Maybe it shouldn't have.

I was starting to think Arlo had changed who he was to keep Dawn, and after my own experience I understood, I sympathized. The difference was I didn't know how he lasted as long as he did, considering I couldn't last a few weeks pretending to be something I wasn't.

The biggest difference, though, was that Rafe hadn't wanted me to change to be with him.

Dawn *had* wanted Arlo to compromise himself for her.

I was happy for my father if he'd found someone he could be himself with. I texted him back, telling him so. As for Dawn, unsurprisingly, I hadn't heard from her since I told her I was done with her. That would always hurt, but not like it used to. It was a dull ache, almost like a phantom pain after an injury had healed.

"Hey, excuse me?" I felt a tap on my shoulder and glanced over it.

A guy in hipster clothes, beanie hat and all, smiled at me. "Yeah?"

"Could you tell me what we're waiting in line for?"

I grinned. "Sure. It's this new bakery the media has been raving about."

"Oh cool. I guess I'll stick it out, then."

"Great. You want a snack? I have a bunch." I opened my purse and held out some candy bars and chips.

"Ooh, Snickers. Thanks!" He eyed me with a flirtatious smile. "Nice *and* pretty. Hard combination to find."

"Oh, you're sweet. My boyfriend thinks so too."

His smile didn't wane as he caught my subtle point. "'Course he does. Thanks for the bar."

"You're welcome." I turned around, straining my neck to see how much longer I had to wait. My client wanted a box of cupcakes dropped off at his office, and I wasn't sure I was going to make it before most of the stuff was sold out.

One would think after Christmas and New Year's, the people of New York might be a little sick of spending money, but no. My line-sitting job was still booming. Still, I made barely enough to pay half the rent on our apartment, so my time as a line sitter would come to its inevitable end. Dating Rafe had changed my entire perspective on commitment. Committing to a career didn't fill me with that sense of fear or entrapment as it once did. In fact, I was eager to find a career that made me want to settle down and stop hopping around from one job to the next. Something stable that fulfilled me. I wasn't one hundred percent on what I wanted for the future, but I'd win-nowed down my list to two.

Counseling or public relations.

I was a people person and I wanted to do something that allowed me to be a people person.

The two options were totally different, obviously, and both would mean going back to school, but the thought didn't scare me anymore. It excited me. I just had to figure out which of them called to me more. I was scared that if I pursued one and hated it, I'd feel like a failure.

For now, I was content juggling my two jobs, plus I'd started working part time as a receptionist at Rafe's clinic. He'd taken on a new vet, named Sarah (ironically), and the vet nurses were run off their feet working with the animals, so Rafe needed help with the reception desk.

It turned out I really loved working at his clinic, and if I didn't think it was healthy for us to have our own things outside of our re-lationship, I might have considered working there full-time. I loved animals and I enjoyed being able to reassure their owners and keep them calm when they were worried and upset. When they needed comfort, I felt useful in a way that mattered to me.

I considered this as I longed for a coffee. Maybe that was what I should focus on when I thought about my future—a job where I felt useful in a way that mattered to me. I smiled to myself even as my brain whirred. Who knew what the future might hold, right? A year ago I was positive that Jack Kerouac-ing across the States was what I wanted, but I knew now, since the longing to travel had faded so quickly, that I'd only been running from the feeling that something was missing.

Now that I had Rafe in my life, I didn't feel the urge to run anymore. Not that I'd entirely given up the idea of travel. I was plan-ning a girls' trip next summer with Kendall. We were going to a concert at Red Rocks Park in Colorado and decided to turn it into a road trip. It wasn't about running. It was about friendship, music, and travel. Rafe thought it was a great idea, but even if he didn't, I'd still be taking that trip.

I swear it was like the man was inside my head and knew when to turn up just as I was thinking about him.

A warm body pressed into my side and I started a little before looking up to the left to find Rafe standing next to me in his wool coat, a red scarf tucked into the collar, his cheeks a little flushed with the winter chill, and his hair mussed by the wind.

Butterflies erupted in my belly at his unexpected arrival, and I felt a pang of sadness at the thought of a day when he no longer inspired them. I hoped that day would never come.

"Hey, you." I grinned up at him. "What are you doing here?"

"I had a break and I knew you'd be out here in the cold, so . . ." He held out a cup of coffee.

"You're my hero." I took it gratefully and gulped the still-hot liquid down. "Ahh. Much better. I love you."

"I can't tell if that was for me or the coffee." he teased.

"Is it okay if it was both?"

Chuckling, he nodded.

"I don't think I'm going to make it." I gestured down the line.

"It's not your problem that people are too lazy to line up for their own baked goods."

"Will you ever stop hating on my job?"

"I don't hate on your job. I hate on a society in which this job has been allowed to flourish."

Snorting, I shook my head at him. "It pays the rent."

He harrumphed at that.

"Did you just come here to be adorably grumpy?"

Rafe rolled his eyes. "I am not adorable."

"But you are grumpy?"

He gave me an unimpressed look. "You know this"—he gestured between us—"is actually perfect."

Confused, I frowned. "For what?"

"For this." He held out a jar of peanut butter and one of jelly.

Immediately, I was thrown back to our second meeting when I embarrassed him to get his attention. I burst out laughing, taking the jars in my free hand. "What is this? A trip down memory lane?"

Rafe took the coffee cup out of my hand and relayed conversationally, "These jars are us."

I waited for him to continue.

"You're the jelly to my peanut butter," he announced with an impressively straight face.

My lips twitched with delight. "I am?"

"Yes. The two things should not work and maybe for some people they don't. But for us, it works. We taste damn good together."

Bemused but thrilled, I nodded. "Agreed."

Suddenly Rafe took a deep breath, looking a little nervous as he took back the jelly and left me with the peanut butter. "Open the lid."

So I did.

I think my heart stopped.

Because nestled into the peanut butter, as if it were sitting in a ring box, was the most unusual engagement ring. An emerald was clasped between two platinum leaves. It was beautiful. Perfect. "Oh, my . . ." I gaped at it, stunned by its meaning.

"From the moment you yelled at me about peanut butter and jelly, you have captivated me," Rafe continued. "I didn't know what it meant at the time. But I knew what it meant within weeks of knowing you. I knew it meant that I wanted to spend the rest of my life with you."

I wrenched my gaze from the ring to Rafe. "You want to marry me?"

His mouth curled at the corner. "It's not every day you find a woman who takes such pleasure in publicly mortifying you."

Laughter, joy, bliss, excitement, fear, excitement, fear . . . it all rushed through me in a tidal wave. But the excitement and joy and bliss and all the good stuff won out. "I want to spend the rest of my life publicly mortifying you."

He raised his eyebrows. "Is that a yes?"

I nodded and opened my mouth to verbalize it, but Rafe hauled me into his arms to kiss me. The peanut butter jar got crushed between us as I laughed. I broke the kiss with a "Watch the ring!"

Looking down, I saw it thankfully was still sitting on top.

"You like it?" he murmured in my ear, still holding me close.

"It's perfect. Though we can't let it sink any farther in there or we'll have to empty the whole jar."

"Well . . ." Rafe kissed his way up my neck to my ear. "We could empty it out on the bedsheets." His voice lowered as he whispered, "I remember a certain fantasy about licking the stuff off your nipples."

And now I was turned on.

I stiffened and pushed him back. "Yup, let the ring sink." I put the lid back on tight and grabbed Rafe's hand. "Let's go."

Eyes alight with laughter, he gestured to the line. "What about the job?"

"I have other duties to perform this afternoon."

"Lucky bastard," the guy behind us muttered, and I snickered, realizing I'd been loud.

Rafe shook his head and wrapped his arm around me. "Let's go, wife."

"Fiancée," I corrected him.

"That's just a formality."

I snorted, holding tight to my jar and my soon-to-be husband.

Star Shine Meadows, fiancée-soon-to-be-wife.

Now that was a title I never thought I'd have.

However, I'd realized this past year that life had a way of giving you gifts you never wanted because you never knew you needed them. Like there was a fate out there plotting to make your life great, if you'd only stop and pay attention to its moves.

That was the way I liked to look at it.

Rafe would say there was a fate out there plotting to make your life shitty, and you had to stop and pay attention to its moves so you could countermove.

But that was okay. That was why he needed me in his life, and vice versa.

He really was the peanut butter to my jelly.

Acknowledgments

Star and Rafe came to me from a desire to write one of my favorite tropes: grumpy meets sunshine. Their story was one of those rare tales that sprouted from a tiny kernel of an idea. Even more rare was how quickly *The Love Plot* spilled from my imagination onto the page. Every day I sat down to write their love story, the words flowed easily and eagerly. Their romance consumed me! I hope their banter-filled interactions and sizzling sexual chemistry are as fun for readers to read as they were for me to write. Moreover, I hope Star is a wonderful reminder to always be ourselves, because we're perfectly imperfect just the way we are.

For the most part, writing is a solitary endeavor, but publishing most certainly is not. I have to thank my fantastic editor, Kerry Donovan, for helping to make me a better writer and storyteller. Thank you to the team at Berkley for your hard work on Star and Rafe's story.

The same must be said for my amazing agent, Lauren Abramo. Lauren, thank you for always having my back and for making it possible for readers all over the world to read my stories!

And thank you to my bestie and PA extraordinaire, Ashleen Walker, for handling all the things and supporting me every day. There are no words for how much I love and appreciate you.

Thank you to every single blogger, Instagrammer, BookToker, and booklover who has helped spread the word about my books. You all are appreciated so much. On that note, thank you to my wonderful ARC review team and all the fantastic readers in my private Facebook group, Sam's Clan McBookish. You're the kindest, most supportive readers a girl could ask for, and I hope you know how much you all mean to me.

In case I don't say it enough, thank you to my family and friends for your never-ending well of support. I love you all.

Finally, to you, my reader, the biggest thank-you of all.

The

Love Plot

Samantha Young

READERS GUIDE

Discussion Questions

1. When we first meet Star, she's determined not to commit herself to any one career. Does the freedom of moving job to job appeal to you?

2. Even though her closest friends, Roger, Kendall, and Jude, have proven to her that commitment can work, Star is stubbornly set against a long-term monogamous relationship because of her parents. Do you sympathize with Star's fear of commitment?

3. Star agrees to fake-date Rafe because he's offering her the financial opportunity to travel. Would you ever agree to fake-date someone? If so, what would the ideal circumstances be?

4. Star is aware of her physical attraction to Rafe before she agrees to fake-date him but doesn't think it'll be a problem because of how different they are. Do you think you could stay in a platonic relationship with someone you were attracted to?

5. Lying to Rafe's family is harder than Star anticipated when she took the job. How difficult do you think you'd find maintaining such a big lie?

6. Once Star and Rafe fall in love, they decide to spare Rafe's family the hurt of telling them the truth about their fake-dating arrangement. Do you think that was the right decision?

7. When Star and Rafe begin dating for real, Star finds herself in an emotional upheaval and makes decisions that compromise who she truly is and wants to be. Did you have empathy for Star when she was attempting to change to fit in with Rafe's family? Was it obvious to you that Rafe was unhappy with those changes?

8. Upon discovering that Arlo has always wanted commitment from Dawn, Star starts questioning her philosophy on life. Have you ever discovered a fact about someone that totally changed your view of them or yourself?

9. Do you think Star was right to finally cut Dawn out of her life? Would you have handled the situation differently?

10. How did you feel about Star's decision to pursue a career and settle down with Rafe? Would you have made the same choice?

Keep reading for a preview of

A Cosmic Kind of Love

by Samantha Young

Hallie

"SO WHAT STUPID THING HAPPENED TO YOU TODAY?"

I stumbled on one of the concrete steps that led up to my apartment as my boyfriend's question echoed off the stairwell walls from the loudspeaker on my phone.

A flush of irritation made itself known in my cheeks even though George's tone was teasing. "Nothing," I replied defensively as I continued climbing, trying not to sound out of breath.

I struggled to hold my phone and my oversized purse with one hand while I opened the door with the other.

"Come on." George chuckled. "Something had to have happened. It's been almost a week since the last one, so that's, like, a record."

"The sandwich doesn't count." I huffed, dumping my bag onto my small dining table, which doubled as my office desk.

"Eating something that makes you nauseated to please a client counts."

So, okay, maybe I ate several salmon-and-cucumber sandwiches at a client meeting even though the slippery, slimy texture of the salmon made me want to vomit. "Please don't take me back there." I gagged, but the sound softened into a sigh of pleasure as I kicked off my high heels and flattened the arches of my feet onto my cool hardwood floors.

"You're telling me you've gone a full week without something ridiculous happening?"

Perhaps I was merely exhausted and low on a sense of humor, but sometimes it seemed like George only stuck around because he found me entertaining. And not in a good way.

Biting back hurt feelings, I wondered if my defensiveness was less about feeling tired and more about the fact that something stupid *had* happened to me today. "Fine." I cringed. "About thirty minutes ago, I was on the subway and I saw this guy standing across from me who was super familiar, and he kept looking over at me."

"Right . . ."

The mortifying moment was doubly awkward as I relived it. I squeezed my eyes closed against the memory, gritting my teeth. "Well, have you ever bumped into someone who you know but you can't place them or remember their name?"

"Yeah, that's the worst."

"Exactly. I'm thinking, *Oh God, I know this guy, it's probably from college, but for the life of me I can't remember his name.* When he looks at me again, kind of squinting, I'm thinking, *Jesus, he knows me and he thinks I'm so rude for not saying hello* . . . So I just cover my ass and blurt out, 'Aren't you going to say hello? It's been forever; it's great to see you again.'"

"And?"

I buried my face in my hands, just moving my fingers from my mouth so George could hear my reply. "He looked at me like I was crazy and said, 'I'm sorry, we've never met before. I have no idea who you are.' Well, I couldn't explain to him who I was because I couldn't remember who *he* was, so we just stood there trying to avoid each other's eyes for the next ten minutes, and just as I got off the subway . . . I remembered where I knew him from."

"Where?"

My cheeks almost blistered my fingers with the heat of my embarrassment. "It was Joe Ashley, the news anchor, whom I have never met before but do watch regularly on TV."

There was a moment of silence, and then the sounds of choked laughter came from my phone. George was laughing so hard a reluctant smile curled the corners of my mouth.

"Oh man, oh babe, I'm sorry." George hee-hawed. "I don't mean to . . . but that's hilarious."

"I aim to entertain," I said dryly, switching on my coffee machine.

"Only you," he snorted. "These things only happen to you."

It certainly felt that way sometimes. I attempted to change the subject back to the reason I'd called him. "Are we still on for dinner tomorrow night?"

"Uh, yeah . . . but I was thinking you could come here and I could cook."

A romantic dinner at his place? My earlier annoyance fled the building. How sweet. How unlike him. It *was* our three-month "anniversary" next week. Maybe he wanted to commemorate it. I grinned, my mood lifting. "That sounds great. What time? Should I bring anything?"

"Uh, six thirty. And just yourself."

Six thirty was early for dinner. *Why* so early? I frowned. "I don't know if I'll have finished work by then."

George snorted again. "Babe, you're not a heart surgeon. You plan parties, for Pete's sake. I'm pretty sure if *I* can be here by six thirty, you can."

I sucked in a breath as his words ignited my anger and the urge to tell him to go screw himself . . . but that infuriating piece of me that hated confrontation squeezed its fist around my throat.

"Hallie, you still there?"

"Yes," I bit out. "I'll try to be there at six thirty."

"Then I guess I'll see you at seven thirty," he cracked. "Night, babe."

My apartment grew silent as George hung up and I stared at my phone, taking a couple of deep breaths to cool my annoyance. Lately, my boyfriend had gotten more and more patronizing. I wanted to believe he had the best intentions and that he was only teasing. But if he didn't have the best intentions and he was just kind of . . . well . . . an asshole . . . then I'd have to break up with him.

I made a coffee and pulled my laptop out of my purse, my stomach seesawing at the thought of breaking things off. I'd been dating since I was fifteen years old, and I'd only ever had to break up with two boyfriends in the past thirteen years. The rest had either broken up with me or ghosted me. Still, the thought of having to break things off with George made me anxious.

Maybe I didn't have to break up with him, I thought, as I sat down at my desk and flipped open my laptop. Maybe I could just tell him I found some of his teasing derogatory and he should do better not to be such a freaking tool.

Suddenly my cell chimed behind me on the counter and then chimed again and again and again.

"What the . . ." I turned to grab the phone, some kind of sixth sense making me dread the sight of the notification banners from my social media apps. Tapping one—

"Oh my God." Nothing could have prepared me for the video someone had tagged me in.

The video someone had tagged my mother in for her prominent role.

I'd totally forgotten she was attending my aunt Julia's bachelor-

ette party tonight. In typical Aunt Julia fashion, she'd forced everyone out on a weeknight to avoid the weekend crowds. Aunt Julia was
my mom's best friend from high school and had been terminally
single for most of my life. Then, three years ago, she met Hopper.
He was a couple of years younger than her, divorced with three
grown kids, and he and Aunt Julia fell madly in love after meeting in
a supermarket, of all places. Now they were finally getting married,
and I couldn't be happier for her.

However, my mom, who'd been divorced from my dad for less
than two years and had to watch him move on to a younger woman,
was in a fragile place right now. So I could be mad at Aunt Julia for
allowing my vulnerable, postdivorce mom to get recorded at the
bachelorette party giving a male stripper a lap dance while sucking
the banana he held in his hand.

Yup.

My mother, ladies and gentlemen.

I shuddered.

Noticing all the shares on the video, I came out of the app and
slammed my phone down on my desk. Part of me wanted to race out
of my apartment, jump in a cab, find my mom, and drag her out of
whatever strip club in Newark they were in.

Yet there were only so many times that I could rescue my mom
and dad from themselves. This was their new reality postdivorce,
and I needed to let go. Maybe if I didn't have a pile of work to get
through, I might run after my mom.

Who would undoubtedly find the online video mortifying once
she sobered up.

Sighing, I grabbed my phone and called my aunt. To my shock,
she answered. The pounding music from the club they were in
slammed down the line.

"Hey, doll face!" Aunt Julia yelled. "I've changed my mind and
you're allowed to come! Do you want the address?"

Aunt Julia had decided she wanted a bachelorette party that allowed her to do whatever the hell she liked without feeling weird in front of me or any of her friends' grown kids. I was relieved to be left out of the invitation.

"No," I replied loudly, "I'm calling because that video of Mom is all over social media!"

"What video?"

"The lap dance! The banana!"

"Oh shit," she cackled. "You're kidding? Okay," she yelled even louder, "Who put the video of Maggie online?"

Realizing she was talking to her friends, I stayed silent.

"Jenna, you creep!" Aunt Julia yelled good-naturedly. "Take it down!"

"It's not funny, AJ!" I called her by the nickname I'd given her as a child.

"Oh, it's kind of funny, honey, if you're anyone but her daughter!"

"Just make sure she doesn't do anything else lewd that ends up online. Have a good night!" I ended the call before she could reply.

It was clear they were all drunk. Aunt Julia was usually on my side when it came to calming Mom in any postdivorce antics—I'd never had to worry about my mother in any way until her marriage fell apart and she started acting unpredictably.

However, there was no reasoning with drunk bachelorettes.

"Shake it off," I whispered to myself, willing my pulse to slow. "You cannot undo what has already been done, but you can focus on your work so you don't lose your job."

I was an event organizer. I worked for one of the best event-management companies in Manhattan: Lia Zhang Events, owned by my boss, Lia Zhang. After college, I'd planned to go backpacking across Asia, a lifelong dream of mine, but the reality was I needed money to pay for that. So I'd gotten a job as a manager at a large

Manhattan hotel, and when the event planner quit three weeks before a big wedding, I'd stepped in to take over. I'd met Lia at the fourth wedding I planned for the hotel, and she was so impressed by my work she offered me a job. The pay was hard to resist because it would take me closer to my backpacking dream.

Four years later, I was still working for Lia, had been promoted to senior event manager, and almost everyone I knew had talked me out of my backpacking trip.

My latest project was planning Darcy Hawthorne's engagement party. She was a true-blue New York socialite. If we got this right, Darcy would more than likely hire us to plan the wedding.

The issue was that Darcy, an environmental lawyer and elegance personified, was marrying her complete opposite. Her fiancé, Matthias, was a French artist and musician. He wanted a "modern, stripped back, yet artistic party with a rock band" while Darcy was all about traditional opulence. She was a flowers-and-string-quartet kind of woman. It was my job as their planner to find a compromise, so I'd asked Darcy and Matthias to email me images and music for inspiration.

I'd been busy at work finalizing plans for another client's spring wedding, so I hadn't had time to look over their emails. I had a lunch meeting with them tomorrow. Hence the late night.

Slamming back coffee, I opened my email and found the couples' separate replies.

Matthias had sent me a helpful Pinterest board. It had to be the artist in him. Most guys I worked with either didn't care about the minute details of the event or didn't know how to communicate what it was they visualized. Clients who were creative, however, were always a godsend because they usually knew how to tell me what they wanted.

While Matthias's board was straight to the point, I discovered

Darcy had sent me a link to an online cloud account where she had several digital folders for me to look at. To my confusion, some folders were named with numbers that read like dates. I opened a folder from a year ago to see it contained a video.

Huh?

Had she sent me YouTube videos for inspiration?

I double-clicked and the video started.

A somewhat familiar man's face took up most of the screen, but behind him I could see a strange, organized jumble of pipes and wires on a white wall. I could hear a loud hum of machine noise in the background.

"Well, here I am, Darce." The man grinned into the camera, a glamorous white-toothed smile that caught my attention as if he'd reached out of the screen to curl his hand around my wrist. "I'm on the International Space Station. I still can't believe it."

Photo by Mark Archibald

Samantha Young is the *New York Times* and *USA Today* bestselling author of the Hart's Boardwalk series and the On Dublin Street series, including *Moonlight on Nightingale Way*, *Echoes of Scotland Street*, *Fall from India Place*, *Before Jamaica Lane*, *Down London Road*, and *On Dublin Street*. She resides in Scotland.

CONNECT ONLINE

AuthorSamanthaYoung.com

🅕 AuthorSamanthaYoung

🅞 AuthorSamanthaYoung

Ready to find
your next great read?

Let us help.

Visit prh.com/nextread